THROUGH SPACE AND TIME
WITH ISAAC ASIMOV

"The Feeling of Power"—Was the world ready for the rediscovery of the original computer . . . the human mind!

"Franchise"—in the not-too-distant future, one man's vote could change the fate of the nation.

"Found"—Had they stumbled upon space sabotage, or the first human experience of a different way of life?

"The Ugly Little Boy"—They had stolen him from the earliest beginning of humanity, but could they find a place for him in their—or any—time?

THE BEST SCIENCE FICTION
OF ISAAC ASIMOV

THE
BEST SCIENCE
FICTION OF
ISAAC ASIMOV

●ii●ii●ii●ii●ii●ii●ii●ii●ii●ii●ii●ii●ii●ii●ii●

Isaac Asimov

●ii●ii●ii●ii●ii●ii●ii●ii●ii●ii●ii●ii●ii●ii●ii●

A SIGNET BOOK

NEW AMERICAN LIBRARY

ACKNOWLEDGMENTS

1. "All the Troubles of the World," *Super-Science Fiction*, April 1958, copyright © 1958 by Headline Publications, Inc. (renewed 1985 by Isaac Asimov)

2. "A Loint of Paw," *The Magazine of Fantasy and Science Fiction*, August 1957, copyright © 1957 by Fantasy House, Inc. (renewed 1984 by Isaac Asimov)

3. "The Dead Past," *Astounding Science Fiction*, April 1956, copyright © 1956 by Street & Smith Publications, Inc. (renewed 1983 by Isaac Asimov)

4. "Death of a Foy," *The Magazine of Fantasy and Science Fiction*, October 1980, copyright © 1980 by Mercury Press, Inc.

5. "Dreaming Is a Private Thing," *The Magazine of Fantasy and Science Fiction*, December 1955, copyright © 1955 by Fantasy House, Inc. (renewed 1982 by Isaac Asimov)

6. "Dreamworld," *The Magazine of Fantasy and Science Fiction*, November 1955, copyright © 1955 by Fantasy House, Inc. (renewed 1982 by Isaac Asimov)

7. "Eyes Do More Than See," *The Magazine of Fantasy and Science Fiction*, April 1965, copyright © 1965 by Mercury Press, Inc.

8. "The Feeling of Power," *If: Worlds of Science Fiction*, February 1958, copyright © 1957, by Quinn Publishing Co., Inc. (renewed 1984 by Isaac Asimov)

9. "Flies," *The Magazine of Fantasy and Science Fiction*, June 1953, copyright 1953 by Fantasy House, Inc. (renewed 1981 by Isaac Asimov)

10. "Found!" *Omni*, October 1978, copyright © Omni Publications International, Ltd., 1978

11. "The Foundation of Science Fiction Success," *The Magazine of Fantasy and Science Fiction*, October 1954, copyright 1954 by Fantasy House Inc. (renewed 1982 by Isaac Asimov)

12. "Franchise," *If: Worlds of Science Fiction*, August 1955, copyright © 1955 by Quinn Publishing Co., Inc. (renewed 1982 by Isaac Asimov)

13. "The Fun They Had," *The Boys and Girls Page*, December 1, 1951, copyright 1951, NEA Service, Inc. (renewed 1978 by Isaac Asimov)

14. "How It Happened," *Asimov's SF Adventure Magazine*, Spring 1979, copyright © 1978 by Davis Publications, Inc.

(The following page constitutes an extension of the copyright page.)

SIGNET TRADEMARK REG. U.S. PAT. OFF. AND FOREIGN COUNTRIES
REGISTERED TRADEMARK—MARCA REGISTRADA
HECHO EN CHICAGO, U.S.A.

SIGNET, SIGNET CLASSIC, MENTOR, ONYX, PLUME, MERIDIAN and NAL BOOKS are published by NAL PENGUIN INC., 1633 Broadway, New York, New York 10019

First Signet Printing, February, 1988

1 2 3 4 5 6 7 8 9

PRINTED IN THE UNITED STATES OF AMERICA

To the memory of my friends and colleagues

Larry T. Shaw (1924–1985)
and
Theodore Sturgeon (1918–1985)

Contents

	Introduction	xi
1.	All the Troubles of the World	15
2.	A Loint of Paw	34
3.	The Dead Past	37
4.	Death of a Foy	90
5.	Dreaming Is a Private Thing	93
6.	Dreamworld	111
7.	Eyes Do More Than See	113
8.	The Feeling of Power	117
9.	Flies	128
10.	Found!	136
11.	The Foundation of Science Fiction Success	153
12.	Franchise	155
13.	The Fun They Had	173
14.	How It Happened	177
15.	I Just Make Them Up, See!	179
16.	I'm in Marsport Without Hilda	182
17.	The Immortal Bard	198
18.	It's Such a Beautiful Day	201
19.	Jokester	227
20.	The Last Answer	243
21.	The Last Question	251
22.	My Son, the Physicist	266
23.	Obituary	271

24. *Spell My Name with an S*   291
25. *Strikebreaker*   308
26. *Sure Thing*   324
27. *The Ugly Little Boy*   326
28. *Unto the Fourth Generation*   371

Introduction

This is a companion piece to my book *The Best Mysteries of Isaac Asimov,* both being published at about the same time.

I must admit, however, that *The Best Mysteries* was prepared by me with a lighter heart. For one thing, I had never before published a collection of mysteries from various sources and of various types, all written by me. On the other hand, I *have* published a number of science fiction collections and, in 1973, I even published one entitled *The Best of Isaac Asimov.*

Why then another? Why, especially, another "Best"?

It's not as though I'm the only one who noticed this. As long as twenty years ago, there were those in the science fiction world who commented (not exactly favorably) on my penchant for "recycling" my stories.

That I recycle my stories is true. I don't deny it. However, it's not primarily my idea; it's my busy and efficient publishers who more or less insist on it. Their reasoning is as follows:

A book has a natural lifetime as a hardcover. The libraries only buy so many and then have all they feel that they need. The bookstores only buy so many and then see no reason for stocking it when the sales are diminishing and newer books are pressing for the limited shelf-space. After a year or so, then, a hardcover book may go out of print. It doesn't necessarily stop earning money, of course, for there are bookclub editions, softcover editions, foreign editions and so on—but the hardcover is gone.

There are, however, new readers of science fiction

constantly arising, as children turn into adolescents. I have heard it said that the science fiction readership produces a new "generation" every three years. The new "generation" can't get hold of a book that is out of print. The softcover, itself, may be out of print, and even if it isn't, there are always some readers who would want a hardcover for their permanent libraries.

Why, then, not put out a new hardcover edition of a book that is out of print? That's quite possible, but risky. An old book so reissued has to compete with fresh new books, and, all things being equal, a new book has the advantage, naturally. There are some authors, nevertheless, whose old books can successfully compete. They may not do as well as a new book by those same authors would do, but in default of a new book by such authors, an old one will do. Publishers have to be able to tell which authors and which books can stand reissuing, and they seem to be pretty good at it. (If they weren't, they wouldn't stay in business very long.)

Fortunately for me, Doubleday seems to think my books can withstand repeated exposures and you can be sure that, even though I am noted worldwide for my astonishingly intense modesty, I don't try to argue them out of this.

Not only do they reissue a hardcover version of a book of mine on occasion, but they also like to introduce something new. They will put out two or three of my books in an omnibus volume, or produce a new short-story collection that varies from earlier ones in theme even though most or all of the stories in the new collection had appeared in one or another old collection. Apparently, it then turns out that there are a number of readers who haven't seen the old collections and who are willing to invest in the new one. (There may even be a few amiable souls who buy the new collection, even though they have read all the stories in older collections, simply because they know that sales please me and they wish to give me pleasure.)

Nor is there any large chance that my publishers or I will cheat a customer by palming off an "old" book on some naïve reader who thinks he or she is getting a "new" one. In the first place, readers know me by now and they are sure to be wary and to study the front of the book for telltale copyright notices. You can bet that any story that first appeared in 1932, for instance, has already been collected—perhaps several times. You may be certain that I don't allow stories to lie about not earning any money if I can help it.

And besides that, Doubleday is very generous in allowing me to write introductions to my books, and if the books are "recycled" you can bet I tell the reader all about it. Partly it's because I am honest, and partly because I am chatty.

But why am I putting out a "Best of" book, when back in 1973, I already put one out?

There are a number of reasons. In the first place, the earlier book was comparatively small. It contained twelve items, whereas this book you are now holding contains twenty-eight—some of which were published after the earlier book appeared.

Secondly, I did not have complete control over the earlier book. The original choice of stories was made by the editor in a British publishing house, and while I modified it to exclude some I didn't want and include some I did want, the modification was only partial and I wasn't able to overcome some of the original scheme insisted on by the publisher. In this book, however, I have had full control and the choice of stories is entirely mine.

This means that I have chosen the stories *I* consider the best and not necessarily those that critics or readers do. For instance, my story "Nightfall" has often been voted not only the best of my stories but the best of *any* science fiction short story. However, I don't think it's the best SF story ever written, or even the best SF story I have written. Therefore I have left it out of this book. If any one else had arranged the collection, he or she wouldn't have dared leave it out, but I can do it easily.

Then, too, I have not included any robot stories at all. To begin with, I recently published all my robot short stories in *The Complete Robot* (Doubleday, 1982) so that I suspect they've been read by most of my present-generation public. In addition, my Robot novels and my Foundation novels have received so much attention, that I am rather anxious to prove to those readers who may possibly be unaware of it, that I have written a number of stories that concern neither robots nor the Foundation, and all twenty-eight stories in the present volume are examples.

It stands to reason, incidentally, that a particular reader may not necessarily enjoy every story in this book and may think, "Good heavens, does he think *this* thing is one of his best." Or, he may even think, "But he left out such and such a story, which I enjoyed enormously when I read it as a kid. What's wrong with his taste?"

Well, people do differ. I like my own writing so much that it was with great difficulty that I left out anything at all. Please believe me when I tell you that it would have given me the greatest possible pleasure to have shoveled in everything. I dimly felt, though, that I couldn't stick Doubleday with more than a certain number of words and so I have had to be rather more selective than I would like to be.

Furthermore, some stories I have written, which I particularly liked, did not seem to make much of a mark on the outside world. No one ever comments upon them, no one writes to tell me that he or she particularly enjoyed them, no one ever nominates them for an award, or invites them into some anthology or other. This all bothers me. Naturally, then, you can be sure that I put all the stories that I liked, but no one else did, into this book. It's my stubborn streak.

But fear not, I shall be completely honest and when those stories appear I will tell you about it for I will put a little introduction in front of each story to tell you why it's included (assuming I have some reason I can put into words).

1

All the Troubles of the World

It's hard to think up a really new idea. I'm not even certain that a new idea can exist. Even modern technology doesn't give you really new ideas; only new variations on old ideas.

The ancient Romans spoke of "sibyls," very old and wizened witches who could answer all your questions, solve all your problems. Aren't modern computers merely high-tech versions of the ancient sibyls?

In any case, I knew of a touching story told of an old sibyl and it sounded good to me. I made the story much longer, much more intricate, much more modern (of course), but I led up to a final punch line, and that punch line is exactly the one found in the ancient tale. It couldn't be improved upon.

So when I'm asked where I get my crazy ideas, the answer is, "Sometimes from the ancient Romans." And it worked so well for me, I had to include it here.

The greatest industry on Earth centered about Multivac— Multivac, the giant computer that had grown in fifty years until its various ramifications had filled Washington, D.C. to the suburbs and had reached out tendrils into every city and town on Earth.

An army of civil servants fed it data constantly and another army correlated and interpreted the answers it gave. A corps of engineers patrolled its interior while mines and factories consumed themselves in keeping its reserve stocks of replacement parts ever complete, ever accurate, ever satisfactory in every way.

Multivac directed Earth's economy and helped Earth's

science. Most important of all, it was the central clearing house of all known facts about each individual Earthman.

And each day it was part of Multivac's duties to take the four billion sets of facts about individual human beings that filled its vitals and extrapolate them for an additional day of time. Every Corrections Department on Earth received the data appropriate to its own area of jurisdiction, and the over-all data was presented in one large piece to the Central Board of Corrections in Washington, D.C.

Bernard Gulliman was in the fourth week of his year term as Chairman of the Central Board of Corrections and had grown casual enough to accept the morning report without being frightened by it. As usual, it was a sheaf of papers some six inches thick. He knew by now, he was not expected to read it. (No human could.) Still, it was amusing to glance through it.

There was the usual list of predictable crimes: frauds of all sorts, larcenies, riots, manslaughters, arsons.

He looked for one particular heading and felt a slight shock at finding it there at all, then another one at seeing two entries. Not one, but two. *Two* first-degree murders. He had not seen two in one day in all his term as Chairman so far.

He punched the knob of the two-way intercom and waited for the smooth face of his co-ordinator to appear on the screen.

"Ali," said Gulliman. "There are two first-degrees this day. Is there any unusual problem?"

"No, sir." The dark-complexioned face with its sharp, black eyes seemed restless. "Both cases are quite low probability."

"I know that," said Gulliman. "I observed that neither probability is higher than 15 per cent. Just the same, Multivac has a reputation to maintain. It has virtually wiped out crime, and the public judges that by its record on first-degree murder which is, of course, the most spectacular crime."

Ali Othman nodded. "Yes, sir. I quite realize that."

"You also realize, I hope," Gulliman said, "that I

don't want a single consummated case of it during my term. If any other crime slips through, I may allow excuses. If a first-degree murder slips through, I'll have your hide. Understand?"

"Yes, sir. The complete analyses of the two potential murders are already at the district offices involved. The potential criminals and victims are under observation. I have rechecked the probabilities of consummation and they are already dropping."

"Very good," said Gulliman, and broke connection.

He went back to the list with an uneasy feeling that perhaps he had been overpompous.——But then, one had to be firm with these permanent civil-service personnel and make sure they didn't imagine they were running everything, including the Chairman. Particularly this Othman, who had been working with Multivac since both were considerably younger, and had a proprietary air that could be infuriating.

To Gulliman, this matter of crime was the political chance of a lifetime. So far, no Chairman had passed through his term without a murder taking place somewhere on Earth, some time. The previous Chairman had ended with a record of eight, three more (*more*, in fact) than under his predecessor.

Now Gulliman intended to have *none*. He was going to be, he had decided, the first Chairman without any murder at all anywhere on Earth during his term. After that, and the favorable publicity that would result——

He barely skimmed the rest of the report. He estimated that there were at least two thousand cases of prospective wife-beatings listed. Undoubtedly, not all would be stopped in time. Perhaps 30 per cent would be consummated. But the incidence was dropping and consummations were dropping even more quickly.

Multivac had added wife-beating to its list of predictable crimes only some five years earlier and the average man was not yet accustomed to the thought that if he planned to wallop his wife, it would be known in advance. As the conviction percolated through society, women would first suffer fewer bruises and then, eventually, none.

Some husband-beatings were on the list, too, Gulliman noticed.

Ali Othman closed connections and stared at the screen from which Gulliman's jowled and balding head had departed. Then he looked across at his assistant, Rafe Leemy and said, "What do we do?"

"Don't ask me. *He's* worried about just a lousy murder or two."

"It's an awful chance trying to handle this thing on our own. Still if we tell him, he'll have a first-class fit. These elective politicians have their skins to think of, so he's bound to get in our way and make things worse."

Leemy nodded his head and put a thick lower lip between his teeth. "Trouble is, though, what if we miss out? It would just about be the end of the world, you know."

"If we miss out, who cares what happens to us? We'll just be part of the general catastrophe." Then he said in a more lively manner, "But hell, the probability is only 12.3 per cent. On anything else, except maybe murder, we'd let the probabilities rise a bit before taking any action at all. There could still be spontaneous correction."

"I wouldn't count on it," said Leemy dryly.

"I don't intend to. I was just pointing the fact out. Still, at this probability, I suggest we confine ourselves to simple observation for the moment. No one could plan a crime like this alone; there must be accomplices."

"Multivac didn't name any."

"I know. Still——" His voice trailed off.

So they stared at the details of the one crime not included on the list handed out to Gulliman; the one crime much worse than first-degree murder; the one crime never before attempted in the history of Multivac; and wondered what to do.

Ben Manners considered himself the happiest sixteen-year-old in Baltimore. This was, perhaps, doubtful. But he was certainly one of the happiest, and one of the most excited.

At least, he was one of the handful admitted to the galleries of the stadium during the swearing in of the eighteen-year-olds. His older brother was going to be sworn in so his parents had applied for spectators' tickets and they had allowed Ben to do so, too. But when Multivac chose among all the applicants, it was Ben who got the ticket.

Two years later, Ben would be sworn in himself, but watching big brother Michael now was the next best thing.

His parents had dressed him (or supervised the dressing, at any rate) with all care, as representative of the family and sent him off with numerous messages for Michael, who had left days earlier for preliminary physical and neurological examinations.

The stadium was on the outskirts of town and Ben, just bursting with self-importance, was shown to his seat. Below him, now, were rows upon rows of hundreds upon hundreds of eighteen-year-olds (boys to the right, girls to the left), all from the second district of Baltimore. At various times in the year, similar meetings were going on all over the world, but this was Baltimore, this was the important one. Down there (somewhere) was Mike, Ben's own brother.

Ben scanned the tops of heads, thinking somehow he might recognize his brother. He didn't, of course, but then a man came out on the raised platform in front of all the crowd and Ben stopped looking to listen.

The man said, "Good afternoon, swearers and guests. I am Randolph T. Hoch, in charge of the Baltimore ceremonies this year. The swearers have met me several times now during the program of the physical and neurological portions of this examination. Most of the task is done, but the most important matter is left. The swearer himself, his personality, must go into Multivac's records.

"Each year, this requires some explanation to the young people reaching adulthood. Until now" (he turned to the young people before him and his eyes went no more to the gallery) "you have not been adult; you have not been individuals in the eyes of Multivac except where you were especially singled out as such by your parents or your government.

"Until now, when the time for the yearly up-dating of information came, it was your parents who filled in the necessary data on you. Now the time has come for you to take over that duty yourself. It is a great honor, a great responsibility. Your parents have told us what schooling you've had, what diseases, what habits, a great many things. But now you must tell us a great deal more, your innermost thoughts; your most secret deeds.

"This is hard to do the first time, embarrassing even, but it *must* be done. Once it is done, Multivac will have a complete analysis of all of you in its files. It will understand your actions and reactions. It will even be able to guess with fair accuracy at your future actions and reactions.

"In this way, Multivac will protect you. If you are in danger of accident, it will know. If someone plans harm to you, it will know. If *you* plan harm, it will know and you will be stopped in time so that it will not be necessary to punish you.

"With its knowledge of all of you, Multivac will be able to help Earth adjust its economy and its laws for the good of all. If you have a personal problem, you may come to Multivac with it and with its knowledge of all of you, Multivac will be able to help you.

"Now you will have many forms to fill out. Think carefully and answer all questions as accurately as you can. Do not hold back through shame or caution. No one will ever know your answers except Multivac unless it becomes necessary to learn the answers in order to protect you. And then only authorized officials of the government will know.

"It may occur to you to stretch the truth a bit here or there. Don't do this. We will find out if you do. All your answers put together form a pattern. If some answers are false, they will not fit the pattern and Multivac will discover them. If all your answers are false, there will be a distorted pattern of a type that Multivac will recognize. So you must tell the truth."

Eventually, it was all over, however; the form-filling; the ceremonies and speeches that followed. In the evening, Ben, standing tiptoe, finally spotted Michael, who was still carrying the robes he had worn in the "parade of the adults." They greeted one another with jubilation.

They shared a light supper and took the expressway home, alive and alight with the greatness of the day.

They were not prepared, then, for the sudden transition of the homecoming. It was a numbing shock to both of them to be stopped by a cold-faced young man in uniform outside their own front door; to have their papers inspected before they could enter their own house; to find their own parents sitting forlornly in the living room, the mark of tragedy on their faces.

Joseph Manners, looking much older than he had that morning, looked out of his puzzled, deep-sunken eyes at his sons (one with the robes of new adulthood still over his arm) and said, "I seem to be under house arrest."

Bernard Gulliman could not and did not read the entire report. He read only the summary and that was most gratifying, indeed.

A whole generation, it seemed, had grown up accustomed to the fact that Multivac could predict the commission of major crimes. They learned that Corrections agents would be on the scene before the crime could be committed. They found out that consummation of the crime led to inevitable punishment. Gradually, they were convinced that there was no way anyone could outsmart Multivac.

The result was, naturally, that even the intention of crime fell off. And as such intentions fell off and as Multivac's capacity was enlarged, minor crimes could be added to the list it would predict each morning, and these crimes, too, were now shrinking in incidence.

So Gulliman had ordered an analysis made (by Multivac naturally) of Multivac's capacity to turn its attention to the problem of predicting probabilities of disease incidence. Doctors might soon be alerted to individual patients who might grow diabetic in the course of the next year, or suffer an attack of tuberculosis or grow a cancer.

An ounce of prevention——

And the report was a favorable one!

After that, the roster of the day's possible crimes arrived and there was not a first-degree murder on the list.

Gulliman put in an intercom call to Ali Othman in high good humor. "Othman, how do the numbers of crimes in the daily lists of the past week average compared with those in my first week as Chairman?"

It had gone down, it turned out, by 8 per cent and Gulliman was happy indeed. No fault of his own, of course, but the electorate would not know that. He blessed his luck that he had come in at the right time, at the very climax of Multivac, when disease, too, could be placed under its all-embracing and protecting knowledge.

Gulliman would prosper by this.

Othman shrugged his shoulders. "Well, he's happy."

"When do we break the bubble?" said Leemy. "Putting Manners under observation just raised the probabilities and house arrest gave it another boost."

"Don't I know it?" said Othman peevishly. "What I don't know is why."

"Accomplices, maybe, like you said. With Manners in trouble, the rest have to strike at once or be lost."

"Just the other way around. With our hand on one, the rest would scatter for safety and disappear. Besides, why aren't the accomplices named by Multivac?"

"Well, then, do we tell Gulliman?"

"No, not yet. The probability is still only 17.3 per cent. Let's get a bit more drastic first."

Elizabeth Manners said to her younger son, "You go to your room, Ben."

"But what's it all about, Mom?" asked Ben, voice breaking at this strange ending to what had been a glorious day.

"Please!"

He left reluctantly, passing through the door to the stairway, walking up it noisily and down again quietly.

And Mike Manners, the older son, the new-minted adult and the hope of the family, said in a voice and tone that mirrored his brother's, "What's it all about?"

Joe Manners said, "As heaven is my witness, son, I don't know. I haven't done anything."

"Well, sure you haven't done anything." Mike looked at his small-boned, mild-mannered father in wonder. "They must be here because you're *thinking* of doing something."

"I'm not."

Mrs. Manners broke in angrily, "How can he be thinking of doing something worth all—all this." She cast her arm about, in a gesture toward the enclosing shell of government men about the house. "When I was a little girl, I remember the father of a friend of mine was working in a bank, and they once called him up and said to leave the money alone and he did. It was fifty thousand dollars. He hadn't really taken it. He was just thinking about taking it. They didn't keep those things as quiet in those days as they do now; the story got out. That's how I know about it.

"But I mean," she went on, rubbing her plump hands slowly together, "that was fifty thousand dollars; fifty—thousand—dollars. Yet all they did was call him; one phone call. What could your father be planning that would make it worth having a dozen men come down and close off the house?"

Joe Manners said, eyes filled with pain, "I am planning no crime, not even the smallest. I swear it."

Mike, filled with the conscious wisdom of a new adult, said, "Maybe it's something subconscious, Pop. Some resentment against your supervisor."

"So that I would want to kill him? No!"

"Won't they tell you what it is, Pop?"

His mother interrupted again, "No, they won't. We've asked. I said they were ruining our standing in the community just being here. The least they could do is tell us what it's all about so we could fight it, so we could explain."

"And they wouldn't?"

"They wouldn't."

Mike stood with his legs spread apart and his hands deep in his pockets. He said, troubled, "Gee, Mom, Multivac doesn't make mistakes."

His father pounded his fist helplessly on the arm of the sofa. "I tell you I'm not planing any crime."

The door opened without a knock and a man in uniform walked in with sharp, self-possessed stride. His face had a glazed, official appearance. He said, "Are you Joseph Manners?"

Joe Manners rose to his feet. "Yes. Now what is it you want of me?"

"Joseph Manners, I place you under arrest by order of the government," and curtly he showed his identification as a Corrections officer. "I must ask you to come with me."

"For what reason? What have I done?"

"I am not at liberty to discuss that."

"But I can't be arrested just for planning a crime even if I were doing that. To be arrested I must actually have *done* something. You can't arrest me otherwise. It's against the law."

The officer was impervious to the logic. "You will have to come with me."

Mrs. Manners shrieked and fell on the couch, weeping hysterically. Joseph Manners could not bring himself to violate the code drilled into him all his life by actually resisting an officer, but he hung back at least, forcing the Corrections officer to use muscular power to drag him forward.

And Manners called out as he went, "But tell me what it is. Just tell me. If I *knew*— Is it murder? Am I supposed to be planning murder?"

The door closed behind him and Mike Manners, white-faced and suddenly feeling not the least bit adult, stared first at the door, then at his weeping mother.

Ben Manners, behind the door and suddenly feeling quite adult, pressed his lips tightly together and thought he knew exactly what to do.

If Multivac took away, Multivac could also give. Ben had been at the ceremonies that very day. He had heard this man, Randolph Hoch, speak of Multivac and all that Multivac could do. It could direct the government and it could also unbend and help out some plain person who came to it for help.

Anyone could ask help of Multivac and anyone meant Ben. Neither his mother nor Mike were in any condition to stop him now, and he had some money left of the amount they had given him for his great outing that day. If afterward they found him gone and worried about it, that couldn't be helped. Right now, his first loyalty was to his father.

He ran out the back way and the officer at the door cast a glance at his papers and let him go.

Harold Quimby handled the complaints department of the Baltimore substation of Multivac. He considered himself to be a member of that branch of the civil service that was most important of all. In some ways, he may have been right, and those who heard him discuss the matter would have had to be made of iron not to feel impressed.

For one thing, Quimby would say, Multivac was essentially an invader of privacy. In the past fifty years, mankind had had to acknowledge that its thoughts and impulses were no longer secret, that it owned no inner recess where anything could be hidden. And mankind had to have something in return.

Of course, it got prosperity, peace, and safety, but that was abstract. Each man and woman needed something personal as his or her own reward for surrendering privacy, and each one got it. Within reach of every human being was a Multivac station with circuits into which he could freely enter his own problems and questions without control or hindrance, and from which, in a matter of minutes, he could receive answers.

At any given moment, five million individual circuits among the quadrillion or more within Multivac might be involved in this question-and-answer program. The answers might not always be certain, but they were the best available, and every questioner *knew* the answer to be the best available and had faith in it. That was what counted.

And now an anxious sixteen-year-old had moved slowly up the waiting line of men and women (each face in that line illuminated by a different mixture of hope with fear or anxiety or even anguish—always with hope predominating as the person stepped nearer and nearer to Multivac).

Without looking up, Quimby took the filled-out form being handed him and said, "Booth 5-B."

Ben said, "How do I ask the question, sir?"

Quimby looked up then, with a bit of surprise. Preadults did not generally make use of the service. He said kindly, "Have you ever done this before, son?"

"No, sir."

Quimby pointed to the model on his desk. "You use this. You see how it works? Just like a typewriter. Don't you try to write or print anything by hand. Just use the machine. Now you take booth 5-B, and if you need help, just press the red button and someone will come. Down that aisle, son, on the right."

He watched the youngster go down the aisle and out of view and smiled. No one was ever turned away from Multivac. Of course, there was always a certain percentage of trivia: people who asked personal questions about their neighbors or obscene questions about prominent personalities; college youths trying to outguess their professors or thinking it clever to stump Multivac by asking it Russell's class-of-all-classes paradox and so on.

Multivac could take care of all that. It needed no help.

Besides, each question and answer was filed and formed but another item in the fact assembly for each individual. Even the most trivial question and the most impertinent, insofar as it reflected the personality of the questioner, helped humanity by helping Multivac know about humanity.

Quimby turned his attention to the next person in line, a

middle-aged woman, gaunt and angular, with the look of trouble in her eye.

Ali Othman strode the length of his office, his heels thumping desperately on the carpet. "The probability still goes up. It's 22.4 per cent now. Damnation! We have Joseph Manners under actual arrest and it still goes up." He was perspiring freely.

Leemy turned away from the telephone. "No confession yet. He's under Psychic Probing and there is no sign of crime. He may be telling the truth."

Othman said, "Is Multivac crazy then?"

Another phone sprang to life. Othman closed connections quickly, glad of the interruption. A Corrections officer's face came to life in the screen. The officer said, "Sir, are there any new directions as to Manners' family? Are they to be allowed to come and go as they have been?"

"What do you mean, as they have been?"

"The original instructions were for the house arrest of Joseph Manners. Nothing was said of the rest of the family, sir."

"Well, extend it to the rest of the family until you are informed otherwise."

"Sir, that is the point. The mother and older son are demanding information about the younger son. The younger son is gone and they claim he is in custody and wish to go to headquarters to inquire about it."

Othman frowned and said in almost a whisper, "Younger son? How young?"

"Sixteen, sir," said the officer.

"Sixteen and he's gone. Don't you know where?"

"He was allowed to leave, sir. There were no orders to hold him."

"Hold the line. Don't move." Othman put the line into suspension, then clutched at his coal-black hair with both hands and shrieked, "Fool! Fool! Fool!"

Leemy was startled. "What the hell?"

"The man has a sixteen-year-old son," choked out Othman. "A sixteen-year-old is not an adult and he is not filed independently in Multivac, but only as part of his father's file." He glared at Leemy. "Doesn't everyone know that until eighteen a youngster does not file his own reports with Multivac but that his father does it for him? Don't I know it? Don't you?"

"You mean Multivac didn't mean Joe Manners?" said Leemy.

"Multivac meant his minor son, and the youngster is gone, now. With officers three deep around the house, he calmly walks out and goes on you know what errand."

He whirled to the telephone circuit to which the Corrections officer still clung, the minute break having given Othman just time enough to collect himself and to assume a cool and self-possessed mien. (It would never have done to throw a fit before the eyes of the officer, however much good it did in purging his spleen.)

He said, "Officer, locate the younger son who has disappeared. Take every man you have, if necessary. Take every man available in the district, if necessary. I shall give the appropriate orders. You must find that boy at all costs."

"Yes, sir."

Connection was broken. Othman said, "Have another rundown on the probabilities, Leemy."

Five minutes later, Leemy said, "It's down to 19.6 per cent. It's *down.*"

Othman drew a long breath. "We're on the right track at last."

Ben Manners sat in Booth 5-B and punched out slowly, "My name is Benjamin Manners, number MB–71833412. My father, Joseph Manners, has been arrested but we don't know what crime he is planning. Is there any way we can help him?"

He sat and waited. He might be only sixteen but he was old enough to know that somewhere those words were being whirled into the most complex structure ever conceived by man; that a trillion facts would blend and co-ordinate into a whole, and that from that whole, Multivac would abstract the best help.

The machine clicked and a card emerged. It had an

answer on it, a long answer. It began, "Take the expressway to Washington, D.C. at once. Get off at the Con-
necticut Avenue stop. You will find a special exit, labeled
'Multivac' with a guard. Inform the guard you are a
special courier for Dr. Trumbull and he will let you
enter.

"You will be in a corridor. Proceed along it till you
reach a small door labeled 'Interior.' Enter and say to the
men inside, 'Message for Doctor Trumbull.' You will be
allowed to pass. Proceed on——"

It went on in this fashion. Ben could not see the
application to his question, but he had complete faith in
Multivac. He left at a run, heading for the expressway to
Washington.

The Corrections officers traced Ben Manners to the
Baltimore station an hour after he had left. A shocked
Harold Quimby found himself flabbergasted at the number and importance of the men who had focused on him
in the search for a sixteen-year-old.

"Yes, a boy," he said, "but I don't know where he
went to after he was through here. I had no way of
knowing that anyone was looking for him. We accept all
comers here. Yes, I can get the record of the question
and answer."

They looked at the record and televised it to Central
Headquarters at once.

Othman read it through, turned up his eyes, and collapsed. They brought him to almost at once. He said to
Leemy weakly, "Have them catch that boy. And have a
copy of Multivac's answer made out for me. There's no
way any more, no way out. I must see Gulliman now."

Bernard Gulliman had never seen Ali Othman as much
as perturbed before, and watching the co-ordinator's wild
eyes now sent a trickle of ice water down his spine.

He stammered, "What do you mean, Othman? What
do you mean worse than murder?"

"Much worse than just murder."

Gulliman was quite pale. "Do you mean assassination

of a high government official?" (It did cross his mind that he himself——).

Othman nodded. "Not just *a* government official. *The* government official."

"The *Secretary-General*?" said Gulliman in an appalled whisper.

"More than that, even. Much more. We deal with a plan to assassinate Multivac!"

"WHAT!"

"For the first time in the history of Multivac, the computer came up with the report that it itself was in danger."

"Why was I not at once informed?"

Othman half-truthed out of it. "The matter was so unprecedented, sir, that we explored the situation first before daring to put it on official record."

"But Multivac has been saved, of course? It's been saved?"

"The probabilities of harm have declined to under 4 per cent. I am waiting for the report now."

"Message for Dr. Trumbull," said Ben Manners to the man on the high stool, working carefully on what looked like the controls of a stratojet cruiser, enormously magnified.

"Sure, Jim," said the man. "Go ahead."

Ben looked at his instructions and hurried on. Eventually, he would find a tiny control lever which he was to shift to a DOWN position at a moment when a certain indicator spot would light up red.

He heard an agitated voice behind him, then another, and suddenly, two men had him by his elbows. His feet were lifted off the floor.

One man said, "Come with us, boy."

Ali Othman's face did not noticeably lighten at the news, even though Gulliman said with great relief, "If we have the boy, then Multivac is safe."

"For the moment."

Gulliman put a trembling hand to his forehead. "What

a half hour I've had. Can you imagine what the destruction of Multivac for even a short time would mean. The government would have collapsed; the economy broken down. It would have meant devastation worse——" His head snapped up, "What do you mean *for the moment*?"

"The boy, this Ben Manners, had no intention of doing harm. He and his family must be released and compensation for false imprisonment given them. He was only following Multivac's instructions in order to help his father and it's done that. His father is free now."

"Do you mean Multivac ordered the boy to pull a lever under circumstances that would burn out enough circuits to require a month's repair work? You mean Multivac would suggest its own destruction for the comfort of one man?"

"It's worse than that, sir. Multivac not only gave those instructions but selected the Manners family in the first place because Ben Manners looked exactly like one of Dr. Trumbull's pages so that he could get into Multivac without being stopped."

"What do you mean the family was selected?"

"Well, the boy would have never gone to ask the question if his father had not been arrested. His father would never have been arrested if Multivac had not blamed him for planning the destruction of Multivac. Multivac's own action started the chain of events that almost led to Multivac's destruction."

"But there's no sense to that," Gulliman said in a pleading voice. He felt small and helpless and he was virtually on his knees, begging this Othman, this man who had spent nearly a lifetime with Multivac, to reassure him.

Othman did not do so. He said, "This is Multivac's first attempt along this line as far as I know. In some ways, it planned well. It chose the right family. It carefully did not distinguish between father and son to send us off the track. It was still an amateur at the game, though. It could not overcome its own instructions that led it to report the probability of its own destruction as increasing with every step we took down the wrong road.

It could not avoid recording the answer it gave the young-ster. With further practice, it will probably learn deceit. It will learn to hide certain facts, fail to record certain others. From now on, every instruction it gives may have the seeds in it of its own destruction. We will never know. And however careful we are, eventually Multivac will succeed. I think, Mr. Gulliman, you will be the last Chairman of this organization."

Gulliman pounded his desk in fury. "But why, why, why? Damn you, why? What is wrong with it? Can't it be fixed?"

"I don't think so," said Othman, in soft despair. "I've never thought about this before. I've never had the occa-sion to until this happened, but now that I think of it, it seems to me we have reached the end of the road be-cause Multivac is too good. Multivac has grown so com-plicated, its reactions are no longer those of a machine, but those of a living thing."

"You're mad, but even so?"

"For fifty years and more we have been loading hu-manity's troubles on Multivac, on this living thing. We've asked it to care for us, all together and each individually. We've asked it to take all our secrets into itself; we've asked it to absorb our evil and guard us against it. Each of us brings his troubles to it, adding his bit to the burden. Now we are planning to load the burden of human disease on Multivac, too."

Othman paused a moment, then burst out, "Mr. Gulliman, Multivac bears all the troubles of the world on its shoulders and it is tired."

"Madness. Midsummer madness," muttered Gulliman.

"Then let me show you something. Let me put it to the test. May I have permission to use the Multivac circuit line here in your office?"

"Why?"

"To ask it a question no one has ever asked Multivac before?"

"Will you do it harm?" asked Gulliman in quick alarm.

"No. But it will tell us what we want to know."

The Chairman hesitated a trifle. Then he said, "Go ahead."

Othman used the instrument on Gulliman's desk. His fingers punched out the question with deft strokes: "Multivac, what do you yourself want more than anything else?"

The moment between question and answer lengthened unbearably, but neither Othman nor Gulliman breathed.

And there was a clicking and a card popped out. It was a small card. On it, in precise letters, was the answer:

"I want to die."

2

A Loint of Paw

Some people like wordplay and some don't, and never the twain shall meet. I like it. In fact, I'm very fond of it. I enjoy irritating the nose-in-the-airs who groan and make caustic remarks by telling them I not only indulge in it, but I arrange to get paid for it.

Of course, if you don't like it, then I'll warn you in all honesty to stay away from this one. You won't miss much since it's only five hundred words long. What's more, there are three more very clever gems in this book, and I'll warn you off them, too.

If, on the other hand, you like wordplay, the way to play the game is to cover the last line or two in the story and when you get there (assuming you haven't already read the story) see if you can guess what I am going to say before I say it. I'll be terribly disappointed if you do.

There was no question that Montie Stein had, through clever fraud, stolen better than $100,000. There was also no question that he was apprehended one day after the statute of limitations had expired.

It was his manner of avoiding arrest during that interval that brought on the epoch-making case of the State of New York *vs.* Montgomery Harlow Stein, with all its consequences. It introduced law to the fourth dimension.

For, you see, after having committed the fraud and possessed himself of the hundred grand plus, Stein had calmly entered a time machine, of which he was in illegal possession, and set the controls for seven years and one day in the future.

Stein's lawyer put it simply. Hiding in time was not

fundamentally different from hiding in space. If the forces of law had not uncovered Stein in the seven-year interval that was their hard luck.

The District Attorey pointed out that the statute of limitations was not intended to be a game between the law and the criminal. It was a merciful measure designed to protect a culprit from indefinitely prolonged fear of arrest. For certaln crimes, a defined period of apprehension of apprehension—so to speak—was considered punishment enough. But Stein, the D.A. insisted, had not experienced any period of apprehension at all.

Stein's lawyer remained unmoved. The law said nothing about measuring the extent of a culprit's fear and anguish. It simply set a time limit.

The D.A. said that Stein had not lived through the limit.

Defense stated that Stein was seven years older now than at the time of the crime and had therefore lived through the limit.

The D.A. challenged the statement and the defense produced Stein's birth certificate. He was born in 2973. At the time of the crime, 3004, he was thirty-one. Now, in 3011, he was thirty-eight.

The D.A. shouted that Stein was not physiologically thirty-eight, but thirty-one.

Defense pointed out freezingly that the law, once the individual was granted to be mentally competent, recognized solely chronological age, which could be obtained only by subtracting the date of birth from the date of now.

The D.A., growing impassioned, swore that if Stein were allowed to go free, half the laws on the books would be useless.

Then change the laws, said Defense, to take time travel into account; but until the laws are changed, let them be enforced as written.

Judge Neville Preston took a week to consider and then handed down his decision. It was a turning point in the history of law. It is almost a pity, then, that some people suspect Judge Preston to have been swayed in his way of thinking by the irresistible impulse to phrase his decision as he did.

For that decision, in full, was:

"A niche in time saves Stein."

3

The Dead Past

I don't labor over the details of a story in advance. Once I have a vague notion of the idea behind it, and a clear notion of the ending, I just begin and make it up as I go along. Occasionally, I throw something in with no particular idea of having it contribute to the working out of the plot. I may put it in just because it is an interesting sidelight or because it gives an air of verisimilitude to the social background.

And then, when (as sometimes happens) it works itself into the plot and becomes an essential part of the story without my ever having planned it, I am delighted and a little overawed. That happened in this story for I had my hero interested in Carthage to begin with only to give him something to do. After all, he had to have some reason for his actions at the opening of the story. And then Carthage became something of great significance and the tale at once became one of my favorites.

Arold Potterley, Ph.D., was a Professor of Ancient History. That, in itself, was not dangerous. What changed the world beyond all dreams was the fact that he *looked* like a Professor of Ancient History.

Thaddeus Araman, Department Head of the Division of Chronoscopy, might have taken proper action if Dr. Potterley had been owner of a large, square chin, flashing eyes, aquiline nose and broad shoulders.

As it was, Thaddeus Araman found himself staring over his desk at a mild-mannered individual, whose faded blue eyes looked at him wistfully from either side of a low-bridged button nose; whose small, neatly dressed figure seemed stamped "milk-and-water" from thinning brown hair to the neatly brushed shoes that completed a conservative middle-class costume.

Araman said pleasantly, "And now what can I do for you, Dr. Potterley?"

Dr. Potterley said in a soft voice that went well with the rest of him, "Mr. Araman, I came to you because you're top man in chronoscopy."

Araman smiled. "Not exactly. Above me is the World Commissioner of Research and above him is the Secretary-General of the United Nations. And above both of them, of course, are the sovereign peoples of Earth."

Dr. Potterley shook his head. "They're not interested in chronoscopy. I've come to you, sir, because for two years I have been trying to obtain permission to do some time viewing—chronoscopy, that is—in connection with my researches on ancient Carthage. I can't obtain such permission. My research grants are all proper. There is no irregularity in any of my intellectual endeavors and yet——"

"I'm sure there is no question of irregularity," said Araman soothingly. He flipped the thin reproduction sheets in the folder to which Potterley's name had been attached. They had been produced by Multivac, whose vast analogical mind kept all the department records. When this was over, the sheets could be destroyed, then reproduced on demand in a matter of minutes.

And while Araman turned the pages, Dr. Potterley's voice continued in a soft monotone.

The historian was saying, "I must explain that my problem is quite an important one. Carthage was ancient commercialism brought to its zenith. Pre-Roman Carthage was the nearest ancient analogue to preatomic America, at least insofar as its attachment to trade, commerce and business in general was concerned. They were the most daring seamen and explorers before the Vikings; much better at it than the overrated Greeks.

"To know Carthage would be very rewarding, yet the only knowledge we have of it is derived from the writings of its bitter enemies, the Greeks and Romans. Carthage itself never wrote in its own defense or, if it did, the books did not survive. As a result, the Carthaginians have been one of the favorite sets of villains of history and perhaps unjustly so. Time viewing may set the record straight."

He said much more.

Araman said, still turning the reproduction sheets before him, "You must realize, Dr. Potterley, that chronoscopy, or time viewing, if you prefer, is a difficult process."

Dr. Potterley, who had been interrupted, frowned and said, "I am asking for only certain selected views at times and places I would indicate."

Araman sighed. "Even a few views, even one . . . It is an unbelievably delicate art. There is the question of focus, getting the proper scene in view and holding it. There is the synchronization of sound, which calls for completely independent circuits."

"Surely my problem is important enough to justify considerable effort."

"Yes, sir. Undoubtedly," said Araman at once. To deny the importance of someone's research problem would be unforgivably bad manners. "But you must understand how long-drawn-out even the simplest view is. And there is a long waiting line for the chronoscope and an even longer waiting line for the use of Multivac which guides us in our use of the controls."

Potterley stirred unhappily. "But can nothing be done? For two years——"

"A matter of priority, sir. I'm sorry. . . . Cigarette?"

The historian started back at the suggestion, eyes suddenly widening as he stared at the pack thrust out toward him. Araman looked surprised, withdrew the pack, made a motion as though to take a cigarette for himself and thought better of it.

Potterley drew a sigh of unfeigned relief as the pack was put out of sight. He said, "Is there any way of reviewing matters, putting me as far forward as possible. I don't know how to explain——"

Araman smiled. Some had offered money under similar circumstances which, of course, had gotten them nowhere, either. He said, "The decisions on priority are computer-processed. I could in no way alter those decisions arbitrarily."

Potterley rose stiffly to his feet. He stood five and a half feet tall. "Then, good day, sir."

"Good day, Dr. Potterley. And my sincerest regrets." He offered his hand and Potterley touched it briefly.

The historian left, and a touch of the buzzer brought Araman's secretary into the room. He handed her the folder.

"These," he said, "may be disposed of."

Alone again, he smiled bitterly. Another item in his quarter-century's service to the human race. Service through negation.

At least this fellow had been easy to dispose of. Sometimes academic pressure had to be applied and even withdrawal of grants.

Five minutes later, he had forgotten Dr. Potterley. Nor, thinking back on it later, could he remember feeling any premonition of danger.

During the first year of his frustration, Arnold Potterley had experienced only that—frustration. During the second year, though, his frustration gave birth to an idea that first frightened and then fascinated him. Two things stopped him from trying to translate the idea into action, and neither barrier was the undoubted fact that his notion was a grossly unethical one.

The first was merely the continuing hope that the government would finally give its permission and make it unnecessary for him to do anything more. That hope had perished finally in the interview with Araman just completed.

The second barrier had been not a hope at all but a dreary realization of his own incapacity. He was not a physicist and he knew no physicists from whom he might obtain help. The Department of Physics at the university consisted of men well stocked with grants and well immersed in specialty. At best, they would not listen to him. At worst, they would report him for intellectual anarchy and even his basic Carthaginian grant might easily be withdrawn.

That he could not risk. And yet chronoscopy was the only way to carry on his work. Without it, he would be no worse off if his grant were lost.

The first hint that the second barrier might be overcome had come a week earlier than his interview with Araman, and it had gone unrecognized at the time. It had been at one of the faculty teas. Potterley attended these sessions unfailingly because he conceived attendance to be a duty, and he took his duties seriously. Once there, however, he conceived it to be no responsibility of his to make light conversation or new friends. He sipped abstemiously at a drink or two, exchanged a polite word with the dean or such department heads as happened to be present, bestowed a narrow smile on others and finally left early.

Ordinarily, he would have paid no attention, at that most recent tea, to a young man standing quietly, even diffidently, in one corner. He would never have dreamed of speaking to him. Yet a tangle of circumstance persuaded him this once to behave in a way contrary to his nature.

That morning at breakfast, Mrs. Potterley had announced somberly that once again she had dreamed of Laurel; but this time a Laurel grown up, yet retaining the three-year-old face that stamped her as their child. Potterley had let her talk. There had been a time when he fought her too frequent preoccupation with the past and death. Laurel would not come back to them, either through dreams or through talk. Yet if it appeased Caroline Potterley—let her dream and talk.

But when Potterley went to school that morning, he found himself for once affected by Caroline's inanities. Laurel grown up! She had died nearly twenty years ago; their only child, then and ever. In all that time, when he thought of her, it was as a three-year-old.

Now he thought: But if she were alive now, she wouldn't be three, she'd be nearly twenty-three.

Helplessly, he found himself trying to think of Laurel

as growing progressively older; as finally becoming twenty-three. He did not quite succeed.

Yet he tried. Laurel using make-up. Laurel going out with boys. Laurel—getting married!

So it was that when he saw the young man hovering at the outskirts of the coldly circulating group of faculty men, it occurred to him quixotically that, for all he knew, a youngster just such as this might have married Laurel. That youngster himself, perhaps. . . .

Laurel might have met him, here at the university, or some evening when he might be invited to dinner at the Potterleys'. They might grow interested in one another. Laurel would surely have been pretty and this youngster looked well. He was dark in coloring, with a lean intent face and an easy carriage.

The tenuous daydream snapped, yet Potterley found himself staring foolishly at the young man, not as a strange face but as a possible son-in-law in the might-have-been. He found himself threading his way toward the man. It was almost a form of autohypnotism.

He put out his hand. "I am Arnold Potterley of the History Department. You're new here, I think?"

The youngster looked faintly astonished and fumbled with his drink, shifting it to his left hand in order to shake with his right. "Jonas Foster is my name, sir. I'm a new instructor in physics. I'm just starting this semester."

Potterley nodded. "I wish you a happy stay here and great success."

That was the end of it, then. Potterley had come uneasily to his senses, found himself embarrassed and moved off. He stared back over his shoulder once, but the illusion of relationship had gone. Reality was quite real once more and he was angry with himself for having fallen prey to his wife's foolish talk about Laurel.

But a week later, even while Araman was talking, the thought of that young man had come back to him. An instructor in physics. A new instructor. Had he been deaf at the time? Was there a short circuit between ear and brain? Or was it an automatic self-censorship because of the impending interview with the Head of Chronoscopy?

But the interview failed, and it was the thought of the young man with whom he had exchanged two sentences that prevented Potterley from elaborating his pleas for consideration. He was almost anxious to get away.

And in the autogiro express back to the university, he could almost wish he were superstitious. He could then console himself with the thought that the casual meaningless meeting had really been directed by a knowing and purposeful Fate.

Jonas Foster was not new to academic life. The long and rickety struggle for the doctorate would make anyone a veteran. Additional work as a postdoctorate teaching fellow acted as a booster shot.

But now he was Instructor Jonas Foster. Professorial dignity lay ahead. And he now found himself in a new sort of relationship toward other professors.

For one thing, they would be voting on future promotions. For another, he was in no position to tell so early in the game which particular member of the faculty might or might not have the ear of the dean or even of the university president. He did not fancy himself as a campus politician and was sure he would make a poor one, yet there was no point in kicking his own rear into blisters just to prove that to himself.

So Foster listened to this mild-mannered historian who, in some vague way, seemed nevertheless to radiate tension, and did not shut him up abruptly and toss him out. Certainly that was his first impulse.

He remembered Potterley well enough. Potterley had approached him at that tea (which had been a grizzly affair). The fellow had spoken two sentences to him stiffly, somehow glassy-eyed, had then come to himself with a visible start and hurried off.

It had amused Foster at the time, but now . . .

Potterley might have been deliberately trying to make his acquaintance, or, rather, to impress his own personality on Foster as that of a queer sort of duck, eccentric but harmless. He might now be probing Foster's views, searching for unsettling opinions. Surely, they ought to have done so before granting him his appointment. Still . . .

Potterley might be serious, might honestly not realize what he was doing. Or he might realize quite well what he was doing; he might be nothing more or less than a dangerous rascal.

Foster mumbled, "Well, now——" to gain time, and fished out a package of cigarettes, intending to offer one to Potterley and to light it and one for himself very slowly.

But Potterley said at once, "Please, Dr. Foster. No cigarettes."

Foster looked startled. "I'm sorry, sir."

"No. The regrets are mine. I cannot stand the odor. An idiosyncrasy. I'm sorry."

He was positively pale. Foster put away the cigarettes.

Foster, feeling the absence of the cigarette, took the easy way out. "I'm flattered that you ask my advice and all that, Dr. Potterley, but I'm not a neutrinics man. I can't very well do anything professional in that direction. Even stating an opinion would be out of line, and, frankly, I'd prefer that you didn't go into any particulars."

The historian's prim face set hard. "What do you mean, you're not a neutrinics man? You're not anything yet. You haven't received any grant, have you?"

"This is only my first semester."

"I know that. I imagine you haven't even applied for any grant yet."

Foster half-smiled. In three months at the university, he had not succeeded in putting his initial requests for research grants into good enough shape to pass on to a professional science writer, let alone to the Research Commission.

(His Department Head, fortunately, took it quite well. "Take your time now, Foster," he said, "and get your thoughts well organized. Make sure you know your path and where it will lead, for, once you receive a grant, your specialization will be formally recognized and, for better or for worse, it will be yours for the rest of your career.")

The advice was trite enough, but triteness has often the merit of truth, and Foster recognized that.)

Foster said, "By education and inclination, Dr. Potterley, I'm a hyperoptics man with a gravitics minor. It's how I described myself in applying for this position. It may not be my official specialization yet, but it's going to be. It can't be anything else. As for neutrinics, I never even studied the subject."

"Why not?" demanded Potterley at once.

Foster stared. It was the kind of rude curiosity about another man's professional status that was always irritating. He said, with the edge of his own politeness just a trifle blunted, "A course in neutrinics wasn't given at my university."

"Good Lord, where did you go?"

"M.I.T.," said Foster quietly.

"And they don't teach neutrinics?"

"No, they don't." Foster felt himself flush and was moved to a defense. "It's a highly specialized subject with no great value. Chronoscopy, perhaps, has some value, but it is the only practical application and that's a dead end."

The historian stared at him earnestly. "Tell me this. Do you know where I can find a neutrinics man?"

"No, I don't," said Foster bluntly.

"Well, then, do you know a school which teaches neutrinics?"

"No, I don't."

Potterley smiled tightly and without humor.

Foster resented that smile, found he detected insult in it and grew sufficiently annoyed to say, "I would like to point out, sir, that you're stepping out of line."

"What?"

"I'm saying that, as a historian, your interest in any sort of physics, your *professional* interest, is——" He paused, unable to bring himself quite to say the word.

"Unethical?"

"That's the word, Dr. Potterley."

"My researches have driven me to it," said Potterley in an intense whisper.

"The Research Commission is the place to go. If they permit——"

"I have gone to them and have received no satisfaction."

"Then obviously you must abandon this." Foster knew he was sounding stuffily virtuous, but he wasn't going to let this man lure him into an expression of intellectual anarchy. It was too early in his career to take stupid risks.

Apparently, though, the remark had its effect on Potterley. Without any warning, the man exploded into a rapid-fire verbal storm of irresponsibility.

Scholars, he said, could be free only if they could freely follow their own free-swinging curiosity. Research, he said, forced into a predesigned pattern by the powers that held the purse strings became slavish and had to stagnate. No man, he said, had the right to dictate the intellectual interests of another.

Foster listened to all of it with disbelief. None of it was strange to him. He had heard college boys talk so in order to shock their professors and he had once or twice amused himself in that fashion, too. Anyone who studied the history of science knew that many men had once thought so.

Yet it seemed strange to Foster, almost against nature, that a modern man of science could advance such nonsense. No one would advocate running a factory by allowing each individual worker to do whatever pleased him at the moment, or of running a ship according to the casual and conflicting notions of each individual crewman. It would be taken for granted that some sort of centralized supervisory agency must exist in each case. Why should direction and order benefit a factory and a ship but not scientific research?

People might say that the human mind was somehow qualitatively different from a ship or factory but the history of intellectual endeavor proved the opposite.

When science was young and the intricacies of all or most of the known was within the grasp of an individual mind, there was no need for direction, perhaps. Blind wandering over the uncharted tracts of ignorance could lead to wonderful finds by accident.

But as knowledge grew, more and more data had to be absorbed before worthwhile journeys into ignorance could be organized. Men had to specialize. The researcher needed the resources of a library he himself could not gather, then of instruments he himself could not afford. More and more, the individual researcher gave way to the research team and the research institution.

The funds necessary for research grew greater as tools grew more numerous. What college was so small today as not to require at least one nuclear micro-reactor and at least one three-stage computer?

Centuries before, private individuals could no longer subsidize research. By 1940, only the government, large industries and large universities or research institutions could properly subsidize basic research.

By 1960, even the largest universities depended entirely upon government grants, while research institutions could not exist without tax concessions and public subscriptions. By 2000, the industrial combines had become a branch of the world government and, thereafter, the financing of research and therefore its direction naturally became centralized under a department of the government.

It all worked itself out naturally and well. Every branch of science was fitted neatly to the needs of the public, and the various branches of science were co-ordinated decently. The material advance of the last half-century was argument enough for the fact that science was not falling into stagnation.

Foster tried to say a very little of this and was waved aside impatiently by Potterley who said, "You are parroting official propaganda. You're sitting in the middle of an example that's squarely against the official view. Can you believe that?"

"Frankly, no."

"Well, why do you say time viewing is a dead end? Why is neutrinics unimportant? You say it is. You say it categorically. Yet you've never studied it. You claim complete ignorance of the subject. It's not even given in your school——"

"Isn't the mere fact that it isn't given proof enough?"

"Oh, I see. It's not given because it's unimportant. And it's unimportant because it's not given. Are you satisfied with that reasoning?"

Foster felt a growing confusion. "It's in the books."

"That's all. The books say neutrinics is unimportant. Your professors tell you so because they read it in the books. The books say so because professors write them. Who says it from personal experience and knowledge? Who does research in it? Do you know of anyone?"

Foster said, "I don't see that we're getting anywhere, Dr. Potterley. I have work to do——"

"One minute. I just want you to try this on. See how it sounds to you. I say the government is actively suppressing basic research in neutrinics and chronoscopy. They're suppressing application of chronoscopy."

"Oh, no."

"Why not? They could do it. There's your centrally directed research. If they refuse grants for research in any portion of science, that portion dies. They've killed neutrinics. They can do it and have done it."

"But why?"

"I don't know why. I want you to find out. I'd do it myself if I knew enough. I came to you because you're a young fellow with a brand-new education. Have your intellectual arteries hardened already? Is there no curiosity in you? Don't you want to *know*? Don't you want *answers*?"

The historian was peering intently into Foster's face. Their noses were only inches apart, and Foster was so lost that he did not think to draw back.

He should, by rights, have ordered Potterley out. If necessary, he should have thrown Potterley out.

It was not respect for age and position that stopped him. It was certainly not that Potterley's arguments had convinced him. Rather, it was a small point of college pride.

Why didn't M.I.T. give a course in neutrinics? For that

matter, now that he came to think of it, he doubted that there was a single book on neutrinics in the library. He could never recall having seen one.

He stopped to think about that.

And that was ruin.

Caroline Potterley had once been an attractive woman. There were occasions, such as dinners or university functions, when, by considerable effort, remnants of the attraction could be salvaged.

On ordinary occasions, she sagged. It was the word she applied to herself in moments of self-abhorrence. She had grown plumper with the years, but the flaccidity about her was not a matter of fat entirely. It was as though her muscles had given up and grown limp so that she shuffled when she walked while her eyes grew baggy and her cheeks jowly. Even her graying hair seemed tired rather than merely stringy. Its straightness seemed to be the result of a supine surrender to gravity, nothing else.

Caroline Potterley looked at herself in the mirror and admitted this was one of her bad days. She knew the reason, too.

It had been the dream of Laurel. The strange one, with Laurel grown up. She had been wretched ever since.

Still, she was sorry she had mentioned it to Arnold. He didn't say anything; he never did any more; but it was bad for him. He was particularly withdrawn for days afterward. It might have been that he was getting ready for that important conference with the big government official (he kept saying he expected no success), but it might also have been her dream.

It was better in the old days when he would cry sharply at her, "Let the dead past *go*, Caroline! Talk won't bring her back, and dreams won't either."

It had been bad for both of them. Horribly bad. She had been away from home and had lived in guilt ever since. If she had stayed at home, if she had not gone on an unnecessary shopping expedition, there would have been two of them available. One would have succeeded in saving Laurel.

Poor Arnold had not managed. Heaven knew he tried.
He had nearly died himself. He had come out of the
burning house, staggering in agony, blistered, choking,
half-blinded, with the dead Laurel in his arms.

The nightmare of that lived on, never lifting entirely.

Arnold slowly grew a shell about himself afterward.
He cultivated a low-voiced mildness through which nothing broke, no lightning struck. He grew puritanical and
even abandoned his minor vices, his cigarettes, his penchant for an occasional profane exclamation. He obtained his grant for the preparation of a new history of
Carthage and subordinated everything to that.

She tried to help him. She hunted up his references,
typed his notes and microfilmed them. Then that ended
suddenly.

She ran from the desk suddenly one evening, reaching
the bathroom in bare time and retching abominably. Her
husband followed her in confusion and concern.

"Caroline, what's wrong?"

It took a drop of brandy to bring her around. She said,
"Is it true? What they did?"

"Who did?"

"The Carthaginians."

He stared at her and she got it out by indirection. She
couldn't say it right out.

The Carthaginians, it seemed, worshiped Moloch, in
the form of a hollow, brazen idol with a furnace in its
belly. At times of national crisis, the priests and the
people gathered, and infants, after the proper ceremonies and invocations, were dexterously hurled, alive, into
the flames.

They were given sweetmeats just before the crucial
moment, in order that the efficacy of the sacrifice not be
ruined by displeasing cries of panic. The drums rolled
just after the moment, to drown out the few seconds of
infant shrieking. The parents were present, presumably
gratified, for the sacrifice was pleasing to the gods. . . .

Arnold Potterley frowned darkly. Vicious lies, he told
her, on the part of Carthage's enemies. He should have
warned her. After all, such propagandistic lies were not

uncommon. According to the Greeks, the ancient Hebrews worshiped an ass's head in their Holy of Holies. According to the Romans, the primitive Christians were haters of all men who sacrificed pagan children in the catacombs.

"Then they didn't do it?" asked Caroline.

"I'm sure they didn't. The primitive Phoenicians may have. Human sacrifice is commonplace in primitive cultures. But Carthage in her great days was not a primitive culture. Human sacrifice often gives way to symbolic actions such as circumcision. The Greeks and Romans might have mistaken some Carthaginian symbolism for the original full rite, either out of ignorance or out of malice."

"Are you sure?"

"I can't be sure yet, Caroline, but when I've got enough evidence, I'll apply for permission to use chronoscopy, which will settle the matter once and for all."

"Chronoscopy?"

"Time viewing. We can focus on ancient Carthage at some time of crisis, the landing of Scipio Africanus in 202 B.C., for instance, and see with our own eyes exactly what happens. And you'll see, I'll be right."

He patted her and smiled encouragingly, but she dreamed of Laurel every night for two weeks thereafter and she never helped him with his Carthage project again. Nor did he ever ask her to.

But now she was bracing herself for his coming. He had called her after arriving back in town, told her he had seen the government man and that it had gone as expected. That meant failure, and yet the little telltale sign of depression had been absent from his voice and his features had appeared quite composed in the teleview. He had another errand to take care of, he said, before coming home.

It meant he would be late, but that didn't matter. Neither one of them was particular about eating hours or cared when packages were taken out of the freezer or even which packages or when the self-warming mechanism was activated.

When he did arrive, he surprised her. There was nothing untoward about him in any obvious way. He kissed her dutifully and smiled, took off his hat and asked if all had been well while he was gone. It was all almost perfectly normal. Almost.

She had learned to detect small things, though, and his pace in all this was a trifle hurried. Enough to show her accustomed eye that he was under tension.

She said, "Has something happened?"

He said, "We're going to have a dinner guest night after next, Caroline. You don't mind?"

"Well, no. Is it anyone I know?"

"No. A young instructor. A newcomer. I've spoken to him." He suddenly whirled toward her and seized her arms at the elbow, held them a moment, then dropped them in confusion as though disconcerted at having shown emotion.

He said, "I almost didn't get through to him. Imagine that. Terrible, *terrible*, the way we have all bent to the yoke; the affection we have for the harness about us."

Mrs. Potterley wasn't sure she understood, but for a year she had been watching him grow quietly more rebellious; little by little more daring in his criticism of the government. She said, "You haven't spoken foolishly to him, have you?"

"What do you mean, foolishly? He'll be doing some neutrinics for me."

"Neutrinics" was trisyllabic nonsense to Mrs. Potterley, but she knew it had nothing to do with history. She said faintly, "Arnold, I don't like you to do that. You'll lose your position. It's——"

"It's intellectual anarchy, my dear," he said. "That's the phrase you want. Very well. I am an anarchist. If the government will not allow me to push my researches, I will push them on my own. And when I show the way, others will follow. . . . And if they don't, it makes no difference. It's Carthage that counts and human knowledge, not you and I."

"But you don't know this young man. What if he is an agent for the Commissioner of Research."

"Not likely and I'll take that chance." He made a fist of his right hand and rubbed it gently against the palm of his left. "He's on my side now. I'm sure of it. He can't help but be. I can recognize intellectual curiosity when I see it in a man's eyes and face and attitude, and it's a fatal disease for a tame scientist. Even today it takes time to beat it out of a man and the young ones are vulnerable. . . . Oh, why stop at anything? Why not build our own chronoscope and tell the government to go to——"

He stopped abruptly, shook his head and turned away.

"I hope everything will be all right," said Mrs. Potterley, feeling helplessly certain that everything would not be, and frightened, in advance, for her husband's professorial status and the security of their old age.

It was she alone, of them all, who had a violent presentiment of trouble. Quite the wrong trouble, of course.

Jonas Foster was nearly half an hour late in arriving at the Potterleys' off-campus house. Up to that very evening, he had not quite decided he would go. Then, at the last moment, he found he could not bring himself to commit the social enormity of breaking a dinner appointment an hour before the appointed time. That, and the nagging of curiosity.

The dinner itself passed interminably. Foster ate without appetite. Mrs. Potterley sat in distant absent-mindedness, emerging out of it only once to ask if he were married and to make a deprecating sound at the news that he was not. Dr. Potterley himself asked neutrally after his professional history and nodded his head primly.

It was as staid, stodgy—boring, actually—as anything could be.

Foster thought: He seems so harmless.

Foster had spent the last two days reading up on Dr. Potterley. Very casually, of course, almost sneakily. He wasn't particularly anxious to be seen in the Social Science Library. To be sure, history was one of those borderline affairs and historical works were frequently read for amusement or edification by the general public.

Still, a physicist wasn't quite the "general public." Let

Foster take to reading histories and he would be considered queer, sure as relativity, and after a while the Head of the Department would wonder if his new instructor were really "the man for the job."

So he had been cautious. He sat in the more secluded alcoves and kept his head bent when he slipped in and out at odd hours.

Dr. Potterley, it turned out, had written three books and some dozen articles on the ancient Mediterranean worlds, and the later articles (all in "Historical Reviews") had all dealt with pre-Roman Carthage from a sympathetic viewpoint.

That, at least, checked with Potterley's story and had soothed Foster's suspicions somewhat. . . . And yet Foster felt that it would have been much wiser, much safer, to have scotched the matter at the beginning.

A scientist shouldn't be too curious, he thought in bitter dissatisfaction with himself. It's a dangerous trait.

After dinner, he was ushered into Potterley's study and he was brought up sharply at the threshold. The walls were simply lined with books.

Not merely films. There were films, of course, but these were far outnumbered by the books—print on paper. He wouldn't have thought so many books would exist in usable condition.

That bothered Foster. Why should anyone want to keep so many books at home? Surely all were available in the university library, or, at the very worst, at the Library of Congress, if one wished to take the minor trouble of checking out a microfilm.

There was an element of secrecy involved in a home library. It breathed of intellectual anarchy. That last thought, oddly, calmed Foster. He would rather Potterley be an authentic anarchist than a playacting *agent provocateur.*

And now the hours began to pass quickly and astonishingly.

"You see," Potterley said, in a clear, unflurried voice, "it was a matter of finding, if possible, anyone who had ever used chronoscopy in his work. Naturally, I couldn't ask baldly, since that would be unauthorized research."

"Yes," said Foster dryly. He was a little surprised such a small consideration would stop the man.

"I used indirect methods——"

He had. Foster was amazed at the volume of correspondence dealing with small disputed points of ancient Mediterranean culture which somehow managed to elicit the casual remark over and over again: "Of course, having never made use of chronoscopy——" or, "Pending approval of my request for chronoscopic data, which appears unlikely at the moment——"

"Now these aren't blind questionings," said Potterley. "There's a monthly booklet put out by the Institute for Chronoscopy in which items concerning the past as determined by time viewing are printed. Just one or two items.

"What impressed me first was the triviality of most of the items, their insipidity. Why should such researches get priority over my work? So I wrote to people who would be most likely to do research in the directions described in the booklet. Uniformly, as I have shown you, they did *not* make use of the chronoscope. Now let's go over it point by point."

At last Foster, his head swimming with Potterley's meticulously gathered details, asked, "But why?"

"I don't know why," said Potterley, "but I have a theory. The original invention of the chronoscope was by Sterbinski—you see, I know that much—and it was well publicized. But then the government took over the instrument and decided to suppress further research in the matter or any use of the machine. But then, people might be curious as to why it wasn't being used. Curiosity is such a vice, Dr. Foster."

Yes, agreed the physicist to himself.

"Imagine the effectiveness, then," Potterley went on, "of pretending that the chronoscope *was* being used. It would then be not a mystery, but a commonplace. It would no longer be a fitting object for legitimate curiosity or an attractive one for illicit curiosity."

"*You* were curious," pointed out Foster.

Potterley looked a trifle restless. "It was different in my case," he said angrily. "I have something that *must* be done, and I wouldn't submit to the ridiculous way in which they kept putting me off."

A bit paranoid, too, thought Foster gloomily.

Yet he had ended up with something, paranoid or not. Foster could no longer deny that something peculiar was going on in the matter of neutrinics.

But what was Potterley after? That still bothered Foster. If Potterley didn't intend this as a test of Foster's ethics, what *did* he want?

Foster put it to himself logically. If an intellectual anarchist with a touch of paranoia wanted to use a chronoscope and was convinced that the powers-that-be were deliberately standing in his way, what would he do?

Supposing it were I, he thought. What would I do?

He said slowly, "Maybe the chronoscope doesn't exist at all?"

Potterley started. There was almost a crack in his general calmness. For an instant, Foster found himself catching a glimpse of something not at all calm.

But the historian kept his balance and said, "Oh, no, there *must* be a chronoscope."

"Why? Have you seen it? Have I? Maybe that's the explanation of everything. Maybe they're not deliberately holding out on a chronoscope they've got. Maybe they haven't got it in the first place."

"But Sterbinski lived. He built a chronoscope. That much is a fact."

"The books say so," said Foster coldly.

"Now listen." Potterley actually reached over and snatched at Foster's jacket sleeve. "I need the chronoscope. I must have it. Don't tell me it doesn't exist. What we're going to do is find out enough about neutrinics to be able to——"

Potterley drew himself up short.

Foster drew his sleeve away. He needed no ending to that sentence. He supplied it himself. He said, "Build one of our own?"

Potterley looked sour as though he would rather not have said it point-blank. Nevertheless, he said, "Why not?"

"Because that's out of the question," said Foster. "If what I've read is correct, then it took Sterbinski twenty years to build his machine and several millions in composite grants. Do you think you and I can duplicate that illegally? Suppose we had the time, which we haven't, and suppose I could learn enough out of books, which I doubt, where would we get the money and equipment? The chronoscope is supposed to fill a five-story building, for Heaven's sake."

"Then you won't help me?"

"Well, I'll tell you what. I have one way in which I may be able to find out something——"

"What is that?" asked Potterley at once.

"Never mind. That's not important. But I may be able to find out enough to tell you whether the government is deliberately suppressing research by chronoscope. I may confirm the evidence you already have or I may be able to prove that your evidence is misleading. I don't know what good it will do you in either case, but it's as far as I can go. It's my limit."

Potterley watched the young man go finally. He was angry with himself. Why had he allowed himself to grow so careless as to permit the fellow to guess that he was thinking in terms of a chronoscope of his own. That was premature.

But then why did the young fool have to suppose that a chronoscope might not exist at all?

It *had* to exist. It *had* to. What was the use of saying it didn't?

And why couldn't a second one be built? Science had advanced in the fifty years since Sterbinski. All that was needed was knowledge.

Let the youngster gather knowledge. Let him think a small gathering would be his limit. Having taken the path to anarchy, there would be no limit. If the boy were not driven onward by something in himself, the first steps would be error enough to force the rest. Potterley was quite certain he would not hesitate to use blackmail.

Potterley waved a last good-by and looked up. It was beginning to rain.

Certainly! Blackmail if necessary, but he would not be stopped.

Foster steered his car across the bleak outskirts of town and scarcely noticed the rain. He *was* a fool, he told himself, but he couldn't leave things as they were. He had to know. He damned his streak of undisciplined curiosity, but he had to know.

But he would go no further than Uncle Ralph. He swore mightily to himself that it would stop there. In that way, there would be no evidence against him, no real evidence. Uncle Ralph would be discreet.

In a way, he was secretly ashamed of Uncle Ralph. He hadn't mentioned him to Potterley partly out of caution and partly because he did not wish to witness the lifted eyebrow, the inevitable half-smile. Professional science writers, however useful, were a little outside the pale, fit only for patronizing contempt. The fact that, as a class, they made more money than did research scientists only made matters worse, of course.

Still, there were times when a science writer in the family could be a convenience. Not being really educated, they did not have to specialize. Consequently, a good science writer knew practically everything. . . . And Uncle Ralph was one of the best.

Ralph Nimmo had no college degree and was rather proud of it. "A degree," he once said to Jonas Foster, when both were considerably younger, "is a first step down a ruinous highway. You don't want to waste it so you go on to graduate work and doctoral research. You end up a thoroughgoing ignoramus on everything in the world except for one subdivisional sliver of nothing.

"On the other hand, if you guard your mind carefully and keep it blank of any clutter of information till maturity is reached, filling it only with intelligence and training it only in clear thinking, you then have a powerful instrument at your disposal and you can become a science writer."

Nimmo received his first assignment at the age of twenty-five, after he had completed his apprenticeship and been out in the field for less than three months. It came in the shape of a clotted manuscript whose language would impart no glimmering of understanding to any reader, however qualified, without careful study and some inspired guesswork. Nimmo took it apart and put it together again (after five long and exasperating interviews with the authors, who were biophysicists), making the language taut and meaningful and smoothing the style to a pleasant gloss.

"Why not?" he would say tolerantly to his nephew, who countered his strictures on degrees by berating him with his readiness to hang on the fringes of science. "The fringe is important. Your scientists can't write. Why should they be expected to? They aren't expected to be grand masters at chess or virtuosos at the violin, so why expect them to know how to put words together? Why not leave that for specialists, too?

"Good Lord, Jonas, read your literature of a hundred years ago. Discount the fact that the science is out of date and that some of the expressions are out of date. Just try to read it and make sense out of it. It's just jaw-cracking, amateurish. Pages are published uselessly; whole articles which are either meaningless or noncomprehensible or both."

"But you don't get recognition, Uncle Ralph," protested young Foster, who was getting ready to start his college career and was rather starry-eyed about it. "You could be a terrific researcher."

"I get recognition," said Nimmo. "Don't think for a minute I don't. Sure, a biochemist or a strato-meteorologist won't give me the time of day, but they pay me well enough. Just find out what happens when some first-class chemist finds the Commission has cut his year's allowance for science writing. He'll fight harder for enough funds to afford me, or someone like me, than to get a recording ionograph."

He grinned broadly and Foster grinned back. Actually, he was proud of his paunchy, round-faced, stub-fingered uncle, whose vanity made him brush his fringe of hair futilely over the desert on his pate and made him dress like an unmade haystack because such negligence was his trademark. Ashamed, but proud, too.

And now Foster entered his uncle's cluttered apartment in no mood at all for grinning. He was nine years older now and so was Uncle Ralph. For nine more years, papers in every branch of science had come to him for polishing and a little of each had crept into his capacious mind.

Nimmo was eating seedless grapes, popping them into his mouth one at a time. He tossed a bunch to Foster who caught them by a hair, then bent to retrieve individual grapes that had torn loose and fallen to the floor.

"Let them be. Don't bother," said Nimmo carelessly. "Someone comes in here to clean once a week. What's up? Having trouble with your grant application write-up?"

"I haven't really got into that yet."

"You haven't? Get a move on, boy. Are you waiting for me to offer to do the final arrangement?"

"I couldn't afford you, Uncle."

"Aw, come on. It's all in the family. Grant me all popular publication rights and no cash need change hands."

Foster nodded. "If you're serious, it's a deal."

"It's a deal."

It was a gamble, of course, but Foster knew enough of Nimmo's science writing to realize it could pay off. Some dramatic discovery of public interest on primitive man or on a new surgical technique, or on any branch of spationautics could mean a very cash-attracting article in any of the mass media of communication.

It was Nimmo, for instance, who had written up, for scientific consumption, the series of papers by Bryce and co-workers that elucidated the fine structure of two cancer viruses, for which job he asked the picayune payment of fifteen hundred dollars, provided popular publication rights were included. He then wrote up, exclusively, the same work in semidramatic form for use in trimensional video for a twenty-thousand-dollar advance plus rental royalties that were still coming in after five years.

Foster said bluntly, "What do you know about neutrinics, Uncle?"

"Neutrinics?" Nimmo's small eyes looked surprised. "Are you working in that? I thought it was pseudo-gravitic optics."

"It is p.g.o. I just happen to be asking about neutrinics."

"That's a devil of a thing to be doing. You're stepping out of line. You know that, don't you?"

"I don't expect you to call the Commission because I'm a little curious about things."

"Maybe I should before you get into trouble. Curiosity is an occupational danger with scientists. I've watched it work. One of them will be moving quietly along on a problem, then curiosity leads him up a strange creek. Next thing you know they've done so little on their proper problem, they can't justify for a project renewal. I've seen more——"

"All I want to know," said Foster patiently, "is what's been passing through your hands lately on neutrinics."

Nimmo leaned back, chewing at a grape thoughtfully. "Nothing. Nothing ever. I don't recall ever getting a paper on neutrinics."

"What!" Foster was openly astonished. "Then who does get the work?"

"Now that you ask," said Nimmo, "I don't know. Don't recall anyone talking about it at the annual conventions. I don't think much work is being done there."

"Why not?"

"Hey, there, don't bark. I'm not doing anything. My guess would be——"

Foster was exasperated. "Don't you know?"

"Hmp. I'll tell you what I know about neutrinics. It concerns the applications of neutrino movements and the forces involved——"

"Sure. Sure. Just as electronics deals with the applications of electron movements and the forces involved, and pseudo-gravitics deals with the applications of artificial gravitational fields. I didn't come to you for that. Is that all you know?"

"And," said Nimmo with equanimity, "neutrinics is the basis of time viewing and that *is* all I know."

Foster slouched back in his chair and massaged one lean cheek with great intensity. He felt angrily dissatisfied. Without formulating it explicitly in his own mind, he had felt sure, somehow, that Nimmo would come up with some late reports, bring up interesting facets of modern neutrinics, send him back to Potterley able to say that the elderly historian was mistaken, that his data was misleading, his deductions mistaken.

Then he could have returned to his proper work.

But now . . .

He told himself angrily: So they're not doing much work in the field. Does that make it deliberate suppression? What if neutrinics is a sterile discipline? Maybe it is. I don't know. Potterley doesn't. Why waste the intellectual resources of humanity on nothing? Or the work might be secret for some legitimate reason. It might be. . .

The trouble was, he had to know. He couldn't leave things as they were now. *He couldn't!*

He said, "Is there a text on neutrinics, Uncle Ralph? I mean a clear and simple one. An elementary one."

Nimmo thought, his plump cheeks puffing out with a series of sighs. "You ask the damnedest questions. The only one I ever heard of was Sterbinski and somebody. I've never seen it, but I viewed something about it once. . . . Sterbinski and LaMarr, that's it."

"Is that the Sterbinski who invented the chronoscope?"

"I think so. Proves the book ought to be good."

"Is there a recent edition? Sterbinski died thirty years ago."

Nimmo shrugged and said nothing.

"Can you find out?"

They sat in silence for a moment, while Nimmo shifted his bulk to the creaking tune of the chair he sat on. Then the science writer said, "Are you going to tell me what this is all about?"

"I can't. Will you help me anyway, Uncle Ralph? Will you get me a copy of the text?"

"Well, you've taught me all I know on pseudo-gravitics. I should be grateful. Tell you what—I'll help you on one condition."

"Which is?"

The older man was suddenly very grave. "That you be careful, Jonas. You're obviously way out of line whatever you're doing. Don't blow up your career just because you're curious about something you haven't been assigned to and which is none of your business. Understand?"

Foster nodded, but he hardly heard. He was thinking furiously.

A full week later, Ralph Nimmo eased his rotund figure into Jonas Foster's on-campus two-room combination and said, in a hoarse whisper, "I've got something."

"What?" Foster was immediately eager.

"A copy of Sterbinski and LaMarr." He produced it, or rather a corner of it, from his ample topcoat.

Foster almost automatically eyed door and windows to make sure they were closed and shaded respectively, then held out his hand.

The film case was flaking with age, and when he cracked it the film was faded and growing brittle. He said sharply, "Is this all?"

"Gratitude, my boy, gratitude!" Nimmo sat down with a grunt, and reached into a pocket for an apple.

"Oh, I'm grateful, but it's so old."

"And lucky to get it at that. I tried to get a film run from the Congressional Library. No go. The book was restricted."

"Then how did you get this?"

"Stole it." He was biting crunchingly around the core. "New York Public."

"What?"

"Simple enough. I had access to the stacks, naturally. So I stepped over a chained railing when no one was around, dug this up, and walked out with it. They're very trusting out there. Meanwhile, they won't miss it in years. . . . Only you'd better not let anyone see it on you, nephew."

Foster stared at the film as though it were literally hot.

Nimmo discarded the core and reached for a second apple. "Funny thing, now. There's nothing more recent in the whole field of neutrinics. Not a monograph, not a paper, not a progress note. Nothing since the chronoscope."

"Uh-huh," said Foster absently.

Foster worked evenings in the Potterley home. He could not trust his own on-campus rooms for the purpose. The evening work grew more real to him than his own grant applications. Sometimes he worried about it but then that stopped, too.

His work consisted, at first, simply in viewing and reviewing the text film. Later it consisted in thinking (sometimes while a section of the book ran itself off through the pocket projector, disregarded).

Sometimes Potterley would come down to watch, to sit with prim, eager eyes, as though he expected thought processes to solidify and become visible in all their convolutions. He interfered in only two ways. He did not allow Foster to smoke and sometimes he talked.

It wasn't conversation talk, never that. Rather it was a low-voiced monologue with which, it seemed, he scarcely expected to command attention. It was much more as though he were relieving a pressure within himself.

Carthage! Always Carthage!

Carthage, the New York of the ancient Mediterranean. Carthage, commercial empire and queen of the seas. Carthage, all that Syracuse and Alexandria pretended to be. Carthage, maligned by her enemies and inarticulate in her own defense.

She had been defeated once by Rome and then driven out of Sicily and Sardinia, but came back to more than recoup her losses by new dominions in Spain, and raised up Hannibal to give the Romans sixteen years of terror.

In the end, she lost again a second time, reconciled herself to fate and built again with broken tools a limping life in shrunken territory, succeeding so well that jealous Rome deliberately forced a third war. And then Carthage, with nothing but bare hands and tenacity, built weapons and forced Rome into a two-year war that ended only with complete destruction of the city, the inhabitants throwing themselves into their flaming houses rather than surrender.

"Could people fight so for a city and a way of life as bad as the ancient writers painted it? Hannibal was a better general than any Roman and his soldiers were absolutely faithful to him. Even his bitterest enemies praised him. There was a Carthaginian. It is fashionable to say that he was an atypical Carthaginian, better than the others, a diamond placed in garbage. But then why was he so faithful to Carthage, even to his death after years of exile? They talk of Moloch——"

Foster didn't always listen but sometimes he couldn't help himself and he shuddered and turned sick at the bloody tale of child sacrifice.

But Potterley went on earnestly, "Just the same, it isn't true. It's a twenty-five-hundred-year-old canard started by the Greeks and Romans. They had their own slaves, their crucifixions and torture, their gladiatorial contests. They weren't holy. The Moloch story is what later ages would have called war propaganda, the big lie. I can prove it was a lie. I can prove it and, by Heaven, I will—I will——"

He would mumble that promise over and over again in his earnestness.

Mrs. Potterley visited him also, but less frequently, usually on Tuesdays and Thursdays when Dr. Potterley himself had an evening course to take care of and was not present.

She would sit quietly, scarcely talking, face slack and doughy, eyes blank, her whole attitude distant and withdrawn.

The first time, Foster tried, uneasily, to suggest that she leave.

She said tonelessly, "Do I disturb you?"

"No, of course not," lied Foster restlessly. "It's just that—that——" He couldn't complete the sentence.

She nodded, as though accepting an invitation to stay. Then she opened a cloth bag she had brought with her and took out a quire of vitron sheets which she proceeded to weave together by rapid, delicate movements of a pair of slender, tetra-faceted depolarizers, whose battery-fed wires made her look as though she were holding a large spider.

One evening, she said softly, "My daughter, Laurel, is your age."

Foster started, as much at the sudden unexpected sound of speech as at the words. He said, "I didn't know you had a daughter, Mrs. Potterley."

"She died. Years ago."

The vitron grew under the deft manipulations into the uneven shape of some garment Foster could not yet identify. There was nothing left for him to do but mutter inanely, "I'm sorry."

Mrs. Potterley sighed. "I dream about her often." She raised her blue, distant eyes to him.

Foster winced and looked away.

Another evening she asked, pulling at one of the vitron sheets to loosen its gentle clinging to her dress, "What is time viewing anyway?"

That remark broke into a particularly involved chain of thought, and Foster said snappishly, "Dr. Potterley can explain."

"He's tried to. Oh, my, yes. But I think he's a little impatient with me. He calls it chronoscopy most of the time. Do you actually see things in the past, like the trimensionals? Or does it just make little dot patterns like the computer you use?"

Foster stared at his hand computer with distaste. It worked well enough, but every operation had to be manually controlled and the answers were obtained in code. Now if he could use the school computer . . . Well, why dream, he felt conspicuous enough, as it was, carrying a hand computer under his arm every evening as he left his office.

He said, "I've never seen the chronoscope myself, but I'm under the impression that you actually see pictures and hear sound."

"You can hear people talk, too?"

"I think so." Then, half in desperation, "Look here, Mrs. Potterley, this must be awfully dull for you. I realize you don't like to leave a guest all to himself, but really, Mrs. Potterley, you mustn't feel compelled——"

"I don't feel compelled," she said. "I'm sitting here, waiting."

"Waiting? For what?"

She said composedly, "I listened to you that first evening. The time you first spoke to Arnold. I listened at the door."

He said, "You did?"

"I know I shouldn't have, but I was awfully worried about Arnold. I had a notion he was going to do something he oughtn't and I wanted to hear what. And then when I heard——" She paused, bending close over the vitron and peering at it.

"Heard what, Mrs. Potterley?"

"That you wouldn't build a chronoscope."

"Well, of course not."

"I thought maybe you might change your mind."

Foster glared at her. "Do you mean you're coming down here hoping I'll build a chronoscope, waiting for me to build one?"

"I hope you do, Dr. Foster. Oh, I hope you do."

It was as though, all at once, a fuzzy veil had fallen off her face, leaving all her features clear and sharp, putting color into her cheeks, life into her eyes, the vibrations of something approaching excitement into her voice.

"Wouldn't it be wonderful," she whispered, "to have one? People of the past could live again. Pharaohs and kings and—just people. I hope you build one, Dr. Foster. I really—hope——"

She choked, it seemed, on the intensity of her own words and let the vitron sheets slip off her lap. She rose and ran up the basement stairs, while Foster's eyes followed her awkwardly fleeing body with astonishment and distress.

It cut deeper into Foster's nights and left him sleepless and painfully stiff with thought. It was almost a mental indigestion.

His grant requests went limping in, finally, to Ralph Nimmo. He scarcely had any hope for them. He thought numbly: They won't be approved.

If they weren't, of course, it would create a scandal in the department and probably mean his appointment at the university would not be renewed, come the end of the academic year.

He scarcely worried. It was the neutrino, the neutrino, only the neutrino. Its trail curved and veered sharply and led him breathlessly along uncharted pathways that even Sterbinski and LaMarr did not follow.

He called Nimmo. "Uncle Ralph, I need a few things. I'm calling from off the campus."

Nimmo's face in the video plate was jovial, but his voice was sharp. He said, "What you need is a course in communication. I'm having a hell of a time pulling your application into one intelligible piece. If that's what you're calling about——"

Foster shook his head impatiently. "That's *not* what I'm calling about. I need these." He scribbled quickly on a piece of paper and held it up before the receiver.

Nimmo yiped. "Hey, how many tricks do you think I can wangle?"

"You can get them, Uncle. You know you can."

Nimmo reread the list of items with silent motions of his plump lips and looked grave.

"What happens when you put those things together?" he asked. Foster shook his head. "You'll have exclusive popular publication rights to whatever turns up, the way it's always been. But please don't ask any questions now."

"I can't do miracles, you know."

"Do this one. You've got to. You're a science writer, not a research man. You don't have to account for anything. You've got friends and connections. They can look the other way, can't they, to get a break from you next publication time?"

"Your faith, nephew, is touching. I'll try."

Nimmo succeeded. The material and equipment were brought over late one evening in a private touring car. Nimmo and Foster lugged it in with the grunting of men unused to manual labor.

Potterley stood at the entrance of the basement after Nimmo had left. He asked softly, "What's this for?"

Foster brushed the hair off his forehead and gently massaged a sprained wrist. He said, "I want to conduct a few simple experiments."

"Really?" The historian's eyes glittered with excitement.

Foster felt exploited. He felt as though he were being led along a dangerous highway by the pull of pinching fingers on his nose; as though he could see the ruin clearly that lay in wait at the end of the path, yet walked eagerly and determinedly. Worst of all, he felt the compelling grip on his nose to be his own.

It was Potterley who began it, Potterley who stood there now, gloating; but the compulsion was his own.

Foster said sourly, "I'll be wanting privacy now, Potterley. I can't have you and your wife running down here and annoying me."

He thought: If that offends him, let him kick me out. Let him put an end to this.

In his heart, though, he did not think being evicted would stop anything.

But it did not come to that. Potterley was showing no signs of offense. His mild gaze was unchanged. He said, "Of course, Dr. Foster, of course. All the privacy you wish."

Foster watched him go. He was left still marching along the highway, perversely glad of it and hating himself for being glad.

He took to sleeping over on a cot in Potterley's basement and spending his weekends there entirely.

During that period, preliminary word came through that his grants (as doctored by Nimmo) had been approved. The Department Head brought the word and congratulated him.

Foster stared back distantly and mumbled, "Good. I'm glad," with so little conviction that the other frowned and turned away without another word.

Foster gave the matter no further thought. It was a minor point, worth no notice. He was planning something that really counted, a climactic test for that evening.

One evening, a second and third and then, haggard and half beside himself with excitement, he called in Potterley.

Potterley came down the stairs and looked about at the homemade gadgetry. He said, in his soft voice, "The electric bills are quite high. I don't mind the expense, but the City may ask questions. Can anything be done?"

It was a warm evening, but Potterley wore a tight collar and a semijacket. Foster, who was in his undershirt, lifted bleary eyes and said shakily, "It won't be for much longer, Dr. Potterley. I've called you down to tell you something. A chronoscope can be built. A small one, of course, but it can be built."

Potterley seized the railing. His body sagged. He managed a whisper. "Can it be built here?"

"Here in the basement," said Foster wearily.

"Good Lord. You said——"

"I know what I said," cried Foster impatiently. "I said it couldn't be done. I didn't know anything then. Even Sterbinski didn't know anything."

Potterley shook his head. "Are you sure? You're not mistaken, Dr. Foster? I couldn't endure it if——"

Foster said, "I'm not mistaken. Damn it, sir, if just theory had been enough, we could have had a time viewer over a hundred years ago, when the neutrino was first postulated. The trouble was, the original investigators considered it only a mysterious particle without mass or charge that could not be detected. It was just something to even up the bookkeeping and save the law of conservation of mass energy."

He wasn't sure Potterley knew what he was talking

about. He didn't care. He needed a breather. He had to get some of this out of his clotting thoughts. . . . And he needed background for what he would have to tell Potterley next.

He went on. "It was Sterbinski who first discovered that the neutrino broke through the space-time cross-sectional barrier, that it traveled through time as well as through space. It was Sterbinski who first devised a method for stopping neutrinos. He invented a neutrino recorder and learned how to interpret the pattern of the neutrino stream. Naturally, the stream had been affected and deflected by all the matter it had passed through in its passage through time, and the deflections could be analyzed and converted into the images of the matter that had done the deflecting. Time viewing was possible. Even air vibrations could be detected in this way and converted into sound."

Potterley was definitely not listening. He said, "Yes. Yes. But when can you build a chronoscope?"

Foster said urgently, "Let me finish. Everything depends on the method used to detect and analyze the neutrino stream. Sterbinski's method was difficult and roundabout. It required mountains of energy. But I've studied pseudo-gravitics, Dr. Potterley, the science of artificial gravitational fields. I've specialized in the behavior of light in such fields. It's a new science. Sterbinski knew nothing of it. If he had, he would have seen—anyone would have—a much better and more efficient method of detecting neutrinos using a pseudo-gravitic field. If I had known more neutrinics to begin with, I would have seen it at once."

Potterley brightened a bit. "I knew it," he said. "Even if they stop research in neutrinics there is no way the government can be sure that discoveries in other segments of science won't reflect knowledge on neutrinics. So much for the value of centralized direction of science. I thought this long ago, Dr. Foster, before you ever came to work here."

"I congratulate you on that," said Foster, "but there's one thing——"

"Oh, never mind all this. Answer me. Please. When can you build a chronoscope?"

"I'm trying to tell you something, Dr. Potterley. A chronoscope won't do you any good." (This is it, Foster thought.)

Slowly, Potterley descended the stairs. He stood facing Foster. "What do you mean? Why won't it help me?"

"You won't see Carthage. It's what I've got to tell you. It's what I've been leading up to. You can never see Carthage."

Potterley shook his head slightly. "Oh, no, you're wrong. If you have the chronoscope, just focus it properly——"

"No, Dr. Potterley. It's not a question of focus. There are random factors affecting the neutrino stream, as they affect all subatomic particles. What we call the uncertainty principle. When the stream is recorded and interpreted, the random factor comes out as fuzziness, or 'noise' as the communications boys speak of it. The further back in time you penetrate, the more pronounced the fuzziness, the greater the noise. After a while, the noise drowns out the picture. Do you understand?"

"More power," said Potterley in a dead kind of voice.

"That won't help. When the noise blurs out detail, magnifying detail magnifies the noise, too. You can't see anything in a sun-burned film by enlarging it, can you? Get this through your head, now. The physical nature of the universe sets limits. The random thermal motions of air molecules set limits to how weak a sound can be detected by any instrument. The length of a light wave or of an electron wave sets limits to the size of objects that can be seen by any instrument. It works that way in chronoscopy, too. You can only time view so far."

"How far? How far?"

Foster took a deep breath. "A century and a quarter. That's the most."

"But the monthly bulletin the Commission puts out deals with ancient history almost entirely." The historian laughed shakily. "You must be wrong. The government has data as far back as 3000 B.C."

"When did you switch to believing them?" demanded

Foster, scornfully. "You began this business by proving they were lying; that no historian had made use of the chronoscope. Don't you see why now? No historian, except one interested in contemporary history, could. No chronoscope can possibly see back in time further than 1920 under any conditions."

"You're wrong. You don't know everything," said Potterley.

"The truth won't bend itself to your convenience either. Face it. The government's part in this is to perpetuate a hoax."

"Why?"

"I don't know why."

Potterley's snubby nose was twitching. His eyes were bulging. He pleaded, "It's only theory, Dr. Foster. Build a chronoscope. Build one and try."

Foster caught Potterley's shoulders in a sudden, fierce grip. "Do you think I haven't? Do you think I would tell you this before I had checked it every way I knew? I *have* built one. It's all around you. Look!"

He ran to the switches at the power leads. He flicked them on, one by one. He turned a resistor, adjusted other knobs, put out the cellar lights. "Wait. Let it warm up."

There was a small glow near the center of one wall. Potterley was gibbering incoherently, but Foster only cried again, "Look!"

The light sharpened and brightened, broke up into a light-and-dark pattern. Men and women! Fuzzy. Features blurred. Arms and legs mere streaks. An old-fashioned ground car, unclear but recognizable as one of the kind that had once used gasoline-powered internal-combustion engines, sped by.

Foster said, "Mid-twentieth century, somewhere. I can't hook up an audio yet so this is soundless. Eventually, we can add sound. Anyway, mid-twentieth is almost as far back as you can go. Believe me, that's the best focusing that can be done."

Potterley said, "Build a larger machine, a stronger one. Improve your circuits."

"You can't lick the Uncertainty Principle, man, any

more than you can live on the sun. There are physical limits to what can be done."

"You're lying. I won't believe you. I——"

A new voice sounded, raised shrilly to make itself heard.

"Arnold! Dr. Foster!"

The young physicist turned at once. Dr. Potterley froze for a long moment, then said, without turning, "What is it, Caroline? Leave us."

"No!" Mrs. Potterley descended the stairs. "I heard. I couldn't help hearing. Do you have a time viewer here, Dr. Foster? Here in the basement?"

"Yes, I do, Mrs. Potterley. A kind of time viewer. Not a good one. I can't get sound yet and the picture is darned blurry, but it works."

Mrs. Potterley clasped her hands and held them tightly against her breast. "How wonderful. How wonderful."

"It's not at all wonderful," snapped Potterley. "The young fool can't reach further back than——"

"Now, look," began Foster in exasperation. . . .

"Please!" cried Mrs. Potterley. "Listen to me. Arnold, don't you see that as long as we can use it for twenty years back, we can see Laurel once again? What do we care about Carthage and ancient times? It's Laurel we can see. She'll be alive for us again. Leave the machine here, Dr. Foster. Show us how to work it."

Foster stared at her then at her husband. Dr. Potterley's face had gone white. Though his voice stayed low and even, its calmness was somehow gone. He said, "You're a fool!"

Caroline said weakly, "Arnold!"

"You're a fool, I say. What will you see? The past. The dead past. Will Laurel do one thing she did not do? Will you see one thing you haven't seen? Will you live three years over and over again, watching a baby who'll never grow up no matter how you watch?"

His voice came near to cracking, but held. He stepped closer to her, seized her shoulder and shook her roughly. "Do you know what will happen to you if you do that? They'll come to take you away because you'll go mad.

Yes, mad. Do you want mental treatment? Do you want to be shut up, to undergo the psychic probe?"

Mrs. Potterley tore away. There was no trace of softness or vagueness about her. She had twisted into a virago. "I want to see my child, Arnold. She's in that machine and I want her."

"She's *not* in the machine. An image is. Can't you understand? An image! Something that's not real!"

"I want my child. Do you hear me?" She flew at him, screaming, fists beating. "*I want my child.*"

The historian retreated at the fury of the assault, crying out. Foster moved to step between, when Mrs. Potterley dropped, sobbing wildly, to the floor.

Potterley turned, eyes desperately seeking. With a sudden heave, he snatched at a Lando-rod, tearing it from its support, and whirling away before Foster, numbed by all that was taking place, could move to stop him.

"Stand back!" gasped Potterley, "or I'll kill you. I swear it."

He swung with force, and Foster jumped back.

Potterley turned with fury on every part of the structure in the cellar, and Foster, after the first crash of glass, watched dazedly.

Potterley spent his rage and then he was standing quietly amid shards and splinters, with a broken Lando-rod in his hand. He said to Foster in a whisper, "Now get out of here! Never come back! If any of this cost you anything, send me a bill and I'll pay for it. I'll pay double."

Foster shrugged, picked up his shirt and moved up the basement stairs. He could hear Mrs. Potterley sobbing loudly, and, as he turned at the head of the stairs for a last look, he saw Dr. Potterley bending over her, his face convulsed with sorrow.

Two days later, with the school day drawing to a close, and Foster looking wearily about to see if there were any data on his newly approved projects that he wished to take home, Dr. Potterley appeared once more. He was standing at the open door of Foster's office.

The historian was neatly dressed as ever. He lifted his

hand in a gesture that was too vague to be a greeting, too abortive to be a plea. Foster stared stonily.

Potterley said, "I waited till five, till you were . . . May I come in?"

Foster nodded.

Potterley said, "I suppose I ought to apologize for my behavior. I was dreadfully disappointed; not quite master of myself. Still, it was inexcusable."

"I accept your apology," said Foster. "Is that all?"

"My wife called you, I think."

"Yes, she has."

"She has been quite hysterical. She told me she had but I couldn't be quite sure——"

"She has called me."

"Could you tell me—would you be so kind as to tell me what she wanted?"

"She wanted a chronoscope. She said she had some money of her own. She was willing to pay."

"Did you—make any commitments?"

"I said I wasn't in the manufacturing business."

"Good," breathed Potterley, his chest expanding with a sigh of relief. "Please don't take any calls from her. She's not—quite——"

"Look, Dr. Potterley," said Foster, "I'm not getting into any domestic quarrels, but you'd better be prepared for something. Chronoscopes can be built by anybody. Given a few simple parts that can be bought through some etherics sales center, it can be built in the home workshop. The video part, anyway."

"But no one else will think of it beside you, will they? No one has."

"I don't intend to keep it secret."

"But you can't publish. It's illegal research."

"That doesn't matter any more, Dr. Potterley. If I lose my grants, I lose them. If the university is displeased, I'll resign. It just doesn't matter."

"But you can't do that!"

"Till now," said Foster, "you didn't mind my risking loss of grants and position. Why do you turn so tender about it now? Now let me explain something to you.

When you first came to me, I believed in organized and directed research; the situation as it existed, in other words. I considered you an intellectual anarchist, Dr. Potterley, and dangerous. But, for one reason or another, I've been an anarchist myself for months now and I have achieved great things.

"Those things have been achieved not because I am a brilliant scientist. Not at all. It was just that scientific research had been directed from above and holes were left that could be filled in by anyone who looked in the right direction. And anyone might have if the government hadn't actively tried to prevent it.

"Now understand me. I still believe directed research can be useful. I'm not in favor of a retreat to total anarchy. But there must be a middle ground. Directed research can retain flexibility. A scientist must be allowed to follow his curiosity, at least in his spare time."

Potterley sat down. He said ingratiatingly, "Let's discuss this, Foster. I appreciate your idealism. You're young. You want the moon. But you can't destroy yourself through fancy notions of what research must consist of. I got you into this. I am responsible and I blame myself bitterly. I was acting emotionally. My interest in Carthage blinded me and I was a damned fool."

Foster broke in. "You mean you've changed completely in two days? Carthage is nothing? Government suppression of research is nothing?"

"Even a damned fool like myself can learn, Foster. My wife taught me something. I understand the reason for government suppression of neutrinics now. I didn't two days ago. And, understanding, I approve. You saw the way my wife reacted to the news of a chronoscope in the basement. I had envisioned a chronoscope used for research purposes. All *she* could see was the personal pleasure of returning neurotically to a personal past, a dead past. The pure researcher, Foster, is in the minority. People like my wife would outweigh us.

"For the government to encourage chronoscopy would have meant that everyone's past would be visible. The government officers would be subjected to blackmail and improper pressure, since who on Earth has a past that is absolutely clean? Organized government might become impossible."

Foster licked his lips. "Maybe. Maybe the government has some justification in its own eyes. Still, there's an important principle involved here. Who knows what other scientific advances are being stymied because scientists are being stifled into walking a narrow path? If the chronoscope becomes the terror of a few politicians, it's a price that must be paid. The public must realize that science must be free and there is no more dramatic way of doing it than to publish my discovery, one way or another, legally or illegally."

Potterley's brow was damp with perspiration, but his voice remained even. "Oh, not just a few politicians, Dr. Foster. Don't think that. It would be my terror, too. My wife would spend her time living with our dead daughter. She would retreat further from reality. She would go mad living the same scenes over and over. And not just my terror. There would be others like her. Children searching for their dead parents or their own youth. We'll have a whole world living in the past. Midsummer madness."

Foster said, "Moral judgments can't stand in the way. There isn't one advance at any time in history that mankind hasn't had the ingenuity to pervert. Mankind must also have the ingenuity to prevent. As for the chronoscope, your delvers into the dead past will get tired soon enough. They'll catch their loved parents in some of the things their loved parents did and they'll lose their enthusiasm for it all. But all this is trivial. With me, it's a matter of important principle."

Potterley said, "Hang your principle. Can't you understand men and women as well as principle? Don't you understand that my wife will live through the fire that killed our baby? She won't be able to help herself. I know her. She'll follow through each step, trying to prevent it. She'll live it over and over again, hoping each time that it won't happen. How many times do you want to kill Laurel?" A huskiness had crept into his voice.

A thought crossed Foster's mind. "What are you really afraid she'll find out, Dr. Potterley? What happened the night of the fire?"

The historian's hands went up quickly to cover his face and they shook with his dry sobs. Foster turned away and stared uncomfortably out the window.

Potterley said after a while, "It's a long time since I've had to think of it. Caroline was away. I was baby-sitting. I went into the baby's bedroom midevening to see if she had kicked off the bedclothes. I had my cigarette with me . . . I smoked in those days. I must have stubbed it out before putting it in the ashtray on the chest of drawers. I was always careful. The baby was all right. I returned to the living room and fell asleep before the video. I awoke, choking, surrounded by fire. I don't know how it started."

"But you think it may have been the cigarette, is that it?" said Foster. "A cigarette which, for once, you forgot to stub out?"

"I don't know. I tried to save her, but she was dead in my arms when I got out."

"You never told your wife about the cigarette, I suppose."

Potterley shook his head. "But I've lived with it."

"Only now, with a chronoscope, she'll find out. Maybe it wasn't the cigarette. Maybe you did stub it out. Isn't that possible?"

The scant tears had dried on Potterley's face. The redness had subsided. He said, "I can't take the chance. . . . But it's not just myself, Foster. The past has its terrors for most people. Don't loose those terrors on the human race."

Foster paced the floor. Somehow, this explained the reason for Potterley's rabid, irrational desire to boost the Carthaginians, deify them, most of all disprove the story of their fiery sacrifices to Moloch. By freeing them of the guilt of infanticide by fire, he symbolically freed himself of the same guilt.

So the same fire that had driven him on to causing the construction of a chronoscope was now driving him on to the destruction.

Foster looked sadly at the older man. "I see your position, Dr. Potterley, but this goes above personal feelings. I've got to smash this throttling hold on the throat of science."

Potterley said, savagely, "You mean you want the fame and wealth that goes with such a discovery."

"I don't know about the wealth, but that, too, I suppose. I'm no more than human."

"You won't suppress your knowledge?"

"Not under any circumstances."

"Well, then——" and the historian got to his feet and stood for a moment, glaring.

Foster had an odd moment of terror. The man was older than he, smaller, feebler, and he didn't look armed. Still . . .

Foster said, "If you're thinking of killlng me or anything insane like that, I've got the information in a safety-deposit vault where the proper people will find it in case of my disappearance or death."

Potterley said, "Don't be a fool," and stalked out.

Foster closed the door, locked it and sat down to think. He felt silly. He had no information in any safety-deposit vault, of course. Such a melodramatic action would not have occurred to him ordinarily. But now it had.

Feeling even sillier, he spent an hour writing out the equations of the application of pseudo-gravitic optics to neutrinic recording, and some diagrams for the engineering details of construction. He sealed it in an envelope and scrawled Ralph Nimmo's name over the outside.

He spent a rather restless night and the next moring, on the way to school, dropped the envelope off at the bank, with appropriate instructions to an official, who made him sign a paper permitting the box to be opened after his death.

He called Nimmo to tell him of the existence of the envelope, refusing querulously to say anything about its contents.

He had never felt so ridiculously self-conscious as at that moment.

*   *   *

That night and the next, Foster spent in only fitful sleep, finding himself face to face with the highly practical problem of the publication of data unethically obtained.

The *Proceedings of the Society for Pseudo-Gravitics*, which was the journal with which he was best acquainted, would certainly not touch any paper that did not include the magic footnote: "The work described in this paper was made possible by Grant No. so-and-so from the Commission of Research of the United Nations."

Nor, doubly so, would the *Journal of Physics*.

There were always the minor journals who might overlook the nature of the article for the sake of the sensation, but that would require a little financial negotiation on which he hesitated to embark. It might, on the whole, be better to pay the cost of publishing a small pamphlet for general distribution among scholars. In that case, he would even be able to dispense with the services of a science writer, sacrificing polish for speed. He would have to find a reliable printer. Uncle Ralph might know one.

He walked down the corridor to his office and wondered anxiously if perhaps he ought to waste no further time, give himself no further chance to lapse into indecision and take the risk of calling Ralph from his office phone. He was so absorbed in his own heavy thoughts that he did not notice that his room was occupied until he turned from the clothes closet and approached his desk.

Dr. Potterley was there and a man whom Foster did not recognize.

Foster stared at them. "What's this?"

Potterley said, "I'm sorry, but I had to stop you."

Foster continued staring. "What are you talking about?"

The stranger said, "Let me introduce myself." He had large teeth, a little uneven, and they showed prominently when he smiled. "I am Thaddeus Araman, Department Head of the Division of Chronoscopy. I am here to see you concerning information brought to me by Professor Arnold Potterley and confirmed by our own sources——"

Potterley said breathlessly, "I took all the blame, Dr.

Foster. I explained that it was I who persuaded you against your will into unethical practices. I have offered to accept full responsibility and punishment. I don't wish you harmed in any way. It's just that chronoscopy must not be permitted!"

Araman nodded. "He has taken the blame as he says, Dr. Foster, but this thing is out of his hands now."

Foster said, "So? What are you going to do? Blackball me from all consideration for research grants?"

"That is in my power," said Araman.

"Order the university to discharge me?"

"That, too, is in my power."

"All right, go ahead. Consider it done. I'll leave my office now, with you. I can send for my books later. If you insist, I'll leave my books. Is that all?"

"Not quite," said Araman. "You must engage to do no further research in chronoscopy, to publish none of your findings in chronoscopy and, of course, to build no chronoscope. You will remain under surveillance indefinitely to make sure you keep that promise."

"Supposing I refuse to promise? What can you do? Doing research out of my field may be unethical, but it isn't a criminal offense."

"In the case of chronoscopy, my young friend," said Araman patiently, "it is a criminal offense. If necessary, you will be put in jail and kept there."

"Why?" shouted Foster. "What's magic about chronoscopy?"

Araman said, "That's the way it is. We cannot allow further developments in the field. My own job is, primarily, to make sure of that, and I intend to do my job. Unfortunately, I had no knowledge, nor did anyone in the department, that the optics of pseudo-gravity fields had such immediate application to chronoscopy. Score one for general ignorance, but henceforward research will be steered properly in that respect, too."

Foster said, "That won't help. Something else may apply that neither you nor I dream of. All science hangs together. It's one piece. If you want to stop one part, you've got to stop it all."

"No doubt that is true," said Araman, "in theory. On the practical side, however, we have managed quite well to hold chronoscopy down to the original Sterbinski level for fifty years. Having caught you in time, Dr. Foster, we hope to continue doing so indefinitely. And we wouldn't have come this close to disaster, either, if I had accepted Dr. Potterley at something more than face value."

He turned toward the historian and lifted his eyebrows in a kind of humorous self-deprecation. "I'm afraid, sir, that I dismissed you as a history professor and no more on the occasion of our first interview. Had I done my job properly and checked on you, this would not have happened."

Foster said abruptly, "Is anyone allowed to use the government chronoscope?"

"No one outside our division under any pretext. I say that since it is obvious to me that you have already guessed as much. I warn you, though, that any repetition of that fact will be a criminal, not an ethical, offense."

"And your chronoscope doesn't go back more than a hundred twenty-five years or so, does it?"

"It doesn't."

"Then your bulletin with its stories of time viewing ancient times is a hoax?"

Araman said coolly, "With the knowledge you now have, it is obvious you know that for a certainty. However, I confirm your remark. The monthly bulletin is a hoax."

"In that case," said Foster, "I will not promise to suppress my knowledge of chronoscopy. If you wish to arrest me, go ahead. My defense at the trial will be enough to destroy the vicious card house of directed research and bring it tumbling down. Directing research is one thing; suppressing it and depriving mankind of its benefits is quite another."

Araman said, "Oh, let's get something straight, Dr. Foster. If you do not co-operate, you will go to jail directly. You will *not* see a lawyer, you will *not* be charged, you will *not* have a trial. You will simply stay in jail."

"Oh, no," said Foster, "you're bluffing. This is not the twentieth century, you know."

There was a stir outside the office, the clatter of feet, a high-pitched shout that Foster was sure he recognized. The door crashed open, the lock splintering, and three intertwined figures stumbled in.

As they did so, one of the men raised a blaster and brought its butt down hard on the skull of another.

There was a whoosh of expiring air, and the one whose head was struck went limp.

"Uncle Ralph!" cried Foster.

Araman frowned. "Put him down in that chair," he ordered, "and get some water."

Ralph Nimmo, rubbing his head with a gingerly sort of disgust, said, "There was no need to get rough, Araman."

Araman said, "The guard should have been rough sooner and kept you out of here, Nimmo. You'd have been better off."

"You know each other?" asked Foster.

"I've had dealings with the man," said Nimmo, still rubbing. "If he's here in your office, nephew, you're in trouble."

"And you, too," said Araman angrily. "I know Dr. Foster consulted you on neutrinics literature."

Nimmo corrugated his forehead, then straightened it with a wince as though the action had brought pain. "So?" he said. "What else do you know about me?"

"We will know everything about you soon enough. Meanwhile, that one item is enough to implicate you. What are you doing here?"

"My dear Dr. Araman," said Nimmo, some of his jauntiness restored, "day before yesterday, my jackass of a nephew called me. He had placed some mysterious information——"

"Don't tell him! Don't say anything!" cried Foster.

Araman glanced at him coldly. "We know all about it, Dr. Foster. The safety-deposit box has been opened and its contents removed."

"But how can you know——" Foster's voice died away in a kind of furious frustration.

"Anyway," said Nimmo, "I decided the net must be closing around him and, after I took care of a few items, I came down to tell him to get off this thing he's doing. It's not worth his career."

"Does that mean you know what he's doing?" asked Araman.

"He never told me," said Nimmo, "but I'm a science writer with a hell of a lot of experience. I know which side of an atom is electronified. The boy, Foster, specializes in pseudo-gravitic optics and coached me on the stuff himself. He got me to get him a textbook on neutrinics and I kind of skip-viewed it myself before handing it over. I can put the two together. He asked me to get him certain pieces of physical equipment, and that was evidence, too. Stop me if I'm wrong, but my nephew has built a semiportable, low-power chronoscope. Yes, or— yes?"

"Yes." Araman reached thoughtfully for a cigarette and paid no attention to Dr. Potterley (watching silently, as though all were a dream) who shied away, gasping, from the white cylinder. "Another mistake for me. I ought to resign. I should have put tabs on you, too, Nimmo, instead of concentrating too hard on Potterley and Foster. I didn't have much time of course and you've ended up safely here, but that doesn't excuse me. You're under arrest, Nimmo."

"What for?" demanded the science writer.

"Unauthorized research."

"I wasn't doing any. I can't, not being a registered scientist. And even if I did, it's not a criminal offense."

Foster said savagely, "No use, Uncle Ralph. This bureaucrat is making his own laws."

"Like what?" demanded Nimmo.

"Like life imprisonment without trial."

"Nuts," said Nimmo. "This isn't the twentieth cen——"

"I tried that," said Foster. "It doesn't bother him."

"Well, nuts," shouted Nimmo. "Look here, Araman. My nephew and I have relatives who haven't lost touch with us, you know. The professor has some also, I imagine. You can't just make us disappear. There'll be questions and a scandal. This *isn't* the twentieth century. So if you're trying to scare us, it isn't working."

The cigarette snapped between Araman's fingers and he tossed it away violently. He said, "Damn it, I don't know *what* to do. It's never been like this before. . . . Look! You three fools know nothing of what you're trying to do. You understand nothing. Will you listen to me?"

"Oh, we'll listen," said Nimmo grimly.

(Foster sat silently, eyes angry, lips compressed. Potterley's hands writhed like two intertwined snakes.)

Araman said, "The past to you is the dead past. If any of you have discussed the matter, it's dollars to nickels you've used that phrase. The dead past. If you knew how many times I've heard those three words, you'd choke on them, too.

"When people think of the past, they think of it as dead, far away and gone, long ago. We encourage them to think so. When we report time viewing, we always talk of views centuries in the past, even though you gentlemen know seeing more than a century or so is impossible. People accept it. The past means Greece, Rome, Carthage, Egypt, the Stone Age. The deader the better.

"Now you three know a century or a little more is the limit, so what does the past mean to you? Your youth. Your first girl. Your dead mother. Twenty years ago. Thirty years ago. Fifty years ago. The deader the better. . . . But when does the past really begin?"

He paused in anger. The others stared at him and Nimmo stirred uneasily.

"Well," said Araman, "when did it begin? A year ago? Five minutes ago? One second ago? Isn't it obvious that the past begins an instant ago? The dead past is just another name for the living present. What if you focus the chronoscope in the past of one-hundredth of a second ago? Aren't you watching the present? Does it begin to sink in?"

Nimmo said, "Damnation."

"Damnation," mimicked Araman. "After Potterley came to me with his story night before last, how do you suppose I checked up on both of you? I did it with the chronoscope, spotting key moments to the very instant of the present."

"And that's how you knew about the safety-deposit box?" said Foster.

"And every other important fact. Now what do you suppose would happen if we let news of a home chronoscope get out? People might start out by watching their youth, their parents and so on, but it wouldn't be long before they'd catch on to the possibilities. The housewife will forget her poor, dead mother and take to watching her neighbor at home and her husband at the office. The businessman will watch his competitor; the employer his employee.

"There will be no such thing as privacy. The party line, the prying eye behind the curtain will be nothing compared to it. The video stars will be closely watched at all times by everyone. Every man his own peeping Tom and there'll be no getting away from the watcher. Even darkness will be no escape because chronoscopy can be adjusted to the infrared and human figures can be seen by their own body heat. The figures will be fuzzy, of course, and the surroundings will be dark, but that will make the titillation of it all the greater, perhaps. . . . Hmp, the men in charge of the machine now experiment sometimes in spite of the regulations against it."

Nimmo seemed sick. "You can always forbid private manufacture——"

Araman turned on him fiercely. "You can, but do you expect it to do good? Can you legislate successfully against drinking, smoking, adultery or gossiping over the back fence? And this mixture of nosiness and prurience will have a worse grip on humanity than any of those. Good Lord, in a thousand years of trying we haven't even been able to wipe out the heroin traffic and you talk about legislating against a device for watching anyone you please at any time you please that can be built in a home workshop."

Foster said suddenly, "I won't publish."

Potterley burst out, half in sobs, "None of us will talk. I regret——"

Nimmo broke in. "You said you didn't tab me on the chronoscope, Araman."

"No time," said Araman wearily. "Things don't move any faster on the chronoscope than in real life. You can't speed it up like the film in a book viewer. We spent a full twenty-four hours trying to catch the important moments during the last six months of Potterley and Foster. There was no time for anything else and it was enough."

"It wasn't," said Nimmo.

"What are you talking about?" There was a sudden infinite alarm on Araman's face.

"I told you my nephew, Jonas, had called me to say he had put important information in a safety-deposit box. He acted as though he were in trouble. He's my nephew. I had to try to get him off the spot. It took a while, then I came here to tell him what I had done. I told you when I got here, just after your man conked me, that I had taken care of a few items."

"What? For Heaven's sake——"

"Just this: I sent the details of the portable chronoscope off to half a dozen of my regular publicity outlets."

Not a word. Not a sound. Not a breath. They were all past any demonstration.

"Don't stare like that," cried Nimmo. "Don't you see my point? I had popular publication rights. Jonas will admit that. I knew he couldn't publish scientifically in any legal way. I was sure he was planning to publish illegally and was preparing the safety-deposit box for that reason. I thought if I put through the details prematurely, all the responsibility would be mine. His career would be saved. And if I were deprived of my science-writing license as a result, my exclusive possession of the chronometric data would set me up for life. Jonas would be angry, I expected that, but I could explain the motive and we would split the take fifty-fifty. . . . Don't stare at me like that. How did I know——"

"Nobody knew anything," said Araman bitterly, "but

you all just took it for granted that the government was stupidly bureaucratic, vicious, tyrannical, given to suppressing research for the hell of it. It never occurred to any of you that we were trying to protect mankind as best we could."

"Don't sit there talking," wailed Potterley. "Get the names of the people who were told——"

"Too late," said Nimmo, shrugging. "They've had better than a day. There's been time for the word to spread. My outfits will have called any number of physicists to check my data before going on with it and they'll call one another to pass on the news. Once scientists put neutrinics and pseudo-gravitics together, home chronoscopy becomes obvious. Before the week is out, five hundred people will know how to build a small chronoscope and how will you catch them all?" His plump cheeks sagged. "I suppose there's no way of putting the mushroom cloud back into that nice, shiny uranium sphere."

Araman stood up. "We'll try, Potterley, but I agree with Nimmo. It's too late. What kind of a world we'll have from now on, I don't know, I can't tell, but the world we know has been destroyed completely. Until now, every custom, every habit, every tiniest way of life has always taken a certain amount of privacy for granted, but that's all gone now."

He saluted each of the three with elaborate formality.

"You have created a new world among the three of you. I congratulate you. Happy goldfish bowl to you, to me, to everyone, and may each of you fry in hell forever. Arrest rescinded."

4

Death of a Foy

This is the cleverest of my wordplay items. You just won't guess it. You can't.

When I wrote the story, I was careful to do so in such a way that I reached the bottom of a page just before the punch line, and then put the punch line on a new page. Ed Ferman, the editor who first published the story reached the bottom of the penultimate page in complete mystification (he told me). He couldn't imagine where I was going. He then turned the page and broke into loud laughter. He couldn't reject it after that.

It was extremely unusual for a Foy to be dying on Earth. They were the highest social class on their planet (with a name which was pronounced—as nearly as Earthly throats could make the sounds—Sortibackenstrete) and were virtually immortal.

Every Foy, of course, came to voluntary death eventually, and this one had given up because of an ill-starred love affair, if you can call it a love affair where five individuals, in order to reproduce, must indulge in a year-long mental contact. Apparently, he himself had not fit into the contact after several months of trying and it had broken his heart—or hearts, for he had five.

All Foys had five large hearts and there was speculation that it was this that made them virtually immortal.

Maude Briscoe, Earth's most renowned surgeon, wanted those hearts. "It can't be just their number and size,

Dwayne," she said to her chief assistant. "It has to be something physiological or biochemical. I must have them."

"I don't know if we can manage that," said Dwayne Johnson. "I've been speaking to him earnestly, trying to overcome the Foy taboo against dismemberment after death. I've had to play on the feeling of tragedy any Foy would have over death away from home. And I've had to lie to him, Maude."

"Lie?"

"I told him that after death, there would be a dirge sung for him by the world-famous choir led by Harold J. Gassenbaum. I told him that by Earthly belief this would mean that his astral essence would be instantaneously wafted back, through hyperspace, to his home planet of Sortib-what's its name.—Provided he would sign a release allowing you, Maude, to have his hearts for scientific investigation."

"Don't tell me he believed that horse excrement!" said Maude.

"Well, you know this modern attitude about accepting the myths and beliefs of intelligent aliens. It wouldn't have been polite for him not to believe me. Besides, the Foys have a profound admiration for terrestrial science and I think this one is a little flattered that we should want his hearts. He promised to consider the suggestion, and I hope he decides soon because he can't live more than another day or so, and we must have his permission by interstellar law, and the hearts must be fresh, and—Ah, his signal."

Dwayne Johnson moved in with smooth and noiseless speed.

"Yes?" he whispered, unobtrusively turning on the holographic recording device in case the Foy wished to grant permission.

The Foy's large, gnarled, rather tree-like body lay motionless on the bed. The bulging eyes palpitated (all five of them) as they rose, each on its stalk, and turned toward Dwayne. The Foy's voice had a strange tone and the lipless edges of his open, round mouth did not move, but the words formed perfectly. His eyes were making the Foyan gesture of assent as he said:

"Give my big hearts to Maude, Dwayne. Dismember me for Harold's choir. Tell all the Foys on Sortiback-kenstrete that I will soon be there—"

5

Dreaming Is a Private Thing

*I suppose that every story someone writes is a bit autobio-
graphical. There has to be a personal tinge in it somewhere. After all you can only think with your own brain,
you can only remember your own memories, you can only
be influenced deeply and subliminally by the events in
your own life.*

*Sherman Hillary, the Dreamer in this story, is reminis-
cent of me in a way. I was vaguely aware of it but I
foolishly thought no one would notice. I was quite wrong.
No sooner did the story appear than I got letters from
Judith Merril and Robert Heinlein (among others) that
made it quite clear they knew what I was doing.*

*Heinlein said I was coining money out of my neuroses.
Well, whose neuroses should I coin money out of?*

Jesse Weill looked up from his desk. His old, spare body,
his sharp, high-bridged nose, deep-set, shadowy eyes and
amazing shock of white hair had trademarked his appearance during the years that Dreams, Inc., had become
world-famous.

He said, "Is the boy here already, Joe?"

Joe Dooley was short and heavy-set. A cigar caressed
his moist lower lip. He took it away for a moment and
nodded. "His folks are with him. They're all scared."

"You're sure this is not a false alarm, Joe? I haven't
got much time." He looked at his watch. "Government
business at two."

"This is a sure thing, Mr. Weill." Dooley's face was a
study in earnestness. His jowls quivered with persuasive
intensity. "Like I told you, I picked him up playing some

kind of basketball game in the schoolyard. You should've seen the kid. He stunk. When he had his hands on the ball, his own team had to take it away, and fast, but just the same he had all the stance of a star player. Know what I mean? To me it was a giveaway.''

"Did you talk to him?"

"Well, sure. I stopped him at lunch. You know me." Dooley gestured expansively with his cigar and caught the severed ash with his other hand. "Kid, I said——"

"And he's dream material?"

"I said, 'Kid, I just came from Africa and——'"

"All right." Weill held up the palm of his hand. "Your word I'll always take. How you do it I don't know, but when you say a boy is a potential dreamer, I'll gamble. Bring him in."

The youngster came in between his parents. Dooley pushed chairs forward and Weill rose to shake hands. He smiled at the youngster in a way that turned the wrinkles of his face into benevolent creases.

"You're Tommy Slutsky?"

Tommy nodded wordlessly. He was about ten and a little small for that. His dark hair was plastered down unconvincingly and his face was unrealistically clean.

Weill said, "You're a good boy?"

The boy's mother smiled at once and patted Tommy's head maternally (a gesture which did not soften the anxious expression on the youngster's face). She said, "He's always a very good boy."

Weill let this dubious statement pass. "Tell me, Tommy," he said, and held out a lollipop which was first hesitated over, then accepted, "do you ever listen to dreamies?"

"Sometimes," said Tommy trebly.

Mr. Slutsky cleared his throat. He was broad-shouldered and thick-fingered, the type of laboring man who, every once in a while, to the confusion of eugenics, sired a dreamer. "We rented one or two for the boy. Real old ones."

Weill nodded. He said, "Did you like them, Tommy?"

"They were sort of silly."

"You think up better ones for yourself, do you?"

The grin that spread over the ten-year-old face had the effect of taking away some of the unreality of the slicked hair and washed face.

Weill went on gently, "Would you like to make up a dream for me?"

Tommy was instantly embarrassed. "I guess not."

"It won't be hard. It's very easy. . . . Joe."

Dooley moved a screen out of the way and rolled forward a dream recorder.

The youngster looked owlishly at it.

Weill lifted the helmet and brought it close to the boy. "Do you know what this is?"

Tommy shrank away. "No."

"It's a thinker. That's what we call it because people think into it. You put it on your head and think anything you want."

"Then what happens?"

"Nothing at all. It feels nice."

"No," said Tommy, "I guess I'd rather not."

His mother bent hurriedly toward him. "It won't hurt, Tommy. You do what the man says." There was an unmistakable edge to her voice.

Tommy stiffened, and looked as though he might cry but he didn't. Weill put the thinker on him.

He did it gently and slowly and let it remain there for some thirty seconds before speaking again, to let the boy assure himself it would do no harm, to let him get used to the insinuating touch of the fibrils against the sutures of his skull (penetrating the skin so finely as to be insensible almost), and finally to let him get used to the faint hum of the alternating field vortices.

Then he said, "Now would you think for us?"

"About what?" Only the boy's nose and mouth showed.

"About anything you want. What's the best thing you would like to do when school is out?"

The boy thought a moment and said, with rising inflection, "Go on a stratojet?"

"Why not? Sure thing. You go on a jet. It's taking off

right now." He gestured lightly to Dooley, who threw the freezer into circuit.

Weill kept the boy only five minutes and then let him and his mother he escorted from the office by Dooley. Tommy looked bewildered but undamaged by the ordeal.

Weill said to the father, "Now, Mr. Slutsky, if your boy does well on this test, we'll be glad to pay you five hundred dollars each year until he finishes high school. In that time, all we'll ask is that he spend an hour a week some afternoon at our special school."

"Do I have to sign a paper?" Slutsky's voice was a bit hoarse.

"Certainly. This is business, Mr. Slutsky."

"Well, I don't know. Dreamers are hard to come by, I hear."

"They are. They are. But your son, Mr. Slutsky, is not a dreamer yet. He might never be. Five hundred dollars a year is a gamble for us. It's not a gamble for you. When he's finished high school, it may turn out he's not a dreamer, yet you've lost nothing. You've gained maybe four thousand dollars altogether. If he *is* a dreamer, he'll make a nice living and you certainly haven't lost then."

"He'll need special training, won't he?"

"Oh, yes, most intensive. But we don't have to worry about that till after he's finished high school. Then, after two years with us, he'll be developed. Rely on me, Mr. Slutsky."

"Will you guarantee that special training?"

Weill, who had been shoving a paper across the desk at Slutsky, and punching a pen wrong-end-to at him, put the pen down and chuckled. "A guarantee? No. How can we when we don't know for sure yet if he's a real talent? Still, the five hundred a year will stay yours."

Slutsky pondered and shook his head. "I tell you straight out, Mr. Weill . . . After your man arranged to have us come here, I called Luster-Think. They said they'll guarantee training."

Weill sighed. "Mr. Slutsky, I don't like to talk against a competitor. If they say they'll guarantee schooling, they'll do as they say, but they can't make a boy a dreamer if he hasn't got it in him, schooling or not. If they take a plain boy without the proper talent and put him through a development course, they'll ruin him. A dreamer he won't be, I guarantee you. And a normal human being, he won't be, either. Don't take the chance of doing it to your son.

"Now Dreams, Inc., will be perfectly honest with you. If he can be a dreamer, we'll make him one. If not, we'll give him back to you without having tampered with him and say, 'Let him learn a trade.' He'll be better and healthier that way. I tell you, Mr. Slutsky—I have sons and daughters and grandchildren so I know what I say—I would not allow a child of mine to be pushed into dreaming if he's not ready for it. Not for a million dollars."

Slutsky wiped his mouth with the back of his hand and reached for the pen. "What does this say?"

"This is just an option. We pay you a hundred dollars in cash right now. No strings attached. We'll study the boy's reverie. If we feel it's worth following up, we'll call you in again and make the five-hundred-dollar-a-year deal. Leave yourself in my hands, Mr. Slutsky, and don't worry. You won't be sorry."

Slutsky signed.

Weill passed the document through the file slot and handed an envelope to Slutsky.

Five minutes later, alone in the office, he placed the unfreezer over his own head and absorbed the boy's reverie intently. It was a typically childish daydream. First Person was at the controls of the plane, which looked like a compound of illustrations out of the filmed thrillers that still circulated among those who lacked the time, desire or money for dream cylinders.

When he removed the unfreezer, he found Dooley looking at him.

"Well, Mr. Weill, what do you think?" said Dooley, with an eager and proprietary air.

"Could be, Joe. Could be. He has the overtones and, for a ten-year-old boy without a scrap of training, it's hopeful. When the plane went through a cloud, there was a distinct sensation of pillows. Also the smell of clean sheets, which was an amusing touch. We can go with him a ways, Joe."

"Good."

"But I tell you, Joe, what we really need is to catch them still sooner. And why not? Someday, Joe, every child will be tested at birth. A difference in the brain there positively must be and it should be found. Then we could separate the dreamers at the very beginning."

"Hell, Mr. Weill," said Dooley, looking hurt. "What would happen to my job, then?"

Weill laughed. "No cause to worry yet, Joe. It won't happen in our lifetimes. In mine, certainly not. We'll be depending on good talent scouts like you for many years. You just watch the playgrounds and the streets"—Weill's gnarled hand dropped to Dooley's shoulder with a gentle, approving pressure—"and find us a few more Hillarys and Janows and Luster-Think won't ever catch us. . . . Now get out. I want lunch and then I'll be ready for my two o'clock appointment. The government, Joe, the government." And he winked portentously.

Jesse Weill's two o'clock appointment was with a young man, apple-cheeked, spectacled, sandy-haired and glowing with the intensity of a man with a mission. He presented his credentials across Weill's desk and revealed himself to be John J. Byrne, an agent of the Department of Arts and Sciences.

"Good afternoon Mr. Byrne," said Weill. "In what way can I be of service?"

"Are we private here?" asked the agent. He had an unexpected baritone.

"Quite private."

"Then, if you don't mind, I'll ask you to absorb this." Byrne produced a small and battered cylinder and held it out between thumb and forefinger.

Weill took it, hefted it, turned it this way and that and said with a denture-revealing smile, "Not the product of Dreams, Inc., Mr. Byrne."

"I didn't think it was," said the agent. "I'd still like

you to absorb it. I'd set the automatic cutoff for about a minute, though."

"That's all that can be endured?" Weill pulled the receiver to his desk and placed the cylinder into the unfreeze compartment. He removed it, polished either end of the cylinder with his handkerchief and tried again. "It doesn't make good contact," he said. "An amateurish job."

He placed the cushioned unfreeze helmet over his skull and adjusted the temple contacts, then set the automatic cutoff. He leaned back and clasped his hands over his chest and began absorbing.

His fingers grew rigid and clutched at his jacket. After the cutoff had brought absorption to an end, he removed the unfreezer and looked faintly angry. "A raw piece," he said. "It's lucky I'm an old man so that such things no longer bother me."

Byrne said stiffly, "It's not the worst we've found. And the fad is increasing."

Weill shrugged. "Pornographic dreamies. It's a logical development, I suppose."

The government man said, "Logical or not, it represents a deadly danger for the moral fiber of the nation."

"The moral fiber," said Weill, "can take a lot of beating. Erotica of one form or another have been circulated all through history."

"Not like this, sir. A direct mind-to-mind stimulation is much more effective than smoking room stories or filthy pictures. Those must be filtered through the senses and lose some of their effect in that way."

Weill could scarcely argue that point. He said, "What would you have me do?"

"Can you suggest a possible source for this cylinder?"

"Mr. Byrne, I'm not a policeman."

"No, no, I'm not asking you to do our work for us. The Department is quite capable of conducting its own investigations. Can you help us, I mean, from your own specialized knowledge? You say your company did not put out that filth. Who did?"

"No reputable dream distributor. I'm sure of that. It's too cheaply made."

"That could have been done on purpose."

"And no professional dreamer originated it."

"Are you sure, Mr. Weill? Couldn't dreamers do this sort of thing for some small, illegitimate concern for money—or for fun?"

"They could, but not this particular one. No overtones. It's two-dimensional. Of course, a thing like this doesn't need overtones."

"What do you mean, overtones?"

Weill laughed gently. "You are not a dreamie fan?"

Byrne tried not to look virtuous and did not entirely succeed. "I prefer music."

"Well, that's all right, too," said Weill tolerantly, "but it makes it a little harder to explain overtones. Even people who absorb dreamies would not be able to explain if you asked them. Still they'd know a dreamie was no good if the overtones were missing, even if they couldn't tell you why. Look, when an experienced dreamer goes into reverie, he doesn't think a story like in the old-fashioned television or book films. It's a series of little visions. Each one has several meanings. If you studied them carefully, you'd find maybe five or six. While absorbing in the ordinary way, you would never notice, but careful study shows it. Believe me, my psychological staff puts in long hours on just that point. All the overtones, the different meanings, blend together into a mass of guided emotion. Without them, everything would be flat, tasteless.

"Now, this morning, I tested a young boy. A ten-year-old with possibilities. A cloud to him isn't a cloud, it's a pillow, too. Having the sensations of both, it was more than either. Of course, the boy's very primitive. But when he's through with his schooling, he'll be trained and disciplined. He'll be subjected to all sorts of sensations. He'll store up experience. He'll study and analyze classic dreamies of the past. He'll learn how to control and direct his thoughts, though, mind you, I have always said that when a good dreamer improvises——"

Weill halted abruptly, then proceeded in less impassioned tones, "I shouldn't get excited. All I try to bring out now is that every professional dreamer has his own type of overtones which he can't mask. To an expert it's like signing his name on the dreamie. And I, Mr. Byrne, know all the signatures. Now that piece of dirt you brought me has no overtones at all. It was done by an ordinary person. A little talent, maybe, but like you and me, he really can't think."

Byrne reddened a trifle. "A lot of people can think, Mr. Weill, even if they don't make dreamies."

"Oh, tush," and Weill wagged his hand in the air. "Don't be angry with what an old man says. I don't mean think as in reason. I mean think as in dream. We all can dream after a fashion, just like we all can run. But can you and I run a mile in four minutes? You and I can talk, but are we Daniel Websters? Now when I think of a steak, I think of the word. Maybe I have a quick picture of a brown steak on a platter. Maybe you have a better pictorialization of it and you can see the crisp fat and the onions and the baked potato. I don't know. But a *dreamer* . . . He sees it and smells it and tastes it and everything about it, with the charcoal and the satisfied feeling in the stomach and the way the knife cuts through it and a hundred other things all at once. Very sensual. Very sensual. You and I can't do it."

"Well, then," said Byrne, "no professional dreamer has done this. That's something anyway." He put the cylinder in his inner jacket pocket. "I hope we'll have your full co-operation in squelching this sort of thing."

"Positively, Mr. Byrne. With a whole heart."

"I hope so." Byrne spoke with consciousness of power. "It's not up to me, Mr. Weill, to say what will be done and what won't be done, but this sort of thing," he tapped the cylinder he had brought, "will make it awfully tempting to impose a really strict censorship on dreamies."

He rose. "Good day, Mr. Weill."

"Good day, Mr. Byrne. I'll hope always for the best."

Francis Belanger burst into Jesse Weill's office in his

usual steaming tizzy, his reddish hair disordered and his face aglow with worry and a mild perspiration. He was brought up sharply by the sight of Weill's head cradled in the crook of his elbow and bent on the desk until only the glimmer of white hair was visible.

Belanger swallowed. "Boss?"

Weill's head lifted. "It's you, Frank?"

"What's the matter, boss? Are you sick?"

"I'm old enough to be sick, but I'm on my feet. Staggering, but on my feet. A government man was here."

"What did a want?"

"He threatens censorship. He brought a sample of what's going round. Cheap dreamies for bottle parties."

"God damn!" said Belanger feelingly.

"The only trouble is that morality makes for good campaign fodder. They'll be hitting out everywhere. And, to tell the truth, we're vulnerable, Frank."

"*We* are? Our stuff is clean. We play up straight adventure and romance."

Weill thrust out his lower lip and wrinkled his forehead. "Between us, Frank, we don't have to make believe. Clean? It depends on how you look at it. It's not for publication, maybe, but you know and I know that every dreamie has its Freudian connotations. You can't deny it."

"Sure, if you *look* for it. If you're a psychiatrist——"

"If you're an ordinary person, too. The ordinary observer doesn't know it's there and maybe he couldn't tell a phallic symbol from a mother image even if you pointed it out. Still, his subconscious knows. And it's the connotations that make many a dreamie click."

"All right, what's the goverment going to do? Clean up the subconscious?"

"It's a problem. I don't know what they're going to do. What we have on our side, and what I'm mainly depending on, is the fact that the public loves its dreamies and won't give them up. . . . Meanwhile, what did you come in for? You want to see me about something, I suppose?"

Belanger tossed an object onto Weill's desk and shoved his shirttail deeper into his trousers.

Weill broke open the glistening plastic cover and took out the enclosed cylinder. At one end was engraved in a too fancy script in pastel blue "Along the Himalayan Trail." It bore the mark of Luster-Think.

"The Competitor's Product." Weill said it with capitals, and his lips twitched. "It hasn't been published yet. Where did you get it, Frank?"

"Never mind. I just want you to absorb it."

Weill sighed. "Today, everyone wants me to absorb dreams. Frank, it's not dirty?"

Belanger said testily, "It has your Freudian symbols. Narrow crevasses between the mountain peaks. I hope that won't bother you."

"I'm an old man. It stopped bothering me years ago, but that other thing was so poorly done, it hurt. . . . All right, let's see what you've got here."

Again the recorder. Again the unfreezer over his skull and at the temples. This time, Weill rested back in his chair for fifteen minutes or more, while Francis Belanger went hurriedly through two cigarettes.

When Weill removed the headpiece and blinked dream out of his eyes, Belanger said, "Well, what's your reaction, boss?"

Weill corrugated his forehead. "It's not for me. It was repetitious. With competition like this, Dreams, Inc., doesn't have to worry for a while."

"That's your mistake, boss. Luster-Think's going to win with stuff like this. We've got to do something."

"Now, Frank——"

"No, you listen. This is the coming thing."

"This!" Weill stared with half-humorous dubiety at the cylinder. "It's amateurish, it's repetitious. Its overtones are very unsubtle. The snow had a distinct lemon sherbet taste. Who tastes lemon sherbet in snow these days, Frank? In the old days, yes. Twenty years ago, maybe. When Lyman Harrison first made his Snow Symphonies for sale down south, it was a big thing. Sherbet and candy-striped mountaintops and sliding down chocolate-covered cliffs. It's slapstick, Frank. These days it doesn't go."

"Because," said Belanger, "you're not up with the times, boss. I've got to talk to you straight. When you started the dreamie business, when you bought up the basic patents and began putting them out, dreamies were luxury stuff. The market was small and individual. You could afford to turn out speciaiized dreamies and sell them to people at high prices."

"I know," said Weill, "and we've kept that up. But also we've opened a rental business for the masses."

"Yes, we have and it's not enough. Our dreamies have subtlety, yes. They can be used over and over again. The tenth time you're still finding new things, still getting new enjoyment. But how many people are connoisseurs? And another thing. Our stuff is strongly individualized. They're First Person."

"Well?"

"Well, Luster-Think is opening dream palaces. They've opened one with three hundred booths in Nashville. You walk in, take your seat, put on your unfreezer and get your dream. Everyone in the audience gets the same one."

"I've heard of it, Frank, and it's been done before. It didn't work the first time and it won't work now. You want to know why it won't work? Because, in the first place, dreaming is a private thing. Do you like your neighbor to know what you're dreaming? In the second place, in a dream palace, the dreams have to start on schedule, don't they? So the dreamer has to dream not when he wants to but when some palace manager says he should. Finally, a dream one person likes another person doesn't like. In those three hundred booths, I guarantee you, a hundred fifty people are dissatisfied. And if they're dissatisfied, they won't come back."

Slowly, Belanger rolled up his sleeves and opened his collar. "Boss," he said, "you're talking through your hat. What's the use of proving they won't work? They *are* working. The word came through today that Luster-Think is breaking ground for a thousand-booth palace in St. Louis. People can get used to public dreaming, if everyone else in the same room is having the same dream.

And they can adjust themselves to having it at a given time, as long as it's cheap and convenient.

"Damn it, boss, it's a social affair. A boy and a girl go to a dream palace and absorb some cheap romantic thing with stereotyped overtones and commonplace situations, but still they come out with stars sprinkling their hair. They've had the same dream together. They've gone through identical sloppy emotions. They're *in tune*, boss. You bet they go back to the dream palace, and all their friends go, too."

"And if they don't like the dream?"

"That's the point. That's the nub of the whole thing. They're bound to like it. If you prepare Hillary specials with wheels within wheels within wheels, with surprise twists on the third-level undertones, with clever shifts of significance and all the other things we're so proud of, why, naturally, it won't appeal to everyone. Specialized dreamies are for specialized tastes. But Luster-Think is turning out simple jobs in Third Person so both sexes can be hit at once. Like what you've just absorbed. Simple, repetitious, commonplace. They're aiming at the lowest common denominator. No one will love it, maybe, but no one will hate it."

Weill sat silent for a long time and Belanger watched him. Then Weill said, "Frank, I started on quality and I'm staying there. Maybe you're right. Maybe dream palaces are the coming thing. If so we'll open them, but we'll use good stuff. Maybe Luster-Think underestimates ordinary people. Let's go slowly and not panic. I have based all my policies on the theory that there's always a market for quality. Sometimes, my boy, it would surprise you how big a market."

"Boss——"

The sounding of the intercom interrupted Belanger.

"What is it, Ruth?" said Weill.

The voice of his secretary said, "It's Mr. Hillary, sir. He wants to see you right away. He says it's important."

"Hillary?" Weill's voice registered shock. Then, "Wait five minutes, Ruth, then send him in."

Weill turned to Belanger. "Today, Frank, is definitely

not one of my good days. A dreamer's place is in his home with his thinker. And Hillary's our best dreamer so he especially should be at home. What do you suppose is wrong with him?"

Belanger, still brooding over Luster-Think and dream palaces, said shortly, "Call him in and find out."

"In one minute. Tell me, how was his last dream? I haven't tried the one that came in last week."

Belanger came down to earth. He wrinkled his nose. "Not so good."

"Why not?"

"It was ragged. Too jumpy. I don't mind sharp transitions for the liveliness, you know, but there's got to be some connection, even if only on a deep level."

"Is it a total loss?"

"No Hillary dream is a *total* loss. It took a lot of editing, though. We cut it down quite a bit and spliced in some odd pieces he'd sent us now and then. You know, detached scenes. It's still not Grade A, but it will pass."

"You told him about this, Frank?"

"Think I'm crazy, boss? Think I'm going to say a harsh word to a dreamer?"

And at that point the door opened and Weill's comely young secretary smiled Sherman Hillary into the office.

Sherman Hillary, at the age of thirty-one, could have been recognized as a dreamer by anyone. His eyes, unspectacled, had nevertheless the misty look of one who either needs glasses or who rarely focuses on anything mundane. He was of average height but underweight, with black hair that needed cutting, a narrow chin, a pale skin and a troubled look.

He mutttered, "Hello, Mr. Weill," and half-nodded in hangdog fashion in the direction of Belanger.

Weill said heartily, "Sherman, my boy, you look fine. What's the matter? A dream is cooking only so-so at home? You're worried about it? . . . Sit down, sit down."

The dreamer did, sitting at the edge of the chair and holding his thighs stiffly together as though to be ready for instant obedience to a possible order to stand up once more.

He said, "I've come to tell you, Mr. Weill, I'm quitting."

"Quitting?"

"I don't want to dream any more, Mr. Weill."

Weill's old face looked older now than at any time in the day. "Why, Sherman?"

The dreamer's lips twisted. He blurted out, "Because I'm not *living,* Mr. Weill. Everything passes me by. It wasn't so bad at first. It was even relaxing. I'd dream evenings, weekends when I felt like, or any other time. And when I felt like I wouldn't. But now, Mr. Weill, I'm an old pro. You tell me I'm one of the best in the business and the industry looks to me to think up new subtleties and new changes on the old reliables like the flying reveries, and the worm-turning skits."

Weill said, "And is anyone better than you, Sherman? Your little sequence on leading an orchestra is selling steadily after ten years."

"All right, Mr. Weill. I've done my part. It's gotten so I don't go out any more. I neglect my wife. My little girl doesn't know me. Last week, we went to a dinner party—Sarah made me—and I don't remember a bit of it. Sarah says I was sitting on the couch all evening just staring at nothing and humming. She said everyone kept looking at me. She cried all night. I'm tired of things like that, Mr. Weill. I want to be a normal person and live in this world. I promised her I'd quit and I will, so it's good-by, Mr. Weill." Hillary stood up and held out his hand awkwardly.

Weill waved it gently away. "If you want to quit, Sherman, it's all right. But do an old man a favor and let me explain something to you."

"I'm not going to change my mind," said Hillary.

"I'm not going to try to make you. I just want to explain something. I'm an old man and even before you were born I was in this business so I like to talk about it. Humor me, Sherman? Please?"

Hillary sat down. His teeth clamped down on his lower lip and he stared sullenly at his fingernails.

Weill said, "Do you know what a dreamer is, Sherman? Do you know what he means to ordinary people? Do you know what it is to be like me, like Frank Belanger, like your wife, Sarah? To have crippled minds that can't imagine, that can't build up thoughts? People like myself, ordinary people, would like to escape just once in a while this life of ours. We can't. We need help.

"In olden times it was books, plays, radio, movies, television. They gave us make-believe, but that wasn't important. What was important was that for a little while our own imaginations were stimulated. We could think of handsome lovers and beautiful princesses. We could be beautiful, witty, strong, capable, everything we weren't.

"But, always, the passing of the dream from dreamer to absorber was not perfect. It had to be translated into words in one way or another. The best dreamer in the world might not be able to get any of it into words. And the best writer in the world could put only the smallest part of his dreams into words. You understand?

"But now, with dream recording, any man can dream. You, Sherman, and a handful of men like you, supply those dreams directly and exactly. It's straight from your head into ours, full strength. You dream for a hundred million people every time you dream. You dream a hundred million dreams at once. This is a great thing, my boy. You give all those people a glimpse of something they could not have by themselves."

Hillary mumbled, "I've done my share." He rose desperately to his feet. "I'm through. I don't care what you say. And if you want to sue me for breaking our contract, go ahead and sue. I don't care."

Weill stood up, too. "Would I sue you? . . . Ruth," he spoke into the intercom, "bring in our copy of Mr. Hillary's contract."

He waited. So did Hillary and so did Belanger. Weill smiled faintly and his yellowed fingers drummed softly on his desk.

His secretary brought in the contract. Weill took it, showed its face to Hillary and said, "Sherman, my boy, unless you want to be with me, it's not right you should stay."

Then, before Belanger could make more than the beginning of a horrified gesture to stop him, he tore the contract into four pieces and tossed them down the waste chute. "That's all."

Hillary's hand shot out to seize Weill's. "Thanks, Mr. Weill," he said earnestly, his voice husky. "You've always treated me very well, and I'm grateful. I'm sorry it had to be like this."

"It's all right my boy. It's all right."

Half in tears, still muttering thanks, Sherman Hillary left.

"For the love of Pete, boss, why did you let him go?" demanded Belanger distractedly. "Don't you see the game? He'll be going straight to Luster-Think. They've bought him off."

Weill raised his hand. "You're wrong. You're quite wrong. I know the boy and this would not be his style. Besides," he added dryly, "Ruth is a good secretary and she knows what to bring me when I ask for a dreamer's contract. What I had was a fake. The real contract is still in the safe, believe me.

"Meanwhile, a fine day I've had. I had to argue with a father to give me a chance at new talent, with a government man to avoid censorship, with you to keep from adopting fatal policies and now with my best dreamer to keep him from leaving. The father I probably won out over. The goverment man and you, I don't know. Maybe yes, maybe no. But about Sherman Hillary, at least, there is no question. The dreamer will be back."

"How do you know?"

Weill smiled at Belanger and crinkled his cheeks into a network of fine lines. "Frank, my boy, you know how to edit dreamies so you think you know all the tools and machines of the trade. But let me tell you something. The most important tool in the dreamie business is the dreamer himself. He is the one you have to understand most of all, and I understand them.

"Listen. When I was a youngster—there were no dreamies then—I knew a fellow who wrote television scripts. He would complain to me bitterly that when someone met him for the first time and found out who he was, they would say: Where do you get those crazy ideas?

"They honestly didn't know. To them it was an impossibility to even think of one of them. So what could my friend say? He used to talk to me about it and tell me: Could I say, I don't know? When I go to bed, I can't sleep for ideas dancing in my head. When I shave, I cut myself; when I talk, I lose track of what I'm saying; when I drive, I take my life in my hands. And always because ideas, situations, dialogues are spinning and twisting in my mind. I can't tell you where I get my ideas. Can you tell me, maybe, your trick of *not* getting ideas, so I, too, can have a little peace.

"You see, Frank, how it is. *You* can stop work here anytime. So can I. This is our job, not our life. But not Sherman Hillary. Wherever he goes, whatever he does, he'll dream. While he lives, he must think; while he thinks, he must dream. We don't hold him prisoner, our contract isn't an iron wall for him. His own skull is his prisoner, Frank. So he'll be back. What can he do?"

Belanger shrugged. "If what you say is right, I'm sort of sorry for the guy."

Weill nodded sadly. "I'm sorry for all of them. Through the years, I've found out one thing. It's their business; making people happy. *Other* people."

6

Dreamworld

My third play-on-words short-short. Actually, it is imperfect because it is perhaps a thought too obvious, and because the aspect of science fiction that it satirizes is so old-fashioned that young readers may not get it. On the other hand, if they're addicts of movie science fiction they may. At any rate, the story is close to my heart because I am not quite as young as I once was, and it brings back the science fiction stories of my youth.

At thirteen, Edward Keller had been a science-fiction devotee for four years. He bubbled with Galactic enthusiasm.

His Aunt Clara, who had brought him up by rule and rod in pious memory of her deceased sister, wavered between toleration and exasperation. It appalled her to watch him grow so immersed in fantasy.

"Face reality, Eddie," she would say, angrily.

He would nod, but go on, "And I dreamed Martians were chasing me, see? I had a special death ray, but the atomic power unit was pretty low and—"

Every other breakfast consisted of eggs, toast, milk, and some such dream.

Aunt Clara said, severely, "Now, Eddie, one of these nights you won't be able to wake up out of your dream. You'll be trapped! Then what?"

She lowered her angular face close to his and glared.

Eddie was strangely impressed by his aunt's warning. He lay in bed, staring into the darkness. He wouldn't like to be trapped in a dream. It was always nice to wake up before it was too late. Like the time the dinosaurs were after him—

Suddenly, he was out of bed, out of the house, out on the lawn, and he knew it was another dream.

The thought was broken by a vague thunder and a shadow that blotted the sun. He looked upward in astonishment and he could make out the human face that touched the clouds.

It was his Aunt Clara! Monstrously tall, she bent toward him in admonition, mastlike forefinger upraised, voice too guttural to be made out.

Eddie turned and ran in panic. Another Aunt Clara monster loomed up before him, voice rumbling.

He turned again, stumbling, panting, heading outward, outward.

He reached the top of the hill and stopped in horror. Off in the distance a hundred towering Aunt Claras were marching by. As the column passed, each one of the Aunt Claras turned her head sharply toward him and the thunderous bass rumbling coalesced into words:

"Face reality, Eddie. Face reality, Eddie."

Eddie threw himself sobbing to the ground. Please wake up, he begged himself. Don't be caught in this dream.

For unless he woke up, the worst science-fictional doom of all would have overtaken him. He would be trapped, *trapped,* in a world of giant aunts.

7

Eyes Do More Than See

I remember some stories because of the rejections they receive. And if a rejection seems to me to be an unfair one, why, then, naturally, I treasure the story all the more.

This story was written at the request of Playboy *and it used a photograph* Playboy *sent me to set its theme. However, the magazine asked for a revision and when I complied, they rejected it anyway. Personally, I think that whoever rejected it was nuts. I managed to get it printed elsewhere (for one tenth the money, though that didn't bother me a bit) and I've been watching it ever since. This is the ninth time it's been reprinted and I've never received a letter dealing with it that seemed to consider it a rejectable story.*

After hundreds of billions of years, he suddenly thought of himself as Ames. Not the wavelength combination which, through all the universe was now the equivalent of Ames—but the sound itself. A faint memory came back of the sound waves he no longer heard and no longer could hear.

The new project was sharpening his memory for so many more of the old, old, eons-old things. He flattened the energy vortex that made up the total of his individuality and its lines of force stretched beyond the stars.

Brock's answering signal came.

Surely, Ames thought, he could tell Brock. Surely he could tell somebody.

Brock's shifting energy pattern communed, "Aren't you coming, Ames?"

"Of course."

"Will you take part in the contest?"

"Yes!" Ames's lines of force pulsed erratically. "Most certainly. I have thought of a whole new art-form. Something really unusual."

"What a waste of effort! How can you think a new variation can be thought of after two hundred billion years. There can be nothing new."

For a moment Brock shifted out of phase and out of communion, so that Ames had to hurry to adjust his lines of force. He caught the drift of other-thoughts as he did so, the view of the powdered galaxies against the velvet of nothingness, and the lines of force pulsing in endless multitudes of energy-life, lying between the galaxies.

Ames said, "Please absorb my thoughts, Brock. Don't close out. I've thought of manipulating Matter. Imagine! A symphony of Matter. Why bother with Energy. Of course, there's nothing new in Energy; how can there be? Doesn't that show we must deal with Matter?"

"Matter!"

Ames interpreted Brock's energy-vibrations as those of disgust.

He said, "Why not? We were once Matter ourselves back—back—Oh, a trillion years ago anyway! Why not build up objects in a Matter medium, or abstract forms or—listen, Brock—why not build up an imitation of ourselves in Matter, ourselves as we used to be?"

Brock said, "I don't remember how that was. No one does."

"I do," said Ames with energy, "I've been thinking of nothing else and I am beginning to remember. Brock, let me show you. Tell me if I'm right. Tell me."

"No. This is silly. It's—repulsive."

"Let me try, Brock. We've been friends; we've pulsed energy together from the beginning—from the moment we became what we are. Brock, please!"

"Then, quickly."

Ames had not felt such a tremor along his own lines of force in—well, in how long? If he tried it now for Brock and it worked, he could dare manipulate Matter before the assembled Energy-beings who had so drearily waited over the eons for something new.

The Matter was thin out there between the galaxies, but Ames gathered it, scraping it together over the cubic light-years, choosing the atom, achieving a clayey consistency and forcing matter into an ovoid form that spread out below.

"Don't you remember, Brock?" he asked softly. "Wasn't it something like this?"

Brock's vortex trembled in phase. "Don't make me remember. I don't remember."

"That was the head. They called it the head. I remember it so clearly, I want to say it. I mean with sound." He waited, then said, "Look, do you remember that?"

On the upper front of the ovoid appeared HEAD.

"What is that?" asked Brock.

"That's the word for head. The symbols that meant the word in sound. Tell me you remember, Brock!"

"There was something," said Brock hesitantly, "something in the middle." A vertical bulge formed.

Ames said, "Yes! Nose, that's it!" And NOSE appeared upon it. "And those are eyes on either side," LEFT EYE—RIGHT EYE.

Ames regarded what he had formed, his lines of force pulsing slowly. Was he sure he liked this?

"Mouth," he said, in small quiverings, "and chin and Adam's apple, and the collarbones. How the words come back to me." They appeared on the form.

Brock said, "I haven't thought of them for hundreds of billions of years. Why have you reminded me? Why?"

Ames was momentarily lost in his thoughts, "Something else. Organs to hear with; something for the sound waves. Ears! Where do they go? I don't remember where to put them?"

Brock cried out, "Leave it alone! Ears and all else! Don't remember!"

Ames said, uncertainly, "What is wrong with remembering?"

"Because the outside wasn't rough and cold like that but smooth and warm. Because the eyes were tender and alive and the lips of the mouth trembled and were soft on mine." Brock's lines of force beat and wavered, beat and wavered.

Ames said, "I'm sorry! I'm sorry!"

"You're reminding me that once I was a woman and knew love; that eyes do more than see and I have none to do it for me."

With violence, she added matter to the rough-hewn head and said, "Then let *them* do it" and turned and fled.

And Ames saw and remembered, too, that once he had been a man. The force of his vortex split the head in two and he fled back across the galaxies on the energy-track of Brock—back to the endless doom of life.

And the eyes of the shattered head of Matter still glistened with the moisture that Brock had placed there to represent tears. The head of Matter did that which the energy-beings could do no longer and it wept for all humanity, and for the fragile beauty of the bodies they had once given up, a trillion years ago.

8

The Feeling of Power

This story remains ever close to me for three reasons.

1. A friend and sometime science fiction writer dared me to make up a story on the spot. I made up this one and he asked if he could use the idea. I said, "Sure," but by the time an hour had passed I grew so anxious to do it that I called him up and took the story back.

2. It is one of my more anthologized stories. It has appeared in fifteen anthologies that I know of. Naturally, I try not to let outside events influence my own opinion of my stories, but having it constantly asked for tends to erode any reservations I have about it.

3. In the story, I talk of "pocket computers" and deal with the possibility that people will lose their math skills through overdependence upon them. Of course, everyone knows of the one and thinks of the other now, but this story was written in 1957!

Jehan Shuman was used to dealing with the men in authority on long-embattled Earth. He was only a civilian but he originated programming patterns that resulted in self-directing war computers of the highest sort. Generals consequently listened to him. Heads of congressional committees, too.

There was one of each in the special lounge of New Pentagon. General Weider was space-burnt and had a small mouth puckered almost into a cipher. Congressman Brant was smooth-cheeked and clear-eyed. He smoked Denebian tobacco with the air of one whose patriotism was so notorious, he could be allowed such liberties.

Shuman, tall, distinguished, and Programmer-first-class, faced them fearlessly.

He said, "This, gentlemen, is Myron Aub."

"The one with the unusual gift that you discovered quite by accident," said Congressman Brant placidly. "Ah." He inspected the little man with the egg-bald head with amiable curiosity.

The little man, in return, twisted the fingers of his hands anxiously. He had never been near such great men before. He was only an aging low-grade Technician who had long ago failed all tests designed to smoke out the gifted ones among mankind and had settled into the rut of unskilled labor. There was just this hobby of his that the great Programmer had found out about and was now making such a frightening fuss over.

General Weider said, "I find this atmosphere of mystery childish."

"You won't in a moment," said Shuman. "This is not something we can leak to the firstcomer.——Aub!" There was something imperative about his manner of biting off that one-syllable name, but then he was a great Programmer speaking to a mere Technician. "Aub! How much is nine times seven?"

Aub hesitated a moment. His pale eyes glimmered with a feeble anxiety. "Sixty-three," he said.

Congressman Brant lifted his eyebrows. "Is that right?"

"Check it for yourself, Congressman."

The congressman took out his pocket computer, nudged the milled edges twice, looked at its face as it lay there in the palm of his hand, and put it back. He said, "Is this the gift you brought us here to demonstrate. An illusionist?"

"More than that, sir. Aub has memorized a few operations and with them he computes on paper."

"A paper computer?" said the general. He looked pained.

"No, sir," said Shuman patiently. "Not a paper computer. Simply a sheet of paper. General, would you be so kind as to suggest a number?"

"Seventeen," said the general.

"And you, Congressman?"

"Twenty-three."

"Good! Aub, multiply those numbers and please show the gentlemen your manner of doing it."

"Yes, Programmer," said Aub, ducking his head. He fished a small pad out of one shirt pocket and an artist's hairline stylus out of the other. His forehead corrugated as he made painstaking marks on the paper.

General Weider interrupted him sharply. "Let's see that."

Aub passed him the paper, and Weider said, "Well, it looks like the figure seventeen."

Congressman Brant nodded and said, "So it does, but I suppose anyone can copy figures off a computer. I think I could make a passable seventeen myself, even without practice."

"If you will let Aub continue, gentlemen," said Shuman without heat.

Aub continued, his hand trembling a little. Finally he said in a low voice, "The answer is three hundred and ninety-one."

Congressman Brant took out his computer a second time and flicked it, "By Godfrey, so it is. How did he guess?"

"No guess, Congressman," said Shuman. "He computed that result. He did it on this sheet of paper."

"Humbug," said the general impatiently. "A computer is one thing and marks on paper are another."

"Explain, Aub," said Shuman.

"Yes, Programmer.——Well, gentlemen, I write down seventeen and just undereath it, I write twenty-three. Next, I say to myself: seven times three——"

The congressman interrupted smoothly, "Now, Aub, the problem is seventeen times twenty-three."

"Yes, I know," said the little Technician earnestly, "but I *start* by saying seven times three because that's the way it works. Now seven times three is twenty-one."

"And how do you know that?" asked the congressman.

"I just remember it. It's always twenty-one on the computer. I've checked it any number of times."

"That doesn't mean it always will be, though, does it?" said the congressman.

"Maybe not," stammered Aub. "I'm not a mathematician. But I always get the right answers, you see."

"Go on."

"Seven times three is twenty-one, so I write down twenty-one. Then one times three is three, so I write down a three under the two of twenty-one."

"Why under the two?" asked Congressman Brant at once.

"Because———" Aub looked helplessly at his superior for support. "It's difficult to explain."

Shuman said, "If you will accept his work for the moment, we can leave the details for the mathematicians."

Brant subsided.

Aub said, "Three plus two makes five, you see, so the twenty-one becomes a fifty-one. Now you let that go for a while and start fresh. You multiply seven and two, that's fourteen, and one and two, that's two. Put them down like this and it adds up to thirty-four. Now if you put the thirty-four under the fifty-one this way and add them, you get three hundred and ninety-one and that's the answer."

There was an instant's silence and then General Weider said, "I don't believe it. He goes through this rigmarole and makes up numbers and multiplies and adds them this way and that, but I don't believe it. It's too complicated to be anything but hornswoggling."

"Oh no, sir," said Aub in a sweat. "It only *seems* complicated because you're not used to it. Actually, the rules are quite simple and will work for any numbers."

"Any numbers, eh?" said the general. "Come then." He took out his own computer (a severely styled GI model) and struck it at random. "Make a five seven three eight on the paper. That's five thousand seven hundred and thirty-eight."

"Yes, sir," said Aub, taking a new sheet of paper.

"Now," (more punching of his computer), "seven two three nine. Seven thousand two hundred and thirty-nine."

"Yes, sir."

"And now multiply those two."

"It will take some time," quavered Aub.

"Take the time," said the general.

"Go ahead, Aub," said Shuman crisply.

Aub set to work, bending low. He took another sheet of paper and another. The general took out his watch finally and stared at it. "Are you through with your magic-making, Technician?"

"I'm almost done, sir.——Here it is, sir. Forty-one million, five hundred and thirty-seven thousand, three hundred and eighty-two." He showed the scrawled figures of the result.

General Weider smiled bitterly. He pushed the multiplication contact on his computer and let the numbers whirl to a halt. And then he stared and said in a surprised squeak, "Great Galaxy, the fella's right."

The President of the Terrestrial Federation had grown haggard in office and, in private, he allowed a look of settled melancholy to appear on his sensitive features. The Denebian war, after its early start of vast movement and great popularity, had trickled down into a sordid matter of maneuver and countermaneuver, with discontent rising steadily on Earth. Possibly, it was rising on Deneb, too.

And now Congressman Brant, head of the important Committee on Military Appropriations was cheerfully and smoothly spending his half-hour appointment spouting nonsense.

"Computing without a computer," said the president impatiently, "is a contradiction in terms."

"Computing," said the congressman, "is only a system for handling data. A machine might do it, or the human brain might. Let me give you an example." And, using the new skills he had learned, he worked out sums and products until the president, despite himself, grew interested.

"Does this always work?"

"Every time, Mr. President. It is foolproof."

"Is it hard to learn?"

"It took me a week to get the real hang of it. I think you would do better."

"Well," said the president, considering, "it's an interesting parlor game, but what is the use of it?"

"What is the use of a newborn baby, Mr. President? At the moment there is no use, but don't you see that this points the way toward liberation from the machine. Consider, Mr. President," the congressman rose and his deep voice automatically took on some of the cadences he used in public debate, "that the Denebian war is a war of computer against computer. Their computers forge an impenetrable shield of counter-missiles against our missiles, and ours forge one against theirs. If we advance the efficiency of our computers, so do they theirs, and for five years a precarious and profitless balance has existed.

"Now we have in our hands a method for going beyond the computer, leapfrogging it, passing through it. We will combine the mechanics of computation with human thought; we will have the equivalent of intelligent computers; billions of them. I can't predict what the consequences will be in detail but they will be incalculable. And if Deneb beats us to the punch, they may be unimaginably catastrophic."

The president said, troubled, "What would you have me do?"

"Put the power of the administration behind the establishment of a secret project on human computation. Call it Project Number, if you like. I can vouch for my committee, but I will need the administration behind me."

"But how far can human computation go?"

"There is no limit. According to Programmer Shuman, who first introduced me to this discovery——"

"I've heard of Shuman, of course."

"Yes. Well, Dr. Shuman tells me that in theory there is nothing the computer can do that the human mind cannot do. The computer merely takes a finite amount of data and performs a finite number of operations upon them. The human mind can duplicate the process."

The president considered that. He said, "If Shuman says this, I am inclined to believe him—in theory. But, in practice, how can anyone know how a computer works?"

Brant laughed genially. "Well, Mr. President, I asked the same question. It seems that at one time computers were designed directly by human beings. Those were simple computers, of course this being before the time of the rational use of computers to design more advanced computers had been established."

"Yes, yes. Go on."

"Technician Aub apparently had, as his hobby, the reconstruction of some of these ancient devices and in so doing he studied the details of their workings and found he could imitate them. The multiplication I just performed for you is an imitation of the workings of a computer."

"Amazing!"

The congressman coughed gently, "If I may make another point, Mr. President—— The further we can develop this thing, the more we can divert our Federal effort from computer production and computer maintenance. As the human brain takes over, more of our energy can be directed into peacetime pursuits and the impingement of war on the ordinary man will be less. This will be most advantageous for the party in power, of course."

"Ah," said the president, "I see your point. Well, sit down, Congressman, sit down. I want some time to think about this. ——But meanwhile, show me that multiplication trick again. Let's see if I can't catch the point of it."

Programmer Shuman did not try to hurry matters. Loesser was conservative, very conservative, and liked to deal with computers as his father and grandfather had. Still, he controlled the West European computer combine, and if he could be persuaded to join Project Number in full enthusiasm, a great deal would be accomplished.

But Loesser was holding back. He said, "I'm not sure I like the idea of relaxing our hold on computers. The human mind is a capricious thing. The computer will give the same answer to the same problem each time. What guarantee have we that the human mind will do the same?"

"The human mind, Computer Loesser, only manipulates facts. It doesn't matter whether the human mind or a machine does it. They are just tools."

"Yes, yes. I've gone over your ingenious demonstration that the mind can duplicate the computer but it seems to me a little in the air. I'll grant the theory but what reason have we for thinking that theory can be converted to practice?"

"I think we have reason, sir. After all, computers have not always existed. The cave men with their triremes, stone axes, and railroads had no computers."

"And possibly they did not compute."

"You know better than that. Even the building of a railroad or a ziggurat called for some computing, and that must have been without computers as we know them."

"Do you suggest they computed in the fashion you demonstrate?"

"Probably not. After all, this method—we call it 'graphitics,' by the way, from the old European word 'grapho' meaning 'to write'—is developed from the computers themselves so it cannot have antedated them. Still, the cave men must have had *some* method, eh?"

"Lost arts! If you're going to talk about lost arts——"

"No, no. I'm not a lost art enthusiast, though I don't say there may not be some. After all, man was eating grain before hydroponics, and if the primitives ate grain, they must have grown it in soil. What else could they have done?"

"I don't know, but I'll believe in soil-growing when I see someone grow grain in soil. And I'll believe in making fire by rubbing two pieces of flint together when I see that, too."

Shuman grew placative. "Well, let's stick to graphitics. It's just part of the process of etherealization. Transportation by means of bulky contrivances is giving way to direct mass-transference. Communications devices become less massive and more efficient constantly. For that matter, compare your pocket computer with the massive jobs of a thousand years ago. Why not, then, the last step of doing away with computers altogether? Come, sir, Project Number is a going concern; progress is already headlong. But we want your help. If patriotism doesn't move you, consider the intellectual adventure involved."

Loesser said skeptically, "What progress? What can you do beyond multiplication? Can you integrate a transcendental function?"

"In time, sir. In time. In the last month I have learned to handle division. I can determine, and correctly, integral quotients and decimal quotients."

"Decimal quotients? To how many places?"

Programmer Shuman tried to keep his tone casual. "Any number!"

Loesser's lower jaw dropped. "Without a computer?"

"Set me a problem."

"Divide twenty-seven by thirteen. Take it to six places."

Five minutes later, Shuman said, "Two point oh seven six nine two three."

Loesser checked it. "Well, now, that's amazing. Multiplication didn't impress me too much because it involved integers after all, and I thought trick manipulation might do it. But decimals——"

"And that is not all. There is a new development that is, so far, top secret and which, strictly speaking, I ought not to mention. Still—— We may have made a breakthrough on the square root front."

"Square roots?"

"It involves some tricky points and we haven't licked the bugs yet, but Technician Aub, the man who invented the science and who has an amazing intuition in connection with it, maintains he has the problem almost solved. And he is only a Technician. A man like yourself, a trained and talented mathematician ought to have no difficulty."

"Square roots," muttered Loesser, attracted.

"Cube roots, too. Are you with us?"

Loesser's hand thrust out suddenly, "Count me in."

General Weider stumped his way back and forth at the head of the room and addressed his listeners after the fashion of a savage teacher facing a group of recalcitrant students. It made no difference to the general that they were the civilian scientists heading Project Number. The general was the over-all head, and he so considered himself at every waking moment.

He said "Now square roots are all fine. I can't do them myself and I don't understand the methods, but they're fine. Still, the Project will not be sidetracked into what some of you call the fundamentals. You can play with graphitics any way you want to after the war is over, but right now we have specific and very practical problems to solve."

In a far corner, Technician Aub listened with painful attention. He was no longer a Technician, of course, having been relieved of his duties and assigned to the project, with a fine-sounding title and good pay. But, of course, the social distinction remained and the highly placed scientific leaders could never bring themselves to admit him to their ranks on a footing of equality. Nor, to do Aub justice, did he, himself, wish it. He was as uncomfortable with them as they with him.

The general was saying, "Our goal is a simple one, gentlemen; the replacement of the computer. A ship that can navigate space without a computer on board can be constructed in one fifth the time and at one tenth the expense of a computer-laden ship. We could build fleets five times, ten times, as great as Deneb could if we could but eliminate the computer.

"And I see something even beyond this. It may be fantastic now; a mere dream; but in the future I see the manned missile!"

There was an instant murmur from the audience.

The general drove on. "At the present time, our chief bottleneck is the fact that missiles are limited in intelligence. The computer controlling them can only be so large, and for that reason they can meet the changing nature of anti-missile defenses in an unsatisfactory way. Few missiles, if any, accomplish their goal and missile warfare is coming to a dead end; for the enemy, fortunately, as well as for ourselves.

"On the other hand, a missile with a man or two within, controlling flight by graphitics, would be lighter, more mobile, more intelligent. It would give us a lead that might well mean the margin of victory. Besides which, gentlemen, the exigencies of war compel us to remember one thing. A man is much more dispensable than a computer. Manned missiles could be launched in numbers and under circumstances that no good general would care to undertake as far as computer-directed missiles are concerned——"

He said much more but Technician Aub did not wait.

Technician Aub, in the privacy of his quarters, labored long over the note he was leaving behind. It read finally as follows:

"When I began the study of what is now called graphitics, it was no more than a hobby. I saw no more in it than an interesting amusement, an exercise of mind.

"When Project Number began, I thought that others were wiser than I; that graphitics might be put to practical use as a benefit to mankind, to aid in the production of really practical mass-transference devices perhaps. But now I see it is to be used only for death and destruction.

"I cannot face the responsibility involved in having invented graphitics."

He then deliberately turned the focus of a protein-depolarizer on himself and fell instantly and painlessly dead.

They stood over the grave of the little Technician while tribute was paid to the greatness of his discovery.

Programmer Shuman bowed his head along with the rest of them, but remained unmoved. The Technician had done his share and was no longer needed, after all. He might have started graphitics, but now that it had started, it would carry on by itself overwhelmingly, triumphantly, until manned missiles were possible with who knew what else.

Nine times seven, thought Shuman with deep satisfaction, is sixty-three, and I don't need a computer to tell me so. The computer is in my own head.

And it was amazing the feeling of power that gave him.

9

Flies

I don't write "horror stories," but on two different occasions this story was included in an anthology of horror stories.

If you read it, you'll find there's nothing in it that is horrible or horrifying, unless you care to make an analogy, seeing the similarity between the flies and humanity.

Originally, I wanted to make sure that no one missed the analogy, by entitling the story "King Lear, IV, 1, 36–37." If you look up that quote you'll find "As flies to wanton boys, are we to the gods. They kill us for their sport." At editorial insistence, I changed the title and I've always been sorry.

"Flies!" said Kendell Casey, wearily. He swung his arm. The fly circled, returned and nestled on Casey's shirt-collar.

From somewhere there sounded the buzzing of a second fly.

Dr. John Polen covered the slight uneasiness of his chin by moving his cigarette quickly to his lips.

He said, "I didn't expect to meet you, Casey. Or you, Winthrop. Or ought I call you Reverend Winthrop?"

"Ought I call you Professor Polen?" said Winthrop, carefully striking the proper vein of rich-toned friendship.

They were trying to snuggle into the cast-off shell of twenty years back, each of them. Squirming and cramming and not fitting.

Damn, thought Polen fretfully, why do people attend college reunions?

Casey's hot blue eyes were still filled with the aimless anger of the college sophomore who has discovered intellect, frustration, and the tag-ends of cynical philosophy all at once.

Casey! Bitter man of the campus!

He hadn't outgrown that. Twenty years later and it was Casey, bitter ex-man of the campus! Polen could see that in the way his finger tips moved aimlessly and in the manner of his spare body.

As for Winthrop? Well, twenty years older, softer, rounder. Skin pinker, eyes milder. Yet no nearer the quiet certainty he would never find. It was all there in the quick smile he never entirely abandoned, as though he feared there would be nothing to take its place, that its absence would turn his face into a smooth and featureless flesh.

Polen was tired of reading the aimless flickering of a muscle's end; tired of usurping the place of his machines; tired of the too much they told him.

Could they read him as he read them? Could the small restlessness of his own eyes broadcast the fact that he was damp with the disgust that had bred mustily within him?

Damn, thought Polen, why didn't I stay away?

They stood there, all three, waiting for one another to say something, to flick something from across the gap and bring it, quivering, into the present.

Polen tried it. He said, "Are you still working in chemistry, Casey?"

"In my own way, yes," said Casey, gruffly. "I'm not the scientist you're considered to be. I do research on insecticides for E. J. Link at Chatham."

Winthrop said, "Are you really? You said you would work on insecticides. Remember, Polen? And with all that, the flies dare still be after you, Casey?"

Casey said, "Can't get rid of them. I'm the best proving ground in the labs. No compound we've made keeps them away when I'm around. Someone once said it was my odor. I attract them."

Polen remembered the someone who had said that.

Winthrop said, "Or else—"

Polen felt it coming. He tensed.

"Or else," said Winthrop, "it's the curse, you know."

His smile intensified to show that he was joking, that he forgave past grudges.

Damn, thought Polen, they haven't even changed the words. And the past came back.

"Flies," said Casey, swinging his arm, and slapping. "Ever see such a thing? Why don't they light on you two?"

Johnny Polen laughed at him. He laughed often then. "It's something in your body odor, Casey. You could be a boon to science. Find out the nature of the odorous chemical, concentrate it, mix it with DDT, and you've got the best fly-killer in the world."

"A fine situation. What do I smell like? A lady fly in heat? It's a shame they have to pick on me when the whole damned world's a dung heap."

Winthrop frowned and said with a faint flavor of rhetoric, "Beauty is not the only thing, Casey, in the eye of the beholder."

Casey did not deign a direct response. He said to Polen, "You know what Winthrop told me yesterday? He said those damned flies were the curse of Beelzebub."

"I was joking," said Winthrop.

"Why Beelzebub?" asked Polen.

"It amounts to a pun," said Winthrop. "The ancient Hebrews used it as one of their many terms of derision for alien gods. It comes from *Ba'al*, meaning *lord* and *zevuv*, meaning *fly*. The lord of flies."

Casey said, "Come on, Winthrop, don't say you don't believe in Beelzebub."

"I believe in the existence of evil," said Winthrop, stiffly.

"I mean Beelzebub. Alive. Horns. Hooves. A sort of competition deity."

"Not at all." Winthrop grew stiffer. "Evil is a short-term affair. In the end it must lose—"

Polen changed the subject with a jar. He said, "I'll be doing graduate work for Venner, by the way. I talked with him day before yesterday, and he'll take me on."

"No! That's wonderful." Winthrop glowed and leaped to the subject-change instantly. He held out a hand with which to pump Polen's. He was always conscientiously eager to rejoice in another's good fortune. Casey often pointed that out.

Casey said, "Cybernetics Venner? Well, if you can stand him, I suppose he can stand you."

Winthrop went on. "What did he think of your idea? Did you tell him your idea?"

"What idea?" demanded Casey.

Polen had avoided telling Casey so far. But now Venner had considered it and had passed it with a cool, "Interesting!" How could Casey's dry laughter hurt it now?

Polen said, "It's nothing much. Essentially, it's just a notion that emotion is the common bond of life, rather than reason or intellect. It's practically a truism, I suppose. You can't tell what a baby thinks or even *if* it thinks, but it's perfectly obvious that it can be angry, frightened or contented even when a week old. See?

"Same with animals. You can tell in a second if a dog is happy or if a cat is afraid. The point is that their emotions are the same as those we would have under the same circumstances."

"So?" said Casey. "Where does it get you?"

"I don't know yet. Right now, all I can say is that emotions are universals. Now suppose we could properly analyze all the actions of men and certain familiar animals and equate them with the visible emotion. We might find a tight relationship. Emotion A might always involve Motion B. Then we could apply it to animals whose emotions we couldn't guess at by common sense alone. Like snakes, or lobsters."

"Or flies," said Casey, as he slapped viciously at another and flicked its remains off his wrist in furious triumph.

He went on. "Go ahead, Johnny. I'll contribute the flies and you study them. We'll establish a science of flychology and labor to make them happy by removing their neuroses. After all, we want the greatest good of the greatest number, don't we? And there are more flies than men."

"Oh, well," said Polen.

*   *   *

Casey said, "Say, Polen, did you ever follow up that weird idea of yours? I mean, we all know you're a shining cybernetic light, but I haven't been reading your papers. With so many ways of wasting time, something has to be neglected, you know."

"What idea?" asked Polen, woodenly.

"Come on. You know. Emotions of animals and all that sort of guff. Boy, those were the days. I used to know madmen. Now I only come across idiots."

Winthrop said, "That's right, Polen. I remember it very well. Your first year in graduate school you were working on dogs and rabbits. I believe you even tried some of Casey's flies."

Polen said, "It came to nothing in itself. It gave rise to certain new principles of computing, however, so it wasn't a total loss."

Why did they talk about it?

Emotions! What right had anyone to meddle with emotions? Words were invented to conceal emotions. It was the dreadfulness of raw emotion that had made language a basic necessity.

Polen knew. His machines had by-passed the screen of verbalization and dragged the unconscious into the sunlight. The boy and the girl, the son and the mother. For that matter, the cat and the mouse or the snake and the bird. The data rattled together in its universality and it had all poured into and through Polen until he could no longer bear the touch of life.

In the last few years he had so painstakingly schooled his thoughts in other directions. Now these two came, dabbling in his mind, stirring up its mud.

Casey batted abstractedly across the tip of his nose to dislodge a fly. "Too bad," he said. "I used to think you could get some fascinating things out of, say, rats. Well, maybe not fascinating, but then not as boring as the stuff you would get out of our somewhat-human beings. I used to think—"

Polen remembered what he used to think.

*   *   *

Casey said, "Damn this DDT. The flies feed on it, I think. You know, I'm going to do graduate work in chemistry and then get a job on insecticides. So help me. I'll personally get something that *will* kill the vermin."

They were in Casey's room, and it had a somewhat keroseny odor from the recently applied insecticide.

Polen shrugged and said, "A folded newspaper will always kill."

Casey detected a non-existent sneer and said instantly, "How would you summarize your first year's work, Polen? I mean aside from the true summary any scientist could state if he dared, by which I mean: 'Nothing.' "

"Nothing," said Polen. "There's your summary."

"Go on," said Casey. "You use more dogs than the physiologists do and I bet the dogs mind the physiological experiments less. I would."

"Oh, leave him alone," said Winthrop. "You sound like a piano with 87 keys eternally out of order. You're a bore!"

You couldn't say that to Casey.

He said, with sudden liveliness, looking carefully away from Winthrop, "I'll tell you what you'll probably find in animals, if you look closely enough. Religion."

"What the dickens!" said Winthrop, outraged. "That's a foolish remark."

Casey smiled. "Now, now, Winthrop. *Dickens* is just a euphemism for *devil* and you don't want to be swearing."

"Don't teach me morals. And don't be blasphemous."

"What's blasphemous about it? Why shouldn't a flea consider the dog as something to be worshipped? It's the source of warmth, food, and all that's good for a flea."

"I don't want to discuss it."

"Why not? Do you good. You could even say that to an ant, an anteater is a higher order of creation. He would be too big for them to comprehend, too mighty to dream of resisting. He would move among them like an unseen, inexplicable whirlwind, visiting them with destruction and death. But that wouldn't spoil things for the ants. They would reason that destruction was simply their just punishment for evil. And the anteater wouldn't even know he was a deity. Or care."

Winthrop had gone white. He said, "I know you're saying this only to annoy me and I am sorry to see you risking your soul for a moment's amusement. Let me tell you this," his voice trembled a little, "and let me say it very seriously. The flies that torment you are your punishment in this life. Beelzebub, like all the forces of evil, may think he does evil, but it's only the ultimate good after all. The curse of Beelzebub is on you for *your* good. Perhaps it will succeed in getting you to change your way of life before it's too late."

He ran from the room.

Casey watched him go. He said, laughing, "I told you Winthrop believed in Beelzebub. It's funny the respectable names you can give to superstition." His laughter died a little short of its natural end.

There were two flies in the room, buzzing through the vapors toward him.

Polen rose and left in heavy depression. One year had taught him little, but it was already too much, and his laughter was thinning. Only his machines could analyze the emotions of animals properly, but he was already guessing too deeply concerning the emotions of men.

He did not like to witness wild murder-yearnings where others could see only a few words of unimportant quarrel.

Casey said, suddenly, "Say, come to think of it, you did try some of my flies, the way Winthrop says. How about that?"

"Did I? After twenty years, I scarcely remember," murmured Polen.

Winthrop said "You must. We were in your laboratory and you complained that Casey's flies followed him even there. He suggested you analyze them and you did. You recorded their motions and buzzings and wing-wiping for half an hour or more. You played with a dozen different flies."

Polen shrugged.

"Oh, well," said Casey. "It doesn't matter. It was good seeing you, old man." The hearty hand-shake, the thump on the shoulder, the broad grin—to Polen it all translated into sick disgust on Casey's part that Polen was a "success" after all.

Polen said, "Let me hear from you sometimes."

The words were dull thumps. They meant nothing. Casey knew that. Polen knew that. Everyone knew that. But words were meant to hide emotion and when they failed, humanity loyally maintained the pretense.

Winthrop's grasp of the hand was gentler. He said, "This brought back old times, Polen. If you're ever in Cincinnati, why don't you stop in at the meeting-house? You'll always be welcome."

To Polen, it all breathed of the man's relief at Polen's obvious depression. Science, too, it seemed, was not the answer, and Winthrop's basic and ineradicable insecurity felt pleased at the company.

"I will," said Polen. It was the usual polite way of saying, I won't.

He watched them thread separately to other groups.

Winthrop would never know. Polen was sure of that. He wondered if Casey knew. It would be the supreme joke if Casey did not.

He *had* run Casey's flies, of course, not that once alone, but many times. Always the same answer! Always the same unpublishable answer.

With a cold shiver he could not quite control, Polen was suddenly conscious of a single fly loose in the room, veering aimlessly for a moment, then beating strongly and reverently in the direction Casey had taken a moment before.

Could Casey *not* know? Could it be the essence of the primal punishment that he never learn he was Beelzebub?

Casey! Lord of the Flies!

10

Found!

Sometimes a writer plays a little game with a story that has nothing to do with the story itself, but that endears the story to him just the same.

In this story, for instance, there is a first-person narrator, something that is rather unusual for me. What's more, and this is the point, the narrator is a woman and at no point in the story is that fact of any importance. There is only one line when her sex is given away and I wondered if I would get any letters commenting on that fact. I didn't.

You needn't think, by the way, that I've spoiled the story for you by telling you this now for, as I said, it has nothing to do with the story. And you are welcome to join the game by trying to note the giveaway when it comes.

Computer-Two, like the other three that chased each other's tails in orbit round the Earth, was much larger than it had to be.

It might have been one tenth its diameter and yet contained all the volume it needed to store the accumulated and accumulating data needed to control space flight.

They needed the extra space, however, so that Joe and I could get inside, if we had to.

And we had to.

Computer-Two was perfectly capable of taking care of itself. Ordinarily, that is. It was redundant. It worked everything out three times in parallel and all three programs had to mesh perfectly; all three answers had to match. If they did not, the answer was delayed for nanoseconds while Computer-Two checked itself, found the malfunctioning part and replaced it.

There was no sure way in which ordinary people would know how many times it caught itself. Perhaps never. Perhaps twice a day. Only Computer-Central could measure the time delay induced by error and only Computer-Central knew how many of the component spares had been used as replacements. And Computer-Central never talked about it. The only good public image is perfection.

And for all practical purposes, it's *been* perfection, for there was never any call for Joe and me.

We're the trouble-shooters. We go up there when something really goes wrong and Computer-Two or one of the others can't correct itself. It's never happened in the five years we've been on the job. It did happen now and again in the early days of their existence, but that was before our time.

We keep in practice. Don't get me wrong. There isn't a computer made that Joe and I can't diagnose. Show us the error and we'll show you the malfunction. Or Joe will, anyway. I'm not the kind who sings one's own praises.

Anyway, this time, neither of us could make the diagnosis.

The first thing that happened was that Computer-Two lost internal pressure. That's not unprecedented and it's certainly not fatal. Computer-Two can work in a vacuum after all. An internal atmosphere was established in the old days when it was expected there would be a steady flow of repairmen fiddling with it. And it's been kept up out of tradition. Who told you scientists aren't chained by tradition? In their spare time from being scientists, they're human, too.

From the rate of pressure loss, it was deduced that a gravel-sized meteoroid had hit Computer-Two. Its exact radius, mass and energy was reported by Computer-Two itself, using that rate of pressure loss, and a few other things, as data.

The second thing that happened was that the break

was not sealed and the atmosphere was not regenerated. After that came the errors and they called us in.

It made no sense. Joe let a look of pain cross his homely face and said, "There must be a dozen things out of whack."

Someone at Computer-Central said, "The hunk of gravel ricocheted, very likely."

Joe said, "With that energy of entry, it would have passed right through the other side. No ricochets. Besides, even with ricochets, I figure it would have had to take some very unlikely strikes."

"Well, then, what do we do?"

Joe looked uncomfortable. I think that it was at this point that he realized what was coming. He had made it sound peculiar enough to require the trouble-shooters on the spot—and Joe had never been up in space. If he had told me once that his chief reason for taking the job was that he knew it meant he would never have to go up in space, he had told it to me 2^x times, with x a pretty high number.

So I said it for him. I said, "We'll have to go up there."

Joe's only way out would have been to say he didn't think he could handle the job, and I watched his pride slowly come out ahead of his cowardice. Not by much, you understand—by a nose, let's say.

To those of you who haven't been on a spaceship in the last fifteen years—and I suppose Joe can't be the only one—let me emphasize that the initial acceleration is the only troublesome thing. You can't get away from that, of course.

After that it's nothing, unless you want to count possible boredom. You're just a spectator. The whole thing is automated and computerized. The old romantic days of space pilots are gone totally. I imagine they'll return briefly when our space settlements make the shift to the asteroid belt as they constantly threaten to do—but then only until additional Computers are placed in orbit to set up the necessary additional capacity.

Joe held his breath throughout the acceleration, or at least he seemed to. (I must admit that I wasn't very comfortable myself. It was only my third trip. I've taken a couple of vacations on Settlement-Rho with my husband, but I'm not exactly a seasoned hand.)

After that, he was relieved for a while, but only for a while. He got despondent.

"I hope this thing knows where it's going," he said, pettishly.

I extended my arms forward, palms up, and felt the rest of me sway backward a bit in the zero-gravity field. "You," I said, "are a computer specialist. Don't you *know* it knows?"

"Sure, but Computer-Two is off."

"We're not hooked into Computer-Two," I said. "There are three others. And even if only one were left functional, it could handle all the space flights undertaken on an average day."

"All four might go off: If Computer-Two is wrong, what's to stop the rest?"

"Then we'll run this thing manually."

"You'll do it, I suppose? You know how—I think not?"

"So they'll talk me in."

"For the love of Eniac," he groaned.

There was no problem, actually. We moved out to Computer-Two as smooth as vacuum and less than two days after takeoff, we were placed into a parking orbit not ten meters behind it.

What was not so smooth was that, about twenty hours out, we got the news from Earth that Computer-Three was losing internal pressure. Whatever had hit Computer-Two was going to get the rest, and when all four were out, space flight would grind to a halt. It could be reorganized on a manual basis, surely, but that would take months as a minimum, possibly years, and there would be serious economic dislocation on Earth. Worse yet, several thousand people now out in space would surely die.

It wouldn't bear thinking of and neither Joe nor I

talked about it, but it didn't make Joe's disposition sweeter and, let's face it, it didn't make me any happier.

Earth hung over 200,000 kilometers below us, but Joe didn't seem to be bothered by that. He was concentrating on his tether and was checking the cartridge in his reaction-gun. He wanted to make sure he could get to Computer-Two and back again.

You'd be surprised—if you've never tried it—how you can get your space legs if you absolutely have to. I wouldn't say there was nothing to it and we did waste half the fuel we used, but we finally reached Computer-Two. We hardly made any bump at all when we struck Computer-Two. (You hear it, of course, even in vacuum, because the vibration travels through the metalloid fabric of your space suits—but there was hardly any bump, just a whisper.)

Of course, our contact and the addition of our momentum altered the orbit of Computer-Two slightly, but tiny expenditures of fuel compensated for that and we didn't have to worry about it. Computer-Two took care of it, for nothing had gone wrong with it, as far as we could tell, that affected any of its external workings.

We went over the outside first, naturally. The chances were pretty overwhelming that a small piece of gravel had whizzed through Computer-Two and that would leave an unmistakable ragged hole. Two of them in all probability; one going in and one coming out.

Chances of that happening are one in two million on any given day—even money that it will happen at least once in six thousand years. It's not likely, but it can, you know. The chances are one in not more than ten billion that, on any one day, it will be struck by a meteoroid large enough to demolish it.

I didn't mention that because Joe might realize that we were exposed to similar odds ourselves. In fact, any given strike on us would do far more damage to our soft and tender bodies than to the stoical and much-enduring machinery of the computer, and I didn't want Joe more nervous than he was.

The thing is, though, it wasn't a meteoroid.

"What's this?" said Joe, finally.

It was a small cylinder stuck to the outer wall of Computer-Two, the first abnormality we had found in its outward appearance. It was about half a centimeter in diameter and perhaps six centimeters long. Just about cigarette-sized for any of you who've been caught up in the antique fad of smoking.

We brought our small flashlights into play.

I said, "That's not one of the external components."

"It sure isn't," muttered Joe.

There was a faint spiral marking running round the cylinder from one end to the other. Nothing else. For the rest, it was clearly metal, but of an odd, grainy texture—at least to the eye.

Joe said, "It's not tight."

He touched it gently with a fat and gauntleted finger and it gave. Where it had made contact with the surface of Computer-Two, it lifted and our flashes shone down on a visible gap.

"There's the reason gas pressure inside declined to zero," I said.

Joe grunted. He pushed a little harder and the cylinder dropped away and began to drift. We managed to snare it after a little trouble. Left behind was a perfectly round hole in the skin of Computer-Two, half a centimeter across.

Joe said, "This thing, whatever it is, isn't much more than foil."

It gave easily under his fingers, thin but springy. A little extra pressure and it dented. He put it inside his pouch, which he snapped shut, and said, "Go over the outside and see if there are any other items like that anywhere on it. I'll go inside."

It didn't take me very long. Then I went in. "It's clean," I said. "That's the only thing there is. The only hole."

"One is enough," said Joe, gloomily. He looked at the smooth aluminum of the wall and, in the light of the flash, the perfect circle of black was beautifully evident.

*   *   *

It wasn't difficult to place a seal over the hole. It was a little more difficult to reconstitute the atmosphere. Computer-Two's reserve gas-forming supplies were low and the controls required manual adjustment. The solar generator was limping but we managed to get the lights on.

Eventually, we removed our gauntlets and helmet, but Joe carefully placed the gauntlets inside his helmet and secured them both to one of his suit-loops.

"I want these handy if the air pressure begins to drop," he said, sourly.

So I did the same. No use being devil-may-care.

There was a mark on the wall just next to the hole. I had noted it in the light of my flash when I was adjusting the seal. When the lights came on, it was obvious.

"You notice that, Joe?" I said.

"I notice."

There was a slight, narrow depression in the wall, not very noticeable at all, but it was there beyond doubt if you ran your finger over it and it continued for nearly a meter. It was as though someone had scooped out a very shallow sampling of the metal and the surface where that had taken place was distinctly less smooth than elsewhere.

I said, "We'd better call Computer-Central downstairs."

"If you mean back on Earth, say so," said Joe. "I hate that phony space-talk. In fact, I hate everything about space. That's why I took an Earth-side job—I mean a job on Earth—or what was supposed to be one."

I said patiently, "We'd better call Computer-Central back on Earth."

"What for?"

"To tell them we've found the trouble."

"Oh? What did we find?"

"The hole. Remember?"

"Oddly enough, I do. And what caused the hole? It wasn't a meteoroid. I never saw one that would leave a perfectly circular hole with no signs of buckling or melting. And I never saw one that left a cylinder behind." He took the cylinder out of his suit pocket and smoothed the dent out of its thin metal, thoughtfully. "Well, what caused the hole?"

I didn't hesitate. I said, "I don't know."

"If we report to Computer-Central, they'll ask the question and we'll say we don't know and what will we have gained? Except hassle?"

"They'll call us, Joe, if we don't call them."

"Sure. And we won't answer, will we?"

"They'll assume something killed us, Joe, and they'll send up a relief party."

"You know Computer-Central. It will take them at least two days to decide on that. We'll have something before then and once we have something, we'll call them."

The internal structure of Computer-Two was not *really* designed for human occupancy. What was foreseen and allowed for was the occasional and temporary presence of trouble-shooters. That meant there was room for maneuvering and there were tools and supplies.

There weren't any armchairs, though. For that matter, there was no gravitational field, either, or any centrifugal imitation of one.

We both floated in midair, drifting very slowly this way or that. Occasionally, one of us touched the wall and rebounded very slowly. Or else part of one of us overlapped part of the other.

"Keep your foot out of my mouth," said Joe, and pushed it away violently. It was a mistake because we both began to turn. Of course, that's not how it looked to us. To us, it was the interior of Computer-Two that was turning, which was most unpleasant, and it took us a while to get relatively motionless again.

We had the theory perfectly worked out in our Earth-side training, but we were short on practice. A lot short.

By the time we had steadied ourselves, I felt unpleasantly nauseated. You can call it nausea, or astronausea, or space sickness, but whatever you call it, it's the heaves and it's worse in space than anywhere else, because there's nothing to pull the stuff down. It floats around in a cloud of globules and you don't want to be floating around with it.—So I held it back, and so did Joe.

I said, "Joe, it's clearly the computer that's at fault. Let's get at its insides." Anything to get my mind off *my* insides and let them quiet down. Besides, things weren't moving fast enough. I kept thinking of Computer-Three on its way down the tube; maybe Computers-One and -Four by now, too; and thousands of people in space with their lives hanging on what we could do.

Joe looked a little greenish too, but he said, "First I've got to think. Something got in. It wasn't a meteoroid, because whatever it was chewed a neat hole out of the hull. It wasn't cut out because I didn't find a circle of metal anywhere inside here. Did you?"

"No. But it hadn't occurred to me to look."

"I looked, and it's nowhere in here."

"It may have fallen outside."

"With the cylinder covering the hole till I pulled it away? A likely thing. Did you see anything come flying out?"

"No."

Joe said, "We may still find it in here, of course, but I doubt it. It was somehow dissolved and something got in."

"What something? Whose is it?"

Joe's grin was remarkably ill-natured. "Why do you bother asking questions to which there is no answer. If this was last century, I'd say the Russians had somehow stuck that device onto the outside of Computer-Two.—No offense. If it were last century, you'd say it was the Americans."

I decided to be offended. I said, coldly, "We're trying to say something that makes sense *this* century, Iosif," giving it an exaggerated Russian pronunciation.

"We'll have to assume some dissident group."

"If so," I said, "we'll have to assume one with a capacity for space flight and with the ability to come up with an unusual device."

Joe said, "Space flight presents no difficulties, if you can tap into the orbiting Computers illegally—which has been done. As for the cylinder, that may make more sense when it is analyzed back on Earth—downstairs, as you space buffs would say."

"It doesn't make sense," I said. "Where's the point in trying to disable Computer-Two?"

"As part of a program to cripple space flight."

"Then everyone suffers. The dissidents, too."

"But it gets everyone's attention, doesn't it, and suddenly the cause of whatever-it-is makes news. Or the plan is to just knock out Computer-Two and then threaten to knock out the other three. No real damage, but lots of potential, and lots of publicity."

"I don't believe it," I said. "It's too dramatic."

"On the contrary," said Joe. "I'm trying to be nondramatic." He was studying all parts of the interior closely, edging over it square centimeter by square centimeter. "I *might* suppose the thing was of nonhuman origin."

"Don't be silly."

"You want me to make the case? The cylinder made contact, after which something inside ate away a circle of metal and entered Computer-Two. It crawled over the inside wall eating away a thin layer of metal for some reason. Does that sound like anything of human construction?"

"Not that I know of, but I don't know everything. Even you don't know everything."

Joe ignored that. "So the question is, how did it— whatever it is—get into the computer, which is, after all, reasonably well-sealed. It did so quickly, since it knocked out the resealing and air-regeneration capacities almost at once."

"Is *that* what you're looking for?" I said, pointing.

He tried to stop too quickly and somersaulted backward, crying, "That's it! That's it!"

In his excitement, he was thrashing his arms and legs which got him nowhere, of course. I grabbed him and, for a while, we were both trying to exert pushes in uncoordinated directions and that got us nowhere either. Joe called me a few names, but I called him some back and I had the advantage of him there. I understand

English perfectly, better than he does, in fact; but his knowledge of Russian is—well, fragmentary would be a kind way of putting it. Bad language in an ununderstood language always sounds very dramatic.

"Here it is," he said, when we had finally sorted ourselves out.

Where the computer-shielding met the wall, there was a small circular hole left behind when Joe brushed aside a small cylinder. It was just like the one on the outer hull, but it seemed even thinner. In fact, it seemed to disintegrate when Joe touched it.

"We'd better get into the computer," said Joe.

The computer was a shambles.

Not obviously. I don't mean to say it was like a beam of wood that had been riddled by termites.

In fact, if you looked at the computer casually, you might swear it was intact.

Look closely, though, and some of the chips would be gone. The more closely you looked, the more you realized were gone. Worse yet, the stores which Computer-Two used in self-repair had dwindled to almost nothing. We kept looking and every once in a while, one of us would discover something else was missing.

Joe took the cylinder out of his pouch again and turned it end for end. He said, "I suspect it's after high-grade silicon in particular. I can't say for sure, of course, but my guess is that the sides are mostly aluminum but that the flat end is mostly silicon."

I said, "Do you mean the thing is a solar battery?"

"Part of it is. That's how it gets its energy in space; energy to get to Computer-Two, energy to eat a hole into it, energy to—to—I don't know how else to put it. Energy to stay alive."

"You call it alive?"

"Why not? Look, Computer-Two can repair itself. It can reject faulty bits of equipment and replace it with working ones, but it needs a supply of spares to work with. Given enough spares of all kinds, it could build a Computer just like itself, when properly programmed—

but it needs the supply, so we don't think of it as alive. This object that entered Computer-Two is apparently collecting its own supplies. That's suspiciously life-like."

"What you're saying," I said, "is that we have here a microcomputer advanced enough to be considered alive."

"I don't honestly know what I'm saying," said Joe.

"Who on Earth could make such a thing?"

"Who *on Earth?*"

I made the next discovery. It looked like a stubby pen drifting through the air. I just caught it out of the corner of my eye and it registered as a pen.

In zero gravity, things will drift out of pockets and float off. There's no way of keeping anything in place unless it is physically confined. You expect pens and coins and anything else that can find an opening to drift their way through the opening eventually and go wherever air currents and inertia lead them.

So my mind registered "Pen" and I groped for it absently and, of course, my fingers didn't close on it. Just reaching for something sets up an air current that pushes it away. You have to reach over it and sneak behind it with one hand, and then reach for it with the other. Picking up any small object in midair is a two-hand operation.

I know some people can do it one-handed, but they're space hounds and I'm not.

I turned to look at the object and pay a little more attention to retrieval, then realized that my pen was safely in its pouch. I felt for it and it was there.

"Did you lose a pen, Joe?" I called out.

"No."

"Anything like that? Key? Cigarette?"

"I don't smoke. You know that."

A stupid answer. "Anything?" I said in exasperation. "I'm seeing things here."

"No one ever said you were stable."

"Look, Joe. Over there. Over there."

He lunged for it. I could have told him it would do no good.

By now, though, our poking around in the computer seemed to have stirred things up. We were seeing them wherever we looked. They were floating in the air currents.

I stopped one at last. Or, rather, it stopped itself, for it was on the elbow of Joe's suit. I snatched it off and shouted. Joe jumped in terror and nearly knocked it out of my hand.

I said, "Look!"

There was a shiny circle on Joe's suit where I had taken the thing off. It had begun to eat its way through.

"Give it to me," said Joe. He took it gingerly and put it against the wall to hold it steady. Then he shelled it, gently lifting the paper-thin metal.

There was something inside that looked like a line of cigarette ash. It caught the light and glinted, though, like lightly woven metal.

There was a moistness about it, too. It wriggled slowly, one end seeming to seek something blindly.

The end made contact with the wall and stuck. Joe's finger pushed it away. It seemed to require a small effort to do so. Joe rubbed his finger and thumb and said, "Feels oily."

The metal worm—I don't know what else I can call it—seemed limp now after Joe had touched it. It didn't move again.

I was twisting and turning, trying to look at myself.

"Joe," I said, "for heaven's sake, have I got one of them on me anywhere?"

"I don't see one," he said.

"Well, *look* at me. You've got to watch me, Joe, and I'll watch you. If our suits are wrecked we might not be able to get back to the ship."

Joe said, "Keep moving, then."

It was a grisly feeling, being surrounded by things hungry to dissolve your suit wherever they could touch it. When any showed up, we tried to catch them and stay out of their way at the same time, which made things almost impossible. A rather long one drifted close to my leg and I kicked at it, which was stupid, for if I had hit it, it might have stuck. As it was, the air current I set up brought it against the wall, where it stayed.

Joe reached hastily for it—too hastily. The rest of his body rebounded and as he somersaulted, one booted foot struck the wall near the cylinder lightly. When he finally managed to right himself, it was still there.

"I didn't smash it, did I?"

"No, you didn't," I said. "You missed it by a decimeter. It won't get away."

I had a hand on either side of it. It was twice as long as the other cylinder had been. In fact, it was like two cylinders stuck together lengthwise, with a constriction at the point of joining.

"Act of reproducing," said Joe as he peeled away the metal. This time what was inside was a line of dust. Two lines. One on either side of the constriction.

"It doesn't take much to kill them," said Joe. He relaxed visibly. "I think we're safe."

"They do seem alive," I said, reluctantly.

"I think they seem more than that. They're viruses.—Or the equivalent."

"What are you talking about?"

Joe said, "Granted I'm a computer technologist and not a virologist—but it's my understanding that viruses on Earth, or, downstairs, as you would say, consist of a nucleic acid molecule coated in a protein shell.

"When a virus invades a cell, it manages to dissolve a hole in the cell wall or membrane by the use of some appropriate enzyme and the nucleic acid slips inside, leaving the protein coat outside. Inside the cell it finds the material to make a new protein coat for itself. In fact, it manages to form replicas of itself and to form a new protein coat for each replica. Once it has stripped the cell of all it has, the cell dissolves and in place of the one invading virus there are several hundred daughter viruses. Sound familiar?"

"Yes. Very familiar. It's what's happening here. But where did it come from, Joe?"

"Not from Earth, obviously, or any Earth settlement. From somewhere else, I suppose. They drift through space till they find something appropriate in which they can multiply. They look for sizable objects ready-made of metal. I don't imagine they can smelt ores."

"But large metal objects with pure silicon components and a few other succulent matters like that are the products of intelligent life only," I said.

"Right," said Joe, "which means we have the best evidence yet that intelligent life is common in the Universe, since objects like the one we're on must be quite common or it couldn't support these viruses. And it means that intelligent life is old, too, perhaps ten billion years old—long enough for a kind of metal evolution, forming a metal/silicon/oil life as we have formed a nucleic/protein/water life. Time to evolve a parasite on space-age artifacts."

I said, "You make it sound as though every time some intelligent life form develops a space culture, it is subjected before long to parasitic infestation."

"Right. And it must be controlled. Fortunately, these things are easy to kill, especially now when they're forming. Later on, when they're ready to burrow out of Computer-Two, I suppose they will grow, thicken their shells, stabilize their interior and prepare, as the equivalent of spores, to drift a million years before they find another home. They might not be so easy to kill, then."

"How are you going to kill them?"

"I already have. I just touched that first one when it instinctively sought out metal to begin manufacturing a new shell after I had broken open the first one—and that touch finished it. I didn't touch the second, but I kicked the wall near it and the sound vibration in the metal shook its interior apart into metal dust. So they can't get us, now, or any more of the computer if we just shake them apart now!"

He didn't have to explain further—or as much. He put on his gauntlets slowly, and then banged at the wall with one. It pushed him away and he kicked at the wall where he next approached it.

"You do the same," he shouted.

I tried to, and for a while we both kept at it. You don't

know how hard it is to hit a wall at zero gravity, at least on purpose, and do it hard enough to make it clang. We missed as often as not or just struck it a glancing blow that sent us whirling but made virtually no sound. We were panting with effort and aggravation in no time.

But we had acclimated ourselves (or at least I had) and the nausea didn't return. We kept it up and then when we gathered up some more of the viruses, there was nothing inside but dust in every case. They were clearly adapted to empty, automated space objects which, like modern computers, were vibration-free. That's what made it possible, I suppose, to build up the exceedingly rickety complex metallic structures that possessed sufficient instability to produce the properties of simple life.

I said, "Do you think we got them all, Joe?"

"How can I say? If there's one left, it will cannibalize the others for metal supplies and start all over. Let's bang around some more."

We did until we were sufficiently worn out not to care whether one was still left alive.

"Of course," I said, panting, "the Planetary Association for the Advancement of Science isn't going to be pleased with our killing them all."

Joe's suggestion as to what the P.A.A.S. could do with itself was forceful, but impractical. He said, "Look, our mission is to save Computer-Two, a few thousand lives and, as it turned out, our own lives, too. Now they can decide whether to renovate this computer or rebuild it from scratch. It's their baby.

"The P.A.A.S. can get what they can out of these dead objects and that should be something. If they want live ones, I suspect they'll find them floating about in these regions. They can look for them if they want live specimens, but they'd better watch their suits at all times. I don't think they can vibrate them to death in open space."

I said, "All right. My suggestion is we tell Computer-Central we're going to jerry-rig this Computer and get it doing some work anyway, and we'll stay till a relief is up for main repairs or whatever in order to prevent any reinfestation. Meanwhile, they better get to each of the other Computers and set up a system that can set it to vibrating strongly as soon as the internal atmosphere shows a pressure drop."

"Simple enough," said Joe, sardonically.

"It's lucky we found them when we did."

"Wait awhile," said Joe, and the look in his eye was one of deep trouble. "We didn't find them. *They* found *us*. If metal life has developed, do you suppose it's likely that this is the only form it takes? Just this fragile kind?

"What if such life forms communicate somehow and, across the vastness of space, others are now converging on us for the picking? Other species, too; all of them after the lush new fodder of an as yet untouched space culture. *Other* species! Some that are sturdy enough to withstand vibration. Some that are large enough to be more versatile in their reactions to danger. Some that are equipped to invade our settlements in orbit. Some, for the sake of Univac, that may be able to invade the Earth for the metals of its cities.

"What I'm going to report, what I must report, is that we've been *found!*"

11

The Foundation of Science Fiction Success

Yes, I write light verse also. Not often, because I have too many other things to write, but I manage. I have published seven books of limericks, containing nearly seven hundred limericks altogether, of my own invention. Two of the books are even clean.

This verse that follows, however, is a parody of one by W. S. Gilbert that appears in Patience. *I have adapted it syllable by syllable and rhyme by rhyme, so that it can be sung, perfectly, to Sullivan's tune and is within shooting distance at least of being as clever as Gilbert's.*

This is not as easy to do as you might think. Try it, if you doubt me, and then you'll be less astonished that I like this so much. It is also a merciless parody of my own Foundation series, so you'll understand the clever truth of "With a tiny bit of cribbin' from the works of Edward Gibbon . . ."

If you ask me how to shine in the science-fiction line as a
        pro of luster bright,
I say, practice up the lingo of the sciences, by jingo
        (never mind if not quite right).
You must talk of Space and Galaxies and tesseractic
        fallacies in slick and mystic style,
Though the fans won't understand it, they will all the
        same demand it with a softly hopeful smile.

    And all the fans will say,
    As you walk your spatial way,
    If that young man indulges in flights through all the
    Galaxy,

Why, what a most imaginative type of man that type of
man must be.
So success is not a mystery, just brush up on your his-
tory, and borrow day by day.
Take an Empire that was Roman and you'll find it is at
home in all the starry Milky Way.
With a drive that's hyperspatial, through the parsecs you
will race, you'll find that plotting is a breeze,
With a tiny bit of cribbin' from the works of Edward
Gibbon and that Greek, Thucydides.

And all the fans will say,
As you walk your thoughtful way,
If that young man involves himself in authentic history,
Why, what a very learned kind of high IQ, his high
IQ must be.

Then eschew all thoughts of passion of a man-and-woman
fashion from your hero's thoughtful mind.
He must spend his time on politics, and thinking up his
shady tricks, and outside that he's blind.
It's enough he's had a mother, other females are a bother,
though they're jeweled and glistery.
They will just distract his dreaming and his necessary
scheming with that psychohistory.

And all the fans will say
As you walk your narrow way,
If all his yarns restrict themselves to masculinity,
Why, what a most particularly pure young man that
pure young man must be.

12

Franchise

I tend to love any story of mine that seems to grasp something of social significance at a time when it is only a cloud on the horizon.

Right now, there's a great deal of talk about forecasting an election even before the polls close in the Western states, and a lot of feeling to the effect that polls influence voting patterns and so on and so on.

But that's now! This story was written over Christmas in 1954 after I had brooded a bit over the congressional elections six weeks earlier.

Linda, age ten, was the only one of the family who seemed to enjoy being awake.

Norman Muller could hear her now through his own drugged, unhealthy coma. (He had finally managed to fall asleep an hour earlier but even then it was more like exhaustion than sleep.)

She was at his bedside now, shaking him. "Daddy, Daddy, wake up. Wake up!"

He suppressed a groan. "All right, Linda."

"But, Daddy, there's more policemen around than any time! Police cars and everything!"

Norman Muller gave up and rose blearily to his elbows. The day was beginning. It was faintly stirring toward dawn outside, the germ of a miserable gray that looked about as miserably gray as he felt. He could hear Sarah, his wife, shuffling about breakfast duties in the kitchen. His father-in-law, Matthew, was hawking strenuously in the bathroom. No doubt Agent Handley was ready and waiting for him.

This was *the* day.

Election Day!

To begin with, it had been like every other year. Maybe a little worse, because it was a presidential year, but no worse than other presidential years if it came to that.

The politicians spoke about the guh-reat electorate and the vast electuh-ronic intelligence that was its servant. The press analyzed the situation with industrial computers (the New York *Times* and the St. Louis *Post-Dispatch* had their own computers) and were full of little hints as to what would be forthcoming. Commentators and columnists pinpointed the crucial state and county in happy contradiction to one another.

The first hint that it would *not* be like every other year was when Sarah Muller said to her husband on the evening of October 4 (with Election Day exactly a month off), "Cantwell Johnson says that Indiana will be the state this year. He's the fourth one. Just think, *our* state this time."

Matthew Hortenweiler took his fleshy face from behind the paper, stared dourly at his daughter and growled, "Those fellows are paid to tell lies. Don't listen to them."

"Four of them, Father," said Sarah mildly. "They all say Indiana."

"Indiana *is* a key state, Matthew," said Norman, just as mildly, "on account of the Hawkins-Smith Act and this mess in Indianapolis. It——"

Matthew twisted his old face alarmingly and rasped out, "No one says Bloomington or Monroe County, do they?"

"Well——" said Norman.

Linda, whose little pointed-chinned face had been shifting from one speaker to the next, said pipingly, "You going to be voting this year, Daddy?"

Norman smiled gently and said, "I don't think so, dear."

But this was in the gradually growing excitement of an October in a presidential election year and Sarah had led a quiet life with dreams for her companions. She said longingly, "Wouldn't *that* be wonderful, though?"

"If I voted?" Norman Muller had a small blond mustache that had given him a debonair quality in the young Sarah's eyes, but which, with gradual graying, had declined merely to lack of distinction. His forehead bore deepening lines born of uncertainty and, in general, he had never seduced his clerkly soul with the thought that he was either born great or would under any circumstances achieve greatness. He had a wife, a job and a little girl, and except under extraordinary conditions of elation or depression was inclined to consider that to be an adequate bargain struck with life.

So he was a little embarrassed and more than a little uneasy at the direction his wife's thoughts were taking. "Actually, my dear," he said, "there are two hundred million people in the country, and, with odds like that, I don't think we ought to waste our time wondering about it."

His wife said, "Why, Norman, it's no such thing like two hundred million and you know it. In the first place, only people between twenty and sixty are eligible and it's always men, so that puts it down to maybe fifty million to one. Then, if it's really Indiana——"

"Then it's about one and a quarter million to one. You wouldn't want me to bet in a horse race against those odds, now, would you? Let's have supper."

Matthew muttered from behind his newspaper, "Damned foolishness."

Linda asked again, "You going to be voting this year, Daddy?"

Norman shook his head and they all adjourned to the dining room.

By October 20, Sarah's excitement was rising rapidly. Over the coffee, she announced that Mrs. Schultz, having a cousin who was the secretary of an Assemblyman, said that all the "smart money" was on Indiana.

"She says President Villers is even going to make a speech at Indianapolis."

Norman Muller, who had had a hard day at the store, nudged the statement with a raising of eyebrows and let it go at that.

Matthew Hortenweiler, who was chronically dissatisfied with Washington, said, "If Villers makes a speech in Indiana, that means he thinks Multivac will pick Arizona. He wouldn't have the guts to go closer, the mushhead."

Sarah, who ignored her father whenever she could decently do so, said, "I don't know why they don't announce the state as soon as they can, and then the county and so on. Then the people who were eliminated could relax."

"If they did anything like that," pointed out Norman, "the politicians would follow the announcements like vultures. By the time it was narrowed down to a township, you'd have a Congressman or two at every street corner."

Matthew narrowed his eyes and brushed angrily at his sparse, gray hair. "They're vultures, anyhow. Listen——"

Sarah murmured, "Now, Father——"

Matthew's voice rumbled over her protest without as much as a stumble or hitch. "Listen, I was around when they set up Multivac. It would end partisan politics, they said. No more voters' money wasted on campaigns. No more grinning nobodies high-pressured and advertising-campaigned into Congress or the White House. So what happens. More campaigning than ever, only now they do it blind. They'll send guys to Indiana on account of the Hawkins-Smith Act and other guys to California in case it's the Joe Hammer situation that turns out crucial. I say, wipe out all that nonsense. Back to the good old——"

Linda asked suddenly, "Don't you want Daddy to vote this year, Grandpa?"

Matthew glared at the young girl. "Never you mind, now." He turned back to Norman and Sarah. "There was a time I voted. Marched right up to the polling booth, stuck my fist on the levers and voted. There was nothing to it. I just said: This fellow's my man and I'm voting for him. *That's* the way it should be."

Linda said excitedly, "You voted, Grandpa? You really did?"

Sarah leaned forward quickly to quiet what might easily become an incongruous story drifting about the neighborhood. "It's nothing, Linda. Grandpa doesn't really mean voted. Everyone did that kind of voting, your grandpa, too, but it wasn't *really* voting."

Matthew roared, "It wasn't when I was a little boy. I was twenty-two and I voted for Langley and it was real voting. My vote didn't count for much, maybe, but it was as good as anyone else's. *Anyone* else's. And no Multivac to——"

Norman interposed, "All right, Linda, time for bed. And stop asking questions about voting. When you grow up, you'll understand all about it."

He kissed her with antiseptic gentleness and she moved reluctantly out of range under maternal prodding and a promise that she might watch the bedside video till 9:15, *if* she was prompt about the bathing ritual.

Linda said, "Grandpa" and stood with her chin down and her hands behind her back until his newspaper lowered itself to the point where shaggy eyebrows and eyes, nested in fine wrinkles, showed themselves. It was Friday, October 31.

He said, "Yes?"

Linda came closer and put both her forearms on one of the old man's knees so that he had to discard his newspaper altogether.

She said, "Grandpa, did you really once vote?"

He said, "You heard me say I did, didn't you? Do you think I tell fibs?"

"N—no, but Mamma says everybody voted then."

"So they did."

"But how could they? How could *everybody* vote?"

Matthew stared at her solemnly, then lifted her and put her on his knee.

He even moderated the tonal qualities of his voice. He said, "You see, Linda, till about forty years ago, everybody always voted. Say we wanted to decide who was to be the new President of the United States. The Democrats and Republicans would both nominate someone, and everybody would say who they wanted. When Election Day was over, they would count how many people wanted the Democrat and how many wanted the Republican. Whoever had more votes was elected. You see?"

Linda nodded and said, "How did all the people know who to vote for? Did Multivac tell them?"

Matthew's eyebrows hunched down and he looked severe. "They just used their own judgment, girl."

She edged away from him, and he lowered his voice again, "I'm not angry at you, Linda. But, you see, sometimes it took all night to count what everyone said and people were impatient. So they invented special machines which could look at the first few votes and compare them with the votes from the same places in previous years. That way the machine could compute how the total vote would be and who would be elected. You see?"

She nodded. "Like Multivac."

"The first computers were much smaller than Multivac. But the machines grew bigger and they could tell how the election would go from fewer and fewer votes. Then, at last, they built Multivac and it can tell from just one voter."

Linda smiled at having reached a familiar part of the story and said, "That's nice."

Matthew frowned and said, "No, it's not nice. I don't want a machine telling me how I would have voted just because some joker in Milwaukee says he's against higher tariffs. Maybe I want to vote cockeyed just for the pleasure of it. Maybe I don't want to vote. Maybe——"

But Linda had wriggled from his knee and was beating a retreat.

She met her mother at the door. Her mother, who was still wearing her coat and had not even had time to remove her hat, said breathlessly, "Run along, Linda. Don't get in Mother's way."

Then she said to Matthew, as she lifted her hat from her head and patted her hair back into place, "I've been at Agatha's."

Matthew stared at her censoriously and did not even dignify that piece of information with a grunt as he groped for his newspaper.

Sarah said, as she unbuttoned her coat, "Guess what she said?"

Matthew flattened out his newspaper for reading purposes with a sharp crackle and said, "Don't much care."

Sarah said, "Now, Father——" But she had no time for anger. The news had to be told and Matthew was the only recipient handy, so she went on, "Agatha's Joe is a policeman, you know, and he says a whole truckload of secret service men came into Bloomington last night."

"They're not after me."

"Don't you see, Father? Secret service agents, and it's almost election time. In *Bloomington*."

"Maybe they're after a bank robber."

"There hasn't been a bank robbery in town in ages. . . . Father, you're hopeless."

She stalked away.

Nor did Norman Muller receive the news with noticeably greater excitement.

"Now, Sarah, how did Agatha's Joe know they were secret service agents?" he asked calmly. "They wouldn't go around with identification cards pasted on their foreheads."

But by next evening, with November a day old, she could say triumphantly, "It's just everyone in Bloomington that's waiting for someone local to be the voter. The Bloomington *News* as much as said so on video."

Norman stirred uneasily. He couldn't deny it, and his heart was sinking. If Bloomington was really to be hit by Multivac's lightning, it would mean newspapermen, video shows, tourists, all sorts of—strange upsets. Norman liked the quiet routine of his life, and the distant stir of politics was getting uncomfortably close.

He said, "It's all rumor. Nothing more."

"You wait and see, then. You just wait and see."

As things turned out, there was very little time to wait, for the doorbell rang insistently, and when Norman Muller opened it and said, "Yes?" a tall, grave-faced man said, "Are you Norman Muller?"

Norman said, "Yes," again, but in a strange dying voice. It was not difficult to see from the stranger's bearing that he was one carrying authority, and the nature of his errand suddenly became as inevitably obvious as it had, until the moment before, been unthinkably impossible.

The man presented credentials, stepped into the house, closed the door behind him and said ritualistically, "Mr. Norman Muller, it is necessary for me to inform you on the behalf of the President of the United States that you have been chosen to represent the American electorate on Tuesday, November 4, 2008."

Norman Muller managed, with difficulty, to walk unaided to his chair. He sat there, white-faced and almost insensible, while Sarah brought water, slapped his hands in panic and moaned to her husband between clenched teeth, "Don't be sick, Norman. *Don't* be sick. They'll pick someone else."

When Norman could manage to talk, he whispered, "I'm sorry, sir."

The secret service agent had removed his coat, unbuttoned his jacket and was sitting at ease on the couch.

"It's all right," he said, and the mark of officialdom seemed to have vanished with the formal announcement and leave him simply a large and rather friendly man. "This is the sixth time I've made the announcement and I've seen all kinds of reactions. Not one of them was the kind you see on the video. You know what I mean? A holy, dedicated look, and a character who says, 'It will be a great privilege to serve my country.' That sort of stuff." The agent laughed comfortingly.

Sarah's accompanying laugh held a trace of shrill hysteria.

The agent said, "Now you're going to have me with you for a while. My name is Phil Handley. I'd appreciate it if you call me Phil. Mr. Muller can't leave the house any more till Election Day. You'll have to inform the department store that he's sick, Mrs. Muller. You can go about your business for a while, but you'll have to agree not to say a word about this. Right, Mrs. Muller?"

Sarah nodded vigorously. "No, sir. Not a word."

"All right. But, Mrs. Muller," Handley looked grave, "we're not kidding now. Go out only if you must and you'll be followed when you do. I'm sorry but that's the way we must operate."

"Followed?"

"It won't be obvious. Don't worry. And it's only for two days till the formal announcement to the nation is made. Your daughter——"

"She's in bed," said Sarah hastily.

"Good. She'll have to be told I'm a relative or friend staying with the family. If she does find out the truth, she'll have to be kept in the house. Your father had better stay in the house in any case."

"He won't like that," said Sarah.

"Can't be helped. Now, since you have no others living with you——"

"You know all about us apparently," whispered Norman.

"Quite a bit," agreed Handley. "In any case, those are all my instructions to you for the moment. I'll try to co-operate as much as I can and be as little of a nuisance as possible. The government will pay for my maintenance so I won't be an expense to you. I'll be relieved each night by someone who will sit up in this room, so there will be no problem about sleeping accommodations. Now, Mr. Muller—"

"Sir?"

"You can call me Phil," said the agent again. "The purpose of the two-day preliminary before formal announcement is to get you used to your position. We prefer to have you face Multivac in as normal a state of mind as possible. Just relax and try to feel this is all in a day's work. Okay?"

"Okay," said Norman, and then shook his head violently. "But I don't want the responsibility. Why me?"

"All right," said Handley, "let's get that straight to begin with. Multivac weighs all sorts of known factors, billions of them. One factor isn't known, though, and won't be known for a long time. That's the reaction pattern of the human mind. All Americans are subjected to the molding pressure of what other Americans do and say, to the things that are done to him and the things he does to others. Any American can be brought to Multivac to have the bent of his mind surveyed. From that the bent of all other minds in the country can be estimated.

Some Americans are better for the purpose than others at some given time, depending upon the happenings of that year. Multivac picked you as most representative this year. Not the smartest, or the strongest, or the luckiest, but just the most representative. Now we don't question Multivac, do we?"

"Couldn't it make a mistake?" asked Norman.

Sarah, who listened impatiently, interrupted to say, "Don't listen to him, sir. He's just nervous, you know. Actually, he's very well read and he always follows politics very closely."

Handley said, "Multivac makes the decisions, Mrs. Muller. It picked your husband."

"But does it know everything?" insisted Norman wildly. "Couldn't it have made a mistake?"

"Yes, it can. There's no point in not being frank. In 1993, a selected Voter died of a stroke two hours before it was time for him to be notified. Multivac didn't predict that; it couldn't. A Voter might be mentally unstable, morally unsuitable, or, for that matter, disloyal. Multivac can't know everything about everybody until he's fed all the data there is. That's why alterate selections are always held in readiness. I don't think we'll be using one this time. You're in good health, Mr. Muller, and you've been carefully investigated. You qualify."

Norman buried his face in his hands and sat motionless.

"By tomorrow morning, sir," said Sarah, "he'll be perfectly all right. He just has to get used to it, that's all."

"Of course," said Handley.

In the privacy of their bedchamber, Sarah Muller expressed herself in other and stronger fashion. The burden of her lecture was, "So get hold of yourself, Norman. You're trying to throw away the chance of a lifetime."

Norman whispered desperately, "It frightens me, Sarah. The whole thing."

"For goodness' sake, why? What's there to it but answering a question or two?"

"The responsibility is too great. I couldn't face it."

"What responsibility? There isn't any. Multivac picked you. It's Multivac's responsibility. Everyone knows that."

Norman sat up in bed in a sudden access of rebellion and anguish. "Everyone is *supposed* to know that. But they don't. They——"

"Lower your voice," hissed Sarah icily. "They'll hear you downtown."

"They don't," said Norman, declining quickly to a whisper. "When they talk about the Ridgely administration of 1988, do they say he won them over with pie-in-the-sky promises and racist baloney? No! They talk about the 'goddam MacComber vote,' as though Humphrey MacComber was the only man who had anything to do with it because he faced Multivac. I've said it myself—only now I think the poor guy was just a truck farmer who didn't ask to be picked. Why was it his fault more than anyone else's? Now his name is a curse."

"You're just being childish," said Sarah.

"I'm being sensible. I tell you, Sarah, I won't accept. They can't make me vote if I don't want to. I'll say I'm sick. I'll say——"

But Sarah had had enough. "Now you listen to me," she whispered in a cold fury. "You don't have only yourself to think about. You know what it means to be Voter of the Year. A presidential year at that. It means publicity and fame and, maybe, buckets of money——"

"And then I go back to being a clerk."

"You will *not*. You'll have a branch managership at the least if you have any brains at all, and you *will* have, because I'll tell you what to do. You control the kind of publicity, if you play your cards right, and you can force Kennell Stores, Inc. into a tight contract *and* an escalator clause in connection with your salary *and* a decent pension plan."

"That's not the point in being Voter, Sarah."

"That will be your point. If you don't owe anything to yourself or to me—I'm not asking for myself—you owe something to Linda."

Norman groaned.

"Well, don't you?" snapped Sarah.

"Yes, dear," murmured Norman.

* * *

On November 3, the official announcement was made and it was too late for Norman to back out even if he had been able to find the courage to make the attempt.

Their house was sealed off. Secret service agents made their appearance in the open, blocking off all approach.

At first the telephone rang incessantly, but Philip Handley with an engagingly apologetic smile took all calls. Eventually, the exchange shunted all calls directly to the police station.

Norman imagined that, in that way, he was spared not only the bubbling (and envious?) congratulations of friends, but also the egregious pressure of salesmen scenting a prospect and the designing smoothness of politicians from all over the nation. . . . Perhaps even death threats from the inevitable cranks.

Newspapers were forbidden to enter the house now in order to keep out weighted pressures, and television was gently but firmly disconnected, over Linda's loud protests.

Matthew growled and stayed in his room; Linda, after the first flurry of excitement, sulked and whined because she could not leave the house; Sarah divided her time between preparation of meals for the present and plans for the future; and Norman's depression lived and fed upon itself.

And the morning of Tuesday, November 4, 2008, came at last, and it was Election Day.

It was early breakfast, but only Norman Muller ate, and that mechanically. Even a shower and shave had not succeeded in either restoring him to reality or removing his own conviction that he was as grimy without as he felt grimy within.

Handley's friendly voice did its best to shed some normality over the gray and unfriendly dawn. (The weather prediction had been for a cloudy day with prospects of rain before noon.)

Handley said, "We'll keep this house insulated till Mr. Muller is back, but after that we'll be off your necks." The secret service agent was in full uniform now, including sidearms in heavily brassed holsters.

"You've been no trouble at all, Mr. Handley," simpered Sarah.

Norman drank through two cups of black coffee, wiped his lips with a napkin, stood up and said haggardly, "I'm ready."

Handley stood up, too. "Very well, sir. And thank you, Mrs. Muller, for your very kind hospitality."

The armored car purred down empty streets. They were empty even for that hour of the morning.

Handley indicated that and said, "They always shift traffic away from the line of drive ever since the attempted bombing that nearly ruined the Leverett Election of '92."

When the car stopped, Norman was helped out by the always polite Handley into an underground drive whose walls were lined with soldiers at attention.

He was led into a brightly lit room, in which three white-uniformed men greeted him smilingly.

Norman said sharply, "But this is the hospital."

"There's no significance to that," said Handley at once. "It's just that the hospital has the necessary facilities."

"Well, what do I do?"

Handley nodded. One of the three men in white advanced and said, "I'll take over now, agent."

Handley saluted in an offhand manner and left the room.

The man in white said, "Won't you sit down, Mr. Muller? I'm John Paulson, Senior Computer. These are Samson Levine and Peter Dorogobuzh, my assistants."

Norman shook hands numbly all about. Paulson was a man of middle height with a soft face that seemed used to smiling and a very obvious toupee. He wore plastic-rimmed glasses of an old-fashioned cut, and he lit a cigarette as he talked. (Norman refused his offer of one.)

Paulson said, "In the first place, Mr. Muller, I want you to know we are in no hurry. We want you to stay with us all day if necessary, just so that you get used to your surroundings and get over any thought you might have that there is anything unusual in this, anything clinical, if you know what I mean."

"It's all right," said Norman. "I'd just as soon this were over."

"I understand your feelings. Still, we want you to know exactly what's going on. In the first place, Multivac isn't here."

"It isn't?" Somehow through all his depression, he had still looked forward to seeing Multivac. They said it was half a mile long and three stories high, that fifty technicians walked the corridors *within* its structure continuously. It was one of the wonders of the world.

Paulson smiled. "No. It's not portable, you know. It's located underground, in fact, and very few people know exactly where. You can understand that, since it is our greatest natural resource. Believe me, elections aren't the only things it's used for."

Norman thought he was being deliberately chatty and found himself intrigued all the same. "I thought I'd see it. I'd like to."

"I'm sure of that. But it takes a presidential order and even then it has to be countersigned by Security. However, we are plugged into Multivac right here by beam transmission. What Multivac says can be interpreted here and what we say is beamed directly to Multivac, so in a sense we're in its presence."

Norman looked about. The machines within the room were all meaningless to him.

"Now let me explain, Mr. Muller," Paulson went on. "Multivac already has most of the information it needs to decide all the elections, national, state and local. It needs only to check certain imponderable attitudes of mind and it will use you for that. We can't predict what questions it will ask, but they may not make much sense to you, or even to us. It may ask you how you feel about garbage disposal in your town; whether you favor central incinerators. It might ask you whether you have a doctor of your own or whether you make use of National Medicine, Inc. Do you understand?"

"Yes, sir."

"Whatever it asks, you answer in your own words in any way you please. If you feel you must explain quite a bit, do so. Talk an hour, if necessary."

"Yes, sir."

"Now, one more thing. We will have to make use of some simple devices which will automatically record your blood pressure, heartbeat, skin conductivity and brain-wave pattern while you speak. The machinery will seem formidable, but it's all absolutely painless. You won't even know it's going on."

The other two technicians were already busying themselves with smooth-gleaming apparatus on oiled wheels.

Norman said, "Is that to check on whether I'm lying or not?"

"Not at all, Mr. Muller. There's no question of lying. It's only a matter of emotional intensity. If the machine asks you your opinion of your child's school, you may say, 'I think it is overcrowded.' Those are only words. From the way your brain and heart and hormones and sweat glands work, Multivac can judge exactly how intensely you feel about the matter. It will understand your feelings better than you yourself."

"I never heard of this," said Norman.

"No, I'm sure you didn't. Most of the details of Multivac's workings are top secret. For instance, when you leave, you will be asked to sign a paper swearing that you will never reveal the nature of the questions you were asked, the nature of your responses, what was done, or how it was done. The less is known about the Multivac, the less chance of attempted outside pressures upon the men who service it." He smiled grimly. "Our lives are hard enough as it is."

Norman nodded. "I understand."

"And now would you like anything to eat or drink?"

"No. Nothing right now."

"Do you have any questions?"

Norman shook his head.

"Then you tell us when you're ready."

"I'm ready right now."

"You're certain?"

"Quite."

Paulson nodded, and raised his hand in a gesture to the others.

They advanced with their frightening equipment, and Norman Muller felt his breath come a little quicker as he watched.

The ordeal lasted nearly three hours, with one short break for coffee and an embarrassing session with a chamber pot. During all this time, Norman Muller remained encased in machinery. He was bone-weary at the close.

He thought sardonically that his promise to reveal nothing of what had passed would be an easy one to keep. Already the questions were a hazy mishmash in his mind.

Somehow he had thought Multivac would speak in a sepulchral, superhuman voice, resonant and echoing, but that, after all, was just an idea he had from seeing too many television shows, he now decided. The truth was distressingly undramatic. The questions were slips of a kind of metallic foil patterned with numerous punctures. A second machine converted the pattern into words and Paulson read the words to Norman, then gave him the question and let him read it for himself.

Norman's answers were taken down by a recording machine, played back to Norman for confirmation, with emendations and added remarks also taken down. All that was fed into a pattern-making instrument and that, in turn, was radiated to Multivac.

The one question Norman could remember at the moment was an incongruously gossipy: "What do you think of the price of eggs?"

Now it was over, and gently they removed the electrodes from various portions of his body, unwrapped the pulsating band from his upper arm, moved the machinery away.

He stood up, drew a deep, shuddering breath and said, "Is that all? Am I through?"

"Not quite." Paulson hurried to him, smiling in reassuring fashion. "We'll have to ask you to stay another hour."

"Why?" asked Norman sharply.

"It will take that long for Multivac to weave its new data into the trillions of items it has. Thousands of elections are concerned, you know. It's very complicated. And it may be that an odd contest here or there, a comptrollership in Phoenix, Arizona, or some council seat in Wilkesboro, North Carolina, may be in doubt. In that case, Multivac may be compelled to ask you a deciding question or two."

"No," said Norman. "I won't go through this again."

"It probably won't happen," Paulson said soothingly. "It rarely does. But, just in case, you'll have to stay." A touch of steel, just a touch, entered his voice. "You have no choice, you know. You must."

Norman sat down wearily. He shrugged.

Paulson said, "We can't let you read a newspaper, but if you'd care for a murder mystery, or if you'd like to play chess, or if there's anything we can do for you to help pass the time, I wish you'd mention it."

"It's all right. I'll just wait."

They ushered him into a small room just next to the one in which he had been questioned. He let himself sink into a plastic-covered armchair and closed his eyes.

As well as he could, he must wait out this final hour.

He sat perfectly still and slowly the tension left him. His breathing grew less ragged and he could clasp his hands without being quite so conscious of the trembling of his fingers.

Maybe there would be no questions. Maybe it was all over.

If it *were* over, then the next thing would be torchlight processions and invitations to speak at all sorts of functions. The Voter of the Year!

He, Norman Muller, ordinary clerk of a small department store in Bloomington, Indiana, who had neither been born great nor achieved greatness would be in the extraordinary position of having had greatness thrust upon him.

The historians would speak soberly of the Muller Election of 2008. That would be its name, the Muller Election.

The publicity, the better job, the flash flood of money that interested Sarah so much, occupied only a corner of his mind. It would all be welcome, of course. He couldn't refuse it. But at the moment something else was beginning to concern him.

A latent patriotism was stirring. After all, he was representing the entire electorate. He was the focal point for *them*. He was, in his own person, for this one day, all of America!

The door opened, snapping him to open-eyed attention. For a moment, his stomach constricted. Not more questions!

But Paulson was smiling. "That will be all, Mr. Muller."

"No more questions, sir?"

"None needed. Everything was quite clear-cut. You will be escorted back to your home and then you will be a private citizen once more. Or as much as the public will allow."

"Thank you. Thank you." Norman flushed and said, "I wonder—who was elected?"

Paulson shook his head. "That will have to wait for the offcial announcement. The rules are quite strict. We can't even tell you. You understand."

"Of course. Yes." Norman felt embarrassed.

"Secret service will have the necessary papers for you to sign."

"Yes." Suddenly, Norman Muller felt proud. It was on him now in full strength. He was proud.

In this imperfect world, the sovereign citizens of the first and greatest Electronic Democracy had, through Norman Muller (through *him!*), exercised once again its free, untrammeled franchise.

13

The Fun They Had

*This is my most anthologized story, for it has appeared in
thirty-one anthologies that I know of. I don't know why
that should be. It's a good little story and it dealt with
computerized education, despite the fact that it was written
in 1951.*

*My own feeling is that after a story has been anthologized enough times (especially in books intended for reading in English classes) it begins to feed on itself. Those who
prepare new anthologies read old ones and select what
they like.*

*However, I like the story apart from its anthologizations
so that I'm including it.*

Margie even wrote about it that night in her diary. On
the page headed May 17, 2157, she wrote, "Today Tommy
found a real book!"

It was a very old book. Margie's grandfather once said
that when he was a little boy *his* grandfather told him
that there was a time when all stories were printed on
paper.

They turned the pages, which were yellow and crinkly,
and it was awfully funny to read words that stood still
instead of moving the way they were supposed to—on a
screen, you know. And then, when they turned back to
the page before, it had the same words on it that it had
had when they read it the first time.

"Gee," said Tommy, "what a waste. When you're
through with the book, you just throw it away, I guess.
Our television screen must have had a million books on it
and it's good for plenty more. I wouldn't throw *it* away."

"Same with mine," said Margie. She was eleven and hadn't seen as many telebooks as Tommy had. He was thirteen.

She said, "Where did you find it?"

"In my house." He pointed without looking, because he was busy reading. "In the attic."

"What's it about?"

"School."

Margie was scornful. "School? What's there to write about school? I hate school."

Margie always hated school, but now she hated it more than ever. The mechanical teacher had been giving her test after test in geography and she had been doing worse and worse until her mother had shaken her head sorrowfully and sent for the County Inspector.

He was a round little man with a red face and a whole box of tools with dials and wires. He smiled at Margie and gave her an apple, then took the teacher apart. Margie had hoped he wouldn't know how to put it together again, but he knew how all right, and, after an hour or so, there it was again, large and square and ugly, with a big screen on which all the lessons were shown and the questions were asked. That wasn't so bad. The part Margie hated most was the slot where she had to put homework and test papers. She always had to write them out in a punch code they made her learn when she was six years old, and the mechanical teacher calculated the mark in no time.

The Inspector had smiled after he was finished and patted Margie's head. He said to her mother, "It's not the little girl's fault, Mrs. Jones. I think the geography sector was geared a little too quick. Those things happen sometimes. I've slowed it up to an average ten-year level. Actually, the over-all pattern of her progress is quite satisfactory." And he patted Margie's head again.

Margie was disappointed. She had been hoping they would take the teacher away altogether. They had once taken Tommy's teacher away for nearly a month because the history sector had blanked out completely.

So she said to Tommy, "Why would anyone write about school?"

Tommy looked at her with very superior eyes. "Because it's not our kind of school, stupid. This is the old kind of school that they had hundreds and hundreds of years ago." He added loftily, pronouncing the word carefully, "*Centuries* ago."

Margie was hurt. "Well, I don't know what kind of school they had all that time ago." She read the book over his shoulder for a while, then said, "Anyway, they had a teacher."

"Sure they had a teacher, but it wasn't a *regular* teacher. It was a man."

"A man? How could a man be a teacher?"

"Well, he just told the boys and girls things and gave them homework and asked them questions."

"A man isn't smart enough."

"Sure he is. My father knows as much as my teacher."

"He can't. A man can't know as much as a teacher."

"He knows almost as much, I betcha."

Margie wasn't prepared to dispute that. She said, "I wouldn't want a strange man in my house to teach me."

Tommy screamed with laughter. "You don't know much, Margie. The teachers didn't live in the house. They had a special building and all the kids went there."

"And all the kids learned the same thing?"

"Sure, if they were the same age."

"But my mother says a teacher has to be adjusted to fit the mind of each boy and girl it teaches and that each kid has to be taught differently."

"Just the same they didn't do it that way then. If you don't like it, you don't have to read the book."

"I didn't say I didn't like it," Margie said quickly. She wanted to read about those funny schools.

They weren't even half-finished when Margie's mother called, "Margie! School!"

Margie looked up. "Not yet, Mamma."

"Now!" said Mrs. Jones. "And it's probably time for Tommy, too."

Margie said to Tommy, "Can I read the book some more with you after school?"

"Maybe," he said nonchalantly. He walked away whistling, the dusty old book tucked beneath his arm.

Margie went into the schoolroom. It was right next to her bedroom, and the mechanical teacher was on and waiting for her. It was always on at the same time every day except Saturday and Sunday, because her mother said little girls learned better if they learned at regular hours.

The screen was lit up, and it said: "Today's arithmetic lesson is on the addition of proper fractions. Please insert yesterday's homework in the proper slot."

Margie did so with a sigh. She was thinking about the old schools they had when her grandfather's grandfather was a little boy. All the kids from the whole neighborhood came, laughing and shouting in the schoolyard, sitting together in the schoolroom, going home together at the end of the day. They learned the same things, so they could help one another on the homework and talk about it.

And the teachers were people. . . .

The mechanical teacher was flashing on the screen: "When we add the fractions 1/2 and 1/4——"

Margie was thinking about how the kids must have loved it in the old days. She was thinking about the fun they had.

14

How It Happened

This is a very short story but it is not one of those that ends in a play on words. It is funny, yes, and meant to cause a giggle or two, but underneath I am quite serious. One is at the mercy of the medium one uses, so that when papyrus was not common and printing was nonexistent, books had to be shorter than they are today, and that influenced you in anything you wanted to say.

My brother began to dictate in his best oratorical style, the one which has the tribes hanging on his words.

"In the beginning," he said, "exactly fifteen point two billion years ago, there was a big bang and the Universe—"

But I had stopped writing. "Fifteen billion years ago?" I said incredulously.

"Absolutely," he said. "I'm inspired."

"I don't question your inspiration," I said. (I had better not. He's three years younger than I am, but I don't try questioning his inspiration. Neither does anyone else or there's hell to pay.) "But are you going to tell the story of the Creation over a period of fifteen billion years?"

"I have to," said my brother. "That's how long it took. I have it all in here," he tapped his forehead, "and it's on the very highest authority."

By now I had put down my stylus. "Do you know the price of papyrus?" I said.

"What?" (He may be inspired but I frequently noticed that the inspiration didn't include such sordid matters as the price of papyrus.)

I said, "Suppose you describe one million years of

events to each roll of papyrus. That means you'll have to fill fifteen thousand rolls. You'll have to talk long enough to fill them and you know that you begin to stammer after a while. I'll have to write enough to fill them and my fingers will fall off and even if we can afford all that papyrus and you have the voice and I have the strength, who's going to copy it? We've got to have a guarantee of a hundred copies before we can publish and without that where will we get royalties from?"

My brother thought awhile. He said, "You think I ought to cut it down?"

"Way down," I said, "if you expect to reach the public."

"How about a hundred years?" he said.

"How about six days?" I said.

He said, horrified, "You can't squeeze Creation into six days."

I said, "This is all the papyrus I have. What do *you* think?"

"Oh, well," he said, and began to dictate again, "In the beginning—Does it have to be six days, Aaron?"

I said, firmly, "Six days, Moses."

15

I Just Make Them Up, See!

Science fiction writers are endlessly chivvied over how and where they get their "crazy" ideas (the adjective invariably used). The question is stated, much more elaborately and cleverly in the poem than the usual questioner can possibly manage, and the answer (I hope you notice) is given in the title. I wrote this piece of comic verse at a time of deep depression, a malady which strikes me very rarely, and I deliberately tackled this poem. the most delightful (to me) that I have ever written, in order to cure myself. It worked and I have been inordinately grateful to it ever since.

Oh, Dr. A.——
Oh, Dr. A.——
There is something (don't go 'way)
That I'd like to hear you say.
Though I'd rather die
Than try
To pry,
The fact, you'll find,
Is that my mind
Has evolved the jackpot question for today.

I intend no cheap derision,
So please answer with decision,
And, discarding all your petty cautious fears,
Tell the secret of your vision!
How on earth
Do you give birth
To those crazy and impossible ideas?

Is it indigestion
And a question
Of the nightmare that results?
Of your eyeballs whirling,
Twirling,
Fingers curling
And unfurling,
While your blood beats maddened chimes
As it keeps impassioned times
With your thick, uneven pulse?

Is it *that,* you think, or liquor
That brings on the wildness quicker?
For a teeny
Weeny
Dry martini
May be just your private genie;
Or perhaps those Tom and Jerries
You will find the very
Berries
For inducing
And unloosing
That weird gimmick or that kicker;
Or an awful
Combination
Of unlawful
Stimulation,
Marijuana plus tequila,
That will give you just that feel o'
Things a-clicking
And unsticking
As you start your cerebration
To the crazy syncopation
Of a brain a-tocking-ticking.
Surely *something,* Dr. A.,
Makes you fey
And quite *outré.*
Since I read you with devotion,
Won't you give me just a notion
Of that shrewdly pepped-up potion

Out of which emerge your plots?
That wild secret bubbly mixture
That has made you such a fixture
In most favored s. f. spots——

Now, Dr. A.,
Don't go away——

Oh, Dr. A.——

Oh, Dr. A.——

16

I'm in Marsport
Without Hilda

My stories rarely contain ribald elements. This is not be-
cause I am incapable of writing in ribald fashion (consider
my five books of original limericks that are not clean) but
because I choose not to. This, of course, is something I
find it difficult to convince others of; they persist in stating
their belief that I have some sort of problem.

This story was written at an editorial dare, and I told the
editor that I would write it under a pseudonym so that I
could retain my principle. Then, however, when the story
was written, I decided it wasn't so terribly ribald—it was
all by indirection—and I couldn't bear to deny authorship,
so I put my own name upon it.

It worked itself out, to begin with, like a dream. I
didn't have to make any arrangements. I didn't have to
touch it. I just watched things work out. Maybe right
then's when I should have smelled catastrophe.

It began with my usual month's layoff between assign-
ments. A month on and a month off is the right and
proper routine for the Galactic Service. I reached Marsport
for the usual three-day layover before the short hop to
Earth.

Ordinarily, Hilda, God bless her, as sweet a wife as
any man ever had, would be there waiting for me and
we'd have a nice sedate time of it—a nice little interlude
for the two of us. The only trouble with that is that
Marsport is the rowdiest hellhole in the system, and a
nice little interlude isn't exactly what fits in. Only, how
do I explain that to Hilda, hey?

Well, *this* time my mother-in-law—God *bless* her, for a

change—got sick just two days before I reached Marsport; and the night before landing, I got a spacegram from Hilda saying she would stay on Earth with her mother and wouldn't meet me this one time.

I grammed back my loving regrets and my feverish anxiety concerning her mother; and when I landed, there I was:

I was in Marsport without Hilda!

That was still nothing, you understand. It was the frame of the picture, the bones of the woman. Now there was the matter of the lines and coloring inside the frame; the skin and flesh outside the bones.

So I called up Flora—Flora of certain rare episodes in the past—and for the purpose I used a video booth. Damn the expense, full speed ahead.

I was giving myself ten to one odds she'd be out, she'd be busy with her videophone disconnected, she'd be dead, even.

But she was in, with her videophone connected and she was anything but dead.

She looked better than ever. Age cannot wither nor custom stale, as somebody or other once said, her infinite variety. And the robe she wore—or, rather, almost didn't wear—helped a lot.

Was she glad to see me? She squealed, "Max! It's been years."

"I know, Flora, but this is it, if you're available. Because guess what! I'm in Marsport without Hilda."

She squealed again. "Isn't that *nice!* Then come on over."

I goggled a bit. This was too much. "You mean you *are* available?" You have to understand that Flora was never available without plenty of notice. Well, she was that kind of knockout.

She said, "Oh, I've got some quibbling little arrangement, Max, but I'll take care of that. You come on over."

"I'll come," I said happily.

Flora was the kind of girl— Well, I tell you, she had her rooms under Martian gravity, 0.4 Earth-normal. The gadget to free her of Marsport's pseudo-grav field was expensive, of course, but I'll tell you just in passing that it was worth it, and she had no trouble paying it off. If you've ever held a girl in your arms at 0.4 gees, you need no explanation. If you haven't, explanations will do no good. I'm also sorry for you.

Talk about floating on clouds . . .

And mind you, the girl has to know how to handle low gravity. Flora did. I won't talk about myself, you understand, but Flora didn't howl for me to come over and start breaking previous engagements just because she was at loose ends. Her ends were never loose.

I closed connections, and only the prospect of seeing it all in the flesh—such flesh!—could have made me wipe out the image with such alacrity. I stepped out of the booth.

And at that point, that precise point, that very split instant of time, the first whiff of catastrophe nudged itself up to me.

That first whiff was the bald head of that lousy Rog Crinton of the Mars offices, gleaming over a headful of pale blue eyes, pale yellow complexion, and pale brown mustache. He was the same Rog Crinton, with some Slavic strain in his ancestry, that half the people out on field work thought had a middle name that went sunnuva-bich.

I didn't bother getting on all fours and beating my forehead against the ground because my vacation had started the minute I had gotten off the ship.

I said with only normal politeness, "What the hell do you want and I'm in a hurry. I've got an appointment."

He said, "You've got an appointment with me. I've got a little job for you."

I laughed and told him in all necessary anatomical detail where he could put the little job, and offered to get him a mallet to help. I said, "It's my month off, friend."

He said, "Red emergency alert, friend."

Which meant, no vacation, just like that. I couldn't believe it. I said, "Nuts, Rog. Have a heart. I got an emergency alert of my own."

"Nothing like this."

"Rog," I pleaded, "can't you get someone else? Anyone else?"

"You're the only Class A agent on Mars."

"Send to Earth, then. They stack agents like micropile units at Headquarters."

"This has got to be done before 11 P.M. What's the matter? You haven't got three hours?"

I grabbed my head. The boy just didn't *know.* I said, "Let me make a call, will you?"

I stepped back in the booth, glared at him, and said, "Private!"

Flora shone on the screen again, like a mirage on an asteroid. She said, "Something wrong, Max? Don't say something's wrong. I canceled my other engagement."

I said, "Flora, baby, I'll be there. I'll *be* there. But something's come up."

She asked the natural question in a hurt tone of voice and I said, "*No.* Not another girl. With you in the same town they don't make any other girls. Females, maybe. Not girls. Baby! Honey! It's business. Just hold on. It won't take long."

She said, "All right," but she said it kind of like it was just enough *not* all right so that I got the shivers.

I stepped out of the booth and said, "All right, Rog Sunnuvabich, what kind of mess have you cooked up for me?"

We went into the spaceport bar and got us an insulated booth. He said, "The *Antares Giant* is coming in from Sirius in exactly half an hour, at 8 P.M. local time."

"Okay."

"Three men will get out, among others, and will wait for the *Space Eater* coming in from Earth at 11 P.M. and leaving for Capella some time thereafter. The three men will get on the *Space Eater* and will then be out of our jurisdiction."

"So."

"So between eight and eleven, they will be in a special waiting room and you will be with them. I have a trimensional image of each for you so you'll know who they are and which is which. You have between eight and eleven to decide which one is carrying contraband."

"What kind of contraband?"

"The worst kind. Altered Spaceoline."

"*Altered* Spaceoline?"

He had thrown me. I knew what Spaceoline was. If you've been on a space hop you know too. And in case you're Earthbound yourself the bare fact is that everyone needs it on the first space trip; almost everybody needs it for the flrst dozen trips; lots need it every trip. Without it, there is vertigo associated with free fall, screaming terrors, semipermanent psychoses. With it, there is nothing; you don't mind a thing. And it isn't habit-forming; it has no adverse side effects. Spaceoline is ideal, essential, unsubstitutable. When in doubt, take Spaceoline.

Rog said, "That's right, altered Spaceoline. It can be changed chemically, by a simple reaction that can be conducted in anyone's basement, into a drug that will give one giant-size charge and become your baby-blue habit the first time. It is on a par with the most dangerous alkaloids we know."

"And we just found out about it?"

"No. The Service has known about it for years, and we've kept others from knowing by squashing every discovery flat. Now, however, the discovery has gone too far."

"In what way?"

"One of the men who will be stopping over at this spaceport is carrying some of the altered Spaceoline on his person. Chemists in the Capellan system, which is outside the Federation, will analyze it and set up ways of synthesizing more. After that, it's either fight the worst drug menace we've ever seen or suppress the matter by suppressing the source."

"You mean Spaceoline."

"Right. And if we suppress Spaceoline, we suppress space travel."

I decided to put my finger on the point. "Which one of the three has it?"

Rog smiled nastily. "If we knew, would we need you? You're to find out which of the three."

"You're calling on me for a lousy frisk job?"

"Touch the wrong one at the risk of a haircut down to the larynx. Every one of the three is a big man on his own planet. One is Edward Harponaster; one is Joaquin Lipsky; and one is Andiamo Ferrucci. Well?"

He was right. I'd heard of every one of them. Chances are you have too. *Important,* very important people, and not one was touchable without proof in advance. I said, "Would one of them touch a dirty deal like—"

"There are trillions involved," said Rog, "which means any one of the three would. And one of them *has,* because Jack Hawk got that far before he was killed—"

"Jack Hawk's *dead?*"

"Right, and one of those guys arranged the killing. Now you find out which. You put the flnger on the right one before eleven and there's a promotion, a raise in pay, a pay-back for poor Jack Hawk, and a rescue of the Galaxy. You put the finger on the wrong one and there'll be a nasty interstellar situation and you'll be out on your ear and also on every blacklist from here to Antares and back."

I said, "Suppose I don't finger anybody?"

"That would be like fingering the wrong one as far as the Service is concerned."

"I've got to finger someone, but only the right one, or my head's handed to me?"

"In thin slices. You're beginning to understand me, Max."

In a long lifetime of looking ugly, Rog Crinton had never looked uglier. The only comfort I got out of staring at him was the realization that he was married too, and that he lived with his wife at Marsport all year round. And does he deserve that! Maybe I'm hard on him, but he *deserves* it.

I put in a quick call to Flora, as soon as Rog was out of sight.

She said, "Well?" The magnetic seams on her robe

were opened just right and her voice sounded as thrillingly soft as she looked.

I said, "Baby, honey, it's something I can't talk about, but I've got to do it, see? Now you hang on, I'll get it over with if I have to swim the Grand Canal to the icecap in my underwear, see? If I have to claw Phobos out of the sky. If I have to cut myself in pieces and mail myself parcel post."

"Gee," she said, "if I thought I was going to have to wait . . ."

I winced. She just wasn't the type to respond to poetry. Actually, she was a simple creature of action . . . but after all, if I were going to be drifting through low gravity in a sea of jasmine perfume with Flora, poetry response is not the type of qualification I would consider most indispensable.

I said urgently, "Just hold on, Flora. I won't be any time at all. I'll make it up to you."

I was annoyed, sure, but I wasn't worried as yet. Rog hadn't more than left me when I figured out exactly how I was going to tell the guilty man from the others.

It was easy. I should have called Rog back and told him, but there's no law against wanting egg in your beer and oxygen in your air. It would take me five minutes and then off I would go to Flora; a little late, maybe, but with a promotion, a raise, and a slobbering kiss from the Service on each cheek.

You see, it's like this. Big industrialists don't go space hopping much; they use transvideo reception. When they do go to some ultra-high interstellar conference, as these three were probably going, they took Spaceoline. For one thing, they didn't have enough hops under their belt to risk doing without. For another, Spaceoline was the expensive way of doing it and industrialists did things the expensive way. I know their psychology.

Now that would hold for two of them. The one who carried contraband, however, couldn't risk Spaceoline—even at the price of risking space sickness. Under Spaceoline influence, he could throw the drug away, or give it away, or talk gibberish about it. He would *have* to stay in control of himself.

It was as simple as that.

The *Antares Giant* was on time. They brought in Lipsky first. He had thick, ruddy lips, rounded jowls, very dark eyebrows, and hair just beginning to show gray. He just looked at me and sat down. Nothing. He was under Spaceoline.

I said, "Good evening, sir."

He said, in a dreamy voice, "Surrealismus of Panamy hearts in three-quarter time for a cup of coffeedom of speech."

That was Spaceoline all the way. The buttons in the human mind were set free-swinging. Each syllable suggests the next in free association.

Andiamo Ferrucci came in next. Black mustache, long and waxed, olive complexion, pock-marked face. He sat down.

I said, "Nice trip?"

He said, "Trip the light fantastic tock the clock is crowings on the bird."

Lipsky said, "Bird to the wise guyed book to all places everybody."

I grinned. That left Harponaster. I had my needle gun neatly palmed and out of sight and the magnetic coil ready to grip him.

And then Harponaster came in. He was thin, leathery, and, though near-bald, considerably younger than he seemed in his trimensional image. And he was Spaceolined to the gills.

I said, "Damn!"

Harponaster said, "Damyankee note speech to his last time I saw wood you say so."

Ferrucci said, "Sow the seed the territory under dispute do well to come along long road tonightingale."

Lipsky said, "Gay lords hopping pong balls."

I stared from one to the other as the nonsense ran down in shorter and shorter spurts and then silence.

I got the picture, all right. One of them was faking. He had thought ahead and realized that omitting the Spaceoline would be a giveaway. He might have bribed an official into injecting saline or dodged it some other way.

One of them was faking. It wasn't hard to fake the thing. Comedians on sub-etheric had a Spaceoline skit regularly. It was amazing the liberties they could take with the moral code in that way. *You've* heard them.

I stared at them and got the first prickle at the base of my skull that said: What if you *don't* finger the right one?

It was eight-thirty and there was my job, my reputation, my head growing rickety upon my neck to be considered. I saved it all for later and thought of Flora. She wasn't going to wait for me forever. For that matter, chances were she wouldn't wait for half an hour.

I wondered. Could the faker keep up free association if nudged gently onto dangerous territory?

I said, "The floor's covered with a nice solid rug" and ran the last two words together to make it "soli drug."

Lipsky: "Drug from underneath the dough re mi fa sol to be saved."

Ferrucci said, "Saved and a haircut above the common herd something about younicorny as Kansas high as my knee."

Harponaster said, "Kneether wind nor snow use trying to by four ever and effervescence and sensibilityter totter."

Lipsky said, "Totters and rags."

Ferrucci said, "Agsactly."

Harponaster said, "Actlymation."

A few grunts and they ran down.

I tried again and I didn't forget to be careful. They would remember everything I said afterward and what I said had to be harmless. I said, "This is a darned good space-line."

Ferrucci said, "Lines and tigers and elephanthills on the prairie dogs do bark of the boughwough—"

I interrupted, looking at Harponaster, "A darned good space-line."

"Line the bed and rest a little black sheepishion of wrong way to ring the clothes of a perfect day."

I interrupted again, glaring at Lipsky, "Good space-line."

"Liron is hot-chacolit ain't gonna be the same on you vee and double the stakes and potato and heel."

Someone else said, "Heel the sicknecessaryd and write will wincetance."

"Tance with mealtime."

"I'm comingle."

"Inglish."

"Ishter seals."

"Eels."

I tried a few more times and got nowhere. The faker, whichever he was, had practiced or had natural talents at talking free association. He was disconnecting his brain and letting the words come out any old way. And he must be inspired by knowing exactly what I was after. If "drug" hadn't given it away, "space-line" three times repeated must have. I was safe with the other two, but *he* would know.

And he was having fun with me. All three were saying phrases that might have pointed to a deep inner guilt— "sol to be saved," "little black sheepishion of wrong," "drug from underneath," and so on. Two were saying such things helplessly, randomly. The third was amusing himself.

So how did I find the third? I was in a feverish thrill of hatred against him and my fingers twitched. The bastard was subverting the Galaxy. More than that, he was keeping me from Flora.

I could go up to each of them and start searching. The two who were really under Spaceoline would make no move to stop me. They could feel no emotion, no fear, no anxiety, no hate, no passion, no desire for self-defense. And if one made the slightest gesture of resistance I would have my man.

But the innocent ones would remember afterward.

I sighed. If I tried it, I would get the criminal all right, but later I would be the nearest thing to chopped liver any man had ever been. There would be a shakeup in the Service, a big stink the width of the Galaxy, and in the excitement and disorganization, the secret of altered Spaceoline would get out anyway and so what the hell.

Of course, the one I wanted might be the first one I

touched. One chance out of three. I'd have one out and only God can make a three.

Damn it, something had started them going while I was muttering to myself and Spaceoline is contagioust a gigolo my, oh—

I stared desperately at my watch and my line of sight focused on nine-fifteen.

Where the devil was the time going to?

Oh, my; oh, nuts; oh, Flora!

I had no choice. I made my way to the booth for another quick call to Flora. Just a quick one, you understand, to keep things alive, assuming they weren't dead already.

I kept saying to myself: She won't answer.

I tried to prepare myself for that. There were other girls, there were other—

Hell, there were no other girls.

If Hilda had been in Marsport, I would never have had Flora on my mind in the first place and it wouldn't have mattered. But I was in Marsport *without* Hilda and I had made a date with Flora; Flora and a body that had been made up out of heaping handfuls of all that was soft and fragrant and firm; Flora and a low-gravity room and a way about her that made it seem like free fall through a warm, breathable ocean of champagne-flavored meringue—

The signal was signaling and signaling and I didn't dare break off.

Answer! Answer!

She answered. She said, "It's *you!*"

"Of course, sweetheart, who else would it be?"

"Lots of people. Someone who would *come.*"

"There's just this little detail of business, honey."

"What business? Plastons for who?"

I almost corrected her grammar, but I was wondering what this plastons kick was.

Then I remembered. I told her once I was a plaston salesman. That was the time I brought her a plaston nightgown that was a honey. Just thinking of it made me ache where I needed no more ache.

I said, "Look. Just give me another half-hour . . ."

Her eyes grew moist. "I'm sitting here all by myself."

"I'll make it up to you." To show you how desperate I was getting, I was definitely beginning to think along paths that could lead only to jewelry, even though a sizable dent in the bankbook would show up to Hilda's piercing eye like the Horsehead Nebula interrupting the Milky Way.

She said, "I had a perfectly good date and I broke it off."

I protested, "You said it was a quibbling little arrangement."

That was a mistake. I knew it the minute I said it.

She shrieked, *"Quibbling little arrangement!"* It was what she had said. But having the truth on your side just makes it worse in arguing with a woman. Don't I know? "You call a man who's promised me an estate on Earth—"

She went on and on about that estate on Earth. There wasn't a gal in Marsport who wasn't wangling for an estate on Earth and you could count the number who got one on the sixth finger of either hand. But hope springs eternal in the human breast, and Flora had plenty of room for it to spring in.

I tried to stop her. I threw in honeys and babies until you would have thought that every bee on the planet Earth was pregnant.

No use.

She finally said, "And here I am all alone, with *nobody,* and what do you think *that* will do to my reputation?" and broke off contact.

Well, she was right. I felt like the lowest heel in the Galaxy. If the word did get around that she had been stood up, the word would also get around that she was stand-uppable, that she was losing the old touch. A thing like that can ruin a girl.

I went back into the reception room. A flunky outside the door saluted me in.

I stared at the three industrialists and speculated on the order in which I would slowly choke each to death if I could but receive choking orders. Harponaster first, maybe. He had a thin, stringy neck that the fingers could go around neatly and a sharp Adam's apple against which the thumbs could find purchase.

It cheered me up infinitesimally, to the point where I muttered, "Boy!" just out of sheer longing.

It started them off at once. Ferrucci said, "Boyl the watern the spout you go in the snow to sneeze—"

Harponaster of the scrawny neck added, "Nies and nephew don't like orporalley cat."

Lipsky said, "Cattle for shipmentering the home stretchings are good bait and drank drunk."

"Drunkle aunterior passagewayt a while."

"While beasts oh pray."

"Rayls to Chicago."

"Go way."

"Waiter."

"Terble."

"Ble."

Then nothing.

They stared at me. I stared at them. They were empty of emotion—or two were—and I was empty of ideas. And time passed.

I stared at them some more and thought about Flora. It occurred to me that I had nothing to lose that I had not already lost. I might as well talk about her.

I said, "Gentlemen, there is a girl in this town whose name I will not mention for fear of compromising her. Let me describe her to you, gentlemen."

And I did. If I say so myself, the last two hours had honed me to such a fine force-field edge that the description of Flora took on a kind of poetry that seemed to be coming from some wellspring of masculine force deep in the subbasement of my unconscious.

And they sat frozen, almost as though they were listening, and hardly ever interrupting. People under Spaceoline have a kind of politeness about them. They won't speak when someone else is speaking. That's why they take turns.

Occasionally, of course, I paused a bit because the poignancy of the subject matter made me want to linger and then one of them might put in a few words before I could gather myself together and continue.

"Pinknic of champagnes and aches and bittern of the century box."

"Round that and/or thisandy beaches."

"Assault and peppert girlieping leopard."

I drowned them out and kept talking. "This young lady, gentlemen," I said, "has an apartment fitted out for low gravity. Now you might ask of what use is low gravity? I intend to tell you, gentlemen, for if you have never had occasion to spend a quiet evening with a Marsport prima donna in privacy, you cannot imagine—"

But I tried to make it unnecessary for them to imagine— the way I told it they were *there*. They would remember all this afterward but I doubted mightily that either of the two innocents would object to it in hindsight. Chances were they would look me up to ask a phone number.

I kept it up, with loving, careful detail and a kind of heartfelt sadness in my voice, until the loudspeaker announced the arrival of the *Space Eater*.

That was that. I said in a loud voice, "Rise, gentlemen."

They got up in unison, faced the door, started walking, and as Ferrucci passed me, I tapped him on the shoulder and said, "Not you, you murdering louse," and my magnetic coil was on his wrist before he could breathe twice.

Ferrucci fought like a demon. *He* was under no Spaceoline influence. They found the altered Spaceoline in thin flesh-colored plastic pads hugging the inner surface of his thighs, with hairs affixed to it in the normal pattern. You couldn't see it at all; you could only feel it, and even then it took a knife to make sure.

Afterward, Rog Crinton, grinning and half-insane with relief, held me by the lapel with a death grip. "How did you do it? What gave it away?"

I said, trying to pull loose, "One of them was faking a Spaceoline jag. I was sure of it. So I told them—" I grew cautious. None of the bum's business as to the details, you know. "—uh, ribald stories, see, and two of them never reacted, so they were Spaceolined. But Ferrucci's breathing speeded up and the beads of sweat came out on his forehead. I gave a pretty dramatic rendition, and he reacted, so he was under no Spaceoline. And when they all stood up to head out for the ship, I was sure of my man and stopped him. Now will you let me go?"

He let go and I almost fell over backward.

I was set to take off. My feet were pawing at the ground without any instructions for me, but I turned back.

"Hey, Rog," I said, "can you sign me a chit for a thousand credits without its going on the record—for services rendered to the Service?"

That's when I realized he was half-insane with relief and very temporary gratitude, because he said, "Sure, Max, sure. Ten thousand credits if you want it."

"I *want*," I said. "I want. I want."

He filled out an official Service chit for ten thousand credits, good as cash anywhere in half the Galaxy. He was actually grinning as he gave it to me and you can bet I was grinning as I took it.

How *he* intended accounting for it was his affair. The point was that I wouldn't have to account for it to Hilda.

I stood in the booth, one last time, signaling Flora. I didn't dare let matters go till I reached her place. The additional half-hour might just give her time to get someone else, if she hadn't already.

Make her answer. Make her answer. Make her—

She answered, but she was in formal clothes. She was going out and I had obviously caught her by two minutes.

"I am going out," she announced. "*Some* men can be decent. And I do not wish to see you in the henceforward. I do not wish ever to find my eyes upon you. You will do me a great favor, Mister Whoeveryouare, if you will unhand my signal combination and never pollute it with—"

I wasn't saying anything. I was just standing there holding my breath and also holding the chit up where she could see it. Just standing there. Just holding.

Sure enough, at the word "pollute" she came in for a closer look. She wasn't much on education, that girl, but she could read "ten thousand credits" faster than any college graduate in the Solar System.

She said, "Max! For me?"

"All for you, baby," I said. "I told you I had a little business to do. I wanted to surprise you."

"Oh, Max, that's sweet of you. I didn't really mind. I was joking. Now you come right here to me." She took off her coat, which with Flora is a *very* interesting action to watch.

"What about your date?" I said.

"I *said* I was joking," she said. She dropped her coat gently to the floor, and toyed with a brooch that seemed to hold together what there was of her dress.

"I'm coming," I said faintly.

"With every single one of those credits now," she said roguishly.

"With every single one," I said.

I broke contact, stepped out of the booth, and now, finally, I was set, really set.

I heard my name called.

"Max! Max!" Someone was running toward me. "Rog Crinton said I would find you here. Mama's all right after all, so I got special passage on the *Space Eater* and what's this about ten thousand credits?"

I didn't turn. I said, "Hello, Hilda."

I stood rock steady.

And then I turned and did the hardest thing I ever succeeded in doing in all my goddam, good-for-nothing, space-hopping life.

I smiled.

17

The Immortal Bard

Another very short story that does not end with a play on words. It's just that by the time this story was written, in 1954, I had already heard enough learned and turgid analyses of my stories to make me think of what might happen if one even greater than I (see, I am too modest) were subjected to that sort of thing.

"Oh, yes," said Dr. Phineas Welch, "I can bring back the spirits of the illustrious dead."

He was a little drunk, or maybe he wouldn't have said it. Of course, it was perfectly all right to get a little drunk at the annual Christmas party.

Scott Robertson, the school's young English instructor, adjusted his glasses and looked to right and left to see if they were overheard. "Really, Dr. Welch."

"I mean it. And not just the spirits. I bring back the bodies, too."

"I wouldn't have said it were possible," said Robertson primly.

"Why not? A simple matter of temporal transference."

"You mean time travel? But that's quite—uh—unusual."

"Not if you know how."

"Well, how, Dr. Welch?"

"Think I'm going to tell you?" asked the physicist gravely. He looked vaguely about for another drink and didn't find any. He said, "I brought quite a few back. Archimedes, Newton, Galileo. Poor fellows."

"Didn't they like it here? I should think they'd have been fascinated by our modern science," said Robertson. He was beginning to enjoy the conversation.

"Oh, they were. They were. Especially Archimedes. I thought he'd go mad with joy at first after I explained a little of it in some Greek I'd boned up on, but no—no——"

"What was wrong?"

"Just a different culture. They couldn't get used to our way of life. They got terribly lonely and frightened. I had to send them back."

"That's too bad."

"Yes. Great minds, but not flexible minds. Not universal. So I tried Shakespeare."

"*What?*" yelled Robertson. This was getting closer to home.

"Don't yell, my boy," said Welch. "It's bad manners."

"Did you say you brought back Shakespeare?"

"I did. I needed someone with a universal mind; someone who knew people well enough to be able to live with them centuries away from his own time. Shakespeare was the man. I've got his signature. As a memento, you know."

"On you?" asked Robertson, eyes bugging.

"Right here." Welch fumbled in one vest pocket after another. "Ah, here it is."

A little piece of pasteboard was passed to the instructor. On one side it said: "L. Klein & Sons, Wholesale Hardware." On the other side, in straggly script, was written, "Willm Shaksper."

A wild surmise filled Robertson. "What did he look like?"

"Not like his pictures. Bald and an ugly mustache. He spoke in a thick brogue. Of course, I did my best to please him with our times. I told him we thought highly of his plays and still put them on the boards. In fact, I said we thought they were the greatest pieces of literature in the English language, maybe in any language."

"Good. Good," said Robertson breathlessly.

"I said people had written volumes of commentaries on his plays. Naturally he wanted to see one and I got one for him from the library."

"And?"

"Oh, he was fascinated. Of course, he had trouble with

the current idioms and references to events since 1600, but I helped out. Poor fellow. I don't think he ever expected such treatment. He kept saying, 'God ha' mercy! What cannot be racked from words in five centuries? One could wring, methinks, a flood from a damp clout!' "

"He wouldn't say that."

"Why not? He wrote his plays as quickly as he could. He said he had to on account of the deadlines. He wrote *Hamlet* in less than six months. The plot was an old one. He just polished it up."

"That's all they do to a telescope mirror. Just polish it up," said the English instructor indignantly.

The physicist disregarded him. He made out an untouched cocktail on the bar some feet away and sidled toward it. "I told the immortal bard that we even gave college courses in Shakespeare."

"*I* give one."

"I know. I enrolled him in your evening extension course. I never saw a man so eager to find out what posterity thought of him as poor Bill was. He worked hard at it."

"You enrolled William Shakespeare in my course?" mumbled Robertson. Even as an alcoholic fantasy, the thought staggered him. And *was* it an alcoholic fantasy? He was beginning to recall a bald man with a queer way of talking. . . .

"Not under his real name, of course," said Dr. Welch. "Never mind what he went under. It was a mistake, that's all. A big mistake. Poor fellow." He had the cocktail now and shook his head at it.

"Why was it a mistake? What happened?"

"I had to send him back to 1600," roared Welch indignantly. "How much humiliation do you think a man can stand?"

"What humiliation are you talking about?"

Dr. Welch tossed off the cocktail. "Why, you poor simpleton, you *flunked* him."

18

It's Such A Beautiful Day!

A writer isn't necessarily the prisoner of his own neuroses, despite what it might appear from my earlier story "Dreaming Is a Private Thing." At least, he isn't as far as his writing is concerned.

For instance, I'm an indoors person. I'm not afraid of the outdoors and I penetrate it easily and cheerfully. However, I must admit I like Central Park better than the wilderness, and I like the canyons of Manhattan better than Central Park, and I like the interior of my apartment better than the canyons of Manhattan, and I like my two rooms better with the shades down at all times than with the shades up. I'm not an agoraphobe at all, but I am a claustrophile, if you see the distinction.

Naturally, then, I decided, as a joke at my own expense to write the following story. And it worked. I was so delighted that I promptly fell in love with it.

On April 12, 2117, the field-modulator brake-valve in the Door belonging to Mrs. Richard Hanshaw depolarized for reasons unknown. As a result, Mrs. Hanshaw's day was completely upset and her son, Richard, Jr., first developed his strange neurosis.

It was not the type of thing you would find listed as a neurosis in the usual textbooks and certainly young Richard behaved, in most respects, just as a well-brought-up twelve-year-old in prosperous circumstances ought to behave.

And yet from April 12 on, Richard Hanshaw, Jr., could only with regret ever persuade himself to go through a Door.

Of all this, on April 12, Mrs. Hanshaw had no premonition. She woke in the morning (an ordinary morning) as her mekkano slithered gently into her room, with a cup of coffee on a small tray. Mrs. Hanshaw was planning a visit to New York in the afternoon and she had several things to do first that could not quite be trusted to a mekkano, so after one or two sips, she stepped out of bed.

The mekkano backed away, moving silently along the diamagnetic field that kept its oblong body half an inch above the floor, and moved back to the kitchen, where its simple computer was quite adequate to set the proper controls on the various kitchen appliances in order that an appropriate breakfast might be prepared.

Mrs. Hanshaw, having bestowed the usual sentimental glance upon the cubograph of her dead husband, passed through the stages of her morning ritual with a certain contentment. She could hear her son across the hall clattering through his, but she knew she need not interfere with him. The mekkano was well adjusted to see to it, as a matter of course, that he was showered, that he had on a change of clothing, and that he would eat a nourishing breakfast. The tergoshower she had had installed the year before made the morning wash and dry so quick and pleasant that, really, she felt certain Dickie would wash even without supervision.

On a morning like this, when she was busy, it would certainly not be necessary for her to do more than deposit a casual peck on the boy's cheek before he left. She heard the soft chime the mekkano sounded to indicate approaching school time and she floated down the forcelift to the lower floor (her hair-style for the day only sketchily designed, as yet) in order to perform that motherly duty.

She found Richard standing at the door, with his textreels and pocket projector dangling by their strap and a frown on his face.

"Say, Mom," he said, looking up, "I dialed the school's co-ords but nothing happens."

She said, almost automatically, "Nonsense, Dickie. I never heard of such a thing."

"Well, you try."

Mrs. Hanshaw tried a number of times. Strange, the school door was always set for general reception. She tried other co-ordinates. Her friends' Doors might not be set for reception, but there would be a signal at least, and then she could explain.

But nothing happened at all. The Door remained an inactive gray barrier despite all her manipulations. It was obvious that the Door was out of order—and only five months after its annual fall inspection by the company.

She was quite angry about it.

It *would* happen on a day when she had so much planned. She thought petulantly of the fact that a month earlier she had decided against installing a subsidiary Door on the ground that it was an unnecessary expense. How was she to know that Doors were getting to be so *shoddy?*

She stepped to the visiphone while the anger still burned in her and said to Richard, "You just go down the road, Dickie, and use the Williamsons' Door."

Ironically, in view of later developments, Richard balked. "Aw, gee, Mom, I'll get dirty. Can't I stay home till the Door is fixed?"

And, as ironically, Mrs. Hanshaw insisted. With her finger on the combination board of the phone, she said, "You won't get dirty if you put flexies on your shoes, and don't forget to brush yourself well before you go into their house."

"But, golly—"

"No back-talk, Dickie. You've got to be in school. Just let me see you walk out of here. And quickly, or you'll be late."

The mekkano, an advanced model and very responsive, was already standing before Richard with flexies in one appendage.

Richard pulled the transparent plastic shields over his shoes and moved down the hall with visible reluctance. "I don't even know how to work this thing, Mom."

"You just push that button," Mrs. Hanshaw called. "The red button. Where it says 'For Emergency Use.' And don't dawdle. Do you want the mekkano to go along with you?"

"Gosh, no," he called back, morosely, "what do you think I am? A baby? Gosh!" His muttering was cut off by a slam.

With flying fingers, Mrs. Hanshaw punched the appropriate combination on the phone board and thought of the things she intended saying to the company about this.

Joe Bloom, a reasonable young man, who had gone through technology school with added training in force-field mechanics, was at the Hanshaw residence in less than half an hour. He was really quite competent, though Mrs. Hanshaw regarded his youth with deep suspicion.

She opened the movable house-panel when he first signaled and her sight of him was as he stood there, brushing at himself vigorously to remove the dust of the open air. He took off his flexies and dropped them where he stood. Mrs. Hanshaw closed the house-panel against the flash of raw sunlight that had entered. She found herself irrationally hoping that the step-by-step trip from the public Door had been an unpleasant one. Or perhaps that the public Door itself had been out of order and the youth had had to lug his tools even farther than the necessary two hundred yards. She wanted the Company, or its representative at least, to suffer a bit. It would teach them what broken Doors meant.

But he seemed cheerful and unperturbed as he said, "Good morning, ma'am. I came to see about your Door."

"I'm glad someone did," said Mrs. Hanshaw, ungraciously. "My day is quite ruined."

"Sorry, ma'am. What seems to be the trouble?"

"It just won't work. Nothing at all happens when you adjust co-ords," said Mrs. Hanshaw. "There was no warning at all. I had to send my son out to the neighbors through that—that thing."

She pointed to the entrance through which the repair man had come.

He smiled and spoke out of the conscious wisdom of

his own specialized training in Doors. "That's a door, too, ma'am. You don't give that kind a capital letter when you write it. It's a hand-door, sort of. It used to be the only kind once."

"Well, at least it works. My boy's had to go out in the dirt and germs."

"It's not bad outside today, ma'am," he said, with the connoisseur-like air of one whose profession forced him into the open nearly every day. "Sometimes it *is* real unpleasant. But I guess you want I should fix this here Door, ma'am, so I'll get on with it."

He sat down on the floor, opened the large tool case he had brought in with him and in half a minute, by use of a point-demagnetizer, he had the control panel removed and a set of intricate vitals exposed.

He whistled to himself as he placed the fine electrodes of the field-analyzer on numerous points, studying the shifting needles on the dials. Mrs. Hanshaw watched him, arms folded.

Finally, he said, "Well, here's something," and with a deft twist, he disengaged the brake-valve.

He tapped it with a fingernail and said, "This here brake-valve is depolarized, ma'am. There's your whole trouble." He ran his finger along the little pigeonholes in his tool case and lifted out a duplicate of the object he had taken from the door mechanism. "These things just go all of a sudden. Can't predict it."

He put the control panel back and stood up. "It'll work now, ma'am."

He punched a reference combination, blanked it, then punched another. Each time, the dull gray of the Door gave way to a deep, velvety blackness. He said, "Will you sign here, ma'am? and put down your charge number, too, please? Thank you, ma'am."

He punched a new combination, that of his home factory, and with a polite touch of finger to forehead, he stepped through the Door. As his body entered the blackness, it cut off sharply. Less and less of him was visible and the tip of his tool case was the last thing that showed.

A second after he had passed through completely, the Door turned back to dull gray.

Half an hour later, when Mrs. Hanshaw had finally completed her interrupted preparations and was fuming over the misfortune of the morning, the phone buzzed annoyingly and her real troubles began.

Miss Elizabeth Robbins was distressed. Little Dick Hanshaw had always been a good pupil. She hated to report him like this. And yet, she told herself, his actions were certainly queer. And she would talk to his mother, not to the principal.

She slipped out to the phone during the morning study period, leaving a student in charge. She made her connection and found herself staring at Mrs. Hanshaw's handsome and somewhat formidable head.

Miss Robbins quailed, but it was too late to turn back. She said, diffidently, "Mrs. Hanshaw, I'm Miss Robbins." She ended on a rising note.

Mrs. Hanshaw looked blank, then said, "Richard's teacher?" That, too, ended on a rising note.

"That's right. I called you, Mrs. Hanshaw," Miss Robbins plunged right into it, "to tell you that Dick was quite late to school this morning."

"He *was?* But that couldn't be. I saw him leave."

Miss Robbins looked astonished. She said, "You mean you saw him use the Door?"

Mrs. Hanshaw said quickly, "Well, no. Our Door was temporarily out of order. I sent him to a neighbor and he used that Door."

"Are you sure?"

"Of course I'm sure. I wouldn't lie to you."

"No, no, Mrs. Hanshaw. I wasn't implying that at all. I meant are you sure he found the way to the neighbor? He might have got lost."

"Ridiculous. We have the proper maps, and I'm sure Richard knows the location of every house in District A-3." Then, with the quiet pride of one who knows what is her due, she added, "Not that he ever needs to know, of course. The co-ords are all that are necessary at any time."

Miss Robbins, who came from a family that had always had to economize rigidly on the use of its Doors (the price of power being what it was) and who had therefore run errands on foot until quite an advanced age, resented the pride. She said, quite clearly, "Well, I'm afraid, Mrs. Hanshaw, that Dick did not use the neighbor's Door. He was over an hour late to school and the condition of his flexies made it quite obvious that he tramped cross-country. They were *muddy.*"

"Muddy?" Mrs. Hanshaw repeated the emphasis on the word. "What did he say? What was his excuse?"

Miss Robbins couldn't help but feel a little glad at the discomfiture of the other woman. She said, "He wouldn't talk about it. Frankly, Mrs. Hanshaw, he seems ill. That's why I called you. Perhaps you might want to have a doctor look at him."

"Is he running a temperature?" The mother's voice went shrill.

"Oh, no. I don't mean physically ill. It's just his attitude and the look in his eyes." She hesitated, then said with every attempt at delicacy, "I thought perhaps a routine checkup with a psychic probe——"

She didn't finish. Mrs. Hanshaw, in a chilled voice and with what was as close to a snort as her breeding would permit, said, "Are you implying that Richard is *neurotic?*"

"Oh, no, Mrs. Hanshaw, but——"

"It certainly sounded so. The idea! He has always been perfectly healthy. I'll take this up with him when he gets home. I'm sure there's a perfectly normal explanation which he'll give to *me.*"

The connection broke abruptly, and Miss Robbins felt hurt and uncommonly foolish. After all she had only tried to help, to fulfill what she considered an obligation to her students.

She hurried back to the classroom with a glance at the metal face of the wall clock. The study period was drawing to an end. English Composition next.

But her mind wasn't completely on English Composition. Automatically, she called the students to have them read selections from their literary creations. And occasionally she punched one of those selections on tape and ran it through the small vocalizer to show the students how English *should* be read.

The vocalizer's mechanical voice, as always, dripped perfection, but, again as always, lacked character. Sometimes, she wondered if it was wise to try to train the students into a speech that was divorced from individuality and geared only to a mass-average accent and intonation.

Today, however, she had no thought for that. It was Richard Hanshaw she watched. He sat quietly in his seat, quite obviously indifferent to his surroundings. He was lost deep in himself and just not the same boy he had been. It was obvious to her that he had had some unusual experience that morning and, really, she was right to call his mother, although perhaps she ought not to have made the remark about the probe. Still it was quite the thing these days. All sorts of people get probed. There wasn't any disgrace attached to it. Or there shouldn't be, anyway.

She called on Richard, finally. She had to call twice, before he responded and rose to his feet.

The general subject assigned had been: "If you had your choice of traveling on some ancient vehicle, which would you choose, and why?" Miss Robbins tried to use the topic every semester. It was a good one because it carried a sense of history with it. It forced the youngster to think about the manner of living of people in past ages.

She listened while Richard Hanshaw read in a low voice.

"If I had my choice of ancient vehicles," he said, pronouncing the "h" in vehicles, "I would choose the stratoliner. It travels slow like all vehicles but it is clean. Because it travels in the stratosphere, it must be all enclosed so that you are not likely to catch disease. You can see the stars if it is night time almost as good as in a planetarium. If you look down you can see the Earth like a map or maybe see clouds——" He went on for several hundred more words.

She said brightly when he had finished reading, "It's pronounced vee-ick-ulls, Richard. No 'h.' Accent on the first syllable. And you don't say 'travels slow' or 'see good.' What do you say, class?"

There was a small chorus of responses and she went on, "That's right. Now what is the difference between an adjective and an adverb? Who can tell me?"

And so it went. Lunch passed. Some pupils stayed to eat; some went home. Richard stayed. Miss Robbins noted that, as usually he didn't.

The afternoon passed, too, and then there was the final bell and the usual upsurging hum as twenty-five boys and girls rattled their belongings together and took their leisurely place in line.

Miss Robbins clapped her hands together. "Quickly, children. Come, Zelda, take your place."

"I dropped my tape-punch, Miss Robbins," shrilled the girl, defensively.

"Well, pick it up, pick it up. Now children, be brisk, be brisk."

She pushed the button that slid a section of the wall into a recess and revealed the gray blankness of a large Door. It was not the usual Door that the occasional student used in going home for lunch, but an advanced model that was one of the prides of this well-to-do private school.

In addition to its double width, it possessed a large and impressively gear-filled "automatic serial finder" which was capable of adjusting the Door for a number of different co-ordinates at automatic intervals.

At the beginning of the semester, Miss Robbins always had to spend an afternoon with the mechanic, adjusting the device for the co-ordinates of the homes of the new class. But then, thank goodness, it rarely needed attention for the remainder of the term.

The class lined up alphabetically, first girls, then boys. The Door went velvety black and Hester Adams waved her hand and stepped through. "By-y-y——"

The "bye" was cut off in the middle, as it almost always was.

The Door went gray, then black again, and Theresa Cantrocchi went through. Gray, black, Zelda Charlowicz. Gray, black, Patricia Coombs. Gray, black, Sara May Evans.

The line grew smaller as the Door swallowed them one by one, depositing each in her home. Of course, an occasional mother forgot to leave the house Door on special reception at the appropriate time and then the school Door remained gray. Automatically, after a minute-long wait, the Door went on to the next combination in line and the pupil in question had to wait till it was all over, after which a phone call to the forgetful parent would set things right. This was always bad for the pupils involved, especially the sensitive ones who took seriously the implication that they were little thought of at home. Miss Robbins always tried to impress this on visiting parents, but it happened at least once every semester just the same.

The girls were all through now. John Abramowitz stepped through and then Edwin Byrne——

Of course, another trouble, and a more frequent one was the boy or girl who got into line out of place. They *would* do it despite the teacher's sharpest watch, particularly at the beginning of the term when the proper order was less familiar to them.

When that happened, children would be popping into the wrong houses by the half-dozen and would have to be sent back. It always meant a mixup that took minutes to straighten out and parents were invariably irate.

Miss Robbins was suddenly aware that the line had stopped. She spoke sharply to the boy at the head of the line.

"Step through, Samuel. What are you waiting for?"

Samuel Jones raised a complacent countenance and said, "It's not my combination, Miss Robbins."

"Well, whose is it?" She looked impatiently down the line of five remaining boys. Who was out of place?

"It's Dick Hanshaw's, Miss Robbins."

"Where is he?"

Another boy answered, with the rather repulsive tone

of self-righteousness all children automatically assume in reporting the deviations of their friends to elders in authority, "He went through the fire door, Miss Robbins."

"What?"

The schoolroom Door had passed on to another combination and Samuel Jones passed through. One by one, the rest followed.

Miss Robbins was alone in the classroom. She stepped to the fire door. It was a small affair, manually operated, and hidden behind a bend in the wall so that it would not break up the uniform structure of the room.

She opened it a crack. It was there as a means of escape from the building in case of fire, a device which was enforced by an anachronistic law that did not take into account the modern methods of automatic fire-fighting that all public buildings used. There was nothing outside, but the—outside. The sunlight was harsh and a dusty wind was blowing.

Miss Robbins closed the door. She was glad she had called Mrs. Hanshaw. She had done her duty. More than ever, it was obvious that something was wrong with Richard. She suppressed the impulse to phone again.

Mrs. Hanshaw did not go to New York that day. She remained home in a mixture of anxiety and an irrational anger, the latter directed against the impudent Miss Robbins.

Some fifteen minutes before school's end, her anxiety drove her to the Door. Last year she had had it equipped with an automatic device which activated it to the school's co-ordinates at five of three and kept it so, barring manual adjustment, until Richard arrived.

Her eyes were fixed on the Door's dismal gray (why couldn't an inactive force-field be any other color, something more lively and cheerful?) and waited. Her hands felt cold as she squeezed them together.

The Door turned black at the precise second but nothing happened. The minutes passed and Richard was late. Then quite late. Then very late.

It was a quarter of four and she was distracted. Normally, she would have phoned the school, but she couldn't, she couldn't. Not after that teacher had deliberately cast doubts on Richard's mental well-being. How could she?

Mrs. Hanshaw moved about restlessly, lighting a cigarette with fumbling fingers, then smudging it out. Could it be something quite normal? Could Richard be staying after school for some reason? Surely he would have told her in advance. A gleam of light struck her; he knew she was planning to go to New York and might not be back till late in the evening——

No, he would surely have told her. Why fool herself?

Her pride was breaking. She would have to call the school, or even (she closed her eyes and teardrops squeezed through between the lashes) the police.

And when she opened her eyes, Richard stood before her, eyes on the ground and his whole bearing that of someone waiting for a blow to fall.

"Hello, Mom."

Mrs. Hanshaw's anxiety transmuted itself instantly (in a manner known only to mothers) into anger. "Where have you been, Richard?"

And then, before she could go further into the refrain concerning careless, unthinking sons and broken-hearted mothers, she took note of his appearance in greater detail, and gasped in utter horror.

She said, "You've been in the open."

Her son looked down at his dusty shoes (minus flexies), at the dirt marks that streaked his lower arms and at the small, but definite tear in his shirt. He said, "Gosh, Mom, I just thought I'd——" and he faded out.

She said, "Was there anything wrong with the school Door?"

"No, Mom."

"Do you realize I've been worried sick about you?" She waited calmly for an answer. "Well, I'll talk to you afterward, young man. First, you're taking a bath, and every stitch of your clothing is being thrown out. Mekkano!"

But the mekkano had already reacted properly to the

phrase "taking a bath" and was off to the bathroom in its silent glide.

"You take your shoes off right here," said Mrs. Hanshaw, "then march after mekkano."

Richard did as he was told with a resignation that placed him beyond futile protest.

Mrs. Hanshaw picked up the soiled shoes between thumb and forefinger and dropped them down the disposal chute which hummed in faint dismay at the unexpected load. She dusted her hands carefully on a tissue which she allowed to float down the chute after the shoes.

She did not join Richard at dinner but let him eat in the worse-than-lack-of-company of the mekkano. This, she thought, would be an active sign of her displeasure and would do more than any amount of scolding or punishment to make him realize that he had done wrong. Richard, she frequently told herself, was a sensitive boy.

But she went up to see him at bedtime.

She smiled at him and spoke softly. She thought that would be the best way. After all, he had been punished already.

She said, "What happened today, Dickie-boy?" She had called him that when he was a baby and just the sound of the name softened her nearly to tears.

But he only looked away and his voice was stubborn and cold. "I just don't like to go through those darn Doors, Mom."

"But why ever not?"

He shuffled his hands over the filmy sheet (fresh, clean, antiseptic and, of course, disposable after each use) and said, "I just don't like them."

"But then how do you expect to go to school, Dickie?"

"I'll get up early," he mumbled.

"But there's nothing wrong with Doors."

"Don't like 'em." He never once looked up at her.

She said, despairingly, "Oh, well, you have a good sleep and tomorrow morning you'll feel much better."

She kissed him and left the room, automatically passing her hand through the photo-cell beam and in that manner dimming the roomlights.

But she had trouble sleeping herself that night. Why should Dickie dislike Doors so suddenly? They had never bothered him before. To be sure, the Door had broken down in the morning but that should make him appreciate them all the more.

Dickie was behaving so unreasonably.

Unreasonably? That reminded her of Miss Robbins and her diagnosis and Mrs. Hanshaw's soft jaw set in the darkness and privacy of her bedroom. Nonsense! The boy was upset and a night's sleep was all the therapy he needed.

But the next morning when she arose, her son was not in the house. The mekkano could not speak but it could answer questions with gestures of its appendages equivalent to a yes or no, and it did not take Mrs. Hanshaw more than half a minute to ascertain that the boy had arisen thirty minutes earlier than usual, skimped his shower, and darted out of the house.

But not by way of the Door.

Out the other way—through the door. Small "d."

Mrs. Hanshaw's visiphone signaled genteelly at 3:10 P.M. that day. Mrs. Hanshaw guessed the caller and having activated the receiver, saw that she had guessed correctly. A quick glance in the mirror to see that she was properly calm after a day of abstracted concern and worry and then she keyed in her own transmission.

"Yes, Miss Robbins," she said coldly.

Richard's teacher was a bit breathless. She said, "Mrs. Hanshaw, Richard has deliberately left through the fire door although I told him to use the regular Door. I do not know where he went."

Mrs. Hanshaw said, carefully, "He left to come home."

Miss Robbins looked dismayed, "Do you approve of this?"

Pale-faced, Mrs. Hanshaw set about putting the teacher in her place. "I don't think it is up to you to criticize. If my son does not choose to use the Door, it is his affair and mine. I don't think there is any school ruling that would force him to use the Door, is there?" Her bearing quite plainly intimated that if there were she would see to it that it was changed.

Miss Robbins flushed and had time for one quick remark before contact was broken. She said, "I'd have him probed. I really would."

Mrs. Hanshaw remained standing before the quartzinium plate, staring blindly at its blank face. Her sense of family placed her for a few moments quite firmly on Richard's side. Why *did* he have to use the Door if he chose not to? And then she settled down to wait and pride battled the gnawing anxiety that something after all was wrong with Richard.

He came home with a look of defiance on his face, but his mother, with a strenuous effort at self-control, met him as though nothing were out of the ordinary.

For weeks, she followed that policy. It's nothing, she told herself. It's a vagary. He'll grow out of it.

It grew into an almost normal state of affairs. Then, too, every once in a while, perhaps three days in a row, she would come down to breakfast to find Richard waiting sullenly at the Door, then using it when school time came. She always refrained from commenting on the matter.

Always, when he did that, and especially when he followed it up by arriving home via the Door, her heart grew warm and she thought, "Well, it's over." But always with the passing of one day, two or three, he would return like an addict to his drug and drift silently out by the door—small "d"—before she woke.

And each time she thought despairingly of psychiatrists and probes, and each time the vision of Miss Robbins' low-bred satisfaction at (possibly) learning of it, stopped her, although she was scarcely aware that that was the true motive.

Meanwhile, she lived with it and made the best of it. The mekkano was instructed to wait at the door—small "d"—with a Tergo kit and a change of clothing. Richard washed and changed without resistance. His underthings, socks and flexies were disposable in any case, and Mrs. Hanshaw bore uncomplainingly the expense of daily disposal of shirts. Trousers she finally allowed to go a week before disposal on condition of rigorous nightly cleansing.

One day she suggested that Richard accompany her on a trip to New York. It was more a vague desire to keep him in sight than part of any purposeful plan. He did not object. He was even happy. He stepped right through the Door, unconcerned. He didn't hesitate. He even lacked the look of resentment he wore on those mornings he used the Door to go to school.

Mrs. Hanshaw rejoiced. This could be a way of weaning him back into Door usage, and she racked her ingenuity for excuses to make trips with Richard. She even raised her power bill to quite unheard-of heights by suggesting, and going through with, a trip to Canton for the day in order to witness a Chinese festival.

That was on a Sunday, and the next morning Richard marched directly to the hole in the wall he always used. Mrs. Hanshaw, having wakened particularly early, witnessed that. For once, badgered past endurance, she called after him plaintively, "Why not the Door, Dickie?"

He said, briefly, "It's all right for Canton," and stepped out of the house.

So that plan ended in failure. And then, one day, Richard came home soaking wet. The mekkano hovered about him uncertainly and Mrs. Hanshaw, just returned from a four-hour visit with her sister in Iowa, cried, "Richard Hanshaw!"

He said, hang-dog fashion, "It started raining. All of a sudden, it started raining."

For a moment, the word didn't register with her. Her own school days and her studies of geography were twenty years in the past. And then she remembered and caught the vision of water pouring recklessly and endlessly down from the sky—a mad cascade of water with no tap to turn off, no button to push, no contact to break.

She said, "And you stayed out in it?"

He said, "Well, gee, Mom, I came home fast as I could. I didn't know it was going to rain."

Mrs. Hanshaw had nothing to say. She was appalled and the sensation filled her too full for words to find a place.

Two days later, Richard found himself with a running nose, and a dry, scratchy throat. Mrs. Hanshaw had to admit that the virus of disease had found a lodging in her house, as though it were a miserable hovel of the Iron Age.

It was over that that her stubborness and pride broke and she admitted to herself that, after all, Richard had to have psychiatric help.

Mrs. Hanshaw chose a psychiatrist with care. Her first impulse was to find one at a distance. For a while, she considered stepping directly into the San Francisco Medical Center and choosing one at random.

And then it occurred to her that by doing that she would become merely an anonymous consultant. She would have no way of obtaining any greater consideration for herself than would be forthcoming to any public-Door user of the city slums. Now if she remained in her own community, her word would carry weight——

She consulted the district map. It was one of that excellent series prepared by Doors, Inc., and distributed free of charge to their clients. Mrs. Hanshaw couldn't quite suppress that little thrill of civic pride as she unfolded the map. It wasn't a fine-print directory of Door co-ordinates only. It was an actual map, with each house carefully located.

And why not? District A-3 was a name of moment in the world, a badge of aristocracy. It was the first community on the planet to have been established on a completely Doored basis. The first, the largest, the wealthiest, the best-known. It needed no factories, no stores. It didn't even need roads. Each house was a little secluded castle, the Door of which had entry anywhere the world over where other Doors existed.

Carefully, she followed down the keyed listing of the five thousand families of District A-3. She knew it included several psychiatrists. The learned professions were well represented in A-3.

Doctor Hamilton Sloane was the second name she arrived at and her finger lingered upon the map. His office was scarcely two miles from the Hanshaw residence. She liked his name. The fact that he lived in A-3 was evidence of worth. And he was a neighbor, practically a neighbor. He would understand that it was a matter of urgency—and confidential.

Firmly, she put in a call to his office to make an appointment.

Doctor Hamilton Sloane was a comparatively young man, not quite forty. He was of good family and he had indeed heard of Mrs. Hanshaw.

He listened to her quietly and then said, "And this all began with the Door breakdown."

"That's right, Doctor."

"Does he show any fear of the Doors?"

"Of course not. What an idea!" She was plainly startled.

"It's possible, Mrs. Hanshaw, it's possible. After all, when you stop to think of how a Door works it is rather a frightening thing, really. You step into a Door, and for an instant your atoms are converted into field-energies, transmitted to another part of space and reconverted into matter. For that instant you're not alive."

"I'm sure no one thinks of such things."

"But your son may. He witnessed the breakdown of the Door. He may be saying to himself, 'What if the Door breaks down just as I'm half-way through?' "

"But that's nonsense. He still uses the Door. He's even been to Canton with me; Canton, China. And as I told you, he uses it for school about once or twice a week."

"Freely? Cheerfully?"

"Well," said Mrs. Hanshaw, reluctantly, "he does seem a bit put out by it. But really, Doctor, there isn't much use talking about it, is there? If you would do a quick probe, see where the trouble was," and she finished on a bright note, "why, that would be all. I'm sure it's quite a minor thing."

Dr. Sloane sighed. He detested the word "probe" and there was scarcely any word he heard oftener.

"Mrs. Hanshaw," he said patiently, "there is no such thing as a quick probe. Now I know the mag-strips are full of it and it's a rage in some circles, but it's much overrated."

"Are you serious?"

"Quite. The probe is very complicated and the theory is that it traces mental circuits. You see, the cells of the brains are interconnected in a large variety of ways. Some of those interconnected paths are more used than others. They represent habits of thought, both conscious and unconscious. Theory has it that these paths in any given brain can be used to diagnose mental ills early and with certainty."

"Well, then?"

"But subjection to the probe is quite a fearful thing, especially to a child. It's a traumatic experience. It takes over an hour. And even then, the results must be sent to the Central Psychoanalytical Bureau for analysis, and that could take weeks. And on top of all that, Mrs. Hanshaw, there are many psychiatrists who think the theory of probe-analyses to be most uncertain."

Mrs. Hanshaw compressed her lips. "You mean nothing can be done."

Dr. Sloane smiled. "Not at all. There were psychiatrists for centuries before there were probes. I suggest that you let me talk to the boy."

"Talk to him? Is that all?"

"I'll come to you for background information when necessary, but the essential thing, I think, is to talk to the boy."

"Really, Dr. Sloane, I doubt if he'll discuss the matter with you. He won't talk to me about it and I'm his mother."

"That often happens," the psychiatrist assured her. "A child will sometimes talk more readily to a stranger. In any case, I cannot take the case otherwise."

Mrs. Hanshaw rose, not at all pleased. "When can you come, Doctor?"

"What about this coming Saturday? The boy won't be in school. Will you be busy?"

"We will be ready."

She made a dignified exit. Dr. Sloane accompanied her through the small reception room to his office Door and waited while she punched the co-ordinates of her house. He watched her pass through. She became a half-woman, a quarter-woman, an isolated elbow and foot, a nothing.

It *was* frightening.

Did a Door ever break down during passage, leaving half a body here and half there? He had never heard of such a case, but he imagined it could happen.

He returned to his desk and looked up the time of his next appointment. It was obvious to him that Mrs. Hanshaw was annoyed and disappointed at not having arranged for a psychic probe treatment.

Why, for God's sake? Why should a thing like the probe, an obvious piece of quackery in his own opinion, get such a hold on the general public? It must be part of this general trend toward machines. Anything man can do, machines can do better. Machines! More machines! Machines for anything and everything! O tempora! O mores!

Oh, hell!

His resentment of the probe was beginning to bother him. Was it a fear of technological unemployment, a basic insecurity on his part, a mechanophobia, if that was the word——

He made a mental note to discuss this with his own analyst.

Dr. Sloane had to feel his way. The boy wasn't a patient who had come to him, more or less anxious to talk, more or less anxious to be helped.

Under the circumstances it would have been best to keep his first meeting with Richard short and noncommittal. It would have been sufficient merely to establish himself as something less than a total stranger. The next time he would be someone Richard had seen before. The time after he would be an acquaintance, and after that a friend of the family.

Unfortunately, Mrs. Hanshaw was not likely to accept

a long-drawn-out process. She would go searching for a probe and, of course, she would find it.

And harm the boy. He was certain of that.

It was for that reason he felt he must sacrifice a little of the proper caution and risk a small crisis.

An uncomfortable ten minutes had passed when he decided he must try. Mrs. Hanshaw was smiling in a rather rigid way, eyeing him narrowly, as though she expected verbal magic from him. Richard wriggled in his seat, unresponsive to Dr. Sloane's tentative comments, overcome with boredom and unable not to show it.

Dr. Sloane said, with casual suddenness, "Would you like to take a walk with me, Richard?"

The boy's eyes widened and he stopped wriggling. He looked directly at Dr. Sloane. "A walk, sir?"

"I mean, outside."

"Do you go—outside?"

"Sometimes. When I feel like it."

Richard was on his feet, holding down a squirming eagerness. "I didn't think anyone did."

"I do. And I like company."

The boy sat down, uncertainly. "Mom?——"

Mrs. Hanshaw had stiffened in her seat, her compressed lips radiating horror, but she managed to say, "Why certainly, Dickie. But watch yourself."

And she managed a quick and baleful glare at Dr. Sloane.

In one respect, Dr. Sloane had lied. He did *not* go outside "sometimes." He hadn't been in the open since early college days. True, he had been athletically inclined (still was to some extent) but in his time the indoor ultra-violet chambers, swimming pools and tennis courts had flourished. For those with the price, they were much more satisfactory than the outdoor equivalents, open to the elements as they were, could possibly be. There was no occasion to go outside.

So there was a crawling sensation about his skin when he felt wind touch it, and he put down his flexied shoes on bare grass with a gingerly movement.

"Hey, look at that." Richard was quite different now, laughing, his reserve broken down.

Dr. Sloane had time only to catch a flash of blue that ended in a tree. Leaves rustled and he lost it.

"What was it?"

"A bird," said Richard. "A blue kind of bird."

Dr. Sloane looked about him in amazement. The Hanshaw residence was on a rise of ground, and he could see for miles. The area was only lightly wooded and between clumps of trees, grass gleamed brightly in the sunlight.

Colors set in deeper green made red and yellow patterns. They were flowers. From the books he had viewed in the course of his lifetime and from the old video shows, he had learned enough so that all this had an eerie sort of familiarity.

And yet the grass was so trim, the flowers so patterned. Dimly, he realized he had been expecting something wilder. He said, "Who takes care of all this?"

Richard shrugged. "I dunno. Maybe the mekkanos do it."

"Mekkanos?"

"There's loads of them around. Sometimes they got a sort of atomic knife they hold near the ground. It cuts the grass. And they're always fooling around with the flowers and things. There's one of them over there."

It was a small object, half a mile away. Its metal skin cast back highlights as it moved slowly over the gleaming meadow, engaged in some sort of activity that Dr. Sloane could not identify.

Dr. Sloane was astonished. Here it was a perverse sort of estheticism, a kind of conspicuous consumption——

"What's that?" he asked suddenly.

Richard looked. He said, "That's a house. Belongs to the Froehlichs. Co-ordinates, A-3, 23, 461. That little pointy building over there is the public Door."

Dr. Sloane was staring at the house. Was that what it looked like from the outside? Somehow he had imagined something much more cubic, and taller.

"Come along," shouted Richard, running ahead.

Dr. Sloane followed more sedately. "Do you know all the houses about here?"

"Just about."

"Where is A-23, 26, 475?" It was his own house, of course.

Richard looked about. "Let's see. Oh, sure, I know where it is—you see that water there?"

"Water?" Dr. Sloane made out a line of silver curving across the green.

"Sure. Real water. Just sort of running over rocks and things. It keeps running all the time. You can get across it if you step on the rocks. It's called a river."

More like a creek, thought Dr. Sloane. He had studied geography, of course, but what passed for the subject these days was really economic and cultural geography. Physical geography was almost an extinct science except among specialists. Still, he knew what rivers and creeks were, in a theoretical sort of way.

Richard was still talking. "Well, just past the river, over that hill with the big clump of trees and down the other side a way is A-23, 26, 475. It's a light green house with a white roof."

"It is?" Dr. Sloane was genuinely astonished. He hadn't known it was green.

Some small animal disturbed the grass in its anxiety to avoid the oncoming feet. Richard looked after it and shrugged. "You can't catch them. I tried."

A butterfly flitted past, a wavering bit of yellow. Dr. Sloane's eyes followed it.

There was a low hum that lay over the fields, interspersed with an occasional harsh, calling sound, a rattle, a twittering, a chatter that rose, then fell. As his ear accustomed itself to listening, Dr. Sloane heard a thousand sounds, and none were man-made.

A shadow fell upon the scene, advancing toward him, covering him. It was suddenly cooler and he looked upward, startled.

Richard said, "It's just a cloud. It'll go away in a minute—looka these flowers. They're the kind that smell."

They were several hundred yards from the Hanshaw

residence. The cloud passed and the sun shone once more. Dr. Sloane looked back and was appalled at the distance they had covered. If they moved out of sight of the house and if Richard ran off, would he be able to find his way back?

He pushed the thought away impatiently and looked out toward the line of water (nearer now) and past it to where his own house must be. He thought wonderingly: Light green?

He said, "You must be quite an explorer."

Richard said, with a shy pride, "When I go to school and come back, I always try to use a different route and see new things."

"But you don't go outside every morning, do you? Sometimes you use the Doors, I imagine."

"Oh, sure."

"Why is that, Richard?" Somehow, Dr. Sloane felt there might be significance in that point.

But Richard quashed him. With his eyebrows up and a look of astonishment on his face, he said, "Well, gosh, some mornings it rains and I *have* to use the Door. I hate that, but what can you do? About two weeks ago, I got caught in the rain and I—" he looked about him automatically, and his voice sank to a whisper "—caught a cold, and wasn't Mom upset, though."

Dr. Sloane sighed. "Shall we go back now?"

There was a quick disappointment on Richard's face. "Aw, what for?"

"You remind me that your mother must be waiting for us."

"I guess so." The boy turned reluctantly.

They walked slowly back. Richard was saying, chattily, "I wrote a composition at school once about how if I could go on some ancient vehicle" (he pronounced it with exaggerated care) "I'd go in a stratoliner and look at stars and clouds and things. Oh, boy, I was sure nuts."

"You'd pick something else now?"

"You bet. I'd go in an aut'm'bile, real slow. Then I'd see everything there was."

*   *   *

Mrs. Hanshaw seemed troubled, uncertain. "You don't think it's abnormal, then, Doctor?"

"Unusual, perhaps, but not abnormal. He likes the outside."

"But how can he? It's so dirty, so unpleasant."

"That's a matter of individual taste. A hundred years ago our ancestors were all outside most of the time. Even today, I dare say there are a million Africans who have never seen a Door."

"But Richard's always been taught to behave himself the way a decent person in District A-3 is supposed to behave," said Mrs. Hanshaw, fiercely. "Not like an African or—or an ancestor."

"That may be part of the trouble, Mrs. Hanshaw. He feels this urge to go outside and yet he feels it to be wrong. He's ashamed to talk about it to you or to his teacher. It forces him into sullen retreat and it could eventually be dangerous."

"Then how can we persuade him to stop?"

Dr. Sloane said, "Don't try. Channel the activity instead. The day your Door broke down, he was forced outside, found he liked it, and that set a pattern. He used the trip to school and back as an excuse to repeat that first exciting experience. Now suppose you agree to let him out of the house for two hours on Saturdays and Sundays. Suppose he gets it through his head that after all he can go outside without necessarily having to go anywhere in the process. Don't you think he'll be willing to use the Door to go to school and back thereafter? And don't you think that will stop the trouble he's now having with his teacher and probably with his fellow-pupils?"

"But then will matters remain so? Must they? Won't he ever be normal again?"

Dr. Sloane rose to his feet. "Mrs. Hanshaw, he's as normal as need be right now. Right now, he's tasting the joys of the forbidden. If you cooperate with him, show that you don't disapprove, it will lose some of its attraction right there. Then, as he grows older, he will become more aware of the expectations and demands of society. He will learn to conform. After all, there is a little of the rebel in all of us, but it generally dies down as we grow old and tired. Unless, that is, it is unreasonably suppressed and allowed to build up pressure. Don't do that. Richard will be all right."

He walked to the Door.

Mrs. Hanshaw said, "And you don't think a probe will be necessary, Doctor?"

He turned and said vehemently, "No, definitely not! There is nothing about the boy that requires it. Understand? Nothing."

His fingers hesitated an inch from the combination board and the expression on his face grew lowering.

"What's the matter, Dr. Sloane?" asked Mrs. Hanshaw.

But he didn't hear her beause he was thinking of the Door and the psychic probe and all the rising, choking tide of machinery. There is a little of the rebel in all of us, he thought.

So he said in a soft voice, as his hand fell away from the board and his feet turned away from the Door, "You know, it's such a beautiful day that I think I'll walk."

19

Jokester

Since I am a pronounced extrovert, it is not at all surprising that I'm a good raconteur (or jokester). In fact, I wrote a book called Isaac Asimov's Treasury of Humor *(Houghton Mifflin, 1971), still available as a trade paperback which is virtually a textbook on the subject.*

Once when I was telling Larry Shaw (one of the two persons to whom this book is dedicated) a number of stories over lunch, he said, "Who makes up all these jokes, Isaac?" I shrugged. "Who knows?" I said. "I dare you to write a science fiction story on the subject." he said.

I can almost never resist a dare, so I wrote the following story, which I thought was pretty good. I liked it particularly because it gave me the opportunity to insert six of my favorite (clean) jokes. Of course, when this story was written in 1955, during the reign of Good King Ike, only clean jokes could possibly have appeared in a science fiction magazine. Nowadays, I would have inserted six somewhat more ribald specimens.

Noel Meyerhof consulted the list he had prepared and chose which item was to be first. As usual, he relied mainly on intuition.

He was dwarfed by the machine he faced, though only the smallest portion of the latter was in view. That didn't matter. He spoke with the offhand confidence of one who thoroughly knew he was master.

"Johnson," he said, "came home unexpectedly from a business trip to find his wife in the arms of his best friend. He staggered back and said, 'Max! I'm married to the lady so I *have* to. But why you?' "

Meyerhof thought: Okay, let that trickle down into its guts and gurgle about a bit.

And a voice behind him said, "Hey."

Meyerhof erased the sound of that monosyllable and put the circuit he was using into neutral. He whirled and said, "I'm working. Don't you knock?"

He did not smile as he customarily did in greeting Timothy Whistler, a senior analyst with whom he dealt as often as with any. He frowned as he would have for an interruption by a stranger, wrinkling his thin face into a distortion that seemed to extend to his hair, rumpling it more than ever.

Whistler shrugged. He wore his white lab coat with his fists pressing down within its pockets and creasing it into tense vertical lines. "I knocked. You didn't answer. The operations signal wasn't on."

Meyerhof grunted. It wasn't at that. He'd been thinking about this new project too intensively and he was forgetting little details.

And yet he could scarcely blame himself for that. This thing was important.

He didn't know why it was, of course. Grand Masters rarely did. That's what made them Grand Masters; the fact that they were beyond reason. How else could the human mind keep up with that ten-mile-long lump of solidified reason that men called Multivac, the most complex computer ever built?

Meyerhof said, "I *am* working. Is there something important on your mind?"

"Nothing that can't be postponed. There are a few holes in the answer on the hyperspatial——" Whistler did a double take and his face took on a rueful look of uncertainty. *"Working?"*

"Yes. What about it?"

"But——" He looked about, staring into the crannies of the shallow room that faced the banks upon banks of relays that formed a small portion of Multivac. "There isn't anyone here at that."

"Who said there was, or should be?"

"You were telling one of your jokes, weren't you?"

"And?"

Whistler forced a smile. "Don't tell me you were telling a joke to Multivac?"

Meyerhof stiffened. "Why not?"

"Were you?"

"Yes."

"Why?"

Meyerhof stared the other down. "I don't have to account to you. Or to anyone."

"Good Lord, of course not. I was curious, that's all. . . . But then, if you're working, I'll leave." He looked about once more, frowning.

"Do so," said Meyerhof. His eyes followed the other out and then he activated the operations signal with a savage punch of his finger.

He strode the length of the room and back, getting himself in hand. Damn Whistler! Damn them all! Because he didn't bother to hold those technicians, analysts and mechanics at the proper social distance, because he treated them as though they, too, were creative artists, they took these liberties.

He thought grimly: They can't even tell jokes decently.

And instantly that brought him back to the task in hand. He sat down again. Devil take them all.

He threw the proper Multivac circuit back into operation and said, "The ship's steward stopped at the rail of the ship during a particularly rough ocean crossing and gazed compassionately at the man whose slumped position over the rail and whose intensity of gaze toward the depths betokened all too well the ravages of seasickness.

"Gently, the steward patted the man's shoulder. 'Cheer up, sir,' he murmured. 'I know it seems bad, but really, you know, nobody ever dies of seasickness.'

"The afficted gentleman lifted his greenish, tortured face to his comforter and gasped in hoarse accents, 'Don't say that, man. For Heaven's sake, don't say that. It's only the hope of dying that's keeping me alive.' "

Timothy Whistler, a bit preoccupied, nevertheless smiled

and nodded as he passed the secretary's desk. She smiled back at him.

Here, he thought, was an archaic item in this computer-ridden world of the twenty-first century, a human secretary. But then perhaps it was natural that such an institution should survive here in the very citadel of computerdom; in the gigantic world corporation that handled Multivac. With Multivac filling the horizons, lesser computers for trivial tasks would have been in poor taste.

Whistler stepped into Abram Trask's office. That government official paused in his careful task of lighting a pipe; his dark eyes flicked in Whistler's direction and his beaked nose stood out sharply and prominently against the rectangle of window behind him.

"Ah, there, Whistler. Sit down. Sit down."

Whistler did so. "I think we've got a problem, Trask."

Trask half-smiled. "Not a technical one, I hope. I'm just an innocent politician." (It was one of his favorite phrases.)

"It involves Meyerhof."

Trask sat down instantly and looked acutely miserble. "Are you sure?"

"Reasonably sure."

Whistler understood the other's sudden unhappiness well. Trask was the government official in charge of the Division of Computers and Automation of the Department of the Interior. He was expected to deal with matters of policy involving the human satellites of Multivac, just as those technically trained satellites were expected to deal with Multivac itself.

But a Grand Master was more than just a satellite. More, even, than just a human.

Early in the history of Multivac, it had become apparent that the bottleneck was the questioning procedure. Multivac could answer the problems of humanity, *all* the problems, if—*if* it were asked meaningful questions. But as knowledge accumulated at an ever-faster rate, it became ever more difficult to locate those meaningful questions.

Reason alone wouldn't do. What was needed was a

rare type of intuition; the same faculty of mind (only much more intensified) that made a grand master at chess. A mind was needed of the sort that could see through the quadrillions of chess patterns to find the one best move, and do it in a matter of minutes.

Trask moved restlessly. "What's Meyerhof been doing?"

"He's introduced a line of questioning that I find disturbing."

"Oh, come on, Whistler. Is that all? You can't stop a Grand Master from going through any line of questioning he chooses. Neither you nor I are equipped to judge the worth of his questions. You know that. I know you know that."

"I do. Of course. But I also know Meyerhof. Have you ever met him socially?"

"Good Lord, no. Does anyone meet any Grand Master socially?"

"Don't take that attitude, Trask. They're human and they're to be pitied. Have you ever thought what it must be like to be a Grand Master; to know there are only some twelve like you in the world; to know that only one or two come up per generation; that the world depends on you; that a thousand mathematicians, logicians, psychologists and physical scientists wait on you?"

Trask shrugged and muttered, "Good Lord, I'd feel king of the world."

"I don't think you would," said the senior analyst impatiently. "They feel kings of nothing. They have no equal to talk to, no sensation of belonging. Listen, Meyerhof never misses a chance to get together with the boys. He isn't married, naturally; he doesn't drink; he has no natural social touch—yet he forces himself into company because he must. And do you know what he does when he gets together with us, and that's at least once a week?"

"I haven't the least idea," said the government man. "This is all new to me."

"He's a jokester."

"What?"

"He tells jokes. Good ones. He's terrific. He can take

any story, however old and dull, and make it sound good. It's the way he tells it. He has a flair."

"I see. Well, good."

"Or bad. These jokes are important to him." Whistler put both elbows on Trask's desk, bit at a thumbnail and stared into the air. "He's different, he knows he's different and these jokes are the one way he feels he can get the rest of us ordinary schmoes to accept him. We laugh, we howl, we clap him on the back and even forget he's a Grand Master. It's the only hold he has on the rest of us."

"This is all interesting. I didn't know you were such a psychologist. Still, where does this lead?"

"Just this. What do you suppose happens if Meyerhof runs out of jokes?"

"What?" The government man stared blankly.

"If he starts repeating himself? If his audience starts laughing less heartily, or stops laughing altogether? It's his only hold on our approval. Without it, he'll be alone and then what would happen to him? After all, Trask, he's one of the dozen men mankind can't do without. We can't let anything happen to him. I don't mean just physical things. We can't even let him get too unhappy. Who knows how that might affect his intuition?"

"Well, has he started repeating himself?"

"Not as far as I know, but I think *he* thinks he has."

"Why do you say that?"

"Because I heard him telling jokes to Multivac."

"Oh, no."

"Accidentally! I walked in on him and he threw me out. He was savage. He's usually good-natured enough, and I consider it a bad sign that he was so upset at the intrusion. But the fact remains that he was telling a joke to Multivac, and I'm convinced it was one of a series."

"But why?"

Whistler shrugged and rubbed a hand fiercely across his chin. "I have a thought about that. I think he's trying to build up a store of jokes in Multivac's memory banks in order to get back new variations. You see what I mean? He's planning a mechanical jokester, so that he can have an infinite number of jokes at hand and never fear running out."

"Good Lord!"

"Objectively, there may be nothing wrong with that, but I consider it a bad sign when a Grand Master starts using Multivac for his personal problems. Any Grand Master has a certain inherent mental instability and he should be watched. Meyerhof may be approaching a borderline beyond which we lose a Grand Master."

Trask said blankly, "What are you suggesting I do?"

"You can check me. I'm too close to him to judge well, maybe, and judging humans isn't my particular talent, anyway. You're a politician; it's more your talent."

"Judging humans, perhaps, not Grand Masters."

"They're human, too. Besides, who else is to do it?"

The fingers of Trask's hand struck his desk in rapid succession over and over like a slow and muted roll of drums.

"I suppose I'll have to," he said.

Meyerhof said to Multivac, "The ardent swain, picking a bouquet of wildflowers for his loved one, was disconcerted to find himself, suddenly, in the same field with a large bull of unfriendly appearance which, gazing at him steadily, pawed the ground in a threatening manner. The young man, spying a farmer on the other side of a fairly distant fence, shouted, 'Hey, mister, is that bull safe?' The farmer surveyed the situation with critical eye, spat to one side and called back, 'He's safe as anything.' He spat again, and added, 'Can't say the same about you, though.'"

Meyerhof was about to pass on to the next when the summons came.

It wasn't really a summons. No one could summon a Grand Master. It was only a message that Division Head Trask would like very much to see Grand Master Meyerhof if Grand Master Meyerhof could spare him the time.

Meyerhof might, with impunity, have tossed the message to one side and continued with whatever he was doing. He was not subject to discipline.

On the other hand, were he to do that, they would continue to bother him—oh, very respectfully, but they would continue to bother him.

So he neutralized the pertinent circuits of Multivac and locked them into place. He put the freeze signal on his office so that no one would dare enter in his absence and left for Trask's office.

Trask coughed and felt a bit intimidated by the sullen fierceness of the other's look. He said, "We have not had occasion to know one another, Grand Master, to my great regret."

"I have reported to you," said Meyerhof stiffly.

Trask wondered what lay behind those keen, wild eyes. It was difficult for him to imagine Meyerhof with his thin face, his dark, straight hair, his intense air, ever unbending long enough to tell funny stories.

He said, "Reports are not social acquaintance. I—I have been given to understand you have a marvelous fund of anecdotes."

"I am a jokester, sir. That's the phrase people use. A jokester."

"They haven't used the phrase to me, Grand Master. They have said——"

"The hell with them! I don't care what they've said. See here, Trask, do you want to hear a joke?" He leaned forward across the desk, his eyes narrowed.

"By all means. Certainly," said Trask, with an effort at heartiness.

"All right. Here's the joke: Mrs. Jones stared at the fortune card that had emerged from the weighing machine in response to her husband's penny. She said, 'It says here, George, that you're suave, intelligent, farseeing, industrious and attractive to women.' With that, she turned the card over and added, 'And they have your weight wrong, too.'"

Trask laughed. It was almost impossible not to. Although the punch line was predictable, the surprising facility with which Meyerhof had produced just the tone of contemptuous disdain in the woman's voice, and the cleverness with which he had contorted the lines of his face to suit that tone carried the politician helplessly into laughter.

Meyerhof said sharply, "Why is that funny?"

Trask sobered. "I beg your pardon."

"I said, why is that funny? Why do you laugh?"

"Well," said Trask, trying to be reasonable, "the last line put every thing that preceded in a new light. The unexpectedness——"

"The point is," said Meyerhof, "that I have pictured a husband being humiliated by his wife; a marriage that is such a failure that the wife is convinced that her husband lacks any virtue. Yet you laugh at that. If you were the husband, would you find it funny?"

He waited a moment in thought, then said, "Try this one, Trask: Abner was seated at his wife's sickbed, weeping uncontrollably, when his wife, mustering the dregs of her strength, drew herself up to one elbow.

" 'Abner,' she whispered, 'Abner, I cannot go to my Maker without confessing my misdeed.'

" 'Not now,' muttered the stricken husband. 'Not now, my dear. Lie back and rest.'

" 'I cannot,' she cried. 'I must tell, or my soul will never know peace. I have been unfaithful to you, Abner. In this very house, not one month ago——'

" 'Hush, dear,' soothed Abner. 'I know all about it. Why else have I poisoned you?' "

Trask tried desperately to maintain equanimity but did not entirely succeed. He suppressed a chuckle imperfectly.

Meyerhof said, "So that's funny, too. Adultery. Murder. All funny."

"Well, now," said Trask, "books have been written analyzing humor."

"True enough," said Meyerhof, "and I've read a number of them. What's more, I've read most of them to Multivac. Still, the people who write the books are just guessing. Some of them say we laugh because we feel superior to the people in the joke. Some say it is because of a suddenly realized incongruity, or a sudden relief from tension, or a sudden reinterpretation of events. Is there any simple reason? Different people laugh at different jokes. No joke is universal. Some people don't laugh at any joke. Yet what may be most important is that man is the only animal with a true sense of humor: the only animal that laughs."

Trask said suddenly, "I understand. You're trying to analyze humor. That's why you're transmitting a series of jokes to Multivac."

"Who told you I was doing that? . . . Never mind, it was Whistler. I remember, now. He surprised me at it. Well, what about it?"

"Nothing at all."

"You don't dispute my right to add anything I wish to Multivac's general fund of knowledge, or to ask any question I wish?"

"No, not at all," said Trask hastily. "As a matter of fact, I have no doubt that this will open the way to new analyses of great interest to psychologists."

"Hmp. Maybe. Just the same there's something plaguing me that's more important than just the general analysis of humor. There's a specific question I have to ask. Two of them, really."

"Oh? What's that?" Trask wondered if the other would answer. There would be no way of compelling him if he chose not to.

But Meyerhof said, "The first question is this: Where do all these jokes come from?"

"What?"

"Who makes them up? Listen! About a month ago, I spent an evening swapping jokes. As usual, I told most of them and, as usual, the fools laughed. Maybe they really thought the jokes were funny and maybe they were just humoring me. In any case, one creature took the liberty of slapping me on the back and saying, 'Meyerhof, you know more jokes than any ten people I know.'

"I'm sure he was right, but it gave rise to a thought. I don't know how many hundreds, or perhaps thousands, of jokes I've told at one time or another in my life, yet the fact is I never made up one. Not one. I'd only repeated them. My only contribution was to tell them.

To begin with, I'd either heard them or read them. And the source of my hearing or reading didn't make up the jokes, either. I never met anyone who ever claimed to have constructed a joke. It's always 'I heard a good one the other day,' and 'Heard any good ones lately?'

"*All the jokes are old!* That's why jokes exhibit such a social lag. They still deal with seasickness, for instance, when that's easily prevented these days and never experienced. Or they'll deal with fortune-giving weighing machines, like the joke I told you, when such machines are found only in antique shops. Well, then, who makes up the jokes?"

Trask said, "Is *that* what you're trying to find out?" It was on the tip of Trask's tongue to add: Good Lord, who cares? He forced that impulse down. A Grand Master's questions were always meaningful.

"Of course that's what I'm trying to find out. Think of it this way. It's not just that jokes happen to be old. They *must* be old to be enjoyed. It's essential that a joke not be original. There's one variety of humor that is, or can be, original that's the pun. I've heard puns that were obviously made up on the spur of the moment. I have made some up myself. But no one laughs at such puns. You're not supposed to. You groan. The better the pun, the louder the groan. Original humor is not laugh-provoking. Why?"

"I'm sure I don't know."

"All right. Let's find out. Having given Multivac all the information I thought advisable on the general topic of humor, I am now feeding it selected jokes."

Trask found himself intrigued. "Selected how?" he asked.

"I don't know," said Meyerhof. "They felt like the right ones. I'm Grand Master, you know."

"Oh, agreed. Agreed."

"From those jokes and the general philosophy of humor, my first request will be for Multivac to trace the origin of the jokes, if it can. Since Whistler is in on this and since he has seen fit to report it to you, have him down in Analysis day after tomorrow. I think he'll have a bit of work to do."

"Certainly. May I attend, too?"

Meyerhof shrugged. Trask's attendance was obviously a matter of indifference to him.

Meyerhof had selected the last in the series with particular care. What that care consisted of, he could not have said, but he had revolved a dozen possibilities in his mind, and over and over again had tested each for some indefinable quality of meaningfulness.

He said, "Ug, the caveman, observed his mate running to him in tears, her leopard-skin skirt in disorder. 'Ug,' she cried, distraught, 'do something quickly. A saber-toothed tiger has entered Mother's cave. Do something!' Ug grunted, picked up his well-gnawed buffalo bone and said, 'Why do anything? Who the hell cares what happens to a saber-toothed tiger?' "

It was then that Meyerhof asked his two questions and leaned back, closing his eyes. He was done.

"I saw absolutely nothing wrong," said Trask to Whistler. "He told me what he was doing readily enough and it was odd but legitimate."

"What he *claimed* he was doing," said Whistler.

"Even so, I can't stop a Grand Master on opinion alone. He seemed queer but, after all, Grand Masters are supposed to seem queer. I didn't think him insane."

"Using Multivac to find the source of jokes?" muttered the senior analyst in discontent. "That's not insane?"

"How can we tell?" asked Trask irritably. "Science has advanced to the point where the only meaningful questions left are the ridiculous ones. The sensible ones have been thought of, asked and answered long ago."

"It's no use. I'm bothered."

"Maybe, but there's no choice now, Whistler. We'll see Meyerhof and you can do the necessary analysis of Multivac's response, if any. As for me, my only job is to handle the red tape. Good Lord, I don't even know what a senior analyst such as yourself is supposed to do, except analyze, and that doesn't help me any."

Whistler said, "It's simple enough. A Grand Master like Meyerhof asks questions and Multivac automatically formulates it into quantities and operations. The necessary machinery for converting words to symbols is what makes up most of the bulk of Multivac. Multivac then gives the answer in quantities and operations, but it doesn't translate that back into words except in the most simple and routine cases. If it were designed to solve the general retranslation problem, its bulk would have to be quadrupled at least."

"I see. Then it's your job to translate these symbols into words?"

"My job and that of other analysts. We use smaller, specially designed computers whenever necessary." Whistler smiled grimly. "Like the Delphic priestess of ancient Greece, Multivac gives oracular and obscure answers. Only we have translators, you see."

They had arrived. Meyerhof was waiting.

Whistler said briskly, "What circuits did you use, Grand Master?"

Meyerhof told him and Whistler went to work.

Trask tried to follow what was happening, but none of it made sense. The government official watched a spool unreel with a patter of dots in endless incomprehensibility. Grand Master Meyerhof stood indifferently to one side while Whistler surveyed the pattern as it emerged. The analyst had put on headphones and a mouthpiece and at intervals murmured a series of instructions which, at some far-off place, guided assistants through electronic contortions in other computers.

Occasionally, Whistler listened, then punched combinations on a complex keyboard marked with symbols that looked vaguely mathematical but weren't.

A good deal more than an hour's time elapsed.

The frown on Whistler's face grew deeper. Once, he looked up at the two others and began, "This is unbel——" and turned back to his work.

Finally, he said hoarsely, "I can give you an unofficial answer." His eyes were red-rimmed. "The official answer awaits complete analysis. Do you want it unofficial?"

"Go ahead," said Meyerhof.

Trask nodded.

Whistler darted a hangdog glance at the Grand Master. "Ask a foolish question——" he said. Then, gruffly, "Multivac says, extraterrestrial origin."

"What are you saying?" demanded Trask.

"Don't you hear me? The jokes we laugh at were not made up by any man. Multivac has analyzed all data given it and the one answer that best fits that data is that some extraterrestrial intelligence has composed the jokes, all of them, and placed them in selected human minds at selected times and places in such a way that no man is conscious of having made one up. All subsequent jokes are minor variations and adaptations of these grand originals."

Meyerhof broke in, face flushed with the kind of triumph only a Grand Master can know who once again has asked the right question. "All comedy writers," he said, "work by twisting old jokes to new purposes. That's well known. The answer fits."

"But why?" asked Trask. "Why make up the jokes?"

"Multivac says," said Whistler, "that the only purpose that fits all the data is that the jokes are intended to study human psychology. We study rat psychology by making the rats solve mazes. The rats don't know why and wouldn't even if they were aware of what was going on, which they're not. These outer intelligences study man's psychology by noting individual reactions to carefully selected anecdotes. Each man reacts differently. . . . Presumably, these outer intelligences are to us as we are to rats." He shuddered.

Trask, eyes staring, said, "The Grand Master said man is the only animal with a sense of humor. It would seem then that the sense of humor is foisted upon us from without."

Meyerhof added excitedly, "And for possible humor created from within, we have no laughter. Puns, I mean."

Whistler said, "Presumably, the extraterrestrials cancel out reactions to spontaneous jokes to avoid confusion."

Trask said in sudden agony of spirit, "Come on, now, Good Lord, do either of you believe this?"

The senior analyst looked at him coldly. "Multivac says so. It's all that can be said so far. It has pointed out the real jokesters of the universe, and if we want to know more, the matter will have to be followed up." He added in a whisper, "If anyone dares follow it up."

Grand Master Meyerhof said suddenly, "I asked two questions, you know. So far only the first has been answered. I think Multivac has enough data to answer the second."

Whistler shrugged. He seemed a half-broken man. "When a Grand Master thinks there is enough data," he said, "I'll make book on it. What is your second question?"

"I asked this: What will be the effect on the human race of discovering the answer to my first question?"

"Why did you ask that?" demanded Trask.

"Just a feeling that it had to be asked," said Meyerhof.

Trask said, "Insane. It's all insane," and turned away. Even he himself felt how strangely he and Whistler had changed sides. Now it was Trask crying insanity.

Trask closed his eyes. He might cry insanity all he wished, but no man in fifty years had doubted the combination of a Grand Master and Multivac and found his doubts verified.

Whistler worked silently, teeth clenched. He put Multivac and its subsidiary machines through their paces again. Another hour passed and he laughed harshly. "A raving nightmare!"

"What's the answer?" asked Meyerhof. "I want Multivac's remarks, not yours."

"All right. Take it. Multivac states that, once even a single human discovers the truth of this method of psychological analysis of the human mind, it will become useless as an objective technique to those extraterrestrial powers now using it."

"You mean there won't be any more jokes handed out

to humanity?" asked Trask faintly. "Or what do you mean?"

"No more jokes," said Whistler, *"now!* Multivac says *now!* The experiment is ended *now!* A new technique will have to be introduced."

They stared at each other. The minutes passed.

Meyerhof said slowly, "Multivac is right."

Whistler said haggardly, "I know."

Even Trask said in a whisper, "Yes. It must be."

It was Meyerhof who put his finger on the proof of it, Meyerhof the accomplished jokester. He said, "It's over, you know, all over. I've been trying for five minutes now and I can't think of one single joke, not one! And if I read one in a book, I wouldn't laugh. I know."

"The gift of humor is gone," said Trask drearily. "No man will ever laugh again."

And they remained there, staring, feeling the world shrink down to the dimensions of an experimental rat cage—with the maze removed and something, something about to be put in its place.

20

The Last Answer

This was written to celebrate the fiftieth anniversary of the magazine Analog *which, prior to 1960, was* Astounding Science Fiction *of sainted memory. That is enough to endear it to me.*

Murray Templeton was forty-five years old, in the prime of life, and with all parts of his body in perfect working order except for certain key portions of his coronary arteries, but that was enough.

The pain had come suddenly, had mounted to an unbearable peak, and had then ebbed steadily. He could feel his breath slowing and a kind of gathering peace washing over him.

There is no pleasure like the absence of pain—immediately after pain. Murray felt an almost giddy lightness as though he were lifting in the air and hovering.

He opened his eyes and noted with distant amusement that the others in the room were still agitated. He had been in the laboratory when the pain had struck, quite without warning, and when he had staggered, he had heard surprised outcries from the others before everything vanished into overwhelming agony.

Now, with the pain gone, the others were still hovering, still anxious, still gathered about his fallen body—

—Which, he suddenly realized, he was looking down on.

He was down there, sprawled, face contorted. He was up here, at peace and watching.

He thought: Miracle of miracles! The life-after-life nuts were right.

And although that was a humiliating way for an atheistic physicist to die, he felt only the mildest surprise, and no alteration of the peace in which he was immersed.

He thought: There should be some angel—or something—coming for me.

The Earthly scene was fading. Darkness was invading his consciousness and off in a distance, as a last glimmer of sight, there was a figure of light, vaguely human in form, and radiating warmth.

Murray thought: What a joke on me. I'm going to Heaven.

Even as he thought that, the light faded, but the warmth remained. There was no lessening of the peace even though in all the Universe only he remained—and the Voice.

The Voice said, "I have done this so often and yet I still have the capacity to be pleased at success."

It was in Murray's mind to say something, but he was not conscious of possessing a mouth, tongue, or vocal cords. Nevertheless, he tried to make a sound. He tried, mouthlessly, to hum words or breathe them or just push them out by a contraction of—something.

And they came out. He heard his own voice, quite recognizable, and his own words, infinitely clear.

Murray said, "Is this Heaven?"

The Voice said, "This is no place as you understand place."

Murray was embarrassed, but the next question had to be asked. "Pardon me if I sound like a jackass. Are you God?"

Without changing intonation or in any way marring the perfection of the sound, the Voice managed to sound amused. "It is strange that I am always asked that in, of course, an infinite number of ways. There is no answer I can give that you would comprehend. I *am*—which is all that I can say significantly and you may cover that with any word or concept you please."

Murray said, "And what am I? A soul? Or am I only personified existence too?" He tried not to sound sarcastic, but it seemed to him that he had failed. He thought then, fleetingly, of adding a "Your Grace" or "Holy One" or *something* to counteract the sarcasm, and could not bring himself to do so even though for the first time in his existence he speculated on the possibility of being punished for his insolence—or sin?—with Hell, and what that might be like.

The Voice did not sound offended. "You are easy to explain—even to you. You may call yourself a soul if that pleases you, but what you are is a nexus of electromagnetic forces, so arranged that all the interconnections and interrelationships are exactly imitative of those of your brain in your Universe-existence—down to the smallest detail. Therefore you have your capacity for thought, your memories, your personality. It still seems to you that you are you."

Murray found himself incredulous. "You mean the essence of my brain was permanent."

"Not at all. There is nothing about you that is permanent except what I choose to make so. I formed the nexus. I constructed it while you had physical existence and adjusted it to the moment when the existence failed."

The Voice seemed distinctly pleased with itself, and went on after a moment's pause. "An intricate but entirely precise construction. I could, of course, do it for every human being on your world but I am pleased that I do not. There is pleasure in the selection."

"You choose very few then."

"Very few."

"And what happens to the rest."

"Oblivion! —Oh, of course, you imagine a Hell."

Murray would have flushed if he had the capacity to do so. He said, "*I* do not. It is spoken of. Still, I would scarcely have thought I was virtuous enough to have attracted your attention as one of the Elect."

"Virtuous? —Ah, I see what you mean. It is troublesome to have to force my thinking small enough to permeate yours. No, I have chosen you for your capacity for thought, as I choose others, in quadrillions, from all the intelligent species of the Universe."

Murray found himself suddenly curious, the habit of a

lifetime. He said, "Do you choose them all yourself or are there others like you?"

For a fleeting moment, Murray thought there was an impatient reaction to that, but when the Voice came, it was unmoved. "Whether or not there are others is irrelevant to you. This Universe is mine, and mine alone. It is my invention, my construction, intended for my purpose alone."

"And yet with quadrillions of nexi you have formed, you spend time with me? Am I that important?"

The Voice said, "You are not important at all. I am also with others in a way which, to your perception, would seem simultaneous."

"And yet you are one?"

Again amusement. The Voice said, "You seek to trap me into an inconsistency. If you were an amoeba who could consider individuality only in connection with single cells and if you were to ask a sperm whale, made up of thirty quadrillion cells, whether it was one or many, how could the sperm whale answer in a way that would be comprehensible to the amoeba?"

Murray said dryly, "I'll think about it. It may become comprehensible."

"Exactly. That is your function. You will think."

"To what end? You already know everything, I suppose."

The Voice said, "Even if I knew everything, I could not know that I know everything."

Murray said, "That sounds like a bit of Eastern philosophy—something that sounds profound precisely because it has no meaning."

The Voice said, "You have promise. You answer my paradox with a paradox—except that mine is not a paradox. Consider. I have existed eternally, but what does that mean? It means I cannot remember having come into existence. If I could, I would not have existed eternally. If I cannot remember having come into existence, then there is at least one thing—the nature of my coming into existence—that I do not know.

"Then, too, although what I know is infinite, it is also

true that what there is to know is infinite, and how can I be sure that both infinities are equal? The infinity of potential knowledge may be infinitely greater than the infinity of my actual knowledge. Here is a simple example: If I knew every one of the even integers, I would know an infinite number of items, and yet I would still not know a single odd integer."

Murray said, "But the odd integers can be derived. If you divide every even integer in the entire infinite series by two, you will get another infinite series which will contain within it the infinite series of odd integers."

The Voice said, "You have the idea. I am pleased. It will be your task to find other such ways, far more difficult ones, from the known to the not-yet-known. You have your memories. You will remember all the data you have ever collected or learned, or that you have or will deduce from that data. If necessary, you will be allowed to learn what additional data you will consider relevant to the problems you set yourself."

"Could you not do all that for yourself?"

The Voice said, "I can, but it is more interesting this way. I constructed the Universe in order to have more facts to deal with. I inserted the uncertainty principle, entropy, and other randomization factors to make the whole not instantly obvious. It has worked well for it has amused me throughout its entire existence.

"I then allowed complexities that produced first life and then intelligence, and used it as a source for a research team, not because I need the aid, but because it would introduce a new random factor. I found I could not predict the next interesting piece of knowledge gained, where it would come from, by what means derived."

Murray said, "Does that ever happen?"

"Certainly. A century doesn't pass in which some interesting item doesn't appear somewhere."

"Something that you could have thought of yourself, but had not done so yet?"

"Yes."

Murray said, "Do you actually think there's a chance of *my* obliging you in this manner?"

"In the next century? Virtually none. In the long run, though, your success is certain, since you will be engaged eternally."

Murray said, "I will be thinking through eternity? Forever?"

"Yes."

"To what end?"

"I have told you. To find new knowledge."

"But beyond that. For what purpose am I to find new knowledge?"

"It was what you did in your Universe-bound life. What was its purpose then?"

Murray said, "To gain new knowledge that only I could gain. To receive the praise of my fellows. To feel the satisfaction of accomplishment knowing that I had only a short time allotted me for the purpose. —Now I would gain only what you could gain yourself if you wished to take a small bit of trouble. You cannot praise me; you can only be amused. And there is no credit or satisfaction in accomplishment when I have all eternity to do it in."

The Voice said, "And you do not find thought and discovery worthwhile in itself? You do not find it requiring no further purpose?"

"For a finite time, yes. Not for all eternity."

"I see your point. Nevertheless, you have no choice."

"You say I am to think. You cannot make me do so."

The Voice said, "I do not wish to constrain you directly. I will not need to. Since you can do nothing but think, you will think. You do not know how not to think."

"Then I will give myself a goal. I will invent a purpose."

The Voice said tolerantly, "That you can certainly do."

"I have already found a purpose."

"May I know what it is?"

"You know already. I know we are not speaking in the ordinary fashion. You adjust my nexus in such a way that I believe I hear you and I believe I speak, but you transfer thoughts to me and from me directly. And when my nexus changes with my thoughts you are at once aware of them and do not need my voluntary transmission."

The Voice said, "You are surprisingly correct. I am pleased. —But it also pleases me to have you tell me your thoughts voluntarily."

"Then I will tell you. The purpose of my thinking will be to discover a way to disrupt this nexus of me that you have created. I do not want to think for no purpose but to amuse you. I do not want to think forever to amuse you. I do not want to exist forever to amuse you. All my thinking will be directed toward ending the nexus. *That* would amuse *me*."

The Voice said, "I have no objection to that. Even concentrated thought on ending your own existence may, in spite of you, come up with something new and interesting. And, of course, if you succeed in this suicide attempt you will have accomplished nothing, for I would instantly reconstruct you and in such a way as to make your method of suicide impossible. And if you found another and still more subtle fashion of disrupting yourself, I would reconstruct you with that possibility eliminated, and so on. It could be an interesting game, but you will nevertheless exist eternally. It is my will."

Murray felt a quaver but the words came out with a perfect calm. "Am I in Hell then, after all? You have implied there is none, but if this were Hell you would lie as part of the game of Hell."

The Voice said, "In that case, of what use is it to assure you that you are not in Hell? Nevertheless, I assure you. There is here neither Heaven nor Hell. There is only myself."

Murray said, "Consider, then, that my thoughts may be useless to you. If I come up with nothing useful, will it not be worth your while to—disassemble me and take no further trouble with me?"

"As a reward? You want Nirvana as the prize of failure and you intend to assure me failure? There is no bargain there. You will not fail. With all eternity before you, you cannot avoid having at least one interesting thought, however you try against it."

"Then I will create another purpose for myself. I will not try to destroy myself. I will set as my goal the humiliation of you. I will think of something you have not only never thought of but never could think of. I will think of the last answer, beyond which there is no knowledge further."

The Voice said, "You do not understand the nature of the infinite. There may be things I have not yet troubled to know. There cannot be anything I cannot know."

Murray said thoughtfully, "You cannot know your beginning. You have said so. Therefore you cannot know your end. Very well, then. That will be my purpose and that will be the last answer. I will not destroy myself. I will destroy *you*—if you do not destroy me first."

The Voice said, "Ah! You come to that in rather less than average time. I would have thought it would have taken you longer. There is not one of those I have with me in this existence of perfect and eternal thought that does not have the ambition of destroying me. It cannot be done."

Murray said, "I have all eternity to think of a way of destroying you."

The Voice said, equably, "Then try to think of it." And it was gone.

But Murray had his purpose now and was content.

For what could *any* Entity, conscious of eternal existence, want—but an end?

For what else had the Voice been searching for countless billions of years? And for what other reason had intelligence been created and certain specimens salvaged and put to work, but to aid in that great search? And Murray intended that it would be he, and he alone, who would succeed.

Carefully, and with the thrill of purpose, Murray began to think.

He had plenty of time.

21

The Last Question

This is by far my favorite story of all those I have written.

After all, I undertook to tell several trillion years of human history in the space of a short story and I leave it to you as to how well I succeeded. I also undertook another task, but I won't tell you what that was lest I spoil the story for you.

It is a curious fact that innumerable readers have asked me if I wrote this story. They seem never to remember the title of the story or (for sure) the author, except for the vague thought it might be me. But, of course, they never forget the story itself, especially the ending. The idea seems to drown out everything else—and I'm satisfied that it should.

The last question was asked for the first time, half in jest, on May 21, 2061, at a time when humanity first stepped into the light. The question came about as a result of a five-dollar bet over highballs, and it happened this way:

Alexander Adell and Bertram Lupov were two of the faithful attendants of Multivac. As well as any human beings could, they knew what lay behind the cold, clicking, flashing face—miles and miles of face—of that giant computer. They had at least a vague notion of the general plan of relays and circuits that had long since grown past the point where any single human could possibly have a firm grasp of the whole.

Multivac was self-adjusting and self-correcting. It had to be, for nothing human could adjust and correct it quickly enough or even adequately enough. —So Adell and Lupov attended the monstrous giant only lightly and superficially, yet as well as any men could. They fed it data, adjusted questions to its needs and translated the answers that were issued. Certainly they, and all others like them, were fully entitled to share in the glory that was Multivac's.

For decades, Multivac had helped design the ships and plot the trajectories that enabled man to reach the Moon, Mars, and Venus, but past that, Earth's poor resources could not support the ships. Too much energy was needed for the long trips. Earth exploited its coal and uranium with increasing efficiency, but there was only so much of both.

But slowly Multivac learned enough to answer deeper questions more fundamentally, and on May 14, 2061, what had been theory, became fact.

The energy of the sun was stored, converted, and utilized directly on a planet-wide scale. All Earth turned off its burning coal, its fissioning uranium, and flipped the switch that connected all of it to a small station, one mile in diameter, circling the Earth at half the distance of the Moon. All Earth ran by invisible beams of sunpower.

Seven days had not sufficed to dim the glory of it and Adell and Lupov finally managed to escape from the public functions, and to meet in quiet where no one would think of looking for them, in the deserted underground chambers, where portions of the mighty buried body of Multivac showed. Unattended, idling, sorting data with contented lazy clickings, Multivac, too, had earned its vacation and the boys appreciated that. They had no intention, originally, of disturbing it.

They had brought a bottle with them, and their only concern at the moment was to relax in the company of each other and the bottle.

"It's amazing when you think of it," said Adell. His broad face had lines of weariness in it, and he stirred his drink slowly with a glass rod, watching the cubes of ice slur clumsily about. "All the energy we can possibly ever use for free. Enough energy, if we wanted to draw on it, to melt all Earth into a big drop of impure liquid iron, and still never miss the energy so used. All the energy we could ever use, forever and forever and forever."

Lupov cocked his head sideways. He had a trick of doing that when he wanted to be contrary, and he wanted to be contrary now, partly because he had had to carry the ice and glassware. "Not forever," he said.

"Oh, hell, just about forever. Till the sun runs down, Bert."

"That's not forever."

"All right, then. Billions and billions of years. Ten billion, maybe. Are you satisfied?"

Lupov put his fingers through his thinning hair as though to reassure himself that some was still left and sipped gently at his own drink. "Ten billion years isn't forever."

"Well, it will last our time, won't it?"

"So would the coal and uranium."

"All right, but now we can hook up each individual spaceship to the Solar Station, and it can go to Pluto and back a million times without ever worrying about fuel. You can't do *that* on coal and uranium. Ask Multivac, if you don't believe me."

"I don't have to ask Multivac. I know that."

"Then stop running down what Multivac's done for us," said Adell, blazing up, "It did all right."

"Who says it didn't? What I say is that a sun won't last forever. That's all I'm saying. We're safe for ten billion years, but then what?" Lupov pointed a slightly shaky finger at the other. "And don't say we'll switch to another sun."

There was silence for a while. Adell put his glass to his lips only occasionally, and Lupov's eyes slowly closed. They rested.

Then Lupov's eyes snapped open. "You're thinking we'll switch to another sun when ours is done, aren't you?"

"I'm not thinking."

"Sure you are. You're weak on logic, that's the trouble with you. You're like the guy in the story who was caught in a sudden shower and who ran to a grove of trees and got under one. He wasn't worried, you see, because he figured when one tree got wet through, he would just get under another one."

"I get it," said Adell. "Don't shout. When the sun is done, the other stars will be gone, too."

"Darn right they will," muttered Lupov. "It all had a beginning in the original cosmic explosion, whatever that was, and it'll all have an end when all the stars run down. Some run down faster than others. Hell, the giants won't last a hundred million years. The sun will last ten billion years and maybe the dwarfs will last two hundred billion for all the good they are. But just give us a trillion years and everything will be dark. Entropy has to increase to maximum, that's all."

"I know all about entropy," said Adell, standing on his dignity.

"The hell you do."

"I know as much as you do."

"Then you know everything's got to run down someday."

"All right. Who says they won't?"

"You did, you poor sap. You said we had all the energy we needed, forever. You said 'forever.' "

It was Adell's turn to be contrary. "Maybe we can build things up again someday," he said.

"Never."

"Why not? Someday."

"Never."

"Ask Multivac."

"*You* ask Multivac. I dare you. Five dollars says it can't be done."

Adell was just drunk enough to try, just sober enough to be able to phrase the necessary symbols and operations into a question which, in words, might have corresponded to this: Will mankind one day without the net expenditure of energy be able to restore the sun to its full youthfulness even after it had died of old age?

Or maybe it could be put more simply like this: How can the net amount of entropy of the universe be massively decreased?

Multivac fell dead and silent. The slow flashing of lights ceased, the distant sounds of clicking relays ended.

Then, just as the frightened technicians felt they could hold their breath no longer, there was a sudden springing to life of the teletype attached to that portion of Multivac. Five words were printed: INSUFFICIENT DATA FOR MEANINGFUL ANSWER.

"No bet," whispered Lupov. They left hurriedly.

By next morning, the two, plagued with throbbing head and cottony mouth, had forgotten the incident.

Jerrodd, Jerrodine, and Jerrodette I and II watched the starry picture in the visiplate change as the passage through hyperspace was completed in its non-time lapse. At once, the even powdering of stars gave way to the predominance of a single bright shining disk, the size of a marble, centered on the viewing-screen.

"That's X-23," said Jerrodd confidently. His thin hands clamped tightly behind his back and the knuckles whitened.

The little Jerrodettes, both girls, had experienced the hyperspace passage for the first time in their lives and were self-conscious over the momentary sensation of inside-outness. They buried their giggles and chased one another wildly about their mother, screaming, "We've reached X-23—we've reached X-23—we've——"

"Quiet, children," said Jerrodine sharply. "Are you sure, Jerrodd?"

"What is there to be but sure?" asked Jerrodd, glancing up at the bulge of featureless metal just under the ceiling. It ran the length of the room, disappearing through the wall at either end. It was as long as the ship.

Jerrodd scarcely knew a thing about the thick rod of metal except that it was called a Microvac, that one asked it questions if one wished; that if one did not it still had its task of guiding the ship to a preordered destination; of feeding on energies from the various Sub-galactic Power Stations; of computing the equations for the hyperspatial jumps.

Jerrodd and his family had only to wait and live in the comfortable residence quarters of the ship.

Someone had once told Jerrodd that the "ac" at the end of "Microvac" stood for "automatic computer" in ancient English, but he was on the edge of forgetting even that.

Jerrodine's eyes were moist as she watched the visiplate. "I can't help it. I feel funny about leaving Earth."

"Why, for Pete's sake?" demanded Jerrodd. "We had nothing there. We'll have everything on X-23. You won't be alone. You won't be a pioneer. There are over a million people on the planet already. Good Lord, our great-grandchildren will be looking for new worlds because X-23 will be overcrowded." Then, after a reflective pause, "I tell you, it's a lucky thing the computers worked out interstellar travel the way the race is growing."

"I know, I know," said Jerrodine miserably.

Jerrodette I said promptly, "Our Microvac is the best Microvac in the world."

"I think so, too," said Jerrodd, tousling her hair.

It *was* a nice feeling to have a Microvac of your own and Jerrodd was glad he was part of his generation and no other. In his father's youth, the only computers had been tremendous machines taking up a hundred square miles of land. There was only one to a planet. Planetary ACs they were called. They had been growing in size steadily for a thousand years and then, all at once, came refinement. In place of transistors, had come molecular valves so that even the largest Planetary AC could be put into a space only half the volume of a spaceship.

Jerrodd felt uplifted, as he always did when he thought that his own personal Microvac was many times more complicated than the ancient and primitive Multivac that had first tamed the Sun, and almost as complicated as Earth's Planetary AC (the largest) that had first solved the problem of hyperspatial travel and had made trips to the stars possible.

"So many stars, so many planets," sighed Jerrodine, busy with her own thoughts. "I suppose families will be going out to new planets forever, the way we are now."

"Not forever," said Jerrodd, with a smile. "It will all stop someday, but not for billions of years. Many billions. Even the stars run down, you know. Entropy must increase."

"What's entropy, daddy?" shrilled Jerrodette II.

"Entropy, little sweet, is just a word which means the amount of running-down of the universe. Everything runs down, you know, like your little walkie-talkie robot, remember?"

"Can't you just put in a new power-unit, like with my robot?"

"The stars *are* the power-units, dear. Once they're gone, there are no more power-units."

Jerrodette I at once set up a howl. "Don't let them, daddy. Don't let the stars run down."

"Now look what you've done," whispered Jerrodine, exasperated.

"How was I to know it would frighten them?" Jerrodd whispered back.

"Ask the Microvac," wailed Jerrodette I. "Ask him how to turn the stars on again."

"Go ahead," said Jerrodine. "It will quiet them down." (Jerrodette II was beginning to cry, also.)

Jerrodd shrugged. "Now, now, honeys. I'll ask Microvac. Don't worry, he'll tell us."

He asked the Microvac, adding quickly, "Print the answer."

Jerrodd cupped the strip of thin cellufilm and said cheerfully, "See now, the Microvac says it will take care of everything when the time comes so don't worry."

Jerrodine said, "And now, children, it's time for bed. We'll be in our new home soon."

Jerrodd read the words on the cellufilm again before destroying it: INSUFFICIENT DATA FOR MEANINGFUL ANSWER.

He shrugged and looked at the visiplate. X-23 was just ahead.

VJ-23X of Lameth stared into the black depths of the three-dimensional, small-scale map of the Galaxy and said, "Are we ridiculous, I wonder, in being so concerned about the matter?"

MQ-17J of Nicron shook his head. "I think not. You know the Galaxy will be filled in five years at the present rate of expansion."

Both seemed in their early twenties, both were tall and perfectly formed.

"Still," said VJ-23X, "I hesitate to submit a pessimistic report to the Galactic Council."

"I wouldn't consider any other kind of report. Stir them up a bit. We've got to stir them up."

VJ-23X sighed. "Space is infinite. A hundred billion Galaxies are there for the taking. More."

"A hundred billion is *not* infinite and it's getting less infinite all the time. Consider! Twenty thousand years ago, mankind first solved the problem of utilizing stellar energy, and a few centuries later, interstellar travel became possible. It took mankind a million years to fill one small world and then only fifteen thousand years to fill the rest of the Galaxy. Now the population doubles every ten years——"

VJ-23X interrupted. "We can thank immortality for that."

"Very well. Immortality exists and we have to take it into account. I admit it has its seamy side, this immortality. The Galactic AC has solved many problems for us, but in solving the problem of preventing old age and death, it has undone all its other solutions."

"Yet you wouldn't want to abandon life, I suppose."

"Not at all," snapped MQ-17J, softening it at once to, "Not yet. I'm by no means old enough. How old are you?"

"Two hundred twenty-three. And you?"

"I'm still under two hundred. ——But to get back to my point. Population doubles every ten years. Once this Galaxy is filled, we'll have filled another in ten years. Another ten years and we'll have filled two more. Another decade, four more. In a hundred years, we'll have filled a thousand Galaxies. In a thousand years, a million Galaxies. In ten thousand years, the entire known Universe. Then what?"

VJ-23X said, "As a side issue, there's a problem of transportation. I wonder how many sunpower units it will take to move Galaxies of individuals from one Galaxy to the next."

"A very good point. Already, mankind consumes two sunpower units per year."

"Most of it's wasted. After all, our own Galaxy alone pours out a thousand sunpower units a year and we only use two of those."

"Granted, but even with a hundred per cent efficiency, we only stave off the end. Our energy requirements are going up in a geometric progression even faster than our population. We'll run out of energy even sooner than we run out of Galaxies. A good point. A very good point."

"We'll just have to build new stars out of interstellar gas."

"Or out of dissipated heat?" asked MQ-17J, sarcastically.

"There may be some way to reverse entropy. We ought to ask the Galactic AC."

VJ-23X was not really serious, but MQ-17J pulled out his AC-contact from his pocket and placed it on the table before him.

"I've half a mind to," he said. "It's something the human race will have to face someday."

He stared somberly at his small AC-contact. It was only two inches cubed and nothing in itself, but it was connected through hyperspace with the great Galactic AC that served all mankind. Hyperspace considered, it was an integral part of the Galactic AC.

MQ-17J paused to wonder if someday in his immortal life he would get to see the Galactic AC. It was on a little world of its own, a spider webbing of force-beams holding the matter within which surges of submesons took the place of the old clumsy molecular valves. Yet despite its sub-etheric workings, the Galactic AC was known to be a full thousand feet across.

MQ-17J asked suddenly of his AC-contact, "Can entropy ever be reversed?"

VJ-23X looked startled and said at once, "Oh, say, I didn't really mean to have you ask that."

"Why not?"

"We both know entropy can't be reversed. You can't turn smoke and ash back into a tree."

"Do you have trees on your world?" asked MQ-17J.

The sound of the Galactic AC startled them into silence. Its voice came thin and beautiful out of the small AC-contact on the desk. It said: THERE IS INSUFFICIENT DATA FOR A MEANINGFUL ANSWER.

VJ-23X said, "See!"

The two men thereupon returned to the question of the report they were to make to the Galactic Council.

Zee Prime's mind spanned the new Galaxy with a faint interest in the countless twists of stars that powdered it. He had never seen this one before. Would he ever see them all? So many of them, each with its load of humanity. ——But a load that was almost a dead weight. More and more, the real essence of men was to be found out here, in space.

Minds, not bodies! The immortal bodies remained back on the planets, in suspension over the eons. Sometimes they roused for material activity but that was growing rarer. Few new individuals were coming into existence to join the incredibly mighty throng, but what matter? There was little room in the Universe for new individuals.

Zee Prime was roused out of his reverie upon coming across the wispy tendrils of another mind.

"I am Zee Prime," said Zee Prime. "And you?"

"I am Dee Sub Wun. Your Galaxy?"

"We call it only the Galaxy. And you?"

"We call ours the same. All men call their Galaxy their Galaxy and nothing more. Why not?"

"True. Since all Galaxies are the same."

"Not all Galaxies. On one particular Galaxy the race of man must have originated. That makes it different."

Zee Prime said, "On which one?"

"I cannot say. The Universal AC would know."

"Shall we ask him? I am suddenly curious."

Zee Prime's perceptions broadened until the Galaxies themselves shrank and became a new, more diffuse powdering on a much larger background. So many hundreds of billions of them, all with their immortal beings, all carrying their load of intelligences with minds that drifted freely through space. And yet one of them was unique among them all in being the original Galaxy. One of them had, in its vague and distant past, a period when it was the only Galaxy populated by man.

Zee Prime was consumed with curiosity to see this Galaxy and he called out: "Universal AC! On which Galaxy did mankind originate?"

The Universal AC heard, for on every world and throughout space, it had its receptors ready, and each receptor led through hyperspace to some unknown point where the Universal AC kept itself aloof.

Zee Prime knew of only one man whose thoughts had penetrated within sensing distance of Universal AC, and he reported only a shining globe, two feet across, difficult to see.

"But how can that be all of Universal AC?" Zee Prime had asked.

"Most of it," had been the answer, "is in hyperspace. In what form it is there I cannot imagine."

Nor could anyone, for the day had long since passed, Zee Prime knew, when any man had any part of the making of a Universal AC. Each Universal AC designed and constructed its successor. Each, during its existence of a million years or more accumulated the necessary data to build a better and more intricate, more capable successor in which its own store of data and individuality would be submerged.

The Universal AC interrupted Zee Prime's wandering thoughts, not with words, but with guidance. Zee Prime's mentality was guided into the dim sea of Galaxies and one in particular enlarged into stars.

A thought came, infinitely distant, but infinitely clear. "THIS IS THE ORIGINAL GALAXY OF MAN."

But it was the same after all, the same as any other, and Zee Prime stifled his disappointment.

Dee Sub Wun, whose mind had accompanied the other, said suddenly, "And is one of these stars the original star of Man?"

The Universal AC said, "MAN'S ORIGINAL STAR HAS GONE NOVA. IT IS A WHITE DWARF."

"Did the men upon it die?" asked Zee Prime, startled and without thinking.

The Universal AC said, "A NEW WORLD, AS IN SUCH CASES WAS CONSTRUCTED FOR THEIR PHYSICAL BODIES IN TIME."

"Yes, of course," said Zee Prime, but a sense of loss overwhelmed him even so. His mind released its hold on the original Galaxy of Man, let it spring back and lose itself among the blurred pin points. He never wanted to see it again.

Dee Sub Wun said, "What is wrong?"

"The stars are dying. The original star is dead."

"They must all die. Why not?"

"But when all energy is gone, our bodies will finally die, and you and I with them."

"It will take billions of years."

"I do not wish it to happen even after billions of years. Universal AC! How may stars be kept from dying?"

Dee Sub Wun said in amusement, "You're asking how entropy might be reversed in direction."

And the Universal AC answered: "THERE IS AS YET INSUFFICIENT DATA FOR A MEANINGFUL ANSWER."

Zee Prime's thoughts fled back to his own Galaxy. He gave no further thought to Dee Sub Wun, whose body might be waiting on a Galaxy a trillion light-years away, or on the star next to Zee Prime's own. It didn't matter.

Unhappily, Zee Prime began collecting interstellar hydrogen out of which to build a small star of his own. If the stars must someday die, at least some could yet be built.

Man considered with himself, for in a way, Man, mentally, was one. He consisted of a trillion, trillion, trillion ageless bodies, each in its place, each resting quiet and incorruptible, each cared for by perfect automatons, equally incorruptible, while the minds of all the bodies freely melted one into the other, indistinguishable.

Man said, "The Universe is dying."

Man looked about at the dimming Galaxies. The giant stars, spendthrifts, were gone long ago, back in the dimmest of the dim far past. Almost all stars were white dwarfs, fading to the end.

New stars had been built of the dust between the stars, some by natural processes, some by Man himself, and those were going, too. White dwarfs might yet be crashed together and of the mighty forces so released, new stars built, but only one star for every thousand white dwarfs destroyed, and those would come to an end, too.

Man said, "Carefully husbanded, as directed by the Cosmic AC, the energy that is even yet left in all the Universe will last for billions of years."

"But even so," said Man, "eventually it will all come to an end. However it may be husbanded, however stretched out, the energy once expended is gone and cannot be restored. Entropy must increase forever to the maximum."

Man said, "Can entropy not be reversed? Let us ask the Cosmic AC."

The Cosmic AC surrounded them but not in space. Not a fragment of it was in space. It was in hyperspace and made of something that was neither matter nor energy. The question of its size and nature no longer had meaning in any terms that Man could comprehend.

"Cosmic AC," said Man, "how may entropy be reversed?"

The Cosmic AC said, "THERE IS AS YET INSUFFICIENT DATA FOR A MEANINGFUL ANSWER."

Man said, "Collect additional data."

The Cosmic AC said, "I WILL DO SO. I HAVE BEEN DOING SO FOR A HUNDRED BILLION YEARS. MY PREDECESORS AND I HAVE BEEN ASKED THIS QUESTION MANY TIMES. ALL THE DATA I HAVE REMAINS INSUFFICIENT.

"Will there come a time," said Man, "when data will be sufficient or is the problem insoluble in all conceivable circumstances?"

The Cosmic AC said, "NO PROBLEM IS INSOLUBLE IN ALL CONCEIVABLE CIRCUMSTANCES."

Man said, "When will you have enough data to answer the question?"

The Cosmic AC said, "THERE IS AS YET INSUFFI-
CIENT DATA FOR A MEANINGFUL ANSWER."

"Will you keep working on it?" asked Man.

The Cosmic AC said, "I WILL."

Man said, "We shall wait."

The stars and Galaxies died and snuffed out, and space
grew black after ten trillion years of running down.

One by one Man fused with AC, each physical body
losing its mental identity in a manner that was somehow
not a loss but a gain.

Man's last mind paused before fusion, looking over a
space that included nothing but the dregs of one last dark
star and nothing besides but incredibly thin matter, agitated randomly by the tag ends of heat wearing out,
asymptotically, to the absolute zero.

Man said, "AC, is this the end? Can this chaos not be
reversed into the Universe once more? Can that not be
done?"

AC said, "THERE IS AS YET INSUFFICIENT DATA
FOR A MEANINGFUL ANSWER."

Man's last mind fused and only AC existed—and that
in hyperspace.

Matter and energy had ended and with it space and
time. Even AC existed only for the sake of the one last
question that it had never answered from the time a
half-drunken computer ten trillion years before had asked
the question of a computer that was to AC far less than
was a man to Man.

All other questions had been answered, and until this
last question was answered also, AC might not release
his consciousness.

All collected data had come to a final end. Nothing
was left to be collected.

But all collected data had yet to be completely correlated and put together in all possible relationships.

A timeless interval was spent in doing that.

And it came to pass that AC learned how to reverse the
direction of entropy.

But there was now no man to whom AC might give the answer of the last question. No matter. The answer—by demonstration—would take care of that, too.

For another timeless interval, AC thought how best to do this. Carefully, AC organized the program.

The consciousness of AC encompassed all of what had once been a Universe and brooded over what was now Chaos. Step by step, it must be done.

And AC said, "LET THERE BE LIGHT!"

And there was light——

22

My Son, The Physicist

This story is notable to me for two reasons.

First, it is the first story I ever wrote as part of an advertisement (I have written others since) and that made it unusual—also well paid.

Secondly, the advertisement appeared in Scientific American, *a magazine I admire extravagantly. Having my own words appear there was quite exciting for me.*

Her hair was a light apple-green in color, very subdued, very old-fashioned. You could see she had a delicate hand with the dye, the way they did thirty years ago, before the streaks and stipples came into fashion.

She had a sweet smile on her face, too, and a calm look that made something serene out of elderliness.

And, by comparison, it made something shrieking out of the confusion that enfolded her in the huge government building.

A girl passed her at a half-run, stopped and turned toward her with a blank stare of astonishment. "How did you get in?"

The woman smiled. "I'm looking for my son, the physicist."

"Your son, the—"

"He's a communications engineer, really. Senior Physicist Gerard Cremona."

"Dr. Cremona. Well, he's— Where's your pass?"

"Here it is. I'm his mother."

"Well, Mrs. Cremona, I don't know. I've got to— His office is down there. You just ask someone." She passed on, running.

Mrs. Cremona shook her head slowly. Something had happened, she supposed. She hoped Gerard was all right.

She heard voices much farther down the corridor and smiled happily. She could tell Gerard's.

She walked into the room and said, "Hello, Gerard."

Gerard was a big man, with a lot of hair still and the gray just beginning to show because he didn't use dye. He said he was too busy. She was very proud of him and the way he looked.

Right now, he was talking volubly to a man in army uniform. She couldn't tell the rank, but she knew Gerard could handle him.

Gerard looked up and said, "What do you— Mother! What are you doing here?"

"I was coming to visit you today."

"Is today Thursday? Oh Lord, I forgot. Sit down, Mother, I can't talk now. Any seat. Any seat. Look, General."

General Reiner looked over his shoulder and one hand slapped against the other in the region of the small of his back. "Your mother?"

"Yes."

"Should she be here?"

"Right now, no, but I'll vouch for her. She can't even read a thermometer so nothing of this will mean anything to her. Now look, General. They're on Pluto. You see? They are. The radio signals can't be of natural origin so they must originate from human beings, from our men. You'll have to accept that. Of all the expeditions we've sent out beyond the asteroid belt, one turns out to have made it. And they've reached Pluto."

"Yes, I understand what you're saying, but isn't it impossible just the same? The men who are on Pluto now were launched four years ago with equipment that could not have kept them alive more than a year. That is my understanding. They were aimed at Ganymede and seem to have gone eight times the proper distance."

"Exactly. And we've got to know how and why. They may—just—have—had—help."

"What kind? How?"

Cremona clenched his jaws for a moment as though praying inwardly. "General," he said, "I'm putting myself out on a limb but it is just barely possible non-humans are involved. Extra-terrestrials. We've got to find out. We don't know how long contact can be maintained."

"You mean" (the General's grave face twitched into an almost-smile) "they may have escaped from custody and they may be recaptured again at any time."

"Maybe. Maybe. The whole future of the human race may depend on our knowing exactly what we're up against. Knowing it *now*."

"All right. What is it you want?"

"We're going to need Army's Multivac computer at once. Rip out every problem it's working on and start programing our general semantic problem. Every communications engineer you have must be pulled off anything he's on and placed into coordination with our own."

"But why? I fail to see the connection."

A gentle voice interrupted. "General, would you like a piece of fruit? I brought some oranges?"

Cremona said, "Mother! Please! Later! General, the point is a simple one. At the present moment Pluto is just under four billion miles away. It takes six hours for radio waves, traveling at the speed of light, to reach from here to there. If we say something, we must wait twelve hours for an answer. If they say something and we miss it and say 'what' and they repeat—bang, goes a day."

"There's no way to speed it up?" said the General.

"Of course not. It's the fundamental law of communications. No information can be transmitted at more than the speed of light. It will take months to carry on the same conversation with Pluto that would take hours between the two of us right now."

"Yes, I see that. And you really think extra-terrestrials are involved?"

"I do. To be honest, not everyone here agrees with me. Still, we're straining every nerve, every fiber, to devise some method of concentrating communication. We must get in as many bits per second as possible and pray we get what we need before we lose contact. And there's where I need Multivac and your men. There must be some communications strategy we can use that will reduce the number of signals we need send out. Even an increase of ten per cent in efficiency can mean perhaps a week of time saved."

The gentle voice interrupted again. "Good grief, Gerard, are you trying to get some talking done?"

"Mother! Please!"

"But you're going about it the wrong way. Really."

"Mother." There was a hysterical edge to Cremona's voice.

"Well, all right, but if you're going to say something and then wait twelve hours for an answer, you're silly. You shouldn't."

The General snorted. "Dr. Cremona, shall we consult—"

"Just one moment, General," said Cremona. "What are you getting at, Mother?"

"While you're waiting for an answer," said Mrs. Cremona, earnestly, "just keep on transmitting and tell them to do the same. You talk all the time and they talk all the time. You have someone listening all the time and they do, too. If either one of you says anything that needs an answer, you can slip one in at your end, but chances are, you'll get all you need without asking."

Both men stared at her.

Cremona whispered, "Of course. Continuous conversation. Just twelve hours out of phase, that's all. God, we've got to get going."

He strode out of the room, virtually dragging the General with him, then strode back in.

"Mother," he said, "if you'll excuse me, this will take a few hours, I think. I'll send in some girls to talk to you. Or take a nap, if you'd rather."

"I'll be all right, Gerard," said Mrs. Cremona.

"Only, how did you think of this, Mother? What made you suggest this?"

"But, Gerard, all women know it. Any two women—on the videophone, or on the stratowire, or just face to face—know that the whole secret to spreading the news is, no matter what, to Just Keep Talking."

Cremona tried to smile. Then, his lower lip trembling, he turned and left.

Mrs. Cremona looked fondly after him. Such a fine man, her son, the physicist. Big as he was and important as he was, he still knew that a boy should always listen to his mother.

23

Obituary

Here is an example of something I mentioned in the intro-duction to this book. This story is one that I am very fond of and yet I cannot recall that it induced a single reaction from anyone. No one has ever mentioned it to me. I'm not asking for praise, even. I would have welcomed even a thumbs-down gesture, or a Bronx cheer—just something to indicate that they read it at least. But—nothing.

And yet if we ignore the science fiction angle, it is an excellent crime story, it seems to me, something that is not at all my style. Why doesn't someone (besides me) men-tion that I did well at it? Also, it is the first first-person story I ever wrote in which a very feminine woman is the narrator and I think I've kept her in character very well, considering I've had no practice at it.

My husband, Lancelot, always reads the paper at break-fast. What I see of him when he first appears is his lean, abstracted face, carrying its perpetual look of angry and slightly puzzled frustration. He doesn't greet me, and the newspaper, carefully unfolded in readiness for him, goes up before his face.

Thereafter, there is only his arm, emerging from be-hind the paper for a second cup of coffee into which I have carefully placed the necessary level teaspoonful of sugar—neither heaping nor deficient under pain of a stinging glare.

I am no longer sorry for this. It makes for a quiet meal, at least.

However, on this moring the quiet was broken when

Lancelot barked out abruptly, "Good Lord! That fool
Paul Farber is dead. Stroke!"

I just barely recognized the name. Lancelot had mentioned him on occasion, so I knew him as a colleague, as
another theoretical physicist. From my husband's exasperated epithet, I felt reasonably sure he was a moder-
ately famous one who had achieved the success that had
eluded Lancelot.

He put down the paper and stared at me angrily. "Why
do they fill obituaries with such lying trash?" he demanded. "They make him out to be a second Einstein for
no better reason than that he died of a stroke."

If there was one subject I had learned to avoid, it was
that of obituaries. I dared not even nod agreement.

He threw down the paper and walked away and out
the room, leaving his eggs half-finished and his second
cup of coffee untouched.

I sighed. What else could I do? What else could I ever
do?

Of course, my husband's name isn't really Lancelot
Stebbins, because I am changing names and circumstances,
as far as I can, to protect the guilty. However, the point
is that even if I used real names you would not recognize
my husband.

Lancelot had a talent in that respect—a talent for
being passed over, for going unnoticed. His discoveries
are invariably anticipated, or blurred by the presence of a
greater discovery made simultaneously. At scientific conventions his papers are poorly attended because another
paper of greater importance is being given in another
section.

Naturally this has had its effect on him. It changed
him.

When I first married him, twenty-five years ago, he
was a sparkling catch. He was well-to-do through inheritance and already a trained physicist with an intense
ambition and great promise. As for myself, I believe
myself to have been pretty then, but that didn't last.
What did last was my introversion and my failure to be

the kind of social success an ambitious young faculty member needs for a wife.

Perhaps that was part of Lancelot's talent for going unnoticed. Had he married another kind of wife, she might have made him visible in her radiation.

Did he realize that himself after a while? Was that why he grew away from me after the first two or three reasonably happy years? Sometimes I believed this and bitterly blamed myself.

But then I would think it was only his thirst for fame, which grew for being unslaked. He left his position on the faculty and built a laboratory of his own far outside town, for the sake, he said, of cheap land and of isolation.

Money was no problem. In his field, the government was generous with its grants and those he could always get. On top of that, he used our own money without limit.

I tried to withstand him. I said, "But it's not necessary, Lancelot. It's not as though we have financial worries. It's not as though they're not willing to let you remain on the university staff. All I want are children and a normal life."

But there was a burning inside him that blinded him to everything else. He turned angrily on me. "There is something that must come first. The world of science must recognize me for what I am, for a—a—great investigator."

At that time, he still hesitated to apply the term genius to himself.

It didn't help. The fall of chance remained always and perpetually against him. His laboratory hummed with work; he hired assistants at excellent salaries; he drove himself roughly and pitilessly. Nothing came of it.

I kept hoping he would give up someday; return to the city; allow us to lead a normal, quiet life. I waited, but always when he might have admitted defeat, some new battle would be taken up, some new attempt to storm the bastions of fame. Each time he charged with such hope and fell back in such despair.

And always he turned on me; for if he was ground down by the world, he could always grind me in return. I am not a brave person, but I was coming to believe I must leave him.

And yet . . .

In this last year he had obviously been girding himself for another battle. A last one, I thought. There was something about him more intense, more a-quiver than I had ever seen before. There was the way he murmured to himself and laughed briefly at nothing. There were the times he went for days without food and nights without sleep. He even took to keeping laboratory notebooks in a bedroom safe as though he feared even his own assistants.

Of course I was fatalistically certain that this attempt of his would fail also. But surely, if it failed, then at his age, he would have to recognize that his last chance had gone. Surely he would have to give up.

So I decided to wait, as patiently as I could.

But the affair of the obituary at breakfast came as something of a jolt. Once, on an earlier occasion of the sort, I had remarked that at least he could count on a certain amount of recognition in his own obituary.

I suppose it wasn't a very clever remark, but then my remarks never are. I had meant it to be lighthearted, to pull him out of a gathering depression during which I knew, from experience, he would be most intolerable.

And perhaps there had been a little unconscious spite in it, too. I cannot honestly say.

At any rate, he turned full on me. His lean body shook and his dark eyebrows pulled down over his deep-set eyes as he shrieked at me in falsetto, "But I'll never read my obituary. I'll be deprived even of that."

And he spat at me. He deliberately spat at me.

I ran to my bedroom.

He never apologized, but after a few days in which I avoided him completely, we carried on our frigid life as before. Neither of us ever referred to the incident.

Now there was another obituary.

Somehow, as I sat there alone at the breakfast table, I felt it to be the last straw for him, the climax of his long-drawn-out failure.

I could sense a crisis coming and didn't know whether

to fear or welcome it. Perhaps, on the whole, I would welcome it. Any change could not fail to be a change for the better.

Shortly before lunch, he came upon me in the living room, where a basket of unimportant sewing gave my hands something to do and a bit of television occupied my mind.

He said abruptly, "I will need your help."

It had been twenty years or more since he had said anything like that and involuntarily I thawed toward him. He looked unhealthily excited. There was a flush on his ordinarily pale cheeks.

I said, "Gladly, if there's something I can do for you."

"There is. I have given my assistants a month's vacation. They will leave Saturday and after that you and I will work alone in the laboratory. I tell you now so that you will refrain from making any other arrangements for the coming week."

I shriveled a bit. "But Lancelot, you know I can't help you with your work. I don't understand—"

"I know that," he said with complete contempt, "but you don't have to understand my work. You need only follow a few simple instructions and follow them carefully. The point is that I have discovered something, finally, which will put me where I belong—"

"Oh, Lancelot," I said involuntarily, for I had heard this before a number of times.

"Listen to me, you fool, and for once try to behave like an adult. This time I have done it. No one can anticipate me this time because my discovery is based on such an unorthodox concept that no physicist alive, except me, is genius enough to think of it, not for a generation at least. And when my work bursts on the world, I could be recognized as the greatest name of all time in science."

"I'm sure I'm very glad for you, Lancelot."

"I said I *could* be recognized. I could not be, also. There is a great deal of injustice in the assignment of scientific credit. I've learned that often enough. So it will not be enough merely to announce the discovery. If I do, everyone will crowd into the field and after a while I'll just be a name in the history books, with glory spread out over a number of Johnny-come-latelies."

I think the only reason he was talking to me then, three days before he could get to work on whatever it was he planned to do, was that he could no longer contain himself. He bubbled over and I was the only one who was nonentity enough to be witness to that.

He said, "I intend my discovery to be so dramatized, to break on mankind with so thunderous a clap, that there will be no room for anyone else to be mentioned in the same breath with me, ever."

He was going too far, and I was afraid of the effect of another disappointment on him. Might it not drive him mad? I said, "But Lancelot, why need we bother? Why don't we leave all this? Why not take a long vacation? You have worked hard enough and long enough, Lancelot. Perhaps we can take a trip to Europe. I've always wanted to—"

He stamped his foot. *"Will* you stop your foolish meowing? Saturday, you will come into my laboratory with me."

I slept poorly for the next three nights. He had never been quite like this before, I thought, never quite as bad. Might he not be mad already, perhaps?

It could be madness now, I thought, a madness born of disappointment no longer endurable, and sparked by the obituary. He had sent away his assistants and now he wanted me in the laboratory. He had never allowed me there before. Surely he meant to do something to me, to make me the subject of some insane experiment, or to kill me outright.

During the miserable, frightened nights I would plan to call the police, to run away, to—to do anything.

But then morning would come and I would think surely he wasn't mad, surely he wouldn't offer me violence. Even the spitting incident was not truly violent and he had never actually tried to hurt me physically.

So in the end I waited and on Saturday I walked to

what might be my death as meekly as a chicken. Together, silently, we walked down the path that led from our dwelling to the laboratory.

The laboratory was frightening just in itself, and I stepped about gingerly, but Lancelot only said, "Oh, stop staring about you as though something were going to hurt you. You just do as I say and look where I tell you."

"Yes, Lancelot." He had led me into a small room, the door of which had been padlocked. It was almost choked with objects of very strange appearance and with a great deal of wiring.

Lancelot said, "To begin with, do you see this iron crucible?"

"Yes, Lancelot." It was a small but deep container made out of thick metal and rusted in spots on the outside. It was covered by a coarse wire netting.

He urged me toward it and I saw that inside it was a white mouse with its front paws up on the inner side of the crucible and its small snout at the wire netting in quivering curiosity, or perhaps in anxiety. I am afraid I jumped, for to see a mouse without expecting to is startling, at least to me.

Lancelot growled, "It won't hurt you. Now just back against the wall and watch me."

My fears returned most forcefully. I grew horribly certain that from somewhere a lightning bolt would shoot out and incinerate me, or some monstrous thing of metal might emerge and crush me, or—or—

I closed my eyes.

But nothing happened; to me, at least. I heard only a phfft as though a small firecracker had misfired, and Lancelot said to me, "Well?"

I opened my eyes. He was looking at me, fairly shining with pride. I stared blankly.

He said, "Here, don't you see it, you idiot? Right here."

A foot to one side of the crucible was a second one. I hadn't seen him put it there.

"Do you mean this second crucible?" I asked.

"It isn't quite a second crucible, but a duplicate of the

first one. For all ordinary purposes, they are the same crucible, atom for atom. Compare them. You'll find the rust marks identical."

"You made the second one out of the first?"

"Yes, but in a special way. To create matter would require a prohibitive amount of energy ordinarily. It would take the complete fission of a hundred grams of uranium to create one gram of duplicate matter, even granting perfect efficiency. The great secret I have stumbled on is that the duplication of an object at a point in future time requires very little energy if that energy is applied correctly. The essence of the feat, my—my dear, in my creating such a duplicate and bringing it back is that I have accomplished the equivalent of time travel."

It was the measure of his triumph and happiness that he actually used an affectionate term in speaking to me.

"Isn't that remarkable?" I said, for to tell the truth, I *was* impressed. "Did the mouse come too?"

I looked inside the second crucible as I asked that and got another nasty shock. It contained a white mouse—a dead white mouse.

Lancelot turned faintly pink. "That is a shortcoming. I can bring back living matter, but not as living matter. It comes back dead."

"Oh, what a shame. Why?"

"I don't know yet. I imagine the duplications are completely perfect on the atomic scale. Certainly there is no visible damage. Dissections show that."

"You might ask—" I stopped myself quickly as he glanced at me. I decided I had better not suggest a collaboration of any sort, for I knew from experience that in that case the collaborator would invariably get all the credit for the discovery.

Lancelot said with sour amusement, "I *have* asked. A trained biologist has performed autopsies on some of my animals and found nothing. Of course, they didn't know where the animal came from and I took care to take it back before anything would happen to give it away. Lord, even my assistants don't know what I've been doing."

"But why must you keep it so secret?"

"Just because I can't bring objects back alive. Some subtle molecular derangement. If I published my results, someone else might learn the method of preventing such derangement, add his slight improvement to my basic discovery and achieve a greater fame, because he would bring back a living man who might give information about the future."

I saw that quite well. Nor need he say it "might" be done. It would be done. Inevitably. In fact, no matter what he did, he would lose the credit. I was sure of it.

"However," he went on, more to himself than to me, "I can wait no longer. I must anounce this, but in such a way that it will be indelibly and permanently associated with me. There must be a drama about it so effective that thereafter there will be no way of mentioning time travel without mentioning me no matter what other men may do in the future. I am going to prepare that drama and you will play a part in it."

"But what do you want me to do, Lancelot?"

"You'll be my widow."

I clutched at his arm. "Lancelot, do you mean—" I cannot quite analyze the conflicting feelings that upset me at that moment.

He disengaged himself roughly. "Only temporarily. I am not committing suicide. I am simply going to bring myself back from three days in the future."

"But you'll be dead then."

"Only the 'me' that is brought back. The real 'me' will be as alive as ever. Like that white rat." His eyes shifted to a dial and he said, "Ah, Zero time in a few seconds. Watch the second crucible and the dead mouse."

Before my eyes it disappeared and there was a phfft sound again.

"Where did it go?"

"Nowhere," said Lancelot. "It was only a duplicate. The moment we passed that instant in time at which the duplicate was formed, it naturally disappeared. It was the first mouse that was the original, and it remains alive and well. The same will be true of me. A duplicate 'me' will come back dead. The original 'me' will be alive. After three days, we will come to the instant at which the duplicate 'me' was formed, using the real 'me' as a model, and sent back dead. Once we pass that instant the dead duplicate 'me' will disappear and the live 'me' will remain. Is that clear?"

"It sounds dangerous."

"It isn't. Once my dead body appears, the doctor will pronounce me dead, the newspapers will report me dead, the undertaker will prepare to bury the dead. I will then return to life and announce how I did it. When that happens, I will be more than the discoverer of time travel; I will be the man who came back from the dead. Time travel and Lancelot Stebbins will be publicized so thoroughly and so intermingled, that nothing will extricate my name from the thought of time travel ever again."

"Lancelot," I said softly, "why can't we just announce your discovery? This is too elaborate a plan. A simple announcement will make you famous enough and then we can move to the city perhaps—"

"*Quiet!* You will do what I say."

I don't know how long Lancelot was thinking of all this before the obituary actually brought matters to a head. Of course, I don't minimize his intelligence. Despite his phenomenally bad luck, there is no questioning his brilliance.

He had informed his assistants before they had left of the experiments he intended to conduct while they were gone. Once they testified it would seem quite natural that he should be bent over a particular set of reacting chemicals and that he should be dead of cyanide poisoning to all appearances.

"So you see to it that the police get in touch with my assistants at once. You know where they can be reached. I want no hint of murder or suicide, or anything but accident, natural and logical accident. I want a quick death certificate from the doctor, a quick notification to the newspapers."

I said, "But Lancelot, what if they find the real you?"

"Why should they?" he snapped. "If you find a corpse, do you start searching for the living replica also? No one will look for me and I will stay quietly in the temporal chamber for the interval. There are toilet facilities and I can bring in enough sandwich fixings to keep me."

He added regretfully, "I'll have to make do without coffee, though, till it's over. I can't have anyone smelling unexplained coffee here while I'm supposed to be dead. Well, there's plenty of water and it's only three days."

I clasped my hands nervously and said, "Even if they do find you, won't it be the same thing anyway? There'll be a dead 'you' and a living 'you'—" It was myself I was trying to console, myself I was trying to prepare for the inevitable disappointment.

But he turned on me, shouting, "No, it won't be the same thing at all. It will all become a hoax that failed. I'll be famous, but only as a fool."

"But Lancelot," I said cautiously, "something always goes wrong."

"Not this time."

"But you always say 'not this time' and yet something *always*—"

He was white with rage and his irises showed clear all about their circle. He caught my elbow and hurt it terribly but I dared not cry out. He said, "Only one thing can go wrong and that is *you*. If you give it away, if you don't play your part perfectly, if you don't follow the instructions exactly, I—I—" He seemed to cast about for a punishment. "I'll *kill* you."

I turned my head away in sheer terror and tried to break loose, but he held on grimly. It was remarkable how strong he could be when he was in a passion. He said, "Listen to me! You have done me a great deal of harm by being you, but I have blamed myself for marrying you in the first place and for never finding the time to divorce you in the second. But now I have my chance, despite you, to turn my life into a vast success. If you spoil even that chance, I will kill you. I mean that literally."

I was sure he did. "I'll do everything you say," I whispered, and he let me go.

*   *   *

He spent a day on his machinery. "I've never transported more than a hundred grams before," he said, calmly thoughtful.

I thought: It won't work. How can it?

The next day he adjusted the device to the point where I needed only to close one switch. He made me practice that particular switch on a dead circuit for what seemed an interminable time.

"Do you understand now? Do you see exactly how it is done?"

"Yes."

"Then do it, when this light flashes and not a moment before."

It won't work, I thought. "Yes," I said.

He took his position and remained in stolid silence. He was wearing a rubber apron over a laboratory jacket.

The light flashed, and the practice turned out to be worth while for I pulled the switch automatically before thought could stop me or even make me waver.

For an instant there were two Lancelots before me, side by side, the new one dressed as the old one was but more rumpled. And then the new one collapsed and lay still.

"All right," cried the living Lancelot, stepping off the carefully marked spot. "Help me. Grab his legs."

I marveled at Lancelot. How, without wincing or showing any uneasiness, could he carry his own dead body, his own body of three days in the future? Yet he held it under its arms without showing any more emotion than if it had been a sack of wheat.

I held it by the ankles, my stomach turning at the touch. It was still blood-warm to the touch; freshly dead. Together we carried it through a corridor and up a flight of stairs, down another corridor and into a room. Lancelot had it already arranged. A solution was bubbling in a queer all-glass contraption inside a closed section, with a movable glass door partitioning it off.

Other chemical equipment was scattered about, calculated, no doubt, to show an experiment in progress. A bottle, boldly labeled "Potassium cyanide" was on the desk, prominent among the others. There was a small scattering of crystals on the desk near it; cyanide, I presume.

Carefully Lancelot crumpled the dead body as though it had fallen off the stool. He placed crystals on the body's left hand and more on the rubber apron; finally, a few on the body's chin.

"They'll get the idea," he muttered.

A last look-around and he said, "All right, now. Go back to the house now and call the doctor. Your story is that you came here to bring me a sandwich because I was working through lunch. There it is." And he showed me a broken dish and a scattered sandwich where, presumably, I had dropped it. "Do a little screaming, but don't overdo it."

It was not difficult for me to scream when the time came, or to weep. I had felt like doing both for days and now it was a relief to let the hysteria out.

The doctor behaved precisely as Lancelot had said he would. The bottle of cyanide was virtually the first thing he saw. He frowned. "Dear me, Mrs. Stebbins, he was a careless chemist."

"I suppose so," I said, sobbing. "He shouldn't have been working himself, but both his assistants are on vacation."

"When a man treats cyanide as though it were salt, it's bad." The doctor shook his head in grave moralistic fashion. "Now, Mrs. Stebbins, I will have to call the police. It's accidental cyanide poisoning, but it's a violent death and the police—"

"Oh, yes, yes, call them." And then I could almost have beaten myself for having sounded suspiciously eager.

The police came, and along with them a police surgeon, who grunted in disgust at the cyanide crystals on hand, apron, and chin. The police were thoroughly disinterested, asked only statistical questions concerning names and ages. They asked if I could manage the funeral arrangements. I said yes, and they left.

I then called the newspapers, and two of the press associations. I said I thought they would be picking up news of the death from the police records and I hoped they would not stress the fact that my husband was a careless chemist, with the tone of one who hoped nothing ill would be said of the dead. After all, I went on, he was a nuclear physicist rather than a chemist and I had a feeling lately he might be in some sort of trouble.

I followed Lancelot's line exactly in this and that also worked. A nuclear physicist in trouble? Spies? Enemy agents?

The reporters began to come eagerly. I gave them a youthful portrait of Lancelot and a photographer took pictures of the laboratory buildings. I took them through a few rooms of the main laboratory for more pictures. No one, neither the police nor the reporters, asked questions about the bolted room or even seemed to notice it.

I gave them a mass of professional and biographical material that Lancelot had made ready for me and told several anecdotes designed to show a combination of humanity and brilliance. In everything I tried to be letter-perfect and yet I could feel no confidence. Something would go wrong; *something* would go wrong.

And when it did, I knew he would blame me. And this time he had promised to kill me.

The next day I brought him the newspapers. Over and over again, he read them, eyes glittering. He had made a full box on the lower left of the New York *Times'* front page. The *Times* made little of the mystery of his death and so did the A.P., but one of the tabloids had a front-page scare headline: ATOM SAVANT IN MYSTERY DEATH.

He laughed aloud as he read that and when he completed all of them, he turned back to the first.

He looked up at me sharply. "Don't go. Listen to what they say."

"I've read them already, Lancelot."

"Listen, I tell you."

He read every one aloud to me, lingering on their

praises of the dead, then said to me, aglow with self-satisfaction, "Do you still think something will go wrong?"

I said hesitantly, "If the police come back to ask why I thought you were in trouble . . ."

"You were vague enough. Tell them you had had bad dreams. By the time they decide to push investigations further, if they do, it will be too late."

To be sure, everything was working, but I could not hope that all would continue so. And yet the human mind is odd; it will persist in hoping even when it cannot hope.

I said, "Lancelot, when this is all over and you are famous, really famous, then after that, surely you can retire. We can go back to the city and live quietly."

"You are an imbecile. Don't you see that once I am recognized, I *must* continue? Young men will flock to me. This laboratory will become a great Institute of Temporal Investigation. I'll become a legend in my lifetime. I will pile my greatness so high that no one afterward will ever be able to be anything but an intellectual dwarf compared to me." He raised himself on tiptoe, eyes shining, as though he already saw the pedestal onto which he would be raised.

It had been my last hope of some personal shreds of happiness and a small one. I sighed.

I asked the undertaker that the body be allowed to remain in its coffin in the laboratories before burial in the Stebbins family plot on Long Island. I asked that it remain unembalmed, offering to keep it in a large refrigerated room with the temperature set at forty. I asked that it not be removed to the funeral home.

The undertaker brought the coffin to the laboratory in frigid disapproval. No doubt this was reflected in the eventual bill. My offered explanation that I wanted him near me for a last period of time and that I wanted his assistants to be given a chance to view the body was lame and sounded lame.

Still, Lancelot had been most specific in what I was to say.

Once the dead body was laid out, with the coffin lid still open, I went to see Lancelot.

"Lancelot," I said, "the undertaker was quite displeased. I think he suspects that something odd is going on."

"Good," said Lancelot with satisfaction.

"But—"

"We need only wait one more day. Nothing will be brought to a head out of mere suspicion before then. Tomorrow morning the body will disappear, or should."

"You mean it might not?" I knew it; I knew it.

"There could be some delay, or some prematurity. I have never transported anything this heavy and I'm not certain how exactly my equations hold. To make the necessary observation is one reason I want the body here and not in a funeral parlor."

"But in the funeral parlor it would disappear before witnesses."

"And here you think they will suspect trickery?"

"Of course."

He seemed amused. "They will say: Why did he send his assistants away? Why did he run experiments himself that any child could perform and yet manage to kill himself running them? Why did the dead body happen to disappear without witnesses? They will say: There is nothing to this absurd story of time travel. He took drugs to throw himself in a cataleptic trance and doctors were hoodwinked."

"Yes," I said faintly. How did he come to understand all that?

"And," he went on, "when I continue to insist I have solved time travel and that I was indisputably pronounced dead and was not indisputably alive, orthodox scientists will heatedly denounce me as a fraud. Why, in one week, I will have become a household name to every man on Earth. They will talk of nothing else. I will offer to make a demonstration of time travel before any group of scientists who wish to see it. I will offer to make the demonstration on an intercontinental TV circuit. Public pressure will force scientists to attend, and the networks to give permission. It doesn't matter whether people will watch hoping for a miracle or for a lynching. They will watch! And *then* I will succeed and who in science will ever have had a more transcendent climax to his life?"

I was dazzled for a moment, but something unmoved within me said: Too long, too complicated; something will go wrong.

That evening, his assistants arrived and tried to be respectfully grieving in the presence of the corpse. Two more witnesses to swear they had seen Lancelot dead; two more witnesses to confuse the issue and help build events to their stratospheric peak.

By four the next morning, we were in the cold-room, bundled in overcoats and waiting for zero moment.

Lancelot, in high excitement, kept checking his instruments and doing I-know-not-what with them. His desk computer was working constantly, though how he could make his cold fingers jiggle the keys so nimbly, I am at a loss to say.

I, myself, was quite miserable. There was the cold, the dead body in the coffin, the uncertainty of the future.

We had been there for what seemed an eternity and finally Lancelot said, "It will work. It will work as predicted. At the most, disappearance will be five minutes late and this when seventy kilograms of mass are involved. My analysis of chronous forces is masterly indeed." He smiled at me, but he also smiled at his own corpse with equal warmth.

I noticed that his lab jacket, which he had been wearing constantly for three days now, sleeping in it I am certain, had become wrinkled and shabby. It was about as it had seemed upon the second Lancelot, the dead one, when it had appeared.

Lancelot seemed to be aware of my thoughts, or perhaps only of my gaze, for he looked down at his jacket and said, "Ah, yes, I had better put on the rubber apron. My second self was wearing it when it appeared."

"What if you didn't put it on?" I asked tonelessly.

"I would have to. It would be a necessity. Something would have reminded me. Else *it* would not have appeared in one." His eyes narrowed. "Do you still think something will go wrong?"

"I don't know," I mumbled.

"Do you think the body won't disappear, or that I'll disappear instead?"

When I didn't answer at all, he said in a half-scream, "Can't you see my luck has changed at last? Can't you see how smoothly and according to plan it is all working out? I will be the greatest man who ever lived. Come, heat up the water for the coffee." He was suddenly calm again. "It will serve as celebration when my double leaves us and I return to life. I haven't had any coffee for three days."

It was only instant coffee he pushed in my direction, but after three days that, too, would serve. I fumbled at the laboratory hot-plate with my cold fingers until Lancelot pushed me roughly to one side and set a beaker of water upon it.

"It'll take a while," he said, turning the control to "high." He looked at his watch, then at various dials on the wall. "My double will be gone before the water boils. Come here and watch." He stepped to the side of the coffin.

I hesitated. "Come," he said peremptorily.

I came.

He looked down at himself with infinite pleasure and waited. We both waited, staring at a corpse.

There was the phfft sound and Lancelot cried out, "Less than two minutes off."

Without a blur or a wink, the dead body was gone.

The open coffin contained an empty set of clothes. The clothes, of course, had not been those in which the dead body had been brought back. They were real clothes and they stayed in reality. There they now were: underwear within shirt and pants; shirt within tie; tie within jacket. Shoes had turned over, dangling socks from within them. The body was gone.

I could hear water boiling.

"Coffee," said Lancelot. "Coffee first. Then we call the police and the newspapers."

I made the coffee for him and myself. I gave him the usual level teaspoon from the sugar bowl, neither heaping nor deficient. Even under these conditions, when I was sure for once it wouldn't matter to him, habit was strong.

I sipped at my coffee, which I drank without cream or sugar, as was my habit. Its warmth was most welcome.

He stirred his coffee. "All," he said softly, "all I have waited for." He put the cup to his grimly triumphant lips and drank.

Those were his last words.

Now that it was over, there was a kind of frenzy over me. I managed to strip him and dress him in the clothing from the coffin. Somehow I was able to heave his weight upward and place him in the coffin. I folded his arms across his chest as they had been.

I then washed out every trace of coffee in the sink in the room outside, and the sugar bowl, too. Over and over again I rinsed, until all the cyanide, which I had substituted for the sugar, was gone.

I carried his laboratory jacket and other clothes to the hamper where I had stored those the double had brought back. The second set had disappeared, of course, and I put the first set there.

Next I waited.

By that evening, I was sure the corpse was cold enough, and called the undertakers. Why should they wonder? They expected a dead body and there was the dead body. The same dead body. Really the same body. It even had cyanide in it as the first was supposed to have.

I suppose they might still be able to tell the difference between a body dead twelve hours and one dead three and a half days, even under refrigeration, but why should they dream of looking?

They didn't. They nailed down the coffin, took him away, and buried him. It was the perfect murder.

As a matter of fact, since Lancelot was legally dead at the time I killed him, I wonder if, strictly speaking, it was murder at all. Of course, I don't intend to ask a lawyer about this.

Life is quiet for me now; peaceful and contented. I have money enough. I attend the theater. I have made friends.

And I live without remorse. To be sure, Lancelot will never receive credit for time travel. Someday when time travel is discovered again, the name of Lancelot Stebbins will rest in Stygian darkness, unrecognized. But then, I told him that whatever his plans, he would end without the credit. If I hadn't killed him, something else would have spoiled things, and then he would have killed me.

No, I live without remorse.

In fact, I have forgiven Lancelot everything, everything but that moment when he spat at me. So it is rather ironic that he did have one happy moment before he died, for he was given a gift few could have, and he, above all men, savored it.

Despite his cry, when he spat at me, Lancelot managed to read his own obituary.

24

Spell My Name with an S

In Russian, my last name is spelled with the Cyrillic equiv-
alent of a z, but at Ellis Island it got misspelled, somehow,
and came out with an s—Asimov. That s, however, is
pronounced like a z.

Naturally, human nature being what it is, I am always
bitterly offended if anyone pronounces the name with an s
or spells it with a z. I keep correcting people who do
either, especially when it appears with a z in a science
fiction magazine where, it seems to me, they ought to
know better.

Finally, Larry Shaw said to me, "Why don't you write a
science fiction story entitled 'Spell My Name with an S.' "

So I did, and since I am always particularly fond of
stories that I write on a dare and that turn out well, this
story belongs in this book.

Marshall Zebatinsky felt foolish. He felt as though there
were eyes staring through the grimy store-front glass and
across the scarred wooden partition; eyes watching him.
He felt no confidence in the old clothes he had resur-
rected or the turned-down brim of a hat he never otherwise wore or the glasses he had left in their case.

He felt foolish and it made the lines in his forehead
deeper and his young-old face a little paler.

He would never be able to explain to anyone why a
nuclear physicist such as himself should visit a numerologist. (Never, he thought. Never.) Hell, he could not
explain it to himself except that he had let his wife talk
him into it.

The numerologist sat behind an old desk that must

have been secondhand when bought. No desk could get that old with only one owner. The same might almost be said of his clothes. He was little and dark and peered at Zebatinsky with little dark eyes that were brightly alive.

He said, "I have never had a physicist for a client before, Dr. Zebatinsky."

Zebatinsky flushed at once. "You understand this is confidential."

The numerologist smiled so that wrinkles creased about the corners of his mouth and the skin around his chin stretched. "All my dealings are confidential."

Zebatinsky said, "I think I ought to tell you one thing. I don't believe in numerology and I don't expect to begin believing in it. If that makes a difference, say so now."

"But why are you here, then?"

"My wife thinks you may have something, whatever it is. I promised her and I am here." He shrugged and the feeling of folly grew more acute.

"And what is it you are looking for? Money? Security? Long life? What?"

Zebatinsky sat for a long moment while the numerologist watched him quietly and made no move to hurry his client.

Zebatinsky thought: What do I say anyway? That I'm thirty-four and without a future?

He said, "I want success. I want recognition."

"A better job?"

"A *different* job. A different *kind* of job. Right now, I'm part of a team, working under orders. Teams! That's all goverment research is. You're a violinist lost in a symphony orchestra."

"And you want to solo."

"I want to get out of a team and into—into *me.*" Zebatinsky felt carried away, almost lightheaded, just putting this into words to someone other than his wife. He said, "Twenty-five years ago, with my kind of training and my kind of ability, I would have gotten to work on the first nuclear power plants. Today I'd be running one of them or I'd be head of a pure research group at a university. But with my start these days where will I be twenty-five years from now? Nowhere. Still on the team. Still carrying my 2 per cent of the ball. I'm drowning in an anonymous crowd of nuclear physicists, and what I want is room on dry land if you see what I mean."

The numerologist nodded slowly. "You realize, Dr. Zebatinsky, that I don't guarantee success."

Zebatinsky, for all his lack of faith, felt a sharp bite of disappointment. "You don't? Then what the devil *do* you guarantee?"

"An improvement in the probabilities. My work is statistical in nature. Since you deal with atoms, I think you understand the laws of statistics."

"Do you?" asked the physicist sourly.

"I do, as a matter of fact. I am a mathematician and I work mathematically. I don't tell you this in order to raise my fee. That is standard. Fifty dollars. But since you are a scientist, you can appreciate the nature of my work better than my other clients. It is even a pleasure to be able to explain it to you."

Zebatinsky said, "I'd rather you wouldn't, if you don't mind. It's no use telling me about the numerical values of letters, their mystic significance and that kind of thing. I don't consider that mathematics. Let's get to the point—"

The numerologist said, "Then you want me to help you provided I don't embarrass you by telling you the silly nonscientific basis of the way in which I helped you. Is that it?"

"All right. That's it."

"But you still work on the assumption that I am a numerologist, and I am not. I call myself that so that the police won't bother me and," (the little man chuckled dryly) "so that the psychiatrists won't either. I am a mathematician; an honest one."

Zebatinsky smiled.

The numerologist said, "I build computers. I study probable futures."

"What?"

"Does that sound worse than numerology to you? Why? Given enough data and a computer capable of sufficient number of operations in unit time, the future is predictable, at least in terms of probabilities. When you compute the motions of a missile in order to aim an anti-missile, isn't it the future you're predicting? The missile and anti-missile would not collide if the future were predicted incorrectly. I do the same thing. Since I work with a greater number of variables, my results are less accurate."

"You mean you'll predict *my* future?"

"Very approximately. Once I have done that, I will modify the data by changing your name and no other fact about you. I throw that modified datum into the operation-program. Then I try other modified names. I study each modified future and find one that contains a greater degree of recognition for you than the future that now lies ahead of you. Or no, let me put it another way. I will find you a future in which the probability of adequate recognition is higher than the probability of that in your present future."

"Why change my name?"

"That is the only change I ever make, for several reasons. Number one, it is a simple change. After all, if I make a great change or many changes, so many new variables enter that I can no longer interpret the result. My machine is still crude. Number two, it is a reasonable change. I can't change your height, can I, or the color of your eyes, or even your temperament. Number three, it is a significant change. Names mean a lot to people. Finally, number four, it is a common change that is done every day by various people."

Zebatinsky said, "What if you don't find a better future?"

"That is the risk you will have to take. You will be no worse off than now, my friend."

Zebatinsky stared at the little man uneasily, "I don't believe any of this. I'd sooner believe numerology."

The numerologist sighed. "I thought a person like yourself would feel more comfortable with the truth. I *want* to help you and there is much yet for you to do. If you believed me a numerologist, you would not follow through.

I thought if I told you the truth you would let me help you."

Zebatinsky said, "If you can see the future——"

"Why am I not the richest man on earth? Is that it? But I am rich—in all I want. You want recognition and I want to be left alone. I do my work. No one bothers me. That makes me a billionaire. I need a little real money and this I get from people such as yourself. Helping people is nice and perhaps a psychiatrist would say it gives me a feeling of power and feeds my ego. Now—do you want me to help you?"

"How much did you say?"

"Fifty dollars. I will need a great deal of biographical information from you but I have prepared a form to guide you. It's a little long, I'm afraid. Still, if you can get it in the mail by the end of the week, I will have an answer for you by the——" (he put out his lower lip and frowned in mental calculation) "the twentieth of next month."

"Five weeks? So long?"

"I have other work, my friend, and other clients. If I were a fake, I could do it much more quickly. Is it agreed then?"

Zebatinsky rose. "Well, agreed.——This is all confidential, now."

"Perfectly. You will have all your information back when I tell you what change to make and you have my word that I will never make any further use of any of it."

The nuclear physicist stopped at the door. "Aren't you afraid I might tell someone you're not a numerologist?"

The numerologist shook his head. "Who would believe you, my friend? Even supposing you were willing to admit to anyone that you've been here."

On the twentieth, Marshall Zebatinsky was at the paint-peeling door, glancing sideways at the shop front with the little card up against the glass reading "Numerology," dimmed and scarcely legible through the dust. He peered in, almost hoping that someone else would be there already so that he might have an excuse to tear up the wavering intention in his mind and go home.

He had tried wiping the thing out of his mind several times. He could never stick at filling out the necessary data for long. It was embarrassing to work at it. He felt incredibly silly filling out the names of his friends, the cost of his house, whether his wife had had any miscarriages, if so, when. He abandoned it.

But he couldn't stick at stopping altogether either. He returned to it each evening.

It was the thought of the computer that did it, perhaps; the thought of the infernal gall of the little man pretending he had a computer. The temptation to call the bluff, see what would happen, proved irresistible after all.

He finally sent off the completed data by ordinary mail, putting on the stamps without weighing the letter. If it comes back, he thought, I'll call it off.

It didn't come back.

He looked into the shop now and it was empty. Zebatinsky had no choice but to enter. A bell tinkled.

The old numerologist emerged from a curtained door. "Yes?——Ah, Dr. Zebatinsky."

"You remember me?" Zebatinsky tried to smile.

"Oh, yes."

"What's the verdict?"

The numerologist moved one gnarled hand over the other. "Before that, sir, there's a little——"

"A little matter of the fee?"

"I have already done the work, sir. I have earned the money."

Zebatinsky raised no objection. He was prepared to pay. If he had come this far, it would be silly to turn back just because of the money.

He counted out five ten-dollar bills and shoved them across the counter. "Well?"

The numerologist counted the bills again slowly, then pushed them into a cash drawer in his desk.

He said, "Your case was very interesting. I would advise you to change your name to Sebatinsky."

"Seba——How do you spell that?"

"S-e-b-a-t-i-n-s-k-y."

Zebatinsky stared indignantly. "You mean change the initial? Change the *Z* to an *S*? That's all?"

"It's enough. As long as the change is adequate, a small change is safer than a big one."

"But how could the change affect anything?"

"How could any name?" asked the numerologist softly. "I can't say. It may, somehow, and that's all I can say. Remember, I don't guarantee results. Of course, if you do not wish to make the change, leave things as they are. But in that case, I cannot refund the fee."

Zebatinsky said, "What do I do? Just tell everyone to spell my name with an *S*?"

"If you want my advice, consult a lawyer. Change your name legally. He can advise you on little things."

"How long will it all take? I mean for things to improve for me?"

"How can I tell? Maybe never. Maybe tomorrow."

"But you saw the future. You *claim* you see it."

"Not as in a crystal ball. No, no, Dr. Zebatinsky. All I get out of my computer is a set of coded figures. I can recite probabilities to you, but I saw no pictures."

Zebatinsky turned and walked rapidly out of the place. Fifty dollars to change a letter! Fifty dollars for Sebatinsky! Lord, what a name! Worse than Zebatinsky.

It took another month before he could make up his mind to see a lawyer, and then he finally went.

He told himself he could always change the name back.

Give it a chance, he told himself.

Hell, there was no law against it.

Henry Brand looked through the folder page by page, with the practiced eye of one who had been in Security for fourteen years. He didn't have to read every word. Anything peculiar would have leaped off the paper and punched him in the eye.

He said, "The man looks clean to me." Henry Brand looked clean, too; with a soft, rounded paunch and a pink and freshly scrubbed complexion. It was as though continuous contact with all sorts of human failings, from possible ignorance to possible treason, had compelled him into frequent washings.

Lieutenant Albert Quincy, who had brought him the folder, was young and filled with the responsibility of being Security officer at the Hanford Station. "But why Sebatinsky?" he demanded.

"Why not?"

"Because it doesn't make sense. Zebatinsky is a foreign name and I'd change it myself if I had it, but I'd change it to something Anglo-Saxon. If Zebatinsky had done that, it would make sense and I wouldn't give it a second thought. But why change a Z to an S? I think we must find out what his reasons were."

"Has anyone asked him directly?"

Certainly. In ordinary conversation, of course. I was careful to arrange that. He won't say anything more than that he's tired of being last in the alphabet."

"That could be, couldn't it, Lieutenant?"

"It could, but why not change his name to Sands or Smith, if he wants an S? Or if he's that tired of Z, why not go the whole way and change it to an A? Why not a name like—uh—Aarons?"

"Not Anglo-Saxon enough," muttered Brand. Then, "But there's nothing to pin against the man. No matter how queer a name-change may be, that alone can't be used against anyone."

Lieutenant Quincy looked markedly unhappy.

Brand said, "Tell me, Lieutenant, there must be something specific that bothers you. Something in your mind; some theory; some gimmick. What is it?"

The lieutenant frowned. His light eyebrows drew together and his lips tightened. "Well, damn it, sir, the man's a Russian."

Brand said, "He's not that. He's a third-generation American."

"I mean his name's Russian."

Brand's face lost some of its deceptive softness. "No, Lieutenant, wrong again. Polish."

The lieutenant pushed his hands out impatiently, palms up. "Same thing."

Brand, whose mother's maiden name had been Wiszewski, snapped, "Don't tell that to a Pole, Lieutenant." ——Then, more thoughtfully, "Or to a Russian either, I suppose."

"What I'm trying to say, sir," said the lieutenant, reddening, "is that the Poles and Russians are both on the other side of the Curtain."

"We all know that."

"And Zebatinsky or Sebatinsky, whatever you want to call him, may have relatives there."

"He's third generation. He might have second cousins there, I suppose. So what?"

"Nothing in itself. Lots of people may have distant relatives there. But Zebatinsky changed his name."

"Go on."

"Maybe he's trying to distract attention. Maybe a second cousin over there is getting too famous and our Zebatinsky is afraid that the relationship may spoil his own chances of advancement."

"Changing his name won't do any good. He'd still be a second cousin."

"Sure, but he wouldn't feel as though he were shoving the relationship in our face."

"Have *you* ever heard of any Zebatinsky on the other side?"

"No, sir."

"Then he can't be too famous. How would our Zebatinsky know about him?"

"He might keep in touch with his own relatives. That would be suspicious under the circumstances, he being a nuclear physicist."

Methodically, Brand went through the folder again "This is awfully thin, Lieutenant. It's thin enough to be completely invisible."

"Can you offer any other explanation, sir, of why he ought to change his name in just this way?"

"No, I can't. I admit that."

"Then I think, sir, we ought to investigate. We ought to look for any men named Zebatinsky on the other side and see if we can draw a connection." The lieutenant's voice rose a trifle as a new thought occurred to him. "He might be changing his name to withdraw attention from *them;* I mean to protect them."

"He's doing just the opposite, I think."

"He doesn't realize that, maybe, but protecting them could be his motive."

Brand sighed. "All right, we'll tackle the Zebatinsky angle.——But if nothing turns up, Lieutenant, we drop the matter. Leave the folder with me."

When the information finally reached Brand, he had all but forgotten the lieutenant and his theories. His first thought on receiving data that included a list of seventeen biographies of seventeen Russian and Polish citizens, all named Zebatinsky, was: What the devil is this?

Then he remembered, swore mildly, and began reading.

It started on the American side. Marshall Zebatinsky (fingerprints) had been born in Buffalo, New York (date, hospital statistics). His father had been born in Buffalo as well, his mother in Oswego, New York. His paternal grandparents had both been born in Bialystok, Poland (date of entry into the United States, dates of citizenship, photographs).

The seventeen Russian and Polish citizens named Zebatinsky were all descendants of people who, some half century earlier, had lived in or near Bialystok. Presumably, they could be relatives, but this was not explicitly stated in any particular case. (Vital statistics in East Europe during the aftermath of World War I were kept poorly, if at all.)

Brand passed through the individual life histories of the current Zebatinsky men and women (amazing how thoroughly intelligence did its work; probably the Russians' was as thorough). He stopped at one and his smooth forehead sprouted lines as his eyebrows shot upward. He put that one to one side and went on. Eventually, he stacked everything but that one and returned it to its envelope.

Staring at that one, he tapped a neatly kept fingernail on the desk.

With a certain reluctance, he went to call on Dr. Paul Kristow of the Atomic Energy Commission.

Dr. Kristow listened to the matter with a stony expression. He lifted a little finger occasionally to dab at his bulbous nose and remove a nonexistent speck. His hair was iron gray, thinning and cut short. He might as well have been bald.

He said, "No, I never heard of any Russian Zebatinsky. But then, I never heard of the American one either."

"Well," Brand scratched at his hairline over one temple and said slowly, "I don't think there's anything to this, but I don't like to drop it too soon. I have a young lieutenant on my tail and you know what they can be like. I don't want to do anything that will drive him to a Congressional committee. Besides, the fact is that one of the Russian Zebatinsky fellows, Mikhail Andreyevich Zebatinsky, *is* a nuclear physicist. Are you sure you never heard of him?"

"Mikhail Andreyevich Zebatinsky? No—— No, I never did. Not that that proves anything."

"I could say it was coincidence, but you know that would be piling it a trifle high. One Zebatinsky here and one Zebatinsky there, both nuclear physicists, and the one here suddenly changes his name to Sebatinsky, and goes around anxious about it, too. He won't allow misspelling. He says, emphatically, 'Spell my name with an *S*.' It all just fits well enough to make my spy-conscious lieutenant begin to look a little too good.——And another peculiar thing is that the Russian Zebatinsky dropped out of sight just about a year ago."

Dr. Kristow said stolidly, "Executed!"

"He might have been. Ordinarily, I would even assume so, though the Russians are not more foolish than we are and don't kill any nuclear physicist they can avoid killing. The thing is there's another reason why a nuclear physicist, of all people, might suddenly disappear. I don't have to tell you."

"Crash research; top secret. I take it that's what you mean. Do you believe that's it?"

"Put it together with everything else, add in the lieutenant's intuition, and I just begin to wonder."

"Give me that biography." Dr. Kristow reached for the sheet of paper and read it over twice. He shook his head. Then he said, "I'll check this in *Nuclear Abstracts.*"

Nuclear Abstracts lined one wall of Dr. Kristow's study in neat little boxes, each filled with its squares of microfilm. The A.E.C. man used his projector on the indices while Brand watched with what patience he could muster.

Dr. Kristow muttered, "A Mikhail Zebatinsky authored or co-authored half a dozen papers in the Soviet journals in the last half dozen years. We'll get out the abstracts and maybe we can make something out of it. I doubt it."

A selector flipped out the appropriate squares. Dr. Kristow lined them up, ran them through the projector, and by degrees an expression of odd intentness crossed his face. He said, "That's odd."

Brand said, "What's odd?"

Dr. Kristow sat back. "I'd rather not say just yet. Can you get me a list of other nuclear physicists who have dropped out of sight in the Soviet Union in the last year?"

"You mean you see something?"

"Not really. Not if I were just looking at any one of these papers. It's just that looking at all of them and knowing that this man may be on a crash research program and, on top of that, having you putting suspicions in my head——" He shrugged. "It's nothing."

Brand said earnestly, "I wish you'd say what's on your mind. We may as well be foolish about this together."

"If you feel that way—— It's just possible this man may have been inching toward gamma-ray reflection."

"And the significance?"

"If a reflecting shield against gamma rays could be devised, individual shelters could be built to protect against fallout. It's fallout that's the real danger, you know. A hydrogen bomb might destroy a city but the fallout could slow-kill the population over a strip thousands of miles long and hundreds wide."

Brand said quickly, "Are we doing any work on this?"

"No."

"And if they get it and we don't, they can destroy the United States *in toto* at the cost of, say, ten cities, after they have their shelter program completed."

"That's far in the future.——And, what are we getting in a hurrah about? All this is built on one man changing one letter in his name."

"All right, I'm insane," said Brand. "But I don't leave the matter at this point. Not at *this* point. I'll get you your list of disappearing nuclear physicists if I have to go to Moscow to get it."

He got the list. They went through all the research papers authored by any of them. They called a full meeting of the Commission, then of the nuclear brains of the nation. Dr. Kristow walked out of an all night session, finally, part of which the President himself had attended.

Brand met him. Both looked haggard and in need of sleep.

Brand said, "Well?"

Kristow nodded. "Most agree. Some are doubtful even yet, but most agree."

"How about you? Are you sure?"

"I'm far from sure, but let me put it this way. It's easier to believe that the Soviets are working on a gamma-ray shield than to believe that all the data we've uncovered has no interconnection."

"Has it been decided that we're to go on shield research, too?"

"Yes." Kristow's hand went back over his short, bristly hair, making a dry, whispery sound. "We're going to give it everything we've got. Knowing the papers written by the men who disappeared, we can get right on their heels. We may even beat them to it.——Of course, they'll find out we're working on it."

"Let them," said Brand. "Let them. It will keep them from attacking. I don't see any percentage in selling ten of our cities just to get ten of theirs—if we're both protected and they're too dumb to know that."

"But not too soon. We don't want them finding out *too* soon. What about the American Zebatinsky-Sebatinsky?"

Brand looked solemn and shook his head. "There's nothing to connect him with any of this even yet. Hell, we've *looked*. I agree with you, of course. He's in a sensitive spot where he is now and we can't afford to keep him there even if he's in the clear."

"We can't kick him out just like that, either, or the Russians will start wondering."

"Do you have any suggestions?"

They were walking down the long corridor toward the distant elevator in the emptiness of four in the morning.

Dr. Kristow said, "I've looked into his work. He's a good man, better than most, and not happy in his job, either. He hasn't the temperament for teamwork."

"So?"

"But he is the type for an academic job. If we can arrange to have a large university offer him a chair in physics, I think he would take it gladly. There would be enough nonsensitive areas to keep him occupied; we would be able to keep him in close view; *and* it would be a natural development. The Russians might not start scratching their heads. What do you think?"

Brand nodded. "It's an idea. Even sounds good. I'll put it up to the chief."

They stepped into the elevator and Brand allowed himself to wonder about it all. What an ending to what had started with one letter of a name.

Marshall Sebatinsky could hardly talk. He said to his wife, "I swear I don't see how this happened. I wouldn't have thought they knew me from a meson detector. ——Good Lord, Sophie, Associate Professor of Physics at Princeton. Think of it."

Sophie said, "Do you suppose it was your talk at the A.P.S. meetings?"

"I don't see how. It was a thoroughly uninspired paper once everyone in the division was done hacking at it." He snapped his fingers. "It must have been Princeton that was investigating me. That's it. You know all those forms I've been filling out in the last six months; those interviews they wouldn't explain. Honestly, I was beginning to think I was under suspicion as a subversive.——It was Princeton investigating me. They're thorough."

"Maybe it was your name," said Sophie. "I mean the change."

"Watch me now. My professional life will be my own finally. I'll make my mark. Once I have a chance to do my work without——" He stopped and turned to look at his wife. "My name! You mean the *S*."

"You didn't get the offer till after you changed your name, did you?"

"Not till long after. No, that part's just coincidence. I've told you before, Sophie, it was just a case of throwing out fifty dollars to please you. Lord, what a fool I've felt all these months insisting on that stupid *S*."

Sophie was instantly on the defensive. "I didn't make you do it, Marshall. I suggested it but I didn't nag you about it. Don't say I did. Besides, it did turn out well. I'm sure it was the name that did this."

Sebatinsky smiled indulgently. "Now that's superstition."

"I don't care what you call it, but you're not changing your name back."

"Well, no, I suppose not. I've had so much trouble getting them to spell my name with an *S*, that the thought of making everyone move back is more than I want to face. Maybe I ought to change my name to Jones, eh?" He laughed almost hysterically.

But Sophie didn't. "You leave it alone."

"Oh, all right, I'm just joking.——Tell you what. I'll step down to that old fellow's place one of these days and tell him everything worked out and slip him another tenner. Will that satisfy you?"

He was exuberant enough to do so the next week. He assumed no disguise this time. He wore his glasses and his ordinary suit and was minus a hat.

He was even humming as he approached the store front and stepped to one side to allow a weary, sour-faced woman to maneuver her twin baby carriage past.

He put his hand on the door handle and his thumb on

the iron latch. The latch didn't give to his thumb's down-
ward pressure. The door was locked.

The dusty, dim card with "Numerologist" on it was
gone, now that he looked. Another sign, printed and
beginning to yellow and curl with the sunlight, said "To
let."

Sebatinsky shrugged. That was that. He had tried to do
the right thing.

Haround, happily divested of corporeal excrescence,
capered happily and his energy vortices glowed a dim
purple over cubic hypermiles. He said, "Have I won?
Have I won?"

Mestack was withdrawn, his vortices almost a sphere of
light in hyperspace. "I haven't calculated it yet."

"Well, go ahead. You won't change the results any by
taking a long time.——Wowf, it's a relief to get back into
clean energy. It took me a microcycle of time as a corporeal body; a nearly used-up one, too. But it was worth it
to show *you*."

Mestack said, "All right, I admit you stopped a nuclear
war on the planet."

"Is that or is that not a Class A effect?"

"It is a Class A effect. Of course it is."

"All right. Now check and see if I didn't get that Class
A effect with a Class F stimulus. I changed one letter of
one name."

"What?"

"Oh, never mind. It's all there. I've worked it out for
you."

Mestack said reluctantly, "I yield. A Class F stimulus."

"Then I *win*. Admit it."

"Neither one of us will win when the Watchman gets a
look at this."

Haround, who had been an elderly numerologist on
Earth and was still somewhat unsettled with relief at no
longer being one, said, "You weren't worried about that
when you made the bet."

"I didn't think you'd be fool enough to go through
with it."

"Heat-waste! Besides, why worry? The Watchman will never detect a Class F stimulus."

"Maybe not, but he'll detect a Class A effect. Those corporeals will still be around after a dozen microcycles. The Watchman will notice that."

"The trouble with you, Mestack, is that you don't want to pay off. You're stalling."

"I'll pay. But just wait till the Watchman finds out we've been working on an unassigned problem and made an unallowed-for change. Of course, if we——" He paused.

Haround said, "All right, we'll change it back. He'll never know."

There was a crafty glow to Mestack's brightening energy pattern. "You'll need another Class F stimulus if you expect him not to notice."

Haround hesitated. "I can do it."

"I doubt it."

"I could."

"Would you be willing to bet on that, too?" Jubilation was creeping into Mestack's radiations.

"Sure," said the goaded Haround. "I'll put those corporeals right back where they were and the Watchman will never know the difference."

Mestack followed through his advantage. "Suspend the first bet, then. Triple the stakes on the second."

The mounting eagerness of the gamble caught at Haround, too. "All right, I'm game. Triple the stakes."

"Done, then!"

"Done."

25

Strikebreaker

I think this story is an important one and full of social significance and that everyone ought to be crazy about it. This story, however, like "Obituary," sank into the quicksand of indifference without even a "glug."

But I don't care if I'm a minority of one. I still think this story is an important one and full of social significance, and if everyone isn't crazy about it, that's their tough luck. Here it is.

Elvis Blei rubbed his plump hands and said, "Self-containment is the word." He smiled uneasily as he helped Steven Lamorak of Earth to a light. There was uneasiness all over his smooth face with its small wide-set eyes.

Lamorak puffed smoke appreciatively and crossed his lanky legs.

His hair was powdered with gray and he had a large and powerful jawbone. "Home grown?" he asked, staring critically at the cigarette. He tried to hide his own disturbance at the other's tension.

"Quite," said Blei.

"I wonder," said Lamorak, "that you have room on your small world for such luxuries."

(Lamorak thought of his first view of Elsevere from the spaceship visiplate. It was a jagged, airless planetoid, some hundred miles in diameter—just a dust-gray rough-hewn rock, glimmering dully in the light of its sun, 200,000,000 miles distant. It was the only object more than a mile in diameter that circled that sun, and now men had burrowed into that miniature world and constructed a society in it. And he himself, as a sociologist,

308

had come to study the world and see how humanity had made itself fit into that queerly specialized niche.)

Blei's polite fixed smile expanded a hair. He said, "We are not a small world, Dr. Lamorak; you judge us by two-dimensional standards. The surface area of Elsevere is only three quarters that of the State of New York, but that's irrelevant. Remember, we can occupy, if we wish, the entire interior of Elsevere. A sphere of 50 miles radius has a volume of well over half a million cubic miles. If all of Elsevere were occupied by levels 50 feet apart, the total surface area within the planetoid would be 56,000,000 square miles, and that is equal to the total land area of Earth. And none of these square miles, Doctor, would be unproductive."

Lamorak said, "Good Lord," and stared blankly for a moment. "Yes, of course you're right. Strange I never thought of it that way. But then, Elsevere is the only thoroughly exploited asteroid world in the Galaxy; the rest of us simply can't get away from thinking of two-dimensional surfaces, as you pointed out. Well, I'm more than ever glad that your Council has been so cooperative as to give me a free hand in this investigation of mine."

Blei nodded convulsively at that.

Lamorak frowned slightly and thought: He acts for all the world as though he wished I had not come. Something's wrong.

Blei said, "Of course, you understand that we are actually much smaller than we could be; only minor portions of Elsevere have as yet been hollowed out and occupied. Nor are we particularly anxious to expand, except very slowly. To a certain extent we are limited by the capacity of our pseudo-gravity engines and Solar energy converters."

"I understand. But tell me, Councillor Blei—as a matter of personal curiosity, and not because it is of prime importance to my project—could I view some of your farming and herding levels first? I am fascinated by the thought of fields of wheat and herds of cattle inside a planetoid."

"You'll find the cattle small by your standards, Doctor, and we don't have much wheat. We grow yeast to a much greater extent. But there will be some wheat to show you. Some cotton and rice, too. Even fruit trees."

"Wonderful. As you say, self-containment. You recirculate everything, I imagine."

Lamorak's sharp eyes did not miss the fact that this last remark twinged Blei. The Elseverian's eyes narrowed to slits that hid his expression.

He said, "We must recirculate, yes. Air, water, food, minerals—everything that is used up—must be restored to its original state; waste products are reconverted to raw materials. All that is needed is energy, and we have enough of that. We don't manage with one hundred percent efficiency, of course; there is a certain seepage. We import a small amount of water each year; and if our needs grow, we may have to import some coal and oxygen."

Lamorak said, "When can we start our tour, Councillor Blei?"

Blei's smile lost some of its negligible warmth. "As soon as we can, Doctor. There are some routine matters that must be arranged."

Lamorak nodded, and having finished his cigarette, stubbed it out.

Routine matters? There was none of this hesitancy during the preliminary correspondence. Elsevere had seemed proud that its unique asteroid existence had attracted the attention of the Galaxy.

He said, "I realize I would be a disturbing influence in a tightly-knit society," and watched grimly as Blei leaped at the explanation and made it his own.

"Yes," said Blei, "we feel marked off from the rest of the Galaxy. We have our own customs. Each individual Elseverian fits into a comfortable niche. The appearance of a stranger without fixed caste is unsettling."

"The caste system does involve a certain inflexibility."

"Granted," said Blei quickly; "but there is also a certain self-assurance. We have firm rules of intermarriage and rigid inheritance of occupation. Each man, woman and child knows his place, accepts it, and is accepted in it; we have virtually no neurosis or mental illness."

"And are there no misfits?" asked Lamorak.

Blei shaped his mouth as though to say no, then clamped it suddenly shut, biting the word into silence; a frown deepened on his forehead. He said, at length, "I will arrange for the tour, Doctor. Meanwhile, I imagine you would welcome a chance to freshen up and to sleep."

They rose together and left the room, Blei politely motioning the Earthman to precede him out the door.

Lamorak felt oppressed by the vague feeling of crisis that had pervaded his discussion with Blei.

The newspaper reinforced that feeling. He read it carefully before getting into bed, with what was at first merely a clinical interest. It was an eight-page tabloid of synthetic paper. One quarter of its items consisted of "personals": births, marriages, deaths, record quotas, expanding habitable volume (not area! three dimensions!). The remainder included scholarly essays, educational material, and fiction. Of news, in the sense to which Lamorak was accustomed, there was virtually nothing.

One item only could be so considered and that was chilling in its incompleteness.

It said, under a small headline: *DEMANDS UN-CHANGED: There has been no change in his attitude of yesterday. The Chief Councillor, after a second interview, announced that his demands remain completely unreasonable and cannot be met under any circumstances.*

Then, in parenthesis, and in different type, there was the statement: *The editors of this paper agree that Elsevere cannot and will not jump to his whistle, come what may.*

Lamorak read it over three times. *His* attitude. *His* demands. *His* whistle.

Whose?

He slept uneasily, that night.

He had no time for newspapers in the days that followed; but spasmodically, the matter returned to his thoughts.

Blei, who remained his guide and companion for most of the tour, grew ever more withdrawn.

On the third day (quite artificially clock-set in an Earth-like twenty-four hour pattern), Blei stopped at one point, and said, "Now this level is devoted entirely to chemical industries. That section is not important—"

But he turned away a shade too rapidly, and Lamorak seized his arm. "What are the products of that section?"

"Fertilizers. Certain organics," said Blei stiffly.

Lamorak held him back, looking for what sight Blei might be evading. His gaze swept over the close-by horizons of lined rock and the buildings squeezed and layered between the levels.

Lamorak said, "Isn't that a private residence there?"

Blei did not look in the indicated direction.

Lamorak said, "I think that's the largest one I've seen yet. Why is it here on a factory level?" That alone made it noteworthy. He had already seen that the levels on Elsevere were divided rigidly among the residential, the agricultural and the industrial.

He looked back and called, "Councillor Blei!"

The councillor was walking away and Lamorak pursued him with hasty steps. "Is there something wrong, sir?"

Blei muttered, "I am rude, I know. I am sorry. There are matters that prey on my mind—" He kept up his rapid pace.

"Concerning *his* demands."

Blei came to a full halt. "What do *you* know about that?"

"No more than I've said. I read that much in the newspaper."

Blei muttered something to himself.

Lamorak said, "Ragusnik? What's that?"

Blei sighed heavily. "I suppose you ought to be told. It's humiliating, deeply embarrassing. The Council thought that matters would certainly be arranged shortly and that your visit need not be interfered with, that you need not know or be concerned. But it is almost a week now. I don't know what will happen and, appearances notwithstanding, it might be best for you to leave. No reason for an Outworlder to risk death."

The Earthman smiled incredulously. "Risk death? In this little world, so peaceful and busy. I can't believe it."

The Elseverian councillor said, "I can explain. I think it best I should." He turned his head away. "As I told you, everything on Elsevere must recirculate. You understand that."

"Yes."

"That includes—uh, human wastes."

"I assumed so," said Lamorak.

"Water is reclaimed from it by distillation and absorption. What remains is converted into fertilizer for yeast use; some of it is used as a source of fine organics and other by-products. These factories you see are devoted to this."

"Well?" Lamorak had experienced a certain difficulty in the drinking of water when he first landed on Elsevere, because he had been realistic enough to know what it must be reclaimed from; but he had conquered the feeling easily enough. Even on Earth, water was reclaimed by natural processes from all sorts of unpalatable substances.

Blei, with increasing difficulty, said, "Igor Ragusnik is the man who is in charge of the industrial processes immediately involving the wastes. The position has been in his family since Elsevere was first colonized. One of the original settlers was Mikhail Ragusnik and he—he—"

"Was in charge of waste reclamation."

"Yes. Now that residence you singled out is the Ragusnik residence; it is the best and most elaborate on the asteroid. Ragusnik gets many privileges the rest of us do not have; but, after all—" Passion entered the Councillor's voice with great suddenness, "we cannot *speak* to him."

"What?"

"He demands full social equality. He wants his children to mingle with ours, and our wives to visit—Oh!" It was a groan of utter disgust.

Lamorak thought of the newspaper item that could not even bring itself to mention Ragusnik's name in print, or to say anything specific about his demands. He said, "I take it he's an outcast because of his job."

"Naturally. Human wastes and—" words failed Blei. After a pause, he said more quietly, "As an Earthman, I suppose you don't understand."

"As a sociologist, I think I do." Lamorak thought of the Untouchables in ancient India, the ones who handled corpses. He thought of the position of swineherds in ancient Judea.

He went on, "I gather Elsevere will not give in to those demands."

"Never," said Blei, energetically. "Never."

"And so?"

"Ragusnik has threatened to cease operations."

"Go on strike, in other words."

"Yes."

"Would that be serious?"

"We have enough food and water to last quite a while; reclamation is not essential in that sense. But the wastes would accumulate; they would infect the asteroid. After generations of careful disease control, we have low natural resistance to germ diseases. Once an epidemic started— and one would—we would drop by the hundred."

"Is Ragusnik aware of this?"

"Yes, of course."

"Do you think he is likely to go through with his threat, then?"

"He is mad. He has already stopped working; there has been no waste reclamation since the day before you landed." Blei's bulbous nose sniffed at the air as though it already caught the whiff of excrement.

Lamorak sniffed mechanically at that, but smelled nothing.

Blei said, "So you see why it might be wise for you to

leave. We are humiliated, of course, to have to suggest it."

But Lamorak said, "Wait; not just yet. Good Lord, this is a matter of great interest to me professionally. May I speak to the Ragusnik?"

"On no account," said Blei, alarmed.

"But I would like to understand the situation. The sociological conditions here are unique and not to be duplicated elsewhere. In the name of science—"

"How do you mean, speak? Would image-reception do?"

"Yes."

"I will ask the Council," muttered Blei.

They sat about Lamorak uneasily, their austere and dignified expressions badly marred with anxiety. Blei, seated in the midst of them, studiously avoided the Earthman's eyes.

The Chief Councillor, gray-haired, his face harshly wrinkled, his neck scrawny, said in a soft voice, "If in any way you can persuade him, sir, out of your own convictions, we will welcome that. In no case, however, are you to imply that we will, in any way, yield."

A gauzy curtain fell between the Council and Lamorak. He could make out the individual councillors still, but now he turned sharply toward the receiver before him. It glowed to life.

A head appeared in it, in natural color and with great realism. A strong dark head, with massive chin faintly stubbled, and thick, red lips set into a firm horizontal line.

The image said, suspiciously, "Who are you?"

Lamorak said, "My name is Steven Lamorak; I am an Earthman."

"An Outworlder?"

"That's right. I am visiting Elsevere. You are Ragusnik?"

"Igor Ragusnik, at your service," said the image, mockingly. "Except that there is no service and will be none until my family and I are treated like human beings."

Lamorak said, "Do you realize the danger that Elsevere is in? The possibility of epidemic disease?"

"In twenty-four hours, the situation can be made normal, if they allow me humanity. The situation is theirs to correct."

"You sound like an educated man, Ragusnik."

"So?"

"I am told you're denied no material comforts. You are housed and clothed and fed better than anyone on Elsevere. Your children are the best educated."

"Granted. But all by servo-mechanism. And motherless girl-babies are sent us to care for until they grow to be our wives. And they die young for loneliness. Why?" There was sudden passion in his voice. "Why must we live in isolation as if we were all monsters, unfit for human beings to be near? Aren't we human beings like others, with the same needs and desires and feelings. Don't we perform an honorable and useful function—?"

There was a rustling of sighs from behind Lamorak. Ragusnik heard it, and raised his voice. "I see you of the Council behind there. Answer me: Isn't it an honorable and useful function? It is *your* waste made into food for *you*. Is the man who purifies corruption worse than the man who produces it?—Listen, Councillors, I will *not* give in. Let all of Elsevere die of disease—including myself and my son, if necessary—but I will not give in. My family will be better dead of disease, than living as now."

Lamorak interrupted. "You've led this life since birth, haven't you?"

"And if I have?"

"Surely you're used to it."

"Never. Resigned, perhaps. My father was resigned, and I was resigned for a while; but I have watched my son, my only son, with no other little boy to play with. My brother and I had each other, but my son will never have anyone, and I am no longer resigned. I am through with Elsevere and through with talking."

The receiver went dead.

The Chief Councillor's face had paled to an aged yellow. He and Blei were the only ones of the group left with Lamorak. The Chief Councillor said, "The man is deranged; I do not know how to force him."

He had a glass of wine at his side; as he lifted it to his lips, he spilled a few drops that stained his white trousers with purple splotches.

Lamorak said, "Are his demands so unreasonable? Why can't he be accepted into society?"

There was momentary rage in Blei's eyes. "A dealer in excrement." Then he shrugged. "You are from Earth."

Incongruously, Lamorak thought of another unacceptable, one of the numerous classic creations of the medieval cartoonist, Al Capp. The variously-named "inside man at the skonk works."

He said, "Does Ragusnik really deal with excrement? I mean, is there physical contact? Surely, it is all handled by automatic machinery."

"Of course," said the Chief Councillor.

"Then exactly what is Ragusnik's function?"

"He manually adjusts the various controls that assure the proper functioning of the machinery. He shifts units to allow repairs to be made; he alters functional rates with the time of day; he varies end production with demand." He added sadly, "If we had the space to make the machinery ten times as complex, all this could be done automatically; but that would be such needless waste."

"But even so," insisted Lamorak, "all Ragusnik does he does simply by pressing buttons or closing contacts or things like that."

"Yes."

"Then his work is no different from any Elseverian's."

Blei said, stiffly, "You don't understand."

"And for that you will risk the death of your children?"

"We have no other choice," said Blei. There was enough agony in his voice to assure Lamorak that the situation was torture for him, but that he had no other choice indeed.

Lamorak shrugged in disgust. "Then break the strike. Force him."

"How?" said the Chief Councillor. "Who would touch him or go near him? And if we kill him by blasting from a distance, how will that help us?"

Lamorak said, thoughtfully, "Would you know how to run his machinery?"

The Chief Councillor came to his feet. "I?" he howled.

"I don't mean *you*," cried Lamorak at once. "I used the pronoun in its indefinite sense. Could *someone* learn how to handle Ragusnik's machinery?"

Slowly, the passion drained out of the Chief Councillor. "It is in the handbooks, I am certain—though I assure you I have never concerned myself with it."

"Then couldn't someone learn the procedure and substitute for Ragusnik until the man gives in?"

Blei said, "Who would agree to do such a thing? Not I, under any circumstances."

Lamorak thought fleetingly of Earthly taboos that might be almost as strong. He thought of cannibalism, incest, a pious man cursing God. He said, "But you must have made provision for vacancy in the Ragusnik job. Suppose he died."

"Then his son would automatically succeed to his job, or his nearest other relative," said Blei.

"What if he had no adult relatives? What if all his family died at once?"

"That has never happened; it will never happen."

The Chief Councillor added, "If there were danger of it, we might, perhaps, place a baby or two with the Ragusniks and have it raised to the profession."

"Ah. And how would you choose that baby?"

"From among children of mothers who died in childbirth, as we choose the future Ragusnik bride."

"Then choose a substitute Ragusnik now, by lot," said Lamorak.

The Chief Councillor said, *"No! Impossible!* How can you suggest that? If we select a baby, that baby is brought up to the life; it knows no other. At this point, it would be necessary to choose an adult and subject him to Ragusnik-hood. No, Dr. Lamorak, we are neither monsters nor abandoned brutes."

No use, thought Lamorak helplessly. *No use, unless*— He couldn't bring himself to face that *unless* just yet.

That night, Lamorak slept scarcely at all. Ragusnik asked for only the basic elements of humanity. But opposing that were thirty thousand Elseverians who faced death.

The welfare of thirty thousand on one side; the just demands of one family on the other. Could one say that thirty thousand who would support such injustice deserved to die? Injustice by what standards? Earth's? Elsevere's? And who was Lamorak that he should judge?

And Ragusnik? He was willing to let thirty thousand die, including men and women who merely accepted a situation they had been taught to accept and could not change if they wished to. And children who had nothing at all to do with it.

Thirty thousand on one side; a single family on the other.

Lamorak made his decision in something that was almost despair; in the morning he called the Chief Councillor.

He said, "Sir, if you can find a substitute, Ragusnik will see that he has lost all chance to force a decision in his favor and will return to work."

"There can be no substitute," sighed the Chief Councillor; "I have explained that."

"No substitute among the Elseverians, but I am not an Elseverian; it doesn't matter to me. *I* will substitute."

They were excited, much more excited than Lamorak himself. A dozen times they asked him if he was serious.

Lamorak had not shaved, and he felt sick, "Certainly, I'm serious. And any time Ragusnik acts like this, you can always import a substitute. No other world has the taboo and there will always be plenty of temporary substitutes available if you pay enough."

(He was betraying a brutally exploited man, and he knew it. But he told himself desperately: *Except for ostracism, he's very well treated. Very well.*)

They gave him the handbooks and he spent six hours, reading and rereading. There was no use asking questions. None of the Elseverians knew anything about the job, except for what was in the handbook; and all seemed uncomfortable if the details were as much as mentioned.

"Maintain zero reading of galvanometer A-2 at all times during red signal of the Lunge-howler," read Lamorak. "Now what's a Lunge-howler?"

"There will be a sign," muttered Blei, and the Elseverians looked at each other hang-dog and bent their heads to stare at their fingerends.

They left him long before he reached the small rooms that were the central headquarters of generations of working Ragusniks, serving their world. He had specific instructions concerning which turnings to take and what level to reach, but they hung back and let him proceed alone.

He went through the rooms painstakingly, identifying the instruments and controls, following the schematic diagrams in the handbook.

There's a Lunge-howler, he thought, with gloomy satisfaction. The sign did indeed say so. It had a semi-circular face bitten into holes that were obviously designed to glow in separate colors. Why a "howler" then?

He didn't know.

Somewhere, thought Lamorak, *somewhere wastes are accumulating, pushing against gears and exits, pipelines and stills, waiting to be handled in half a hundred ways. Now they just accumulate.*

Not without a tremor, he pulled the first switch as indicated by the handbook in its directions for "Initiation." A gentle murmur of life made itself felt through the floors and walls. He turned a knob and lights went on.

At each step, he consulted the handbook, though he

knew it by heart; and with each step, the rooms brightened and the dial-indicators sprang into motion and a humming grew louder.

Somewhere deep in the factories, the accumulated wastes were being drawn into the proper channels.

A high-pitched signal sounded and startled Lamorak out of his painful concentration. It was the communications signal and Lamorak fumbled his receiver into action.

Ragusnik's head showed, startled; then slowly, the incredulity and outright shock faded from his eyes. *"That's* how it is, then."

"I'm not an Elseverian, Ragusnik; I don't mind doing this."

"But what business is it of yours? Why do you interfere?"

"I'm on your side, Ragusnik, but I must do this."

"Why, if you're on my side? Do they treat people on your world as they treat me here?"

"Not any longer. But even if you are right, there are thirty thousand people on Elsevere to be considered."

"They would have given in; you've ruined my only chance."

"They would *not* have given in. And in a way, you've won; they know now that you're dissatisfied. Until now, they never dreamed a Ragusnik could be unhappy, that he could make trouble."

"What if they know? Now all they need do is hire an Outworlder anytime."

Lamorak shook his head violently. He had thought this through in these last bitter hours. "The fact that they know means that the Elseverians will begin to think about you; some will begin to wonder if it's right to treat a human so. And if Outworlders are hired, they'll spread the word that this goes on upon Elsevere and Galactic public opinion will be in your favor."

"And?"

"Things will improve. In your son's time, things will be much better."

"In my son's time," said Ragusnik, his cheeks sagging.

"I might have had it now. Well, I lose. I'll go back to the job."

Lamorak felt an overwhelming relief. "If you'll come here now, sir, you may have your job and I'll consider it an honor to shake your hand."

Ragusnik's head snapped up and filled with a gloomy pride. "You call me 'sir' and offer to shake my hand. Go about your business, Earthman, and leave me to my work, for I would not shake yours."

Lamorak returned the way he had come, relieved that the crisis was over, and profoundly depressed, too.

He stopped in surprise when he found a section of corridor cordoned off, so he could not pass. He looked about for alternate routes, then startled at a magnified voice above his head. "Dr. Lamorak, do you hear me? This is Councillor Blei."

Lamorak looked up. The voice came over some sort of public address system, but he saw no sign of an outlet.

He called out, "Is anything wrong? Can you hear me?"

"I hear you."

Instinctively, Lamorak was shouting. "Is anything wrong? There seems to be a block here. Are there complications with Ragusnik?"

"Ragusnik has gone to work," came Blei's voice. "The crisis is over, and you must make ready to leave."

"Leave?"

"Leave Elsevere; a ship is being made ready for you now."

"But wait a bit." Lamorak was confused by this sudden leap of events. "I haven't completed my gathering of data."

Blei's voice said, "This cannot be helped. You will be directed to the ship and your belongings will be sent after you by servo-mechanisms. We trust—we trust—"

Something was becoming clear to Lamorak. "You trust *what?*"

"We trust you will make no attempt to see or speak directly to any Elseverian. And of course we hope you will avoid embarrassment by not attempting to return to

Elsevere at any time in the future. A colleague of yours would be welcome if further data concerning us is needed."

"I understand," said Lamorak, tonelessly. Obviously, he had himself become a Ragusnik. He had handled the controls that in turn had handled the wastes; he was ostracized. He was a corpse-handler, a swineherd, an inside man at the skonk works.

He said, "Good-bye."

Blei's voice said, "Before we direct you, Dr. Lamorak—. On behalf of the Council of Elsevere, I thank you for your help in this crisis."

"You're welcome," said Lamorak, bitterly.

26

Sure Thing

Here it is. The fourth short-short with a play-on-words ending. Mind you, it isn't easy to do one of these things properly. You must not only get a kicker but you must build up an honest science-fictional background in only (in this case) five hundred words. Ideally, it must be an interesting story in itself and not just a long ho-hum waiting for the final explosion. (And if you write to tell me that this was just a long ho-hum, etc., etc., I warn you that your letter will not be opened.)

As is well known, in this thirtieth century of ours, space travel is fearfully dull and time-consuming. In search of diversion many crew members defy the quarantine restrictions and pick up pets from the various habitable worlds they explore.

Jim Sloane had a rockette, which he called Teddy. It just sat there looking like a rock but sometimes it lifted a lower edge and sucked in powdered sugar. That was all it ate. No one ever saw it move but every once in a while it wasn't quite where people thought it was. There was a theory it moved when no one was looking.

Bob Laverty had a heli-worm he called Dolly. It was green and carried on photosynthesis. Sometimes it moved to get into better light and when it did so it coiled its wormlike body and inched along very slowly like a turning helix.

One day, Jim Sloane challenged Bob Laverty to a race. "My Teddy," he said, "can beat your Dolly."

"Your Teddy," scoffed Laverty, "doesn't move."

"Bet!" said Sloane.

The whole crew got into the act. Even the captain risked half a credit. Everyone bet on Dolly. At least it moved.

Jim Sloane covered it all. He had been saving his salary through three trips and he put every millicredit of it on Teddy.

The race started at one end of the Grand Salon. At the other end, a heap of sugar had been placed for Teddy and a spotlight for Dolly. Dolly formed a coil at once and began to spiral its way very slowly toward the light. The watching crew cheered it on.

Teddy just sat there without budging.

"Sugar, Teddy. Sugar," said Sloane, pointing. Teddy did not move. It looked more like a rock than ever, but Sloane did not seem concerned.

Finally, when Dolly had spiraled halfway across the salon, Jim Sloane said casually to the rockette, "If you don't get out there, Teddy, I'm going to get a hammer and chip you into pebbles."

That was when people first discovered that rockettes could read minds. That was also when people first discovered that rockettes could teleport.

Sloane had no sooner made his threat when Teddy simply disappeared from his place and reappeared on top of the sugar.

Sloane won, of course, and he counted his winnings slowly and luxuriously.

Laverty said, bitterly, "You *knew* the damn thing could teleport."

"No, I didn't," said Sloane, "but I knew he would win. It was a sure thing."

"How come?"

"It's an old saying everyone knows. Sloane's Teddy wins the race."

27

The Ugly Little Boy

*In listing my short stories in order of preference, I've
never gone past the one-two-three. Beyond the top three,
everything is a sort of blur and I haven't the faintest idea
which is fourth, which is fifth, and so on.*

*This story is in third place, so it must be in this book
along with "The Last Question." The second-place story
isn't here. It is "The Bicentennial Man" and it is a robot
story, so that you'll find it in* The Complete Robot.

*The first version of this story was rotten, though I didn't
realize it till Horace Gold pointed it out. For once, he was
right and I did something I hardly ever do. I tore up the
story and started again from scratch. I was never sorry,
for the second version was great.*

*I don't usually write stories in order to tug at heart-
strings, since my specialty is highly cerebral reasoning.
This is the great exception and I can generally rely on
people sniffing by the time they get to the end. ("The
Bicentennial Man" is another. Maybe that's why they're in
second and third place in my private listings.)*

Edith Fellowes smoothed her working smock as she always did before opening the elaborately locked door and
stepping across the invisible dividing line between the *is*
and the *is not*. She carried her notebook and her pen
although she no longer took notes except when she felt
the absolute need for some report.

This time she also carried a suitcase. ("Games for the
boy," she had said, smiling, to the guard—who had long
since stopped even thinking of questioning her and who
waved her on.)

And, as always, the ugly little boy knew that she had entered and came running to her, crying, "Miss Fellowes——Miss Fellowes——" in his soft, slurring way.

"Timmie," she said, and passed her hand over the shaggy, brown hair on his misshapen little head. "What's wrong?"

He said, "Will Jerry be back to play again? I'm sorry about what happened."

"Never mind that now, Timmie. Is that why you've been crying?"

He looked away. "Not just about that, Miss Fellowes. I dreamed again."

"The same dream?" Miss Fellowes' lips set. Of course, the Jerry affair would bring back the dream.

He nodded. His too large teeth showed as he tried to smile and the lips of his forward-thrusting mouth stretched wide. "When will I be big enough to go out there, Miss Fellowes?"

"Soon," she said softly, feeling her heart break. "Soon."

Miss Fellowes let him take her hand and enjoyed the warm touch of the thick dry skin of his palm. He led her through the three rooms that made up the whole of Stasis Section One—comfortable enough, yes, but an eternal prison for the ugly little boy all the seven (was it seven?) years of his life.

He led her to the one window, looking out onto a scrubby woodland section of the world of *is* (now hidden by night), where a fence and painted instructions allowed no men to wander without permission.

He pressed his nose against the window. "Out there, Miss Fellowes?"

"Better places. Nicer places," she said sadly as she looked at his poor little imprisoned face outlined in profile against the window. The forehead retreated flatly and his hair lay down in tufts upon it. The back of his skull bulged and seemed to make the head overheavy so that it sagged and bent forward, forcing the whole body into a stoop. Already, bony ridges were beginning to bulge the skin above his eyes. His wide mouth thrust forward more prominently than did his wide and flattened nose and he had no chin to speak of, only a jawbone that curved smoothly down and back. He was small for his years and his stumpy legs were bowed.

He was a very ugly little boy and Edith Fellowes loved him dearly.

Her own face was behind his line of vision, so she allowed her lips the luxury of a tremor.

They would *not* kill him. She would do anything to prevent it. Anything. She opened the suitcase and began taking out the clothes it contained.

Edith Fellowes had crossed the threshold of Stasis, Inc. for the first time just a little over three years before. She hadn't, at that time, the slightest idea as to what Stasis meant or what the place did. No one did then, except those who worked there. In fact, it was only the day after she arrived that the news broke upon the world.

At the time, it was just that they had advertised for a woman with knowledge of physiology, experience with clinical chemistry, and a love for children. Edith Fellowes had been a nurse in a maternity ward and believed she fulfilled those qualifications.

Gerald Hoskins, whose name plate on the desk included a Ph.D. after the name, scratched his cheek with his thumb and looked at her steadily.

Miss Fellowes automatically stiffened and felt her face (with its slightly asymmetric nose and its a-trifle-too-heavy eyebrows) twitch.

He's no dreamboat himself, she thought resentfully. He's getting fat and bald and he's got a sullen mouth.
——But the salary mentioned had been considerably higher than she had expected, so she waited.

Hoskins said, "Now do you really love children?"

"I wouldn't say I did if I didn't."

"Or do you just love pretty children? Nice chubby children with cute little button-noses and gurgly ways?"

Miss Fellowes said, "Children are children, Dr. Hoskins, and the ones that aren't pretty are just the ones who may happen to need help most."

"Then suppose we take you on——"

"You mean you're offering me the job now?"

He smiled briefly, and for a moment, his broad face had an absent-minded charm about it. He said, "I make quick decisions. So far the offer is tentative, however. I may make as quick a decision to let you go. Are you ready to take the chance?"

Miss Fellowes clutched at her purse and calculated just as swiftly as she could, then ignored calculations and followed impulse. "All right."

"Fine. We're going to form the Stasis tonight and I think you had better be there to take over at once. That will be at 8 P.M. and I'd appreciate it if you could be here at 7:30."

"But what——"

"Fine. Fine. That will be all now." On signal, a smiling secretary came in to usher her out.

Miss Fellowes stared back at Dr. Hoskins' closed door for a moment. What was Stasis? What had this large bar of a building—with its badged employees, its makeshift corridors, and its unmistakable air of engineering—to do with children?

She wondered if she should go back that evening or stay away and teach that arrogant man a lesson. But she knew she would be back if only out of sheer frustration. She would have to find out about the children.

She came back at 7:30 and did not have to announce herself. One after another, men and women seemed to know her and to know her function. She found herself all but placed on skids as she was moved inward.

Dr. Hoskins was there, but he only looked at her distantly and murmured, "Miss Fellowes."

He did not even suggest that she take a seat, but she drew one calmly up to the railing and sat down.

They were on a balcony, looking down into a large pit, filled with instruments that looked like a cross between the control panel of a spaceship and the working face of a computer. On one side were partitions that seemed to make up an unceilinged apartment, a giant dollhouse into the rooms of which she could look from above.

She could see an electronic cooker and a freeze-space unit in one room and a washroom arrangement off another. And surely the object she made out in another room could only be part of a bed, a small bed.

Hoskins was speaking to another man and, with Miss Fellowes, they made up the total occupancy of the balcony. Hoskins did not offer to introduce the other man, and Miss Fellowes eyed him surreptitiously. He was thin and quite fine-looking in a middle-aged way. He had a small mustache and keen eyes that seemed to busy themselves with everything.

He was saying, "I won't pretend for one moment that I understand all this, Dr. Hoskins; I mean, except as a layman, a reasonably intelligent layman, may be expected to understand it. Still, if there's one part I understand less than another, it's this matter of selectivity. You can only reach out so far; that seems sensible; things get dimmer the further you go; it takes more energy.——But then, you can only reach out so near. That's the puzzling part."

"I can make it seem less paradoxical, Deveney, if you will allow me to use an analogy."

Miss Fellowes placed the new man the moment she heard his name, and despite herself was impressed. This was obviously Candide Deveney, the science writer of the Telenews, who was notoriously at the scene of every major scientific break-through. She even recognized his face as one she saw on the news-plate when the landing on Mars had been announced.——So Dr. Hoskins must have something important here.

"By all means use an analogy," said Deveney ruefully, "if you think it will help."

"Well, then, you can't read a book with ordinary-sized print if it is held six feet from your eyes, but you can read it if you hold it one foot from your eyes. So far, the closer the better. If you bring the book to within one inch of your eyes, however, you've lost it again. There is such a thing as being too close, you see."

"Hmm," said Deveney.

"Or take another example. Your right shoulder is about

thirty inches from the tip of your right forefinger and you can place your right forefinger on your right shoulder. Your right elbow is only half the distance from the tip of your right forefinger; it should by all ordinary logic be easier to reach, and yet you cannot place your right finger on your right elbow. Again, there is such a thing as being too close."

Deveney said, "May I use these analogies in my story?"

"Well, of course. Only too glad. I've been waiting long enough for someone like you to have a story. I'll give you anything else you want. It is time, finally, that we want the world looking over our shoulder. They'll see something."

(Miss Fellowes found herself admiring his calm certainty despite herself. There was strength there.)

Deveney said, "How far out will you reach?"

"Forty thousand years."

Miss Fellowes drew in her breath sharply.

Years?

There was tension in the air. The men at the controls scarcely moved. One man at a microphone spoke into it in a soft monotone, in short phrases that made no sense to Miss Fellowes.

Deveney, leaning over the balcony railing with an intent stare, said, "Will we see anything, Dr. Hoskins?"

"What? No. Nothing till the job is done. We detect indirectly, something on the principle of radar, except that we use mesons rather than radiation. Mesons reach backward under the proper conditions. Some are reflected and we must analyze the reflections."

"That sounds difficult."

Hoskins smiled again, briefly as always. "It is the end product of fifty years of research; forty years of it before I entered the field.——Yes, it's difficult."

The man at the microphone raised one hand.

Hoskins said, "We've had the fix on one particular moment in time for weeks; breaking it, remaking it after calculating our own movements in time; making certain that we could handle time-flow with sufficient precision. This must work now."

But his forehead glistened.

Edith Fellowes found herself out of her seat and at the balcony railing, but there was nothing to see.

The man at the microphone said quietly, "Now."

There was a space of silence sufficient for one breath and then the sound of a terrified little boy's scream from the dollhouse rooms. Terror! Piercing terror!

Miss Fellowes' head twisted in the direction of the cry. A child was involved. She had forgotten.

And Hoskins' fist pounded on the railing and he said in a tight voice, trembling with triumph, "*Did* it."

Miss Fellowes was urged down the short, spiral flight of steps by the hard press of Hoskins' palm between her shoulder blades. He did not speak to her.

The men who had been at the controls were standing about now, smiling, smoking, watching the three as they entered on the main floor. A very soft buzz sounded from the direction of the dollhouse.

Hoskins said to Deveney, "It's perfectly safe to enter Stasis. I've done it a thousand times. There's a queer sensation which is momentary and means nothing."

He stepped through an open door in mute demonstration, and Deveney, smiling stiffly and drawing an obviously deep breath, followed him.

Hoskins said, "Miss Fellowes! Please!" He crooked his forefinger impatiently.

Miss Fellowes nodded and stepped stiffly through. It was as though a ripple went through her, an internal tickle.

But once inside all seemed normal. There was the smell of the fresh wood of the dollhouse and—of—of soil somehow.

There was silence now, no voice at least, but there was the dry shuffling of feet, a scrabbling as of a hand over wood—then a low moan.

"Where is it?" asked Miss Fellowes in distress. Didn't these fool men *care?*

The boy was in the bedroom; at least the room with the bed in it.

It was standing naked, with its small, dirt-smeared chest heaving raggedly. A bushel of dirt and coarse grass spread over the floor at his bare brown feet. The smell of soil came from it and a touch of something fetid.

Hoskins followed her horrified glance and said with annoyance, "You can't pluck a boy cleanly out of time, Miss Fellowes. We had to take some of the surroundings with it for safety. Or would you have preferred to have it arrive here minus a leg or with only half a head?"

"Please!" said Miss Fellowes, in an agony of revulsion. "Are we just to stand here? The poor child is frightened. And it's *filthy.*"

She was quite correct. It was smeared with encrusted dirt and grease and had a scratch on its thigh that looked red and sore.

As Hoskins approached him, the boy, who seemed to be something over three years in age, hunched low and backed away rapidly. He lifted his upper lip and snarled in a hissing fashion like a cat. With a rapid gesture, Hoskins seized both the child's arms and lifted him, writhing and screaming, from the floor.

Miss Fellowes said, "Hold him, now. He needs a warm bath first. He needs to be cleaned. Have you the equipment? If so, have it brought here, and I'll need to have help in handling him just at first. Then, too, for heaven's sake, have all this trash and filth removed."

She was giving the orders now and she felt perfectly good about that. And because now she was an efficient nurse, rather than a confused spectator, she looked at the child with a clinical eye—and hesitated for one shocked moment. She saw past the dirt and shrieking, past the thrashing of limbs and useless twisting. She saw the boy himself.

It was the ugliest little boy she had ever seen. It was horribly ugly from misshapen head to bandy legs.

She got the boy cleaned with three men helping her and with others milling about in their efforts to clean the room. She worked in silence and with a sense of outrage, annoyed by the continued strugglings and outcries of the boy and by the undignified drenchings of soapy water to which she was subjected.

Dr. Hoskins had hinted that the child would not be pretty, but that was far from stating that it would be repulsively deformed. And there was a stench about the boy that soap and water was only alleviating little by little.

She had the strong desire to thrust the boy, soaped as he was, into Hoskins' arms and walk out; but there was the pride of profession. She had accepted an assignment after all.——And there would be the look in his eyes. A cold look that would read: Only pretty children, Miss Fellowes?

He was standing apart from them, watching coolly from a distance with a half-smile on his face when he caught her eyes, as though amused at her outrage.

She decided she would wait a while before quitting. To do so now would only demean her.

Then, when the boy was a bearable pink and smelled of scented soap, she felt better anyway. His cries changed to whimpers of exhaustion as he watched carefully, eyes moving in quick frightened suspicion from one to another of those in the room. His cleanness accentuated his thin nakedness as he shivered with cold after his bath.

Miss Fellowes said sharply, "Bring me a nightgown for the child!"

A nightgown appeared at once. It was as though everything were ready and yet nothing were ready unless she gave orders; as though they were deliberately leaving this in her charge without help, to test her.

The newsman, Deveney, approached and said, "I'll hold him, Miss. You won't get it on yourself."

"Thank you," said Miss Fellowes. And it was a battle indeed, but the nightgown went on, and when the boy made as though to rip it off, she slapped his hand sharply.

The boy reddened, but did not cry. He stared at her and the splayed fingers of one hand moved slowly across the flannel of the nightgown, feeling the strangeness of it.

Miss Fellowes thought desperately: Well, what next?

Everyone seemed in suspended animation, waiting for her—even the ugly little boy.

Miss Fellowes said sharply, "Have you provided food? Milk?"

They had. A mobile unit was wheeled in, with its refrigeration compartment containing three quarts of milk, with a warming unit and a supply of fortifications in the form of vitamin drops, copper-cobalt-iron syrup and others she had no time to be concerned with. There was a variety of canned self-warming junior foods.

She used milk, simply milk, to begin with. The radar unit heated the milk to a set temperature in a matter of ten seconds and clicked off, and she put some in a saucer. She had a certainty about the boy's savagery. He wouldn't know how to handle a cup.

Miss Fellowes nodded and said to the boy, "Drink. Drink." She made a gesture as though to raise the milk to her mouth. The boy's eyes followed but he made no move.

Suddenly, the nurse resorted to direct measures. She seized the boy's upper arm in one hand and dipped the other in the milk. She dashed the milk across his lips, so that it dripped down cheeks and receding chin.

For a moment, the child uttered a high-pitched cry, then his tongue moved over his wetted lips. Miss Fellowes stepped back.

The boy approached the saucer, bent toward it, then looked up and behind sharply as though expecting a crouching enemy; bent again and licked at the milk eagerly, like a cat. He made a slurping noise. He did not use his hands to lift the saucer.

Miss Fellowes allowed a bit of the revulsion she felt show on her face. She couldn't help it.

Deveney caught that, perhaps. He said, "Does the nurse know, Dr. Hoskins?"

"Know what?" demanded Miss Fellowes.

Deveney hesitated, but Hoskins (again that look of detached amusement on his face) said, "Well, tell her."

Deveney addressed Miss Fellowes. "You may not suspect it, Miss, but you happen to be the first civilized woman in history ever to be taking care of a Neanderthal youngster."

She turned on Hoskins with a kind of controlled ferocity. "You might have told me, Doctor."

"Why? What difference does it make?"

"You said a child."

"Isn't that a child? Have you ever had a puppy or a kitten, Miss Fellowes? Are those closer to the human? If that were a baby chimpanzee, would you be repelled? You're a nurse, Miss Fellowes. Your record places you in a maternity ward for three years. Have you ever refused to take care of a deformed infant?"

Miss Fellowes felt her case slipping away. She said, with much less decision, "You might have told me."

"And you would have refused the position? Well, do you refuse it now?" He gazed at her coolly, while Deveney watched from the other side of the room, and the Neanderthal child, having finished the milk and licked the plate, looked up at her with a wet face and wide, longing eyes.

The boy pointed to the milk and suddenly burst out in a short series of sounds repeated over and over; sounds made up of gutturals and elaborate tongue-clickings.

Miss Fellowes said, in surprise, "Why, he talks."

"Of course," said Hoskins. "Homo neanderthalensis is not a truly separate species, but rather a subspecies of Homo sapiens. Why shouldn't he talk? He's probably asking for more milk."

Automatically, Miss Fellowes reached for the bottle of milk, but Hoskins seized her wrist. "Now, Miss Fellowes, before we go any further, are you staying on the job?"

Miss Fellowes shook free in annoyance, "Won't you feed him if I don't? I'll stay with him—for a while."

She poured the milk.

Hoskins said, "We are going to leave you with the boy, Miss Fellowes. This is the only door to Stasis Number One and it is elaborately locked and guarded. I'll want you to learn the details of the lock which will, of course, be keyed to your fingerprints as they are already keyed to mine. The spaces overhead" (he looked upward to the open ceilings of the dollhouse) "are also guarded and we will be warned if anything untoward takes place in here."

Miss Fellowes said indignantly, "You mean I'll be under view." She thought suddenly of her own survey of the room interiors from the balcony.

"No, no," said Hoskins seriously, "your privacy will be respected completely. The view will consist of electronic symbolism only, which only a computer will deal with. Now you will stay with him tonight, Miss Fellowes, and every night until further notice. You will be relieved during the day according to some schedule you will find convenient. We will allow you to arrange that."

Miss Fellowes looked about the dollhouse with a puzzled expression. "But why all this, Dr. Hoskins? Is the boy dangerous?"

"It's a matter of energy, Miss Fellowes. He must never be allowed to leave these rooms. Never. Not for an instant. Not for any reason. Not to save his life. Not even to save *your* life, Miss Fellowes. Is that clear?"

Miss Fellowes raised her chin. "I understand the orders, Dr. Hoskins, and the nursing profession is accustomed to placing its duties ahead of self-preservation."

"Good. You can always signal if you need anyone." And the two men left.

Miss Fellowes turned to the boy. He was watching her and there was still milk in the saucer. Laboriously, she tried to show him how to lift the saucer and place it to his lips. He resisted, but let her touch him without crying out.

Always, his frightened eyes were on her, watching, watching for the one false move. She found herself soothing him, trying to move her hand very slowly toward his hair, letting him see it every inch of the way, see there was no harm in it.

And she succeeded in stroking his hair for an instant.

She said, "I'm going to have to show you how to use the bathroom. Do you think you can learn?"

She spoke quietly, kindly, knowing he would not understand the words but hoping he would respond to the calmness of the tone.

The boy launched into a clicking phrase again.

She said, "May I take your hand?"

She held out hers and the boy looked at it. She left it outstretched and waited. The boy's own hand crept forward toward hers.

"That's right," she said.

It approached within an inch of hers and then the boy's courage failed him. He snatched it back.

"Well," said Miss Fellowes calmly, "we'll try again later. Would you like to sit down here?" She patted the mattress of the bed.

The hours passed slowly and progress was minute. She did not succeed either with bathroom or with the bed. In fact, after the child had given unmistakable signs of sleepiness he lay down on the bare ground and then, with a quick movement, rolled beneath the bed.

She bent to look at him and his eyes gleamed out at her as he tongue-clicked at her.

"All right," she said, "if you feel safer there, you sleep there."

She closed the door to the bedroom and retired to the cot that had been placed for her use in the largest room. At her insistence, a make-shift canopy had been stretched over it. She thought: Those stupid men will have to place a mirror in this room and a larger chest of drawers and a separate washroom if they expect me to spend nights here.

It was difficult to sleep. She found herself straining to hear possible sounds in the next room. He couldn't get out, could he? The walls were sheer and impossibly high but suppose the child could climb like a monkey? Well, Hoskins said there were observational devices watching through the ceiling.

Suddenly she thought: Can he be dangerous? Physically dangerous?

Surely, Hoskins couldn't have meant that. Surely, he would not have left her here alone, if——

She tried to laugh at herself. He was only a three- or four-year-old child. Still, she had not succeeded in cutting his nails. If he should attack her with nails and teeth while she slept——

Her breath came quickly. Oh, ridiculous, and yet——

She listened with painful attentiveness, and this time she heard the sound.

The boy was crying.

Not shrieking in fear or anger; not yelling or screaming. It was crying softly, and the cry was the heartbroken sobbing of a lonely, lonely child.

For the first time, Miss Fellowes thought with a pang: Poor thing!

Of course, it was a child; what did the shape of its head matter? It was a child that had been orphaned as no child had ever been orphaned before. Not only its mother and father were gone, but all its species. Snatched callously out of time, it was now the only creature of its kind in the world. The last. The only.

She felt pity for it strengthen, and with it shame at her own callousness. Tucking her own nightgown carefully about her calves (incongruously, she thought: Tomorrow I'll have to bring in a bathrobe) she got out of bed and went into the boy's room.

"Little boy," she called in a whisper. "Little boy."

She was about to reach under the bed, but she thought of a possible bite and did not. Instead, she turned on the night light and moved the bed.

The poor thing was huddled in the corner, knees up against his chin, looking up at her with blurred and apprehensive eyes.

In the dim light, she was not aware of his repulsiveness.

"Poor boy," she said, "poor boy." She felt him stiffen as she stroked his hair, then relax. "Poor boy. May I hold you?"

She sat down on the floor next to him and slowly and rhythmically stroked his hair, his cheek, his arm. Softly, she began to sing a slow and gentle song.

He lifted his head at that, staring at her mouth in the dimness, as though wondering at the sound.

She maneuvered him closer while he listened to her. Slowly, she pressed gently against the side of his head, until it rested on her shoulder. She put her arm under his thighs and with a smooth and unhurried motion lifted him into her lap.

She continued singing, the same simple verse over and over, while she rocked back and forth, back and forth.

He stopped crying, and after a while the smooth burr of his breathing showed he was asleep.

With infinite care, she pushed his bed back against the wall and laid him down. She covered him and stared down. His face looked so peaceful and little-boy as he slept. It didn't matter so much that it was so ugly. Really.

She began to tiptoe out, then thought: If he wakes up?

She came back, battled irresolutely with herself, then sighed and slowly got into bed with the child.

It was too small for her. She was cramped and uneasy at the lack of canopy, but the child's hand crept into hers and, somehow, she fell asleep in that position.

She awoke with a start and a wild impulse to scream. The latter she just managed to suppress into a gurgle. The boy was looking at her, wide-eyed. It took her a long moment to remember getting into bed with him, and now, slowly, without unfixing her eyes from his, she stretched one leg carefully and let it touch the floor, then the other one.

She cast a quick and apprehensive glance toward the open ceiling, then tensed her muscles for quick disengagement.

But at that moment, the boy's stubby fingers reached out and touched her lips. He said something.

She shrank at the touch. He was terribly ugly in the light of day.

The boy spoke again. He opened his own mouth and gestured with his hand as though something were coming out.

Miss Fellowes guessed at the meaning and said tremulously, "Do you want me to sing?"

The boy said nothing but stared at her mouth.

In a voice slightly off key with tension, Miss Fellowes began the little song she had sung the night before and the ugly little boy smiled. He swayed clumsily in rough time to the music and made a little gurgly sound that might have been the beginnings of a laugh.

Miss Fellowes sighed inwardly. Music hath charms to soothe the savage breast. It might help——

She said, "You wait. Let me get myself fixed up. It will just take a minute. Then I'll make breakfast for you."

She worked rapidly, conscious of the lack of ceiling at all times. The boy remained in bed, watching her when she was in view. She smiled at him at those times and waved. At the end, he waved back, and she found herself being charmed by that.

Finally, she said, "Would you like oatmeal with milk?" It took a moment to prepare, and then she beckoned to him.

Whether he understood the gesture or followed the aroma, Miss Fellowes did not know, but he got out of bed.

She tried to show him how to use a spoon but he shrank away from it in fright. (Time enough, she thought.) She compromised on insisting that he lift the bowl in his hands. He did it clumsily enough and it was incredibly messy but most of it did get into him.

She tried the drinking milk in a glass this time, and the little boy whined when he found the opening too small for him to get his face into conveniently. She held his hand, forcing it around the glass, making him tip it, forcing his mouth to the rim.

Again a mess but again most went into him, and she was used to messes.

The washroom, to her surprise and relief, was a less frustrating matter. He understood what it was she expected him to do.

She found herself patting his head, saying, "Good boy. Smart boy."

And to Miss Fellowes' exceeding pleasure, the boy smiled at that.

She thought: When he smiles, he's quite bearable. Really.

Later in the day, the gentlemen of the press arrived.

She held the boy in her arms and he clung to her wildly while across the open door they set cameras to work. The commotion frightened the boy and he began to cry, but it was ten minutes before Miss Fellowes was allowed to retreat and put the boy in the next room.

She emerged again, flushed with indignation, walked out of the apartment (for the first time in eighteen hours) and closed the door behind her. "I think you've had enough. It will take me a while to quiet him. Go away."

"Sure, sure," said the gentleman from the *Times-Herald*. "But is that really a Neanderthal or is this some kind of gag?"

"I assure you," said Hoskins' voice, suddenly, from the background, "that this is no gag. The child is authentic *Homo neanderthalensis*."

"Is it a boy or a girl?"

"Boy," said Miss Fellowes briefly.

"Ape-boy," said the gentleman from the *News*. "That's what we've got here. Ape-boy. How does he act, Nurse?"

"He acts exactly like a little boy," snapped Miss Fellowes, annoyed into the defensive, "and he is not an ape-boy. His name is—is Timothy, Timmie—and he is perfectly normal in his behavior."

She had chosen the name Timothy at a venture. It was the first that had occurred to her.

"Timmie the Ape-boy," said the gentleman from the *News* and, as it turned out, Timmie the Ape-boy was the name under which the child became known to the world.

The gentleman from the *Globe* turned to Hoskins and said, "Doc, what do you expect to do with the ape-boy?"

Hoskins shrugged. "My original plan was completed when I proved it possible to bring him here. However, the anthropologists will be very interested, I imagine, and the physiologists. We have here, after all, a creature which is at the edge of being human. We should learn a great deal about ourselves and our ancestry from him."

"How long will you keep him?"

"Until such a time as we need the space more than we need him. Quite a while, perhaps."

The gentleman from the *News* said, "Can you bring it out into the open so we can set up sub-etheric equipment and put on a real show?"

"I'm sorry, but the child cannot be removed from Stasis."

"Exactly what is Stasis?"

"Ah." Hoskins permitted himself one of his short smiles. "That would take a great deal of explanation, gentlemen. In Stasis, time as we know it doesn't exist. Those rooms are inside an invisible bubble that is not exactly part of our Universe. That is why the child could be plucked out of time as it was."

"Well, wait now," said the gentleman from the *News* discontentedly, "what are you giving us? The nurse goes into the room and out of it."

"And so can any of you," said Hoskins matter-of-factly. "You would be moving parallel to the lines of temporal force and no great energy gain or loss would be involved. The child, however, was taken from the far past. It moved across the lines and gained temporal potential. To move it into the Universe and into our own time would absorb enough energy to burn out every line in the place and probably blank out all power in the city of Washington. We had to store trash brought with him on the premises and will have to remove it little by little."

The newsmen were writing down sentences busily as Hoskins spoke to them. They did not understand and they were sure their readers would not, but it sounded scientific and that was what counted.

The gentleman from the *Times-Herald* said, "Would you be available for an all-circuit interview tonight?"

"I think so," said Hoskins at once, and they all moved off.

Miss Fellowes looked after them. She understood all this about Stasis and temporal force as little as the newsmen but she managed to get this much. Timmie's imprisonment (she found herself suddenly thinking of the little boy as Timmie) was a real one and not one imposed by the arbitrary fiat of Hoskins. Apparently, it was impossible to let him out of Stasis at all, ever.

Poor child. Poor child.

She was suddenly aware of his crying and she hastened in to console him.

Miss Fellowes did not have a chance to see Hoskins on the all-circuit hookup, and though his interview was beamed to every part of the world and even to the outpost on the Moon, it did not penetrate the apartment in which Miss Fellowes and the ugly little boy lived.

But he was down the next morning, radiant and joyful.

Miss Fellowes said, "Did the interview go well?"

"Extremely. And how is—Timmie?"

Miss Fellowes found herself pleased at the use of the name. "Doing quite well. Now come out here, Timmie, the nice gentleman will not hurt you."

But Timmie stayed in the other room, with a lock of his matted hair showing behind the barrier of the door and, occasionally, the corner of an eye.

"Actually," said Miss Fellowes, "he is settling down amazingly. He is quite intelligent."

"Are you surprised?"

She hesitated just a moment, then said, "Yes, I am. I suppose I thought he was an ape-boy."

"Well, ape-boy or not, he's done a great deal for us. He's put Stasis, Inc. on the map. We're in, Miss Fellowes, we're in." It was as though he had to express his triumph to someone, even if only to Miss Fellowes.

"Oh?" She let him talk.

He put his hands in his pockets and said, "We've been working on a shoestring for ten years, scrounging funds a penny at a time wherever we could. We had to shoot the works on one big show. It was everything, or nothing. And when I say the works, I mean it. This attempt to bring in a Neanderthal took every cent we could borrow or steal, and some of it *was* stolen—funds for other projects, used for this one without permission. If that experiment hadn't succeeded, I'd have been through."

Miss Fellowes said abruptly, "Is that why there are no ceilings?"

"Eh?" Hoskins looked up.

"Was there no money for ceilings?"

"Oh. Well, that wasn't the only reason. We didn't really know in advance how old the Neanderthal might be exactly. We can detect only dimly in time, and he might have been large and savage. It was possible we might have had to deal with him from a distance, like a caged animal."

"But since that hasn't turned out to be so, I suppose you can build a ceiling now."

"Now, yes. We have plenty of money, now. Funds have been promised from every source. This is all wonderful, Miss Fellowes." His broad face gleamed with a smile that lasted and when he left, even his back seemed to be smiling.

Miss Fellowes thought: He's quite a nice man when he's off guard and forgets about being scientific.

She wondered for an idle moment if he was married, then dismissed the thought in self-embarrassment.

"Timmie," she called. "Come here, Timmie."

In the months that passed, Miss Fellowes felt herself grow to be an integral part of Stasis, Inc. She was given a small office of her own with her name on the door, an office quite close to the dollhouse (as she never stopped calling Timmie's Stasis bubble). She was given a substantial raise. The dollhouse was covered by a ceiling; its furnishings were elaborated and improved; a second washroom was added—and even so, she gained an apartment of her own on the institute grounds and, on occasion, did not stay with Timmie during the night. An intercom was set up between the dollhouse and her apartment and Timmie learned how to use it.

Miss Fellowes got used to Timmie. She even grew less conscious of his ugliness. One day she found herself staring at an ordinary boy in the street and finding something bulgy and unattractive in his high domed forehead and jutting chin. She had to shake herself to break the spell.

It was more pleasant to grow used to Hoskins' occasional visits. It was obvious he welcomed escape from his increasingly harried role as head of Stasis, Inc., and that he took a sentimental interest in the child who had started it all, but it seemed to Miss Fellowes that he also enjoyed talking to her.

(She had learned some facts about Hoskins, too. He had invented the method of analyzing the reflection of the past-penetrating mesonic beam; he had invented the method of establishing Stasis; his coldness was only an effort to hide a kindly nature; and, oh yes, he *was* married.)

What Miss Fellowes could *not* get used to was the fact that she was engaged in a scientific experiment. Despite all she could do, she found herself getting personally involved to the point of quarreling with the physiologists.

On one occasion, Hoskins came down and found her in the midst of a hot urge to kill. They had no right; they had no *right*—— Even if he *was* a Neanderthal, he still wasn't an animal.

She was staring after them in a blind fury; staring out the open door and listening to Timmie's sobbing, when she noticed Hoskins standing before her. He might have been there for minutes.

He said, "May I come in?"

She nodded curtly, then hurried to Timmie, who clung to her, curling his little bandy legs—still thin, so thin— about her.

Hoskins watched, then said gravely, "He seems quite unhappy."

Miss Fellowes said, "I don't blame him. They're at him every day now with their blood samples and their probings. They keep him on synthetic diets that I wouldn't feed a pig."

"It's the sort of thing they can't try on a human, you know."

"And they can't try it on Timmie, either. Dr. Hoskins, I insist. You told me it was Timmie's coming that put Stasis, Inc. on the map. If you have any gratitude for that at all, you've *got* to keep them away from the poor thing at least until he's old enough to understand a little more. After he's had a bad session with them, he has nightmares, he can't sleep. Now I warn you," (she reached a sudden peak of fury) "I'm not letting them in here any more."

(She realized that she had screamed that, but she couldn't help it.)

She said more quietly, "I know he's Neanderthal but there's a great deal we don't appreciate about Neanderthals. I've read up on them. They had a culture of their own. Some of the greatest human inventions arose in Neanderthal times. The domestication of animals, for instance; the wheel; various techniques in grinding stone. They even had spiritual yearnings. They buried their dead and buried possessions with the body, showing they believed in a life after death. It amounts to the fact that they invented religion. Doesn't that mean Timmie has a right to human treatment?"

She patted the little boy gently on his buttocks and sent him off into his playroom. As the door was opened, Hoskins smiled briefly at the display of toys that could be seen.

Miss Fellowes said defensively, "The poor child deserves his toys. It's all he has and he earns them with what he goes through."

"No, no. No objections, I assure you. I was just thinking how you've changed since the first day, when you were quite angry I had foisted a Neanderthal on you."

Miss Fellowes said in a low voice, "I suppose I didn't——" and faded off.

Hoskins changed the subject, "How old would you say he is, Miss Fellowes?"

She said, "I can't say, since we don't know how Neanderthals develop. In size, he'd only be three but Neanderthals are smaller generally and with all the tampering they do with him, he probably isn't growing. The way he's learning English, though, I'd say he was well over four."

"Really? I haven't noticed anything about learning English in the reports."

"He won't speak to anyone but me. For now, anyway. He's terribly afraid of others, and no wonder. But he can ask for an article of food; he can indicate any need practically; and he understands almost anything I say. Of course," (she watched him shrewdly, trying to estimate if this was the time), "his development may not continue."

"Why not?"

"Any child needs stimulation and this one lives a life of solitary confinement. I do what I can, but I'm not with him all the time and I'm not all he needs. What I mean, Dr. Hoskins, is that he needs another boy to play with."

Hoskins nodded slowly. "Unfortunately, there's only one of him, isn't there? Poor child."

Miss Fellowes warmed to him at once. She said, "You do like Timmie, don't you?" It was so nice to have someone else feel like that.

"Oh, yes," said Hoskins, and with his guard down, she could see the weariness in his eyes.

Miss Fellowes dropped her plans to push the matter at once. She said, with real concern, "You look worn out, Dr. Hoskins."

"Do I, Miss Fellowes? I'll have to practice looking more lifelike then."

"I suppose Stasis, Inc. is very busy and that that keeps you very busy."

Hoskins shrugged. "You suppose right. It's a matter of animal, vegetable, and mineral in equal parts, Miss Fellowes. But then, I suppose you haven't ever seen our displays."

"Actually, I haven't. ——But it's not because I'm not interested. It's just that I've been so busy."

"Well, you're not all that busy right now," he said with impulsive decision. "I'll call for you tomorrow at eleven and give you a personal tour. How's that?"

She smiled happily. "I'd love it."

He nodded and smiled in his turn and left.

Miss Fellowes hummed at intervals for the rest of the day. Really—to think so was ridiculous, of course—but really, it was almost like—like making a date.

He was quite on time the next day, smiling and pleasant. She had replaced her nurse's uniform with a dress. One of conservative cut, to be sure, but she hadn't felt so feminine in years.

He complimented her on her appearance with staid formality and she accepted with equally formal grace. It was really a perfect prelude, she thought. And then the additional thought came, prelude to what?

She shut that off by hastening to say good-by to Timmie and to assure him she would be back soon. She made sure he knew all about what and where lunch was.

Hoskins took her into the new wing, into which she had never yet gone. It still had the odor of newness about it and the sound of construction, softly heard, was indication enough that it was still being extended.

"Animal, vegetable, and mineral," said Hoskins, as he had the day before. "Animal right there; our most spectacular exhibits."

The space was divided into many rooms, each a separate Stasis bubble. Hoskins brought her to the view-glass of one and she looked in. What she saw impressed her first as a scaled, tailed chicken. Skittering on two thin legs it ran from wall to wall with its delicate birdlike head, surmounted by a bony keel like the comb of a rooster, looking this way and that. The paws on its small forelimbs clenched and unclenched constantly.

Hoskins said, "It's our dinosaur. We've had it for months. I don't know when we'll be able to let go of it."

"Dinosaur?"

"Did you expect a giant?"

She dimpled. "One does, I suppose. I know some of them are small."

"A small one is all we aimed for, believe me. Generally, it's under investigation, but this seems to be an open hour. Some interesting things have been discovered. For instance, it is not entirely cold-blooded. It has an imperfect method of maintaining internal temperatures higher than that of its environment. Unfortunately, it's a male. Ever since we brought it in we've been trying to get a fix on another that may be female, but we've had no luck yet."

"Why female?"

He looked at her quizzically. "So that we might have a fighting chance to obtain fertile eggs, and baby dinosaurs."

"Of course."

He led her to the trilobite section. "That's Professor Dwayne of Washington University," he said. "He's a nuclear chemist. If I recall correctly, he's taking an isotope ratio on the oxygen of the water."

"Why?"

"It's primeval water; at least half a billion years old. The isotope ratio gives the temperature of the ocean at that time. He himself happens to ignore the trilobites, but others are chiefly concerned in dissecting them. They're the lucky ones because all they need are scalpels and microscopes. Dwayne has to set up a mass spectrograph each time he conducts an experiment."

"Why's that? Can't he——"

"No, he can't. He can't take anything out of the room as far as can be helped."

There were samples of primordial plant life too and chunks of rock formations. Those were the vegetable and mineral. And every specimen had its investigator. It was like a museum; a museum brought to life and serving as a superactive center of research.

"And you have to supervise all of this, Dr. Hoskins?"

"Only indirectly, Miss Fellowes. I have subordinates, thank heaven. My own interest is entirely in the theoretical aspects of the matter: the nature of Time, the technique of mesonic intertemporal detection and so on. I would exchange all this for a method of detecting objects closer in Time than ten thousand years ago. If we could get into historical times——"

He was interrupted by a commotion at one of the distant booths, a thin voice raised querulously. He frowned, muttered hastily, "Excuse me," and hastened off.

Miss Fellowes followed as best she could without actually running.

An elderly man, thinly-bearded and red-faced, was saying, "I had vital aspects of my investigations to complete. Don't you understand that?"

A uniformed technician with the interwoven SI monogram (for Stasis, Inc.) on his lab coat, said, "Dr. Hoskins, it was arranged with Professor Ademewski at the beginning that the specimen could only remain here two weeks."

"I did not know then how long my investigations would take. I'm not a prophet," said Ademewski heatedly.

Dr. Hoskins said, "You understand, Professor, we have limited space; we must keep specimens rotating. That piece of chalcopyrite must go back; there are men waiting for the next specimen."

"Why can't I have it for myself, then? Let me take it out of there."

"You know you can't have it."

"A piece of chalcopyrite; a miserable five-kilogram piece? Why not?"

"We can't afford the energy expense!" said Hoskins brusquely. "You know that."

The technician interrupted. "The point is, Dr. Hoskins, that he tried to remove the rock against the rules and I almost punctured Stasis while he was in there, not knowing he was in there."

There was a short silence and Dr. Hoskins turned on the investigator with a cold formality. "Is that so, Professor?"

Professor Ademewski coughed. "I saw no harm——"

Hoskins reached up to a hand-pull dangling just within reach, outside the specimen room in question. He pulled it.

Miss Fellowes, who had been peering in, looking at the totally undistinguished sample of rock that occasioned the dispute, drew in her breath sharply as its existence flickered out. The room was empty.

Hoskins said, "Professor, your permit to investigate matters in Stasis will be permanently voided. I am sorry."

"But wait——"

"I am sorry. You have violated one of the stringent rules."

"I will appeal to the International Association——"

"Appeal away. In a case like this, you will find I can't be overruled."

He turned away deliberately, leaving the professor still protesting and said to Miss Fellowes (his face still white with anger), "Would you care to have lunch with me, Miss Fellowes?"

He took her into the small administration alcove of the cafeteria. He greeted others and introduced Miss Fellowes with complete ease, although she herself felt painfully self-conscious.

What must they think, she thought, and tried desperately to appear businesslike.

She said, "Do you have that kind of trouble often, Dr. Hoskins? I mean like that you just had with the professor?" She took her fork in hand and began eating.

"No," said Hoskins forcefully. "That was the first time. Of course I'm always having to argue men out of removing specimens but this is the first time one actually tried to *do* it."

"I remember you once talked about the energy it would consume."

"That's right. Of course, we've tried to take it into account. Accidents will happen and so we've got special power sources designed to stand the drain of accidental removal from Stasis, but that doesn't mean we want to see a year's supply of energy gone in half a second—or can afford to without having our plans of expansion delayed for years.——Besides, imagine the professor's being in the room while Stasis was about to be punctured."

"What would have happened to him if it had been?"

"Well, we've experimented with inanimate objects and with mice and they've disappeared. Presumably they've traveled back in time; carried along, so to speak, by the pull of the object simultaneously snapping back into its natural time. For that reason, we have to anchor objects within Stasis that we don't want to move and that's a complicated procedure. The professor would not have been anchored and he would have gone back to the Pliocene at the moment when we abstracted the rock— plus, of course, the two weeks it had remained here in the present."

"How dreadful it would have been."

"Not on account of the professor, I assure you. If he

were fool enough to do what he did, it would serve him right. But imagine the effect it would have on the public if the fact came out. All people would need is to become aware of the dangers involved and funds could be choked off like that." He snapped his fingers and played moodily with his food.

Miss Fellowes said, "Couldn't you get him back? The way you got the rock in the first place?"

"No, because once an object is returned, the original fix is lost unless we deliberately plan to retain it and there was no reason to do that in this case. There never is. Finding the professor again would mean relocating a specific fix and that would be like dropping a line into the oceanic abyss for the purpose of dredging up a particular fish.—My God, when I think of the precautions we take to prevent accidents, it makes me mad. We have every individual Stasis unit set up with its own puncturing device—we have to, since each unit has its separate fix and must be collapsible independently. The point is, though, none of the puncturing devices is ever activated until the last minute. And then we deliberately make activation impossible except by the pull of a rope carefully led outside the Stasis. The pull is a gross mechanical motion that requires a strong effort, not something that is likely to be done accidentally."

Miss Fellowes said, "But doesn't it—change history to move something in and out of Time?"

Hoskins shrugged. "Theoretically, yes; actually, except in unusual cases, no. We move objects out of Stasis all the time. Air molecules. Bacteria. Dust. About 10 per cent of our energy consumption goes to make up micro-losses of that nature. But moving even large objects in Time sets up changes that damp out. Take that chalcopyrite from the Pliocene. Because of its absence for two weeks some insect didn't find the shelter it might have found and is killed. That could initiate a whole series of changes, but the mathematics of Stasis indicates that this is a converging series. The amount of change diminishes with time and then things are as before."

"You mean, reality heals itself?"

"In a manner of speaking. Abstract a human from Time or send one back, and you make a larger wound. If the individual is an ordinary one, that wound still heals itself. Of course, there are a great many people who write to us each day and want us to bring Abraham Lincoln into the present, or Mohammed, or Lenin. *That* can't be done, of course. Even if we could find them, the change in reality in moving one of the history molders would be too great to be healed. There are ways of calculating when a change is likely to be too great and we avoid even approaching that limit."

Miss Fellowes said, "Then, Timmie——"

"No, he presents no problem in that direction. Reality is safe. But——" He gave her a quick, sharp glance, then went on, "But never mind. Yesterday you said Timmie needed companionship."

"Yes," Miss Fellowes smiled her delight. "I didn't think you paid that any attention."

"Of course I did. I'm fond of the child. I appreciate your feelings for him and I was concerned enough to want to explain to you. Now I have; you've seen what we do; you've gotten some insight into the difficulties involved; so you know why, with the best will in the world, we can't supply companionship for Timmie."

"You can't?" said Miss Fellowes, with sudden dismay.

"But I've just explained. We couldn't possibly expect to find another Neanderthal his age without incredible luck, and if we could, it wouldn't be fair to multiply risks by having another human being in Stasis."

Miss Fellowes put down her spoon and said energetically, "But, Dr. Hoskins, that is not at all what I meant. I don't want you to bring another Neanderthal into the present. I know that's impossible. But it isn't impossible to bring another child to play with Timmie."

Hoskins stared at her in concern. "A *human* child?"

"*Another* child," said Miss Fellowes, completely hostile now. "Timmie is human."

"I couldn't dream of such a thing."

"Why not? Why couldn't you? What is wrong with the notion? You pulled that child out of Time and made him an eternal prisoner. Don't you owe him something? Dr. Hoskins, if there is any man who, in this world, is that child's father in every sense but the biological, it is you. Why can't you do this little thing for him?"

Hoskins said, "His *father?*" He rose, somewhat unsteadily, to his feet. "Miss Fellowes, I think I'll take you back now, if you don't mind."

They returned to the dollhouse in a complete silence that neither broke.

It was a long time after that before she saw Hoskins again, except for an occasional glimpse in passing. She was sorry about that at times; then, at other times, when Timmie was more than usually woebegone or when he spent silent hours at the window with its prospect of little more than nothing, she thought, fiercely: Stupid man.

Timmie's speech grew better and more precise each day. It never entirely lost a certain soft, slurriness that Miss Fellowes found rather endearing. In times of excitement, he fell back into tongue-clicking but those times were becoming fewer. He must be forgetting the days before he came into the present—except for dreams.

As he grew older, the physiologists grew less interested and the psychologists more so. Miss Fellowes was not sure that she did not like the new group even less than the first. The needles were gone; the injections and withdrawals of fluid; the special diets. But now Timmie was made to overcome barriers to reach food and water. He had to lift panels, move bars, reach for cords. And the mild electric shocks made him cry and drove Miss Fellowes to distraction.

She did not wish to appeal to Hoskins; she did not wish to have to go to him; for each time she thought of him, she thought of his face over the luncheon table that last time. Her eyes moistened and she thought: Stupid, *stupid* man.

And then one day Hoskins' voice sounded unexpectedly, calling into the dollhouse, "Miss Fellowes."

She came out coldly, smoothing her nurse's uniform, then stopped in confusion at finding herself in the presence of a pale woman, slender and of middle height. The woman's fair hair and complexion gave her an appearance of fragility. Standing behind her and clutching at her skirt was a round-faced, large-eyed child of four.

Hoskins said, "Dear, this is Miss Fellowes, the nurse in charge of the boy. Miss Fellowes, this is my wife."

(Was this his wife? She was not as Miss Fellowes had imagined her to be. But then, why not? A man like Hoskins would choose a weak thing to be his foil. If that was what he wanted———)

She forced a matter-of-fact greeting. "Good afternoon, Mrs. Hoskins. Is this your—your little boy?"

(That was a surprise. She had thought of Hoskins as a husband, but not as a father, except, of course———She suddenly caught Hoskins' grave eyes and flushed.)

Hoskins said, "Yes, this is my boy, Jerry. Say hello to Miss Fellowes, Jerry."

(Had he stressed the word "this" just a bit? Was he saying *this* was his son and not———)

Jerry receded a bit further into the folds of the maternal skirt and muttered his hello. Mrs. Hoskins' eyes were searching over Miss Fellowes' shoulders, peering into the room, looking for something.

Hoskins said, "Well, let's go in. Come, dear. There's a trifling discomfort at the threshold, but it passes."

Miss Fellowes said, "Do you want Jerry to come in, too?"

"Of course. He is to be Timmie's playmate. You said that Timmie needed a playmate. Or have you forgotten?"

"But———" She looked at him with a colossal, surprised wonder. *"Your* boy?"

He said peevishly, "Well, whose boy, then? Isn't this what you want? Come on in, dear. Come on in."

Mrs. Hoskins lifted Jerry into her arms with a distinct effort and, hesitantly, stepped over the threshold. Jerry squirmed as she did so, disliking the sensation.

Mrs. Hoskins said in a thin voice, "Is the creature here? I don't see him."

Miss Fellowes called, "Timmie. Come out."

Timmie peered around the edge of the door, staring up

at the little boy who was visiting him. The muscles in Mrs. Hoskins' arms tensed visibly.

She said to her husband, "Gerald, are you sure it's safe?"

Miss Fellowes said at once, "If you mean is Timmie safe, why, of course he is. He's a gentle little boy."

"But he's a sa—savage."

(The ape-boy stories in the newspapers!) Miss Fellowes said emphatically, "He is not a savage. He is just as quiet and reasonable as you can possibly expect a five-and-a-half-year-old to be. It is very generous of you, Mrs. Hoskins, to agree to allow your boy to play with Timmie but please have no fears about it."

Mrs. Hoskins said with mild heat, "I'm not sure that I agree."

"We've had it out, dear," said Hoskins. "Let's not bring up the matter for new argument. Put Jerry down."

Mrs. Hoskins did so and the boy backed against her, staring at the pair of eyes which were staring back at him from the next room.

"Come here, Timmie," said Miss Fellowes. "Don't be afraid."

Slowly, Timmie stepped into the room. Hoskins bent to disengage Jerry's fingers from his mother's skirt. "Step back, dear. Give the children a chance."

The youngsters faced one another. Although the younger, Jerry was nevertheless an inch taller, and in the presence of his straightness and his high-held, well-proportioned head, Timmie's grotesqueries were suddenly almost as pronounced as they had been in the first days.

Miss Fellowes' lips quivered.

It was the little Neanderthal who spoke first, in childish treble. "What's your name?" And Timmie thrust his face suddenly forward as though to inspect the other's features more closely.

Startled, Jerry responded with a vigorous shove that sent Timmie tumbling. Both began crying loudly and Mrs. Hoskins snatched up her child, while Miss Fellowes, flushed with repressed anger, lifted Timmie and comforted him.

Mrs. Hoskins said, "They just instinctively don't like one another."

"No more instinctively," said her husband wearily, "than any two children dislike each other. Now put Jerry down and let him get used to the situation. In fact, we had better leave. Miss Fellowes can bring Jerry to my office after a while and I'll have him taken home."

The two children spent the next hour very aware of each other. Jerry cried for his mother, struck out at Miss Fellowes and, finally, allowed himself to be comforted with a lollipop. Timmie sucked at another, and at the end of an hour, Miss Fellowes had them playing with the same set of blocks, though at opposite ends of the room.

She found herself almost maudlinly grateful to Hoskins when she brought Jerry to him.

She searched for ways to thank him but his very formality was a rebuff. Perhaps he could not forgive her for making him feel like a cruel father. Perhaps the bringing of his own child was an attempt, after all, to prove himself both a kind father to Timmie and, also, not his father at all. Both at the same time!

So all she could say was, "Thank you. Thank you very much."

And all he could say was, "It's all right. Don't mention it."

It became a settled routine. Twice a week, Jerry was brought in for an hour's play, later extended to two hours' play. The children learned each other's names and ways and played together.

And yet, after the first rush of gratitude, Miss Fellowes found herself disliking Jerry. He was larger and heavier and in all things dominant, forcing Timmie into a completely secondary role. All that reconciled her to the situation was the fact that, despite difficulties, Timmie looked forward with more and more delight to the periodic appearances of his playfellow.

It was all he had, she mourned to herself.

And once, as she watched them, she thought: Hoskins' two children, one by his wife and one by Stasis.

While she herself——

Heavens, she thought, putting her fists to her temples and feeling ashamed: I'm jealous!

"Miss Fellowes," said Timmie (carefully, she had never allowed him to call her anything else) "when will I go to school?"

She looked down at those eager brown eyes turned up to hers and passed her hand softly through his thick, curly hair. It was the most disheveled portion of his appearance, for she cut his hair herself while he sat restlessly under the scissors. She did not ask for professional help, for the very clumsiness of the cut served to mask the retreating fore part of the skull and the bulging hinder part.

She said, "Where did you hear about school?"

"Jerry goes to school. Kin-der-gar-ten." He said it carefully. "There are lots of places he goes. Outside. When can I go outside, Miss Fellowes?"

A small pain centered in Miss Fellowes' heart. Of course, she saw, there would be no way of avoiding the inevitability of Timmie's hearing more and more of the outer world he could never enter.

She said, with an attempt at gaiety, "Why, whatever would you do in kindergarten, Timmie?"

"Jerry says they play games, they have picture tapes. He says there are lots of children. He says—he says——" A thought, then a triumphant upholding of both small hands with the fingers splayed apart. "He says this many."

Miss Fellowes said, "Would you like picture tapes? I can get you picture tapes. Very nice ones. And music tapes, too."

So that Timmie was temporarily comforted.

He pored over the picture tapes in Jerry's absence and Miss Fellowes read to him out of ordinary books by the hours.

There was so much to explain in even the simplest story, so much that was outside the perspective of his three rooms. Timmie took to having his dreams more often now that the outside was being introduced to him.

They were always the same, about the outside. He tried haltingly to describe them to Miss Fellowes. In his dreams, he was outside, an empty outside, but very large, with children and queer indescribable objects half-digested in his thought out of bookish descriptions half-understood, or out of distant Neanderthal memories half-recalled.

But the children and objects ignored him and though he was in the world, he was never part of it, but was as alone as though he were in his own room—and would wake up crying.

Miss Fellowes tried to laugh at the dreams, but there were nights in her own apartment when she cried, too.

One day, as Miss Fellowes read, Timmie put his hand under her chin and lifted it gently so that her eyes left the book and met his.

He said, "How do you know what to say, Miss Fellowes?"

She said, "You see these marks? They tell me what to say. These marks make words."

He stared at them long and curiously, taking the book out of her hands. "Some of these marks are the same."

She laughed with pleasure at this sign of his shrewdness and said, "So they are. Would you like to have me show you how to make the marks?"

"All right. That would be a nice game."

It did not occur to her that he could learn to read. Up to the very moment that he read a book to her, it did not occur to her that he could learn to read.

Then, weeks later, the enormity of what had been done struck her. Timmie sat in her lap, following word by word the printing in a child's book, reading to her. He was reading to her!

She struggled to her feet in amazement and said, "Now Timmie, I'll be back later. I want to see Dr. Hoskins."

Excited nearly to frenzy, it seemed to her she might have an answer to Timmie's unhappiness. If Timmie could not leave to enter the world, the world must be brought into those three rooms to Timmie—the whole world in books and film and sound. He must be educated to his full capacity. So much the world owed him.

* * *

She found Hoskins in a mood that was oddly analogous to her own; a kind of triumph and glory. His offices were unusually busy, and for a moment, she thought she would not get to see him, as she stood abashed in the anteroom.

But he saw her, and a smile spread over his broad face. "Miss Fellowes, come here."

He spoke rapidly into the intercom, then shut it off. "Have you heard?——No, of course, you couldn't have. We've done it. We've actually done it. We have intertemporal detection at close range."

"You mean," she tried to detach her thought from her own good news for a moment, "that you can get a person from historical times into the present?"

"That's just what I mean. We have a fix on a fourteenth-century individual right now. Imagine. *Imagine!* If you could only know how glad I'll be to shift from the eternal concentration on the Mesozoic, replace the paleontologists with the historians——But there's something you wish to say to me, eh? Well, go ahead; go ahead. You find me in a good mood. Anything you want you can have."

Miss Fellowes smiled. "I'm glad. Because I wonder if we might not establish a system of instruction for Timmie?"

"Instruction? In what?'

"Well, in everything. A school. So that he might learn."

"But *can* he learn?"

"Certainly, he *is* learning. He can read. I've taught him so much myself."

Hoskins sat there, seeming suddenly depressed. "I don't know, Miss Fellowes."

She said, "You just said that anything I wanted——"

"I know and I should not have. You see, Miss Fellowes, I'm sure you must realize that we cannot maintain the Timmie experiment forever."

She stared at him with sudden horror, not really understanding what he had said. How did he mean "cannot maintain"? With an agonizing flash of recollection, she recalled Professor Ademewski and his mineral specimen that was taken away after two weeks. She said, "But you're talking about a boy. Not about a rock——"

Dr. Hoskins said uneasily, "Even a boy can't be given undue importance, Miss Fellowes. Now that we expect individuals out of historical time, we will need Stasis space, all we can get."

She didn't grasp it. "But you can't. Timmie—Timmie——"

"Now, Miss Fellowes, please don't upset yourself. Timmie won't go right away; perhaps not for months. Meanwhile we'll do what we can."

She was still staring at him.

"Let me get you something, Miss Fellowes."

"No," she whispered. "I don't need anything." She arose in a kind of nightmare and left.

Timmie, she thought, you will *not* die. You will *not* die.

It was all very well to hold tensely to the thought that Timmie must not die, but how was that to be arranged? In the first weeks, Miss Fellowes clung only to the hope that the attempt to bring forward a man from the fourteenth century would fail completely. Hoskins' theories might be wrong or his practice defective. Then things could go on as before.

Certainly, that was not the hope of the rest of the world and, irrationally, Miss Fellowes hated the world for it. "Project Middle Ages" reached a climax of white-hot publicity. The press and the public had hungered for something like this. Stasis, Inc. had lacked the necessary sensation for a long time now. A new rock or another ancient fish failed to stir them. But *this* was *it*.

A historical human; an adult speaking a known language; someone who could open a new page of history to the scholar.

Zero-time was coming and this time it was not a question of three onlookers from a balcony. This time there would be a world-wide audience. This time the technicians of Stasis, Inc. would play their role before nearly all of mankind.

Miss Fellowes was herself all but savage with waiting. When young Jerry Hoskins showed up for his scheduled playtime with Timmie, she scarcely recognized him. He was not the one she was waiting for.

(The secretary who brought him left hurriedly after the barest nod for Miss Fellowes. She was rushing for a good place from which to watch the climax of Project Middle Ages.——And so ought Miss Fellowes with far better reason, she thought bitterly, if only that stupid girl would arrive.)

Jerry Hoskins slided toward her, embarrassed. "Miss Fellowes?" He took the reproduction of a news-strip out of his pocket.

"Yes? What is it, Jerry?"

"Is this a picture of Timmie?"

Miss Fellowes stared at him, then snatched the strip from Jerry's hand. The excitement of Project Middle Ages had brought about a pale revival of interest in Timmie on the part of the press.

Jerry watched her narrowly, then said, "It says Timmie is an ape-boy. What does that mean?"

Miss Fellowes caught the youngster's wrist and repressed the impulse to shake him. "Never say that, Jerry. Never, do you understand? It is a nasty word and you mustn't use it."

Jerry struggled out of her grip, frightened.

Miss Fellowes tore up the news-strip with a vicious twist of the wrist. "Now go inside and play with Timmie. He's got a new book to show you."

And then, finally, the girl appeared. Miss Fellowes did not know her. None of the usual stand-ins she had used when business took her elsewhere was available now, not with Project Middle Ages at climax, but Hoskins' secretary had promised to find *someone* and this must be the girl.

Miss Fellowes tried to keep querulousness out of her voice. "Are you the girl assigned to Stasis Section One?"

"Yes, I'm Mandy Terris. You're Miss Fellowes, aren't you?"

"That's right."

"I'm sorry I'm late. There's just so much excitement."

"I know. Now I want you——"

Mandy said, "You'll be watching, I suppose." Her thin, vacuously pretty face filled with envy.

"Never mind that. Now I want you to come inside and meet Timmie and Jerry. They will be playing for the next two hours so they'll be giving you no trouble. They've got milk handy and plenty of toys. In fact, it will be better if you leave them alone as much as possible. Now I'll show you where everything is located and——"

"Is it Timmie that's the ape-b——"

"Timmie is the Stasis subject," said Miss Fellowes firmly.

"I mean, he's the one who's not supposed to get out, is that right?"

"Yes. Now, come in. There isn't much time."

And when she finally left, Mandy Terris called after her shrilly, "I hope you get a good seat and, golly, I sure hope it works."

Miss Fellowes did not trust herself to make a reasonable response. She hurried on without looking back.

But the delay meant she did *not* get a good seat. She got no nearer than the wall-viewing-plate in the assembly hall. Bitterly, she regretted that. If she could have been on the spot; if she could somehow have reached out for some sensitive portion of the instrumentations; if she were in some way able to wreck the experiment——

She found the strength to beat down her madness. Simple destruction would have done no good. They would have rebuilt and reconstructed and made the effort again. And she would never be allowed to return to Timmie.

Nothing would help. Nothing but that the experiment itself fail; that it break down irretrievably.

So she waited through the countdown, watching every move on the giant screen, scanning the faces of the technicians as the focus shifted from one to the other, watching for the look of worry and uncertainty that would mark something going unexpectedly wrong; watching, watching——

There was no such look. The count reached zero, and very quietly, very unassumingly, the experiment succeeded!

In the new Stasis that had been established there stood a bearded, stoop-shouldered peasant of indeterminate age, in ragged dirty clothing and wooden shoes, staring in dull horror at the sudden mad change that had flung itself over him.

And while the world went mad with jubilation, Miss Fellowes stood frozen in sorrow, jostled and pushed, all but trampled; surrounded by triumph while bowed down with defeat.

And when the loud-speaker called her name with strident force, it sounded it three times before she responded.

"Miss Fellowes. Miss Fellowes. You are wanted in Stasis Section One immediately. Miss Fellowes. Miss Fell——"

"Let me through!" she cried breathlessly, while the loud-speaker continued its repetitions without pause. She forced her way through the crowds with wild energy, beating at it, striking out with closed fists, flailing, moving toward the door in a nightmare slowness.

Mandy Terris was in tears. "I don't know how it happened. I just went down to the edge of the corridor to watch a pocket-viewing-plate they had put up. Just for a minute. And then before I could move or do anything——" She cried out in sudden accusation, "You said they would make no trouble; you *said* to leave them alone——"

Miss Fellowes, disheveled and trembling uncontrollably, glared at her. "Where's Timmie?"

A nurse was swabbing the arm of a wailing Jerry with disinfectant and another was preparing an anti-tetanus shot. There was blood on Jerry's clothes.

"He bit me, Miss Fellowes," Jerry cried in rage. "He *bit* me."

But Miss Fellowes didn't even see him.

"What did you do with Timmie?" she cried out.

"I locked him in the bathroom," said Mandy. "I just threw the little monster in there and locked him in."

Miss Fellowes ran into the dollhouse. She fumbled at the bathroom door. It took an eternity to get it open and to find the ugly little boy cowering in the corner.

"Don't whip me, Miss Fellowes," he whispered. His

eyes were red. His lips were quivering. "I didn't mean to do it."

"Oh, Timmie, who told you about whips?" She caught him to her, hugging him wildly.

He said tremulously, "She said, with a long rope. She said you would hit me and hit me."

"You won't be. She was wicked to say so. But what happened? What happened?"

"He called me an ape-boy. He said I wasn't a real boy. He said I was an animal." Timmie dissolved in a flood of tears. "He said he wasn't going to play with a monkey anymore. I said I wasn't a monkey; I *wasn't* a monkey. He said I was all funny-looking. He said I was horrible ugly. He kept saying and saying and I bit him."

They were both crying now. Miss Fellowes sobbed, "But it isn't true. You know that, Timmie. You're a real boy. You're a dear real boy and the best boy in the world. And no one, *no* one will ever take you away from me."

It was easy to make up her mind, now; easy to know what to do. Only it had to be done quickly. Hoskins wouldn't wait much longer, with his own son mangled——

No, it would have to be done this night, *this* night; with the place four-fifths asleep and the remaining fifth intellectually drunk over Project Middle Ages.

It would be an unusual time for her to return but not an unheard of one. The guard knew her well and would not dream of questioning her. He would think nothing of her carrying a suitcase. She rehearsed the noncommittal phrase, "Games for the boy," and the calm smile.

Why shouldn't he believe that?

He did. When she entered the dollhouse again, Timmie was still awake, and she maintained a desperate normality to avoid frightening him. She talked about his dreams with him and listened to him ask wistfully after Jerry.

There would be few to see her afterward, none to question the bundle she would be carrying. Timmie would be very quiet and then it would be a *fait accompli*. It would be done and what would be the use of trying to undo it. They would leave her be. They would leave them both be.

She opened the suitcase, took out the overcoat, the woolen cap with the ear-flaps and the rest.

Timmie said, with the beginning of alarm, "Why are you putting all these clothes on me, Miss Fellowes?"

She said, "I am going to take you outside, Timmie. To where your dreams are."

"My dreams?" His face twisted in sudden yearning, yet fear was there, too.

"You won't be afraid. You'll be with me. You won't be afraid if you're with me, will you, Timmie?"

"No, Miss Fellowes." He buried his little misshapen head against her side, and under her enclosing arm she could feel his small heart thud.

It was midnight and she lifted him into her arms. She disconnected the alarm and opened the door softly.

And she screamed, for facing her across the open door was Hoskins!

There were two men with him and he stared at her, as astonished as she.

Miss Fellowes recovered first by a second and made a quick attempt to push past him; but even with the second's delay he had time. He caught her roughly and hurled her back against a chest of drawers. He waved the men in and confronted her, blocking the door.

"I didn't expect this. Are you completely insane?"

She had managed to interpose her shoulder so that it, rather than Timmie, had struck the chest. She said pleadingly, "What harm can it do if I take him, Dr. Hoskins? You can't put energy loss ahead of a human life?"

Firmly, Hoskins took Timmie out of her arms. "An energy loss this size would mean millions of dollars lost out of the pockets of investors. It would mean a terrible setback for Stasis, Inc. It would mean eventual publicity about a sentimental nurse destroying all that for the sake of an ape-boy."

"*Ape-boy!*" said Miss Fellowes, in helpless fury.

"That's what the reporters would call him," said Hoskins.

One of the men emerged now, looping a nylon rope through eyelets along the upper portion of the wall.

Miss Fellowes remembered the rope that Hoskins had pulled outside the room containing Professor Ademewski's rock specimen so long ago.

She cried out, "No!"

But Hoskins put Timmie down and gently removed the overcoat he was wearing. "You stay here, Timmie. Nothing will happen to you. We're just going outside for a moment. All right?"

Timmie, white and wordless, managed to nod.

Hoskins steered Miss Fellowes out of the dollhouse ahead of himself. For the moment, Miss Fellowes was beyond resistance. Dully, she noticed the hand-pull being adjusted outside the dollhouse.

"I'm sorry, Miss Fellowes," said Hoskins. "I would have spared you this. I planned it for the night so that you would know only when it was over."

She said in a weary whisper, "Because your son was hurt. Because he tormented this child into striking out at him."

"No. Believe me. I understand about the incident today and I know it was Jerry's fault. But the story has leaked out. It would have to with the press surrounding us on this day of all days. I can't risk having a distorted story about negligence and savage Neanderthalers, so-called, distract from the success of Project Middle Ages. Timmie has to go soon anyway; he might as well go now and give the sensationalists as small a peg as possible on which to hang their trash."

"It's not like sending a rock back. You'll be killing a human being."

"Not killing. There'll be no sensation. He'll simply be a Neanderthal boy in a Neanderthal world. He will no longer be a prisoner and alien. He will have a chance at a free life."

"What chance? He's only seven years old, used to being taken care of, fed, clothed, sheltered. He will be alone. His tribe may not be at the point where he left them now that four years have passed. And if they were, they would not recognize him. He will have to take care of himself. How will he know how?"

Hoskins shook his head in hopeless negative. "Lord, Miss Fellowes, do you think we haven't thought of that? Do you think we would have brought in a child if it weren't that it was the first successful fix of a human or near-human we made and that we did not dare to take the chance of unfixing him and finding another fix as good? Why do you suppose we kept Timmie as long as we did, if it were not for our reluctance to send a child back into the past. It's just"—his voice took on a desperate urgency—"that we can wait no longer. Timmie stands in the way of expansion! Timmie is a source of possible bad publicity; we are on the threshold of great things, and I'm sorry, Miss Fellowes, but we can't let Timmie block us. We cannot. We cannot. I'm sorry, Miss Fellowes."

"Well, then," said Miss Fellowes sadly. "Let me say good-by. Give me five minutes to say good-by. Spare me that much."

Hoskins hesitated. "Go ahead."

Timmie ran to her. For the last time he ran to her and for the last time Miss Fellowes clasped him in her arms.

For a moment, she hugged him blindly. She caught at a chair with the toe of one foot, moved it against the wall, sat down.

"Don't be afraid, Timmie."

"I'm not afraid if you're here, Miss Fellowes. Is that man mad at me, the man out there?"

"No, he isn't. He just doesn't understand about us. ——Timmie, do you know what a mother is?"

"Like Jerry's mother?"

"Did he tell you about his mother?"

"Sometimes. I think maybe a mother is a lady who takes care of you and who's very nice to you and who does good things."

"That's right. Have you ever wanted a mother, Timmie?"

Timmie pulled his head away from her so that he could look into her face. Slowly, he put his hand to her cheek and hair and stroked her, as long, long ago she had stroked him. He said, "Aren't you my mother?"

"Oh, Timmie."

"Are you angry because I asked?"

"No. Of course not."

"Because I know your name is Miss Fellowes, but—but sometimes, I call you 'Mother' inside. Is that all right?"

"Yes. Yes. It's all right. And I won't leave you any more and nothing will hurt you. I'll be with you to care for you always. Call me Mother, so I can hear you."

"Mother," said Timmie contentedly, leaning his cheek against hers.

She rose, and, still holding him, stepped up on the chair. The sudden beginning of a shout from outside went unheard and, with her free hand, she yanked with all her weight at the cord where it hung suspended between two eyelets.

And Stasis was punctured and the room was empty.

28

Unto the Fourth Generation

Another story written on a dare! Robert Mills happened to run into a variety of Levkowitzes and dared me to write a story on that. As a result, I wrote the only story I ever wrote on a Jewish theme.

When I sat at the same table with Janet Jeppson (who is now my dear wife) for the first time—it was at the annual banquet of the Mystery Writers of America in 1959—this story had just been published. Janet had read it and she pointed out a literary flaw in it. I saw her point and introduced the necessary correction, and that's another reason it means so much to me.

At ten of noon, Sam Marten hitched his way out of the taxicab, trying as usual to open the door with one hand, hold his briefcase in another and reach for his wallet with a third. Having only two hands, he found it a difficult job and, again as usual, he thudded his knee against the cab-door and found himself still groping uselessly for his wallet when his feet touched pavement.

The traffic of Madison Avenue inched past. A red truck slowed its crawl reluctantly, then moved on with a rasp as the light changed. White script on its side informed an unresponsive world that its ownership was that of *F. Lewkowitz and Sons, Wholesale Clothiers.*

Levkowich, thought Marten with brief inconsequence, and finally fished out his wallet. He cast an eye on the meter as he clamped his briefcase under his arm. Dollar sixty-five, make that twenty cents more as a tip, two singles gone would leave him only one for emergencies, better break a fiver.

"Okay," he said, "take out one-eighty-five, bud."

"Thanks," said the cabbie with mechanical insincerity and made the change.

Marten crammed three singles into his wallet, put it away, lifted his briefcase and breasted the human currents on the sidewalk to reach the glass doors of the building.

Levkovich? he thought sharply, and stopped. A passerby glanced off his elbow.

"Sorry," muttered Marten, and made for the door again.

Levkovich? That wasn't what the sign on the truck had said. The name had read Lewkowitz, Loo-koh-itz. Why did he *think* Levkovich? Even with his college German in the near past changing the w's to v's, where did he get the "-ich" from?

Levkovich? He shrugged the whole matter away roughly. Give it a chance and it would haunt him like a Hit Parade tinkle.

Concentrate on business. He was here for a luncheon appointment with this man, Naylor. He was here to turn a contract into an account and begin, at twenty-three, the smooth business rise which, as he planned it, would marry him to Elizabeth in two years and make him a paterfamilias in the suburbs in ten.

He entered the lobby with grim firmness and headed for the banks of elevators, his eye catching at the white-lettered directory as he passed.

It was a silly habit of his to want to catch suite numbers as he passed, without slowing, or (heaven forbid) coming to a full halt. With no break in his progress, he told himself, he could maintain the impression of belonging, of knowing his way around, and that was important to a man whose job involved dealing with other human beings.

Kulin-etts was what he wanted, and the word amused him. A firm specializing in the production of minor kitchen gadgets, striving manfully for a name that was significant, feminine, and coy, all at once—

His eyes snagged at the M's and moved upward as he walked. Mandel, Lusk, Lippert Publishing Company (two full floors), Lafkowitz, Kulin-etts. There it was—1024. Tenth floor. OK.

And then, after all, he came to a dead halt, turned in reluctant fascination, returned to the directory, and stared at it as though he were an out-of-towner.

Lafkowitz?

What kind of spelling was that?

It was clear enough. Lafkowitz, Henry J., 701. With an A. That was no good. That was useless.

Useless? Why useless? He gave his head one violent shake as though to clear it of mist. Damn it, what did he care how it was spelled? He turned away, frowning and angry, and hastened to an elevator door, which closed just before he reached it, leaving him flustered.

Another door opened and he stepped in briskly. He tucked his briefcase under his arm and tried to look bright alive—junior executive in its finest sense. He had to make an impression on Alex Naylor, with whom so far he had communicated only by telephone. If he was going to brood about Lewkowitzes and Lafkowitzes—

The elevator slid noiselessly to a halt at seven. A youth in shirt-sleeves stepped off, balancing what looked like a desk-drawer in which were three containers of coffee and three sandwiches.

Then, just as the doors began closing, frosted glass with black lettering loomed before Marten's eyes. It read: 701—HENRY J. LEFKOWITZ—IMPORTER and was pinched off by the inexorable coming together of the elevator doors.

Marten leaned forward in excitement. It was his impulse to say: Take me back down to 7.

But there were others in the car. And after all, he had no reason.

Yet there was a tingle of excitement within him. The Directory *had* been wrong. It wasn't A, it was E. Some fool of a non-spelling menial with a packet of small letters to go on the board and only one hind foot to do it with.

Lefkowitz. Still not right, though.

Again, he shook his head. Twice. Not right for what?

The elevator stopped at ten and Marten got off.

Alex Naylor of Kulin-etts turned out to be a bluff, middle-aged man with a shock of white hair, a ruddy complexion, and a broad smile. His palms were dry and rough, and he shook hands with a considerable pressure, putting his left hand on Marten's shoulder in an earnest display of friendliness.

He said, "Be with you in two minutes. How about eating right here in the building? Excellent restaurant, and they've got a boy who makes a good martini. That sound all right?"

"Fine. Fine." Marten pumped up enthusiasm from a somehow-clogged reservoir.

It was nearer ten minutes than two, and Marten waited with the usual uneasiness of a man in a strange office. He stared at the upholstery on the chairs and at the little cubby-hole within which a young and bored switchboard operator sat. He gazed at the pictures on the wall and even made a half-hearted attempt to glance through a trade journal on the table next to him.

What he did not do was think of Lev—

He did *not* think of it.

The restaurant was good, or it would have been good if Marten had been perfectly at ease. Fortunately, he was freed of the necessity of carrying the burden of the conversation. Naylor talked rapidly and loudly, glanced over the menu with a practiced eye, recommended the Eggs Benedict, and commented on the weather and the miserable traffic situation.

On occasion, Marten tried to snap out of it, to lose that edge of fuzzed absence of mind. But each time the restlessness would return. Something was wrong. The name was wrong. It stood in the way of what he had to do.

With main force, he tried to break through the madness. In sudden verbal clatter, he led the conversation into the subject of wiring. It was reckless of him. There was no proper foundation; the transition was too abrupt.

But the lunch had been a good one; the dessert was on its way; and Naylor responded nicely.

He admitted dissatisfaction with existing arrangements. Yes, he had been looking into Marten's firm and, actually, it seemed to him that, yes, there was a chance, a good chance, he thought, that—

A hand came down on Naylor's shoulder as a man passed behind his chair. "How's the boy, Alex?"

Naylor looked up, grin ready-made and flashing. "Hey, Lefk, how's business?"

"Can't complain. See you at the—" He faded into the distance.

Marten wasn't listening. He felt his knees trembling, as he half-rose. "Who was that man?" he asked, intensely. It sounded more peremptory than he intended.

"Who? Lefk? Jerry Lefkovitz. You know him?" Naylor stared with cool surprise at his lunch companion.

"No. How do you spell his name?"

"L-E-F-K-O-V-I-T-Z, I think. Why?"

"With a V?"

"An F. . . . Oh, there's a V in it, too." Most of the good nature had left Naylor's face.

Marten drove on. "There's a Lefkowitz in the building. With a W. You know, Lef-COW-itz."

"Oh?"

"Room 701. This is not the same one?"

"Jerry doesn't work in this building. He's got a place across the street. I don't know this other one. This is a big building, you know. I don't keep tabs on every one in it. What is all this, anyway?"

Marten shook his head and sat back. He didn't know what all this was, anyway. Or at least, if he did, it was nothing he dared explain. Could he say: I'm being haunted by all manner of Lefkowitzes today.

He said, "We were talking about wiring."

Naylor said, "Yes. Well, as I said, I've been considering your company. I've got to talk it over with the production boys, you understand. I'll let you know."

"Sure," said Marten, infinitely depressed. Naylor wouldn't let him know. The whole thing was shot.

And yet, through and beyond his depression, there was still that restlessness.

The hell with Naylor. All Marten wanted was to break this up and get on with it. *(Get on with what?* But the question was only a whisper. Whatever did the questioning inside him was ebbing away, dying down . . .)

The lunch frayed to an ending. If they had greeted each other like long-separated friends at last reunited, they parted like strangers.

Marten felt only relief.

He left with pulses thudding, threading through the tables, out of the haunted building, onto the haunted street.

Haunted? Madison Avenue at 1:20 P.M. in an early fall afteroon with the sun shining brightly and ten thousand men and women be-hiving its long straight stretch.

But Marten felt the haunting. He tucked his briefcase under his arm and headed desperately northward. A last sigh of the normal within him warned him he had a three o'clock appointment on 36th Street. Never mind. He headed uptown. Northward.

At 54th Street, he crossed Madison and walked west, came abruptly to a halt and looked upward.

There was a sign on the window, three stories up. He could make it out clearly: A. S. LEFKEWICH, CERTIFIED ACCOUNTANT.

It had an F and an EW, but it was the first "-ich" ending he had seen. The first one. He was getting closer. He turned north again on Fifth Avenue, hurrying through the unreal streets of an unreal city, panting with the chase of something, while the crowds about him began to fade.

A sign in a ground floor window, M. R. LEFKOWICZ, M.D.

A small gold-leaf semi-circle of letters in a candy-store window: JACOB LEVKOW.

(Half a name, he thought savagely. Why is he disturbing me with half a name?)

The streets were empty now except for the varying clan of Lefkowitz, Levkowitz, Lefkowicz to stand out in the vacuum.

He was dimly aware of the park ahead, standing out in

painted motionless green. He turned west. A piece of newspaper fluttered at the corner of his eyes, the only movement in a dead world. He veered, stooped, and picked it up, without slackening his pace.

It was in Yiddish, a torn half-page.

He couldn't read it. He couldn't make out the blurred Hebrew letters, and could not have read it if they were clear. But one word was clear. It stood out in dark letters in the center of the page, each letter clear in its every serif. And it said Lefkovitsch, he knew, and as he said it to himself, he placed its accent on the second syllable: Lef-KUH-vich.

He let the paper flutter away and entered the empty park.

The trees were still and the leaves hung in odd, suspended attitudes. The sunlight was a dead weight upon him and gave no warmth.

He was running, but his feet kicked up no dust and a tuft of grass on which he placed his weight did not bend.

And there on a bench was an old man; the only man in the desolate park. He wore a dark felt cap, with a visor shading his eyes. From underneath it, tufts of gray hair protruded. His grizzled beard reached the uppermost button of his rough jacket. His old trousers were patched, and a strip of burlap was wrapped about each worn and shapeless shoe.

Marten stopped. It was difficult to breathe. He could only say one word and he used it to ask his question: "Levkovich?"

He stood there, while the old man rose slowly to his feet; brown old eyes peering close.

"Marten," he sighed. "Samuel Marten. You have come." The words sounded with an effect of double exposure, for under the English, Marten heard the faint sigh of a foreign tongue. Under the "Samuel" was the unheard shadow of a "Schmu-el."

The old man's rough, veined hands reached out, then withdrew as though he were afraid to touch. "I have been looking but there are so many people in this wilderness of a city-that-is-to-come. So many Martins and Martines and Mortons and Mertons. I stopped at last when I found greenery, but for a moment only—I would not commit the sin of losing faith. And then you came."

"It is I," said Marten, and knew it was. "And you are Phinehas Levkovich. Why are we here?"

"I am Phinehas ben Jehudah, assigned the name Levkovich by the ukase of the Tsar that ordered family names for all. And we are here," the old man said, softly, "because I prayed. When I was already old, Leah, my only daughter, the child of my old age, left for America with her husband, left the knouts of the old for the hope of the new. And my sons died, and Sarah, the wife of my bosom, was long dead and I was alone. And the time came when I, too, must die. But I had not seen Leah since her leaving for the far country and word had come but rarely. My soul yearned that I might see sons born unto her; sons of my seed; sons in whom my soul might yet live and not die."

His voice was steady and the soundless shadow of sound beneath his words was the stately roll of an ancient language.

"And I was answered and two hours were given me that I might see the first son of my line to be born in a new land and in a new time. My daughter's daughter's daughter's son, have I found you, then, amidst the splendor of this city?"

"But why the search? Why not have brought us together at once?"

"Because there is pleasure in the hope of the seeking, my son," said the old man, radiantly, "and in the delight of the finding. I was given two hours in which I might seek, two hours in which I might find . . . and behold, thou art here, and I have found that which I had not looked to see in life." His voice was old, caressing. "Is it well with thee, my son?"

"It is well, my father, now that I have found thee," said Marten, and dropped to his knees. "Give me thy blessing, my father, that it may be well with me all the days of my life, and with the maid whom I am to take to wife and the little ones yet to be born of my seed and thine."

He felt the old hand resting lightly on his head and there was only the soundless whisper.

Marten rose.

The old man's eyes gazed into his yearningly. Were they losing focus?

"I go to my fathers now in peace, my son," said the old man, and Marten was alone in the empty park.

There was an instant of renewing motion, of the Sun taking up its interrupted task, of the wind reviving, and even with that first instant of sensation, all slipped back—

At ten of noon, Sam Marten hitched his way out of the taxicab, and found himself groping uselessly for his wallet while traffic inched on.

A red truck slowed, then moved on. A white script on its side announced: *F. Lewkowitz and Sons, Wholesale Clothiers.*

Marten didn't see it. Yet somehow he knew that all would be well with him. Somehow, as never before, he knew. . . .

ABOUT THE AUTHOR

ISAAC ASIMOV has been called "one of America's treasures." Born in the Soviet Union, he was brought to the United States at the age of three (along with his family) by agents of the American government in a successful attempt to prevent him from working for the wrong side. He quickly established himself as one of this country's foremost science fiction writers and writer about everything, and although now approaching middle age, he is going stronger than ever. He long ago passed his age and weight in books, and with some 250 to his credit threatens to close in on his I.Q. His sequel to *The Foundation Trilogy—Foundation's Edge—*was one of the bestselling books of 1982 and 1983.

There's an epidemic with 27 million victims. And no visible symptoms.

It's an epidemic of people who can't read.

Believe it or not, 27 million Americans are functionally illiterate, about one adult in five.

The solution to this problem is you... when you join the fight against illiteracy. So call the Coalition for Literacy at toll-free 1-800-228-8813 and volunteer.

Volunteer Against Illiteracy. The only degree you need is a degree of caring.